Dark Overlord's Clan

THE CHILDREN OF THE GODS
BOOK FORTY

I. T. LUCAS

Dark Overlord's Clan is a work of fiction! Names, characters, places and incidents are products of the author's imagination or are used fictitiously and are not to be construed as real. Any similarity to actual persons, organizations and/or events is purely coincidental.

Copyright © 2020 by I. T. Lucas

All rights reserved.

No part of this book may be reproduced in any form or by any electronic or mechanical means, including information storage and retrieval systems, without written permission from the author, except for the use of brief quotations in a book review.

Published by Evening Star Press

Kalugal

Kalugal opened his eyes and glanced at the brightening sky through the bedroom's open window. The rising sun was painting the dark blue canvas with pink and orange hues, blending them into soft peaches and purples. The sight was magnificent to behold, but its beauty paled in comparison to the one sleeping peacefully next to him.

Jacki.

His mate.

His love.

His life.

With her arm draped over his middle, her leg thrown over his thighs, and her nose buried in the crook of his neck, Jacki had claimed him as hers, and he couldn't be happier about it.

His heart overflowing with gratitude and love, Kalugal caressed her back and leaned to kiss her forehead.

Precious.

He hadn't expected the connection to be so strong. Love had always seemed like a soft emotion to him, but the power of that softness was nearly overwhelming.

The metaphysical sphere that contained who he was had grown, and Jacki had become an integral part of it. Kalugal's self-definition had changed. He was no longer an individual but a part of a greater whole.

Except, he hadn't lost any of himself in the process. He'd gained a new dimension of feeling, of thinking, of being.

Was that how his mother felt about his father?

No wonder Areana stayed with Navuh. She loved him despite who he was and what he did. Perhaps she didn't know the full extent of his evil deeds, but she must be aware of at least some of it. If what Areana felt toward his father was as strong as what Kalugal was feeling towards Jacki, then leaving Navuh was simply impossible.

Was that the powerful bond between immortal mates that Kian and Amanda had been talking about?

But how could it have already formed? Jacki was still human, and it wasn't supposed to happen so fast.

Or was it just the beginning, and the bond hadn't even reached its full strength yet?

How much stronger could it possibly get?

Already, Kalugal couldn't fathom one hour without Jacki, let alone his life without her.

Leaning, he nuzzled her lush hair and inhaled deeply. Her scent was intoxicating, and it wasn't the perfume he'd bought for her or the shampoo she used, it was just her.

His woman.

With a sigh, Kalugal kissed the top of Jacki's head and contemplated the best way to sneak out of bed without waking her up.

As much as he would have loved to stay and just hold her, duty called. His mother should hear the good news about his upcoming wedding from him and not from Annani, which meant that he had to beat his aunt to it.

The discovery of his real heritage still made Kalugal's head spin.

Not only was he the son of a goddess, but he was also the nephew of the formidable head of the clan. Annani and Areana were only half-sisters, but since they were the last goddesses on the planet, the half was irrelevant in the grand scheme of things.

Jacki kept referring to him as a demigod, but despite Kalugal's natural arrogance, he hadn't internalized it yet. In his mind, he'd always been and still was the second most powerful immortal ever born, and he was good with that.

Demigod seemed like too much.

He didn't deserve the title, at least not yet. Perhaps when he took over control of the entire world, he would be more comfortable with it.

Carefully untangling himself from Jacki's arms and legs, Kalugal slid out of bed and took his phone with him to the bathroom.

Regrettably, Tuesday wasn't his turn for Areana's daily call, but he hoped that given the occasion, Annani would allow him to switch days with her. The problem was that he couldn't contact the goddess directly and had to arrange it through Kian.

It was six-fifteen in the morning, and hopefully, his cousin was up already. The guy was grumpy even when fully rested. If Kalugal woke him up, Kian might refuse to arrange the call.

Making as little noise as possible, he finished up in the bathroom and then ducked into the walk-in closet for a robe.

After quietly closing the door between the bedroom and the master sitting room, Kalugal loaded the coffeemaker, sat on the couch, and typed up a text to Kian.

Good morning. My apologies for the early text. I wish to share the happy news about my upcoming wedding with my mother, and I was wondering whether Annani would be willing to switch days with me. Please let me know if that can be arranged.

Long minutes passed as Kalugal waited for Kian to answer, but the time wasn't wasted. The coffee had finished brewing, and when Kian's return text finally arrived, Kalugal was sipping on his second cup.

No problem. Annani sends her congratulations and regrets not officiating over your wedding. When Areana's call comes in, I'll have William patch it through to you.

Kalugal typed back. *Thank you. And thank the goddess for me.*

A quick glance at the time revealed that it was six-thirty. Areana's daily call came at precisely seven every morning, which meant that he had half an hour to plan how he was going to condense everything he wanted to tell his mother into a ten-minute conversation.

Except, Kalugal's thoughts kept wandering in other directions.

He was practically already mated to Jacki, and by tonight it would be official, but he still hadn't shared his plans and aspirations with her.

Kalugal feared that she would find them objectionable.

It wasn't necessary to have that conversation today, but eventually he wanted to share everything with Jacki, even things that he wasn't sure would ever come to fruition.

Right now, Kalugal's world domination ideas seemed far removed from him, and if he didn't believe wholeheartedly that his rule would improve the lives of billions and secure the future of humans and immortals alike, he would have shrugged it off.

Why shoulder such a monumental undertaking?

Let someone else save the world.

Except, there was no one else.

Annani and Kian's hearts were in the right place, but they were going about it the wrong way. They believed in gentle nudges, supplying ideology and technology and hoping that humans would take it from there.

But that was not going to happen, or rather not happen soon enough. Humanity would destroy itself in one way or another long before it reached enlightenment, and it would take immortals down with it.

He'd thought that he had more time, but things were moving faster than he'd anticipated.

Technology was a double-edged sword.

In the right hands it was a blessing, but the problem was that it didn't discriminate, serving both benevolent and malevolent masters equally well.

When his phone rang, Kalugal shook himself out of his morbid reveries and planted a smile on his face. He wanted his mother to hear how happy he was, and that required his expression to match the sentiment.

"I'm patching you through," William said.

A moment later, Areana came on the line. "Kalugal? Is everything all right?"

"Hello, Mother. I have exciting news that I want to share with you. I'm getting married tonight."

Areana gasped. "Are you doing it to secure the alliance? Who is the bride? Someone important in Annani's clan? One of her daughters, perhaps?"

His mother sounded so hopeful and excited.

He should have expected that. Naturally, Areana thought that the rushed wedding had something to do with the summit. The truth was that if Annani had unmated daughters, that would have been a good move despite them being cousins. In that, Areana and Annani being only half-sisters was beneficial, and marriage between their children wasn't genetically problematic.

On the contrary, a child born to him and Annani's daughter would be extremely powerful. But Kalugal had met Jacki first, and she was the one for him.

Leaning back, he crossed his legs and smiled. "Jacqueline is not part of the clan, and at the moment, she is still human. But not for long."

"She is a Dormant?"

"Indeed. She is also an immune, which means that I can't compel her or thrall her or influence her mind in any way. I can just love and cherish her and hope that's enough."

Areana laughed, the otherworldly sound sending goosebumps up his arms. "I can see the appeal. She is a challenge."

"In more ways than one. She is also smart, direct, beautiful, and the least demanding female I've ever encountered."

Except when it came to commitment, but Kalugal didn't want to share that with his mother, lest she think that Jacki had manipulated him to marry her.

Jacki didn't want his money, and she wasn't interested in a cushy life as a rich man's wife either. She wanted to earn her keep, and she was willing to work hard for it.

The one thing she refused to compromise on was his soul. Jacki demanded his love, devotion, and loyalty.

Others though, and that included his mother, might think that she was after his money, or after the immortality he could give her, and that she'd maneuvered him into marrying her.

The opposite was true.

His soul might be priceless, but it wasn't an asset Jacki could or would ever sell, and in exchange, she'd given him hers.

In Kalugal's opinion, the bargain was skewed in his favor.

He was getting much more than he was giving away.

Jacki

As the cobwebs of sleep dissipated, the first thing that Jacki became aware of was the muscular chest her nose was pressed against, and the second was the steady heartbeat within it.

Kalugal.

Her fiancé, the love of her life, her first and last lover.

Or was he her husband now?

They'd already exchanged pledges last night, had consummated those pledges with mind-blowing lovemaking, and tonight they were going to make it official.

Jacki was a virgin no more, and as far as she was concerned, waiting for the right man had been one of the best decisions she'd ever made. The other one had been ditching the government program despite the fabulous salary.

Both had brought her to where she was now. In bed with the best man on the planet.

Not a man, a demigod.

Were they now Mr. and Mrs. Demigod?

With a soft chuckle, Jacki threw her arm around Kalugal and pulled him on top of her.

Naturally, he helped. "Good morning, my love." He dipped his head and kissed her. "Did you sleep well?"

"Best night of my life." She ran her hands over his muscled back. "You've been keeping secrets from me."

He cocked a brow. "Like what?"

"Like the fabulous physique that you were hiding under those cashmere sweaters and suit jackets. The entire time I've been here, I haven't seen you working out even once, and yet there isn't an ounce of fat on you, and every muscle is defined as if it was sculpted by an artist." Jacki pretended to narrow her eyes at him. "Were you sneaking out to the gym in the middle of the night?"

"I'm afraid not." Kalugal affected an apologetic expression. "I've been neglecting that aspect of my daily routine, and if I don't resume it soon, I might become flabby, and you won't want my body anymore." Swiveling his hips, he rubbed his erection against her center.

Jacki's laugh was deep and throaty. "I'll always want you. Besides, you probably don't need to do anything to look like that." She squeezed his bottom and arched up. "Demigods don't get fat."

"Says who?" He smoothed his hand up her ribcage and cupped her breast.

She stifled a moan. "In every myth and legend, gods and demigods are flawless, seducing unsuspecting maidens left and right. Training is never mentioned."

"Unfortunately, that's not true." He thumbed her nipple. "I can get away with doing very little to maintain my fabulous physique, but if I try really hard, I can get fat." He assumed a frown. "I will if that's what you desire." No longer bracing on his forearms, he let her feel the full weight of his athletic body.

Jacki wasn't a small woman, but even though Kalugal was slim, all those muscles were heavy. The weight on top of her was more than she'd expected, and yet it was just right.

"Don't you dare gain or lose an ounce. You are perfect the way you are." She squeezed his muscled bottom again.

Smiling, Kalugal exposed his fangs, which had elongated significantly since they had started their mutual teasing. "Is this an invitation, my Jacqueline?"

As if she needed to answer that.

Just the sight of those fangs was enough to trigger a gush of moisture that he could surely feel as well as smell.

After last night, she would never again look upon his fangs with fear. In fact, she would probably get wet every time Kalugal flashed them at her.

Just as he'd promised, the bite had left no mark on her, and if she hadn't just seen his fangs again this morning, she would have thought the bite hadn't happened and she'd dreamt it.

Jacki wasn't sore either, which was most likely thanks to the healing properties of the venom as well.

Which reminded her that she hadn't seen Kalugal's manhood yet. She'd definitely felt it, though, and the fit had been perfect. But she wanted to see, and touch, and lick, and suck...

The images triggered another outpouring of wetness.

"What do you think?" She arched up a little, rubbing her center against his hard shaft.

His smile turned into a fanged smirk. "I think that it's a yes." He dipped his head and kissed her.

She was already so wet that he could have penetrated her right away, but Kalugal had other ideas. Kissing a trail down her neck, he lingered a moment over the spot he'd bitten last night, licked it, and then sucked the skin in.

Jacki giggled. "There is no trace of your bite, so you want to mark me with a hickey?"

"I wish I could." He kissed the spot. "But nothing will be left of it after I bite you again." His voice dropped an octave.

"I can't wait," she whispered and turned her head sideways.

"Not yet, my love." He chuckled. "First, I need to worship at my goddess's temple." He slid further down, his lips hovering a fraction of an inch over her straining nipple.

Grasping his hair, Jacki pulled his head down to her breast. "The temple awaits your tribute."

Kian

As Kian glanced around the conference table, he felt a stab of guilt for not including Lokan in the strategy meeting.

The truth was that the Guardian briefing had nothing to do with the summit, and therefore should be of no interest to Lokan, but his cousin might disagree. After all, he'd offered his help numerous times and had taken part in missions.

Except, Kian needed to finalize the details of securing his people during Jacki and Kalugal's wedding, and having Lokan there would have made everyone uncomfortable.

Or maybe just him.

He still didn't fully trust Lokan, especially with anything that had to do with Kalugal.

The brothers weren't close, and they interacted more like distant acquaintances than family members. But blood is thicker than water, and Kian had no doubt that when push came to shove, Lokan would side with Kalugal.

The problem was that when Lokan found out about the meeting, he would feel excluded, and that wasn't good either. If Kian wanted Lokan's loyalty, he needed to show the guy that he was part of the team.

Under different circumstances, Kian might have compromised in the name of diplomacy, but this time there was too much at stake to risk it. He was about to walk into Kalugal's compound with Syssi, Amanda, and some of his best friends.

Hell, who was he kidding. This entire thing was one big compromise in the name of diplomacy.

Agreeing to attend the fucking wedding had been a leap of faith on his part, and now it was giving him a mental ulcer.

Perhaps he could convince Syssi not to come?

She could use nausea as an excuse, or fatigue, or some other pregnancy-related syndrome, and bow out gracefully. He would be much less stressed if Syssi went home instead of attending the wedding in Kalugal's mansion.

Yeah, good luck with that.

"Good luck with what?" Yamanu asked.

Kian hadn't been aware of speaking out loud. "Convincing Syssi to go home instead of coming with us to the wedding."

He was answered with a collective murmur of agreement.

Apparently, every mated male in the room felt the same. None of them wanted to expose their mates to even a whiff of danger.

Yamanu clapped Kian on the back. "We are all nervous, but it's going to be okay. The Fates brought us to this fork in the road for a reason. We could have chosen to keep going alone, like we have done up till now, or to take a risk and walk toward a new beginning. As much as I would love for Mey to be safely back in the village, I don't regret bringing her with me."

Kian shook his head. "I wish I had your faith. Nevertheless, let's continue. How many drones do we have on hand?"

"Seven," Turner said. "We had five already, and I'm getting two more delivered. I figured seven would look better in formation."

Kian frowned. "Who is going to operate them?"

Flying drones was not easy, and since he'd promised Kalugal an air show, the operators needed to be skilled in more than the basics.

Turner smiled. "I decided that it would be best if all of them were operated from the village. I'm not taking chances with Kalugal and his compulsion. If he somehow manages to get the cuff off, I want the drone operators to be out of his mental reach. William sent a signal booster that we will put on the balcony of the rented house. He, Roni, and Charlie are going to handle the drones from the safety of the village, and in view mode only. No sound."

"Good. But that's three operators. We need seven."

"I thought so too, but William explained that all seven drones will be controlled by the computer, following a program that he wrote for the occasion. If something happens and the need to use the drones in attack mode arises, the three of them will take over. There is no need for all seven drones to attack at once. We are covering a backyard, not a city block."

Kian shook his head. "I don't like it. Tell William to get at least two more operators. I know it's overkill, but I'd rather err on the side of caution."

"You're the boss."

Kian turned to Magnus. "What about your men? We didn't decide yet where to station them. I'm debating whether to have you join us at the party. The advantage is that you and your men will be right there if I need you. The other option is having you patrol outside."

"Kalugal is not going to allow us to keep our weapons on his property," Magnus said. "I'd rather stay outside with the men and, if needed, rush in fully armed. We can wear earplugs and communicate via text like we did before. That way, if Kalugal somehow manages to pull a magic trick, get rid of the cuff, and command everyone to freeze, we won't be affected."

"Good plan." Kian rapped his fingers on the table. "Stay in the rented house. I don't want him to see you patrolling."

"Why not? He knows we're out there."

"Diplomacy, my friend. I want to pretend that I trust him. He will know it's a lie, but he'll pretend to believe it, and everyone will feel good about themselves. The houses are so close that you can get there in under a minute."

"That's true," Magnus conceded.

"I suggest that as an added precaution, Kian and Brundar should wear earpieces," Turner said. "You both have long hair, so they won't be conspicuous."

Kian grimaced. "It's going to be a pain to hear everyone sound the same, but you're right."

"I'll wear mine too," Anandur said. "I don't care if Kalugal sees them. I'm your bodyguard, and my job is to protect you."

"Aren't you all forgetting something?" Magnus asked.

Kian glanced at Turner, but the guy shrugged. "There is always something. What did we miss?"

"I might be wrong, but I was under the impression that Kalugal went home without the cuff. When are you going to put it on him?"

Kian shook his head. "I can't believe I forgot about that. I should have asked him to keep wearing it." He pulled out his phone. "He'll have to come here."

"On his wedding day?" Anandur huffed out a breath. "Magnus can meet Kalugal outside the gate and put the cuff on him." He looked at the Guardian. "Just wear your earplugs and take a couple of men with you."

Magnus nodded. "I have no problem with that."

"Let me check with Kalugal first," Kian said. "As Anandur pointed out, it's the guy's wedding day, and we should make an effort to accommodate him."

Anandur chuckled. "All in the name of diplomacy."

"That's right," Kian agreed. "But we are also doing this for Jacki."

Syssi

The squealing started as soon as Mey and Jin walked through the door. Actually, Jin was making most of the noise and hugging everyone as if she hadn't seen them for months, but Mey contributed a few more joyous sounds of her own.

When it was Syssi's turn to get crushed in Jin's arms, she was glad that the girl wasn't immortal yet. Jin was surprisingly strong for a human.

Chuckling, she hugged the girl back. "Welcome to our home away from home."

"I'm so happy." Jin released her and wiped tears from her eyes. "I missed you all so much."

Behind her, Arwel shook his head. "You saw everyone on Friday, and it's only Tuesday."

"I know. But Jacki is getting married, and it makes me emotional." Jin wiped away another tear. "I can't wait to see her. She is going to be such a beautiful bride. Thank you so much for loaning her your wedding dress. Last night, Jacki emailed me a picture of herself wearing it, and she looked absolutely gorgeous."

"It's my pleasure."

"Where is Yamanu?" Amanda asked.

"Downstairs at the briefing," Arwel said. "I should head there as well." He glanced at Jin. "You don't need me here, right?"

She pecked him on the cheek. "You can go."

The Guardian looked relieved, which wasn't surprising given that he was the only male in the room. Nevertheless, he hesitated. "You're safe up here. Kian had Roni hack into the hotel's surveillance cameras, and if any suspicious activity is spotted, we will take care of whoever they are before they can get up here."

"I'm not concerned." Jin kissed his cheek again. "Go, have fun with the boys."

As the door closed behind the Guardian, Amanda sauntered over to the sisters and put a hand on each of their shoulders. "Do you need to rest a little, or are you ready to try the saris on? We have a lot of work to do."

Syssi glanced at her watch. "It's eight-thirty in the morning. We have plenty of time."

The party was scheduled to start at nine in the evening, but they were going over there a couple of hours earlier than that to help Jacki get ready. And while the ladies fussed over the bride, the guys were going to throw the groom a mini bachelor party.

It had been Kian's idea to surprise Kalugal and his men with premium whiskey and fine cigars. Despite being wary of his cousin, Kian must have grown fond of him to come up with that. Or maybe it was just another attempt at diplomacy, which Kian had been experimenting with since the whole thing with Kalugal had started.

In either case, Syssi was sure that the gesture would be appreciated, and sharing in a pre-wedding celebration would further the spirit of cooperation between their people.

"We have a lot of work to do." Amanda repeated as she herded the ladies toward the bedroom.

"It won't take us that long to get ready." Syssi followed the procession. "Can I make you girls coffee? Something to eat?"

Mey waved a dismissive hand. "I'm good. I prepared breakfast to go, and we had coffee and sandwiches on the plane."

"I would like some tea if it's not too much trouble." Jin rubbed a hand over the front of her neck. "My throat feels scratchy, and tea helps."

"How long have you been having these symptoms?" Bridget asked.

Jin waved a hand. "Since Arwel and I went up to the mountains. I don't know if it's allergies or if it's the freaking motor home's fault. It was either too cold or too hot inside, and we couldn't get the temperature right."

"Do you have a fever? Are you coughing? Do you have a runny nose?

Jin smiled. "Relax. I don't have a fever, and I'm not coughing. It's just an allergy."

"Do you usually get allergies this time of year?"

"Sometimes, but only mildly. I guess it depends on where I am."

Bridget shook her head. "Just in case, let me take your temperature."

As the doctor left to bring the tools of her trade, Amanda unfolded the two remaining saris. "Everyone has already picked theirs, and these are the only ones left."

Jin reached for the pink one. "Are they all this gaudy?"

"They are beautiful." Mey patted her back. "A sari without the vibrant colors is not a sari. Besides, we are both lucky to have the right coloring to pull it off. Dark hair goes with everything."

Amanda handed Jin a pink, long-sleeved T-shirt. "You can use this instead of the tiny one that comes with the outfit. The wedding is outdoors, and it gets quite chilly here at night."

"Thank you." Jin put the shirt on the bed and whipped her blouse over her head. "Mey brought me a long-sleeved T-shirt too, but it's probably not electric pink."

She pulled the shirt on and glanced at the mirror mounted over the dresser. "Good fit." She unfurled the sari and eyed it suspiciously. "How do you put this thing on?"

"I'll show you." Amanda took the long swathe of fabric and expertly wrapped it around Jin. "I also brought safety pins to hold it in place."

"I guess the yellow one is mine." Mey picked up the last sari. "Not my favorite color, but it will do."

"I can switch with you," Syssi offered. "Do you prefer purple?"

Mey looked at her hopefully. "After red, that's my favorite color. But are you sure? Yellow might be too pale for you."

"It has pink embroidery." Syssi took the sari from Mey. "It might work."

"You see?" Amanda waved a hand. "That's why we needed to start early. I also have to do everyone's makeup, and Callie has to do everyone's hair."

"You don't have to," Syssi said. "We can do it ourselves."

Amanda glanced at Wonder, who suddenly looked panicked. "Not everyone can, and if I'm doing it for one, I might as well do it for everybody." She grinned. "When I'm done, you are all going to look fabulous."

"Oh, boy." Syssi groaned. "Now I know why you need ten hours to get us ready."

Simmons

After checking the GPS, Simmons turned left and looked at his friend. "I'm sorry, Elijah, but a drive-through is our only option." He smiled. "I haven't eaten a hamburger in ages, and I'm actually looking forward to it."

"I don't eat beef." Roberts rolled his window down. "I need to watch my cholesterol."

"One hamburger will not make much of a difference." Simmons cast him a sidelong glance. "It has been how many years since your bypass?"

"Four, and I don't intend on having another one. I need to keep my arteries clean."

Simmons shrugged. "What's the point of prolonging life when you can't enjoy it?"

"I enjoy myself plenty. I happen to love fish. Besides, I allow myself a steak once a month. That's good enough for me."

"What are you going to order then? They don't have fish burgers."

"What about Mexican food? I can eat a bean burrito."

Simmons waved a hand. "Be my guest. Find a Mexican drive-through."

"I shall do that." Elijah pulled out his phone.

Unlike his friend, Simmons didn't have any underlying health conditions, but he wasn't a young man either, so perhaps he should start watching his diet as well. The problem was that he loved the finer things in life, and he hated putting restrictions on the things that brought him pleasure. But taking his continued good health for granted was irresponsible.

At his age, he didn't have a lot of time left to realize his dreams.

The paranormal division he and Elijah had envisioned many years ago was finally happening, and everything had been working splendidly so far. Even the trainee escape hadn't been such a big loss because, other than Jin, their talents were not very impressive.

But the progress was too slow.

At the current rate of recruitment, he and Elijah might not see the division reach its full potential during their lifetimes.

That was why the success of tonight's mission was so critical.

With one fell swoop, they might bring into the program a bunch of new recruits that would have taken them a couple of years to collect using their regular methods.

"Turn right at the next light," Elijah said. "I found a drive-through taco place."

"I had my heart set on a hamburger, but perhaps I should start watching what I eat as well."

Roberts snorted. "I doubt you'll last a week. You love the good life too much."

"Would you like to bet?"

Elijah laughed. "With you? Never. You'll do anything to win."

That was true. He loved a challenge, and winning was nonnegotiable.

After eating their meal in the restaurant's parking lot, Simmons checked the GPS again. "We are meeting my guy in a warehouse on Elliot Street." He put the gearshift in drive.

"Doesn't he have an office?"

"Renting space anywhere in the Bay Area is costly, so Hector works from his home office. For this mission, he's subletting a place from a friend."

"Where does he keep his weapons?"

Simmons shrugged. "I don't know, and I don't care. Maybe he has a self-storage somewhere."

"Could be." Roberts took a sip from his diet drink. "What I'm worried about is that he doesn't sound professional."

"I told you he's a small operator. Besides, what we need from him doesn't require special ops training. Although he has it."

Pulling into a parking spot in front of a warehouse, Simmons pointed at the row of black vans parked one next to the other. "I guess those are ours."

Roberts grimaced. "The thought of riding in one of these all the way back to West Virginia instead of flying is unappealing, to say the least. My hemorrhoids are going to give me hell. Maybe you can stay with the team, and I'll fly back?"

"I wish it was possible, but I need you. We are driving back with tranquilized cargo. Your job is to make sure that we bring them in alive. I don't want to lose any on the way."

Roberts sighed. "I get it. I just don't like it." He released the safety belt and got out.

After locking the rental, Simmons walked up to the door and pressed the intercom button. "We are here to see Hector."

"Doctors Simmons and Roberts?"

He recognized Hector's voice. "That's us."

The door opened, and Simmons walked in first. "Any new recon?"

"Yes." Hector motioned for them to follow him to a back room. "I sent one of my guys with a camera drone to check on what they had going in the backyard." He pulled out two plastic chairs for them.

"Did he find anything interesting?" Roberts asked.

Hector sat behind the dingy metal desk. "It seems like we are going to crash a wedding. The tables are covered in white tablecloths, and there are flower arrangements on each one. They've also built an elevated platform, which I suppose is for the actual ceremony."

"That's good news for us. We don't have to hunt for the terrorists one by one."

Hector lifted his hands in the air. "I don't need to know who they are, and I don't want to know. As long as I'm getting paid, I don't ask questions."

"Smart man." Simmons pulled an envelope out of his suit pocket. "This is half of what we've agreed on. You'll get the other half when you deliver the cargo to West Virginia."

Wendy

In her room, Wendy lay on her belly and flipped through the selection of movies on the server. Whoever had downloaded them had apparently never heard of anime or cartoons because there were none.

She needed something to distract her from the bad mood that had snuck up on her unexpectedly.

Things had been going well with Vlad, and for a couple of hours, she'd felt great. But then Jin had told them that Jacki was getting married and that she and Arwel were leaving for the wedding.

Why wasn't Wendy invited?

Was it because of what she had done?

Everyone else seemed willing to forgive her, so why not Jacki?

Besides, what did Jacki care about her betraying the organization? They weren't her people. She was marrying the guy who Jin had tethered, a supposed threat, and a potential enemy much worse than Wendy.

What was the deal with that anyway? Jacki had just met the guy and was already marrying him?

And what about Richard?

He hadn't done anything wrong, and yet Jacki hadn't invited him either.

There was a knock on the door. "Can I come in?" Vlad asked.

"It's open."

Wendy didn't bother to move. She was fully dressed, her bed was made, and she was lying on it facing the television, with her socked feet pointing at the headboard.

Vlad sat on the bed next to her. "Why are you in your room?"

She shrugged. "I'm trying to find something to watch."

"What's wrong?"

"Why do you think that something is wrong with me? I just want some decent entertainment, but there is nothing on this freaking server." She dropped the remote and turned sideways to look at Vlad.

"You told me that you watch things to keep out of your own head, so I assumed something is going on up there."

He tapped her temple with his finger. "Do you want to talk about it?"

Wendy shrugged. "Jacki is getting married, and she didn't invite Richard or me. She has known us a lot longer than she has known Jin, but she invited her."

"Richard doesn't seem to mind."

Wendy rolled her eyes. "The guy has the emotional spectrum of a gnat. Besides, he had the hots for Jacki, so he's probably not too keen on seeing her hooking up with another guy."

Vlad chuckled. "I think Jacki is old news for Richard. He and Ingrid were hooking up right in front of her."

Closing her eyes, Wendy plopped on her back. "Maybe I'm jealous. Jacki was like me. She stayed away from guys, and everyone thought that she was not into men. I even suspected that she might have been abused, and that's why she didn't want to enter a relationship. But apparently, we were all wrong. She just waited for the right guy. A rich and powerful dude that even the mighty Kian fears."

Vlad didn't say anything, but she sensed his hurt feelings.

Flopping to her side, Wendy opened her eyes and looked at him. "Why are you offended? Jacki wasn't your friend."

"I don't care about not being invited to the wedding. What I care about is you being jealous of Jacki because she is marrying a rich and successful guy. How do you think it makes me feel?"

"It has nothing to do with you."

He arched a brow. "Really? If I were rich and powerful, would you still be jealous of Jacki?"

Rolling her eyes, Wendy sat up, lifted on her knees, and wrapped her arms around Vlad's neck. "You are such a silly boy. My jealousy has nothing to do with whom she is marrying. It's just that Jacki is over whatever issues she had, and I'm not. She has good friends that want to celebrate with her, and I don't." She leaned and kissed his lips lightly. "But I have you, so I shouldn't complain, right?"

Vlad let out a breath, scooped her into his strong arms, and put her on his lap. "Yes, you do. And if you stop brooding in your room so much, you'll notice that there are three other guys out there who think of you as a friend."

"Bowen hates my guts."

"No, he doesn't. He was angry at you, but so was I. In fact, I think he got over it before I did."

"What makes you think that?"

"He was the one who pointed out to me that you are just a young girl, and that you might have called the director because you were scared of living like a fugitive. He said that not everyone is brave."

Wendy put her cheek on Vlad's chest. "He's right, you know. Everything I did was motivated by fear. I'm a big fat coward."

"You are not fat."

She lifted her eyes. "So, you agree with the rest?"

"You're not big, either. In fact, you're quite tiny." He lifted her hand and kissed her pointer finger. "Your hands are so small and delicate." He kissed her pinky.

"But I'm a coward."

"You were a coward. You no longer are."

Vlad

Wendy sighed. "I'm still scared."

"But you are not letting fear rule you, and that's brave."

Lifting her hand, she smiled and cupped his cheek. "How are you so sweet?"

Sweet wasn't the adjective Vlad wanted Wendy to associate with him. He would have preferred sexy, manly, handsome, but perhaps thinking of him as sweet was what made it easier for Wendy to let him in.

Her main fear was falling in love with a guy who might turn abusive, and sweet was the opposite of that.

"My mom made me from sugar and spice and everything nice."

Wendy chuckled. "That's what girls are made from. Boys are made from snips and snails and puppy-dogs' tails."

"That's so sexist." Vlad pretended offense. "No wonder you didn't like boys. Is that the original rhyme?"

"I'm afraid so."

"Then, I need to thank my mom for ignoring it and sticking to the sugar and spice and everything nice." He smiled. "She would always kiss and tickle me when she said that."

Wendy's eyes misted with tears. "She sounds so nice. I wish she hadn't canceled. I would have liked to meet her."

"You said that you were afraid of my mom giving you the stink eye."

"I still am, but I'm also curious to meet her. Your mother sounds so awesome. She's creative and compassionate, and she is also a great mom." Wendy sighed. "I need more good people in my life."

Wrapping his arms tighter around her, he kissed the top of her head.

Wendy was lonely, and she felt friendless. Right now, he was the only friend she had, but perhaps he could change that.

If Kian agreed, and there was no reason why he shouldn't, Vlad could invite people over. The more of the clan Wendy met, the more friends she made, the less isolated she would feel.

"I have an idea. I can invite Jackson and Tessa to come over. Maybe Roni and Sylvia too. Jackson is my age, and

Roni is yours. Tessa and Sylvia are a little older, but they are cool."

"Jackson is your best friend, right? Vanessa's son."

"Yes."

"And Tessa is his girlfriend?"

"That's right."

"What are their talents?"

Damn. He had to make something up quickly. "Jackson has a knack for business. He sees opportunities where no one else does. The bakery I work in belongs to him."

"That's impressive for a twenty-year-old. What about his girlfriend? What's her talent?"

"Compassion."

Wendy laughed. "That's not a talent."

"She works at a detective agency, so I assume that she has some spying abilities. I don't know what each person in our organization can do, and if they don't volunteer the information, it's considered impolite to ask."

That should do it. From now on, he could claim not to know.

"I'm glad that you told me that I shouldn't ask them. But I can ask you, right? What about the other couple? Roni and Sylvia?"

"Roni is a gifted hacker. Sylvia can fritz out electronics at will and with precision."

"Do you think Kian would allow them to come?"

"I don't see why not."

"Do they know what I've done?"

"Jackson does, so I assume that Tessa does as well. And Roni kind of knows everything that goes on, so yeah, he and Sylvia probably know too."

Wendy grimaced. "Then maybe it's not a good idea."

"That's fear talking. My friends are good people, and they are not the kind who hold grudges. Everyone makes mistakes, and I'm sure each of them has a story they are not proud of. Besides, I'm the one who got duped, so if anyone has a reason to feel embarrassed, it's me."

"I'm sorry," Wendy murmured into his shirt.

"I've already forgiven you, so you don't need to keep apologizing."

She lifted her head and smiled. "I can make it up to you."

The mischief in her eyes and the slight whiff of her arousal were enough to trigger a response he couldn't let her notice, and it wasn't the club he'd sprouted in his pants.

He really needed to tell Wendy the truth already.

"I'll take an IOU. Bowen is waiting for us with lunch, and you know how grouchy he gets when he's hungry."

"Why didn't you say so before?" Wendy slid out of his arms. "I'm hungry."

"Yeah, me too."

Kian

As Anandur stopped in front of the rented house, Syssi looked out the window. "I thought that Kalugal's place would be more impressive."

Kian opened the passenger back door. "This is the house that we are using as our base of operations. Kalugal's place is just around the corner."

"Are you going to be long? Jacki is waiting for us."

"I only need a few minutes to check on the guys and make sure that everything is ready, but I want you to stay in the house while I put the cuff on Kalugal. I'll text you when it's okay to come."

"Wasn't Magnus supposed to do that?"

"There was a change of plans." Kian got out and walked around to open the door for Syssi.

Except for Lokan and Carol, who had gone gift-hunting, Kian expected the rest of their party to arrive shortly.

Everyone had been instructed to stop by the rented house first. Turner, who had just parked behind their car, had Bridget, Wonder and Callie with him.

Pulling her sweater tight around her, Syssi shook her head. "I really don't want to get out of the car before I have to. It's cold outside, and this sari is so difficult to move in. Can I stay here while you take care of the cuff? You can go with Anandur and Brundar, and I will drive up when you give the signal."

He took her hand and kissed it. "Please, humor me. I don't want you out here in the car when I'm doing that. This wedding is giving me a phantom ulcer. I can't shake the feeling that it's a trap."

Syssi smiled indulgently. "Fine, my loving and overprotective husband. But just so you know, when we get back home, I'm going to limit your playtime with Turner. He's infecting you with his paranoia."

Passing them by on the way to Turner's car, Anandur chuckled.

"Very funny." Kian glared at him. "Do you want Wonder to wait in the house? Or do you want her to accompany us to meet Kalugal?"

"I want her to wait in the house."

"That's what I thought."

Amanda sauntered over. "How long do we have to wait here?"

"Only until I put the cuff on Kalugal and the drones are up in the air." Kian wrapped his arm around Syssi's shoulders and headed toward the house.

"Do they have enough juice to last that long?" Dalhu asked.

Turner had his arm around Bridget as they walked up the front steps. "We need to change the batteries every hour or so. But since we have seven drones, we will rotate them, so there are always at least three in the air."

"I thought they ran on fuel," Amanda said.

"The big ones that can fire missiles do. These are small. Think of them as flying cameras with machine guns."

"Operating them is like playing a video game," Anandur said. "That's why Roni, who has no flight or combat experience, can operate these beauties better than Charlie."

Turner nodded. "That's the future of warfare."

Syssi shivered. "Can we continue this fascinating discussion inside? It's cold out here."

"Of course." Shrugging his jacket off, Kian was angry at himself for not thinking of giving it to his wife sooner.

Thankfully, it was warmer inside the house, and as the ladies and the brothers got comfortable in the living room, Kian, Turner, and Magnus went out to the backyard to check the drones.

Four black birds were perched on the grassy area, while the other three were stationed on the second-floor balcony.

The original five had been manufactured by one of the clan's subsidiaries, and Kian knew that they would perform well. The additional two Turner had gotten might not be of the same caliber, but since they were only needed for the airshow, they would do.

"Where did you get the other drones?" Kian asked.

"They are on loan from a friend," Turner said. "He wanted to charge an insane amount for them, but when I explained that they were only going to be used for an airshow, he agreed to lower the price."

"Good job." Kian clapped him on the back. "I don't want to spend too much on this."

"It's the clan's wedding gift to Kalugal."

"True, but I like the idea of doing it in-house and saving a bundle."

Magnus nodded. "William is unbelievable. Overnight, he was able to write a computer program to control all seven drones from the village and perform tricks that they weren't designed for."

"Quite impressive," Turner agreed. "I'm usually not a sentimental guy, but I'm glad that we are doing this for them. If not for the airshow, Kalugal and Jacki's celebration would have felt as if it was taking place on a battlefield."

Kian chuckled. "The saying about killing two birds with one stone has never been more apt."

Behind them the French door opened, and Yamanu stepped out. "When do you want me to start shrouding?"

"When the drones start flying."

"I can do that from there." Yamanu pointed at an outdoor chaise.

"There is no need for you to stay here. You can shroud from inside Kalugal's property. Since he needs the party and the drones shrouded, he has no reason to move against you. I'm sure that you want to be with Mey."

"I do. Thank you."

Kian turned to Magnus. "Are your men ready?"

"Yes, sir. They are all wearing earplugs." He pulled a pair out of his pocket. "I removed mine to talk to you, but I'm going to put them in as soon as you leave. From that moment on, text messages only."

Kian nodded. "It's time to put the cuff on Kalugal."

"Shouldn't we start flying the drones already?" Magnus asked.

"Not yet. Once Yamanu is inside Kalugal's property, he will start shrouding, and I'll give William the go signal."

Kalugal

As had been agreed, Kalugal opened the gate and stepped out to greet Kian, who'd arrived with his two bodyguards and another man Kalugal hadn't met before.

"Good evening, cousin. Thank you for coming." He offered Kian his hand.

As a show of trust, he had come out alone. His men were all in the backyard, and Rufsur was spitting nails, but Kalugal knew what he was doing. The time for suspicion was over, and the more trust he showed, the more Kian would be forced to reciprocate.

"You're welcome." Kian shook what was offered. "This is Yamanu." He motioned for the tall guy to step forward. "He is the shrouder I told you about."

"Congratulations." The guy flashed him a big smile and extended a hand the size of a tennis racquet. "We haven't met before, but I was shrouding your property when the exchange took place."

"You did an excellent job." Kalugal shook the guy's hand.

"Thank you."

Kian pulled the cuff out of his pocket. "May I?"

As Kalugal offered his wrist, Anandur chuckled. "You'd better start shrouding this, Yamanu. The neighbors might think that something kinky is going on."

"I'm already shrouding us," Kalugal said.

"I wish you'd told me that you were doing that." Kian snapped the cuff closed around his wrist.

"I thought you could feel it."

"My mind was on other things." Kian motioned at the gate. "Leave it open. I want to park our cars inside."

"Naturally. Where is the rest of your party?"

"They are coming." Kian pulled out his phone and typed up a text.

Kalugal shook his head. "A phone? Where are your earpieces?"

"Right here." Kian tapped his ear. "Did you think I'd come without them?"

That was disappointing.

"I was hoping you would trust me enough to forgo them. Wearing the earpieces in a social setting must be confusing."

"It is. You and my wife sound the same, and that's disturbing."

Kalugal nodded. "I can imagine. How does it work? Can you hear music?"

Kian shook his head. "The software recognizes speech and translates it. It doesn't translate anything else."

"Well, look on the bright side. You're not going to hear the damn drones buzzing overhead."

"True. There is that."

As the other two cars pulled up to the curb, Anandur got behind the wheel of the one Kian had arrived in, waited until the other cars were parked, and then followed.

"Don't close the gate yet." Kian started toward the new arrivals. "Your brother and Carol are on their way."

"Of course." Kalugal followed Kian to welcome his guests.

Opening the driver's side door of one of the cars, Kian offered his wife a hand up, but the other three ladies didn't wait for their mates to assist them.

Although perhaps they should have. The beautiful saris they were all wearing seemed difficult to walk in, probably because they were unaccustomed to the traditional Indian outfit.

"Welcome to my home." Kalugal dipped his head as he shook Syssi's hand first and then Bridget's, Callie's, and lastly, Wonder's.

Then the occupants of the other car spilled out. Amanda, Dalhu, Arwel, Jin, and another woman who looked like an older version of Jin. No doubt that was Mey, Jin's sister.

Dalhu rounded the car, opened the trunk, pulled out a large canvas, and walked over to Kalugal.

"You couldn't have finished the portrait so fast. Oil paints need time to dry."

"I used acrylics. They dry fast." Dalhu handed him the portrait.

"Thank you." Kalugal turned it around. "Simply unbelievable. You are truly talented and incredibly fast."

As he looked at Jacki's beautiful face in the painting, he noticed that even though her expression was happy, she seemed tense, and he knew now what had caused it. Amanda had told her about the bond, scaring her that it might not happen between them.

At first, Kalugal had been angry at Kian's sister for needlessly worrying Jacki before the wedding. But he'd forgiven her. As a result, he and Jacki had already exchanged pledges in private. They had also consummated their mating the night before.

Later tonight, they would repeat their pledges and embellish upon them for their family and friends' benefit.

What a concept.

A family. He actually had one.

Kalugal looked up from the portrait. "When are Lokan and Carol arriving?"

"They will be here shortly," Kian said. "Carol refused to come without a wedding gift, and they went hunting for one."

As the drones started buzzing overhead, both of them lifted their heads, and Kian pointed. "That's the clan's gift to you. The drones will film the wedding from several angles, and we will later edit the footage to create a keepsake for Jacki and you."

"A wonderful idea. Thank you. But you've already given us the greatest gift by coming here and bringing Jacki's friends with you."

Kian nodded but said nothing.

Except, his pinched expression said it all.

His cousin hoped that he wouldn't regret his decision.

Jacki

The bubble bath was supposed to be calming, but it wasn't working.

Nothing was.

The nervous butterflies in Jacki's stomach kept flapping their wings and making her nauseous no matter what she tried.

Thanks to Kalugal's wondrous venom, she'd had a couple of restful hours after their morning lovemaking session, and the effect had lingered even after she'd floated down from the cloud of euphoria.

But since breakfast, she'd been stressed out of her mind for no good reason.

She and Kalugal had already checked off all of the important boxes yesterday, so the event later today was just a party for their friends.

The flower centerpieces had come out great, her dress was beautiful, Amanda and the other ladies were coming to help her get ready, and Kalugal was outside, making sure that every last detail was precisely as he wanted it.

Her mate was a bit of a perfectionist, but that was okay with her. Kalugal had discriminating taste, and yet he'd chosen her, which meant that she was the best.

At least as far as he was concerned.

Don't get too full of yourself, Jacqueline Redford.

Shaking her head, Jacki got out of the tub and reached for a towel. She'd just realized that she was getting married to a man whose last name she didn't know.

Did he even have one?

In some parts of the globe, people used the given names of their parents instead of last names. Maybe that was what Kalugal was going to use in his pledge.

I, Kalugal, son of Navuh and Areana, take thee, Jacqueline, daughter of Jane and John Doe, to be my wife.

Yeah, it could have worked if she knew her parents' names. But she was about three years old when she'd been found, and she didn't know her mother's name. She'd been just Mommy.

But that wasn't the only problem.

Jacki wanted her pledge to Kalugal to be special, but all she'd come up with was a variation on the traditional one. It expressed everything she wanted to say to him, but it wasn't original.

A knock on the door made her jump. "Who is it?"

"It's Jin. Can I come in?"

Jacki rushed to the door, unlocked it, and pulled her best friend into a fierce hug. "You have no idea how happy I am to see you."

Jin kissed her cheek. "You'd better put a robe on. Everyone is here already, and Amanda is freaking out that it's late and that you are not going to be ready on time."

"They are here?" Jacki tightened the towel around her. "Where?"

"In the sitting room. Callie is raiding your bar and mixing drinks for everyone. I hope that's okay."

"Of course. That's what it's for."

"This master bedroom is like a separate apartment." Jin followed Jacki into the closet. "Which is great since there are so many guys living in this house. You can have drinks with your hubby without leaving the bedroom."

Jacki pulled out a robe, dropped the towel, and shrugged it on. "I'd better put on some underwear." She pulled out her lingerie drawer and chose a pair of white panties.

Leaning against the dresser, Jin folded her arms over her chest. "Are all your things in Kalugal's closet?"

"They are now." Jacki pulled on the panties. "I officially moved into the master bedroom this morning."

Jin lifted a brow. "And unofficially?"

Jacki felt her cheeks getting warm. "Last night."

Letting out an ear-splitting squeal, Jin pulled Jacki into her arms. "Congratulations!" She kissed her on both cheeks.

Jacki pushed her away and slapped her arm. "Shh, Jin. Could you have been any louder? The entire household, including everyone outside, must have heard you."

"So what? They don't know what it's about." She leaned closer. "How was it?"

"Mind-blowing."

Jin put a hand over her heart. "Isn't the venom awesome? I bet it took care of the pain right away."

"There was no pain."

"Seriously? I still remember my first time with a guy, and it wasn't much fun."

Jacki smirked. "Kalugal isn't just any guy."

"Yeah, you're right." Jin took her elbow. "You scored a demigod. Good for you."

Thinking back to what Jin had said, Jacki frowned. "What did you mean by first time with a guy? Did you have some other first with a girl?"

Jin laughed. "Not a girl. I don't swing that way. I experimented with a toy first."

"Really? Where did you get it?"

"In a store."

"Damn, you have guts, girl. I would have never walked into a sex store and bought something. How old were you?"

"Seventeen."

"Gutsy." And outspoken.

All the ladies must have heard Jin's story, and as they walked into the master sitting room, Jacki's suspicion was confirmed. Their friends were trying to hide their smirks, except for Amanda, who grinned like a proud mama.

Handing Jin a drink, she clapped her on the back. "You are my kind of girl, Jin Levine." She gave Jacki another one. "We should get started."

As a gust of wind ruffled Jacki's hair, she noticed that the balcony's door was open.

Syssi was out there, looking over the railing at the backyard. "Amanda, come see what Kalugal's men have done."

Jacki followed Amanda and Jin outside, but she stayed a little back so the men wouldn't see her standing there in her silk robe and no bra on.

"Not bad for a bunch of guys," Amanda said. "I'm impressed."

"I think it's beautiful." Jin leaned over the railing next to Syssi.

"It's all Kalugal's work," Jacki said. "He has exquisite taste."

Turning to look at her over her shoulder, Syssi smiled. "Of course he does. He chose you."

Kalugal

"What's all that?" Kalugal looked at the two crates Kian's bodyguards pulled out of the trunk. "Are those whiskey bottles?"

"Indeed. It's a tradition." Kian clapped him on the back. "While the ladies are helping the bride get ready, the men entertain the groom. I brought enough quality whiskey and cigars for all your men." He lifted a shopping bag with the Davidoff symbol embossed on its front.

That was unexpected. "Thank you."

For a brief moment, Kalugal's suspicious mind came up with several not so friendly motives for Kian's gesture, but he shoved them aside. As he'd told Rufsur, he was taking a leap of faith and trusting that his cousin's intentions were good.

Besides, given how good immortals' sense of smell was, sneaking poison into whiskey without them sniffing it out was nearly impossible. Not that Kian had any reason to do that.

"Where do you want us to put them?" Anandur asked.

"If we are going to smoke cigars, I suggest the back veranda."

"Good call." Kian waved a hand. "Lead the way."

As Kalugal was about to step inside, another car pulled up to the open gate and was stopped by the guards.

"That is Carol and Lokan," Kian said.

After signaling the guards to let them in, Kalugal walked over to welcome his brother and his mate.

"I'm sorry for the late arrival." Carol pulled him down for a hug. "But finding a gift was a bitch."

Lokan opened the trunk and pulled out a large box. "I'll get you a proper present later. This is just something small for now." He handed him the box. "Careful with that. It's fragile."

"Thank you. But you've already given me the best present by being here. My wedding is attended by my brother and my cousins and their mates. That wasn't even a dream a couple of weeks ago. Suddenly, I have a family to share my happy moments with, and it feels good."

Everything he'd said was true, but it had been intended for Kian's ears as much as Carol's and Lokan's.

"That's so nice of you to say." Wiping a tear off her cheek, Carol sighed. "I'm so glad that we can be here to celebrate with you."

Kalugal handed the box to Shamash. "If you want to join the ladies upstairs, Shamash can take you there."

"Definitely." Carol flashed the guy a bright smile. "After you, sunshine. That's the meaning of your name, isn't it?"

"It is. Do you speak the old language?"

"Just a few words." She threaded her arm through his.

Kalugal motioned for the others to follow him. "Most of my men are busy with preparations, but I can save the whiskey and cigars for them to enjoy later."

"No problem." Kian fell into step with him. "Did you choose your groomsmen already?"

"I did." Kalugal stepped out onto the back veranda. "My two lieutenants will accompany me, and I'll be honored if you and Lokan join."

"Of course," Lokan said. "I would have been offended if you didn't include me."

Kian chuckled. "I wouldn't, but I'm glad you did. So how is it going to work?"

"The groomsmen and I are going to wait on the podium for Jacki and the bridesmaids to arrive. Once they do, the bridesmaids will move to stand on the right side of the podium, and the groomsmen will move to the left. Jacki and I will take the center, say our pledges, and then the party will begin."

"Sounds good to me." Kian put the Davidoff bag on the table next to the two crates and pulled out one fat cigar. "Are you ready to start your bachelor pre-party celebration?"

Kalugal glanced at the tables out on lawn, then at the buffet table that was set up with warmers but no food yet, and the outdoor bar, of which Hivak was in charge.

"It seems like everything is ready except for the food. So yeah, why not. I could use a relaxing moment."

"Nervous?" Kian asked as he cut the tip of the cigar off and handed it to Kalugal along with a lighter.

"I am." Kalugal lit up and took a puff. "This is a good cigar. Very smooth." He leaned against the table. "I don't know why I have that uneasy feeling, though. It's like I'm forgetting something."

"Do you have the music ready?" Anandur asked.

"I do."

"And is the bar stocked with good booze?"

"It is."

"Then the rest is unimportant." Anandur took the cigar Kian handed him. "Even if your cook burns the food, as long as there is good music and good drinks, everyone will be happy."

As the French doors opened and Rufsur stepped out onto the veranda, Kalugal motioned for him to join the party. "Kian brought cigars and whiskey."

"Much appreciated." Rufsur took the cigar Anandur handed him. "Should I tell Atzil to send out the appetizers?"

"Not yet. Let's enjoy our cigars first." Kalugal took a puff. "Tell whoever is not busy to join us."

"I'll send a group text." Rufsur pulled out his phone.

Kalugal could have done it himself, but he wanted a few quiet moments before the rest of his men joined in.

As Anandur opened one of the whiskey bottles, Kalugal motioned to Hivak to bring shot glasses and then looked at Arwel. "How is mated life, my friend?"

"Excellent. How is yours?"

Kalugal took a puff of his cigar. "Jacki chasing after Rufsur and me to save your ass was the best thing that has ever happened to me, so in a way, I owe my happiness to you."

Arwel chuckled. "Following that logic, you owe your happiness to the crazy gunman. He was the trigger for everything. If not for him, I would have never rushed into the club, and you would have never known that you'd been tethered."

"And we wouldn't be standing here, puffing on cigars and drinking fine whiskey." Anandur poured them all drinks, and Hivak helped pass them around.

"To the lovely bride." Anandur lifted his glass.

"I'll drink to that," Kian said. "And to the Fates who have orchestrated everything."

"To the Fates," Kalugal echoed the salute.

Jacki

"Ready?" Jin asked.

Jacki lifted a shaky hand to her coifed hair. "Is it time?"

Why was she so unreasonably anxious? This was supposed to be the happiest day of her life, but instead of joy, she was battling a feeling of impending doom.

"No touching!" Amanda warned. "Callie, make Jacki another drink."

"Coming up."

Taking her hand, Amanda led Jacki to the couch. "Sit down and tell me your worst fears."

When Jacki didn't say anything, Amanda took her hands in hers and gave them a little encouraging squeeze. "Come on. Are you afraid you're going to trip over your dress?"

"It can happen."

"No, it can't because Jin and Mey are going to have their arms threaded through yours, and if you trip, they'll catch you. Next."

"I'll forget the words of my pledge or confuse them."

"Then you'll make them up on the spot. I love you forever and ever, you are the best thing that ever happened to me, yadda, yadda."

Callie handed Jacki the drink. "Shamash said that they are waiting for us to give them the signal. As soon as we do, they'll play the 'Wedding March'."

"Careful on the lipstick," Amanda warned.

Jacki took a long sip from the drink and handed it back to Callie. "Let's do it. The sooner it's over, the sooner I can take these shoes off and start enjoying myself."

"Is that the problem?" Amanda asked. "If they pinch your toes or bother you in any way, you'd better wear the low-heeled ones. No one is going to see your shoes under the dress."

"That's okay. I like the way they make me look." She lifted her hand. "I have this ugly cuff on that I can't take off, but the dress is beautiful, and I look statuesque in these four-inch heels. So maybe no one will pay attention to the mismatched jewelry." Jacki pushed to her feet and plastered a smile on her face. "Let's do it, ladies."

"One moment." Syssi got in front of her, blocking her way. "Do you love Kalugal?"

"With all my heart."

"Does he love you back."

"Yes."

"Do you want to spend eternity with him?"

"Yes."

"Then take a deep breath and focus on that. As you go down the stairs, look at Kalugal. He'll be waiting for you on the podium with a big smile on his face and even bigger love in his heart. He is the only one you'll see."

Jacki let out a breath. "Thank you. That actually helps." She turned to Callie. "Can you tell Shamash that we are ready?"

"Of course." Callie opened the door and conveyed the message.

Amanda clapped her hands. "Line up, ladies."

Jin and Mey took their spots flanking Jacki, Syssi and Carol were next, and behind them were Wonder and Callie.

The way they'd planned it, Amanda and Bridget, who had chosen not to participate as bridesmaids, would go down using the interior staircase and join their mates at the tables. Jacki and her bridesmaids would use the exterior stairs that led from the master bedroom's balcony straight down to the back yard, which meant that from the moment that Jacki stepped out on the balcony, all eyes would be on her.

No pressure.

Following Syssi's advice, she took a deep breath and thought about Kalugal. The moment she stepped through the balcony's French doors, she would search for him, and when she found him, she would focus on him until she reached the podium.

As the music started, Jin and Mey threaded their arms through hers and practically lifted her.

That wasn't going to work.

Jacki wasn't a prisoner being escorted to her execution, she was a bride about to pledge her eternal love to the best man on the planet.

"That's okay, ladies. I'm not scared anymore. In fact, I'll go first, and you can follow me."

Jin cast her a worried look. "Are you sure? What about the shoes? You might trip."

"I'll be fine. Let's go."

Jacki squared her shoulders and walked out on the balcony with her head held high.

As a cheer went up, followed by clapping, she smiled and waved her hand like a celebrity or a princess. "Thank you!"

The stairs were about six feet wide and turned in a slight arc. Taking them carefully one at the time, Jacki looked at Kalugal, who was smiling and gazing at her adoringly, precisely as Syssi had predicted.

But he wasn't the only one smiling. All of their guests were grinning as well, their well-wishing so palpable that it suffused Jacki with warmth and gratitude.

Kalugal was making all of her wishes come true, even those she hadn't dared to dream.

She was so lucky.

Lifting her face heavenward, Jacki offered a quick thank you to the Fates. Whether it was the mythological matchmakers that the clan believed in or some other higher power who had granted her and Kalugal such a boon, Jacki was grateful for the kindness that had been bestowed on them. Then she also added a quick prayer for her successful transition and an eternity of love.

Kalugal

As the traditional wedding march began playing through the loudspeakers, signaling that Jacki was ready, Kalugal took his place on the podium.

Standing with Lokan on one side and Kian on the other, he was surrounded by family. His best friends, Phinas and Rufsur, stood behind his brother, and Welgost and Ruvon behind Kian.

Above, the drones were buzzing, and he heard the murmurs of admiration for the display, but Kalugal didn't spare them a single glance. His eyes were glued to the second floor's balcony.

When Jacki stepped out, his heart skipped a beat. She looked like a queen, regal, resplendent, and her smile was bright enough to light up the sky.

When a cheer went up, she waved and then looked straight at him, holding his eyes as she descended the stairs.

His mate, his love.

Everything receded into the background, the sights, the sounds, the bridesmaids in their colorful saris, even the cold breeze ruffling his hair. All Kalugal could see was his queen advancing toward him, bathed in light and shining like a star.

Logically, he knew that the glow was the result of the spotlights directed at her and reflecting off her white wedding gown. But reality didn't matter to him at the moment. All he wanted was for Jacki to feel as resplendent as she looked.

As she climbed the two steps up to the podium, the bridesmaids and groomsmen stepped down, leaving the stage clear for the two of them.

"My love." Kalugal offered Jacki his hand.

"I'm here with you for evermore."

An approving murmur rose like a wave and washed over their guests.

"As am I." Kalugal lifted Jacki's hand and kissed it. "Would you like to start?" he whispered.

They hadn't planned who was going first, and Kalugal wasn't sure what was customary.

Jacki nodded and cleared her throat. "I, Jacqueline Redford, take you, Kalugal, son of Areana and Navuh, to be my mate, and I promise in front of these witnesses to have and to hold you from this day forward, for better, for worse, for richer, for poorer, in joy and in sorrow. I will love, cherish, and honor you all the days of my life."

It was perfect, and Kalugal couldn't help but lean and kiss her cheek. "I love you."

As a round of applause began, he lifted his hand. "I'm not finished, people."

He waited until it was quiet again. "I, Kalugal, take you, my beautiful Jacqueline, to be my mate, my wife, my everything. I promise in front of all these witnesses, our family and friends, to love you, provide for you, protect you, and make you happy to the best of my ability. I will love, cherish, and honor you all the days of my life. I may now kiss the bride." He pulled Jacki into his arms and kissed the living daylights out of her.

The applause was deafening, and as someone tapped his shoulder, Kalugal ignored the tap and kept on kissing his mate.

"Look up," Kian said in his ear. "You are missing it."

As he let go of Jacki's mouth, they both looked up to the sky.

Jacki gasped. "It's beautiful!"

The drones had painted a big heart in the sky, and as the pink smoke started to fade, another drone passed through it and unfurled a banner. It said 'Congratulations, Jacki and Kalugal.' Two red hearts flanked the message.

Looking over his shoulder at his cousin, Kalugal mouthed, "Thank you."

"You're welcome."

The drone with the banner made a couple more passes over the backyard, and then the other six put up an impressive airshow, flying in formation and performing aerobatics.

It must have taken a lot of effort for the clan to plan and execute such a professional display in such a short time. And to think that just a few weeks ago they were on opposite sides of the fence.

Now, they were one big happy family.

Naturally, that was an exaggeration, but it was his wedding night, and Kalugal was allowed his fantasies. The real world could wait for tomorrow.

Besides, Kian, Lokan, and he were on the right path, and today's wishful thinking could be tomorrow's reality.

Simmons

"Kajeck Zolotovsky." Simmons read the name from the printed page he pulled out of the file folder. "That's the name of the owner on record. Age thirty-eight, single, emigrated from Russia eleven years ago, initially lived in New York, then eight years later he moved here and bought the house." He lifted his head and looked at Roberts. "Sounds like a fake to me, but everything checked out."

"Why does it sound fake?" Roberts asked.

"Just a gut feeling."

"What does your gut tell you now?"

"That we are going to succeed."

"I hope you are right." Roberts shifted in his seat. "Your guy is taking too long. What's keeping him?"

"We will soon find out."

While Hector made one last pass by the mansion, the rest of them parked two streets over, waiting for his report. Simmons didn't expect any surprises, but it was important to scope the place right before the attack.

Because of the party, additional security might be employed, or perhaps guests were still arriving, or food was being delivered. They had to verify that the party was going full swing and that the paranormals were busy before proceeding with their plan.

Except, Hector was taking longer than expected, and six identical vans parked in a row attracted attention. Simmons wasn't overly worried about that. If anyone came to investigate, he had a cover story prepared. So far, though, it was a quiet night, and only one car had passed by them without slowing down.

"Here he is," Roberts said.

Simmons rolled down his window.

As Hector stopped and rolled his down as well, his expression didn't bode well. "The party must have been canceled. There is no one there, and all the tables and chairs are gone."

That didn't make sense. Only several hours ago, the mansion's backyard was set up for a wedding.

"Perhaps they've moved it inside?"

Hector shook his head. "There is no music, and the house is dark. They are either not there or sleeping."

There could be only one logical explanation for what Hector was reporting. Someone must've gotten hold of the guy's brain again and hypnotized him not to see the party.

"Hold on a moment, Hector." Simmons rolled the window back up. "They've messed with him again. The tables and chairs were still there when he made his previous rounds six hours ago, and four hours ago, and people were putting tablecloths, serve ware, and decorative flower arrangements on the tables. The party is happening right now, but he just can't see it."

"How do you want to proceed?" Roberts asked.

"Just as we planned. Hector's men will knock on the neighbors' doors and explain that an emergency sound system is going to be deployed and not to worry. Once we fire the cannon, they will drive up to the property and collect the talents."

"Perhaps we should take a look first? What if he's right?"

"He's not. But sure. Let's make a quick drive-by."

He rolled the window down. "Wait here. Roberts and I are going to check what's going on."

"Suit yourself. There is nothing there."

The house was less than a five-minute drive away, and as soon as Simmons turned into the street, he heard music playing.

He turned to Roberts. "Do you hear that? They are playing the 'Wedding March'."

Roberts eyed him as if he were insane. "What music?"

"You can't hear it?"

"No."

Simmons rolled down the window. "How about now?"

"Nothing."

The music wasn't loud, but Roberts would have to be deaf not to hear it. Maybe his friend needed a hearing aid?

As a buzzing sound from above caught his attention, Simmons looked up and saw a bunch of drones flying in formation over the property. "Elijah, open your window and look up."

His friend did as he asked, pushed his head out, and looked to the sky. "What am I supposed to see?"

"Drones flying in formation. Oh, look at that. Two just painted a giant heart with smoke."

Roberts shook his head. "Edgar, I worry about you. There are no drones, no music, and there isn't a single light in any of the windows. The entire property looks deserted."

"I know what I'm seeing, Elijah. They must have a powerful hypnotist who is manipulating everybody's minds, and I'm the only one who sees and hears what's going on because I'm immune."

He looked up at the sky again. "One of the drones has a banner that says, 'Congratulations Jacki and Kalugal.' It seems that our Jacki is the one getting married."

Elijah was still looking at him as if he were missing a screw. "No one can hypnotize or compel people remotely to see or not to see, to hear or not to hear something. And if they have someone like that, we shouldn't mess with them. We should cancel the mission."

"I'm not canceling anything. Unless that master hypnotist is an alien from outer space, he or she still has the same ears as everyone else. When we activate the device, all of them will go down no matter what paranormal talents they have or how powerful they are."

"Let's assume for a moment that you are right, and that there is really a party going on out there, and that you haven't lost your mind. We shoot the cannon, we collect the talents, drug them, and bring them to our facility. How are you going to contain someone that powerful? The others can be compelled by the recruiter, but the hypnotist probably not."

Simmons snorted. "Come on, Elijah. You know precisely what can be done to convince a reluctant talent to cooperate. It has been successfully done to condition elite operatives and still is. Between the drugs, the brainwashing, and if needed, sensory deprivation and pain, most minds can be bent to serve their masters. And if they don't, they break."

Kian

As soon as Jacki and Kalugal finished exchanging their vows, everyone erupted in cheers and applause, which Kian saw but couldn't hear. But he could certainly feel his phone vibrating in his pocket.

He pulled it out and read the message from Magnus.

A couple of vans drove by the mansion. One stopped for a couple of minutes, a guy stuck his head out the window, and then the van drove away. Is Kalugal waiting for deliveries?

Kian typed back. *I'll ask.*

Leaning closer to Syssi, he whispered in her ear, "I need to ask Rufsur something. I'll be back in a minute."

She nodded.

He found Kalugal's second-in-command on the veranda, supervising the men bringing out food to the buffet table.

"Rufsur." He lifted a hand to get the guy's attention. "Are you waiting for deliveries?"

"No, why?" Rufsur walked over.

"My men saw a couple of vans drive by the property."

"Let me check with our security." Rufsur pulled out his phone and called. "Did you see a couple of vans driving by?"

He waited for a response that Kian couldn't hear with his earpieces in.

"My guys saw them too, but they figured that the neighbors were waiting for a delivery, and the driver was checking the address. In this neighborhood, deliveries are frequent."

Kian arched a brow. "This late at night?"

"You'd be surprised. Nowadays, people can get even weed delivered to their doorstep, and then when they get the munchies, they can order food."

Kian didn't know that, but he wasn't about to admit it and let Rufsur think that he was ignorant about current trends.

"Nevertheless, I would suggest that your men stay alert and let you know as soon as they see another van near the house. I'll tell mine to do the same."

Rufsur moved aside to let one of his men pass with a tray of appetizers. "How good is your shrouder? Is he really blocking everything?"

"Whoever drives by will see a house with no lights in the windows, and he will hear nothing."

"Impressive."

"Indeed." Kian clapped him on the back. "I'll let you get back to your work. Just stay alert."

Walking back toward his table, Kian typed a message to Magnus, instructing the Guardian to alert him immediately if another van showed up. With that done, he pulled up the app controlling his earpiece and scrolled to the voice selection William had included.

Wearing the earpieces during the summit had been okay, but it was annoying in a social setting. After Kalugal and Jacki had exchanged their vows, Kian had been contemplating removing them entirely.

He was almost certain that Kalugal had no nefarious intentions and that the earpieces were unnecessary, but then Magnus's message arrived, and Kian decided to leave them in just in case the vans actually belonged to Kalugal's men.

Counting the number of them attending the party, Kian had taken into account that some were on duty, and others were helping in the kitchen, and the number Kalugal had given him checked out.

Except, his cousin could have lied, and he could have had more men hiding in the bunker and outside the property. The vans making rounds next to the house could belong to Kalugal, and it could be that the reason they were out there was to check where Kian's men were stationed before launching an attack.

It seemed like a far-fetched scenario, and if he told Syssi about his suspicions, she would probably accuse him of paranoia. But the earpieces were staying in, and he was going to keep an eye on his cousin at all times.

The one thing Kian did, though, was to change the computerized voice from male to female, so when Syssi spoke to him, she wouldn't sound like a man. It had been most disturbing to hear her say that she loved him in a man's voice, and even more so when she'd complimented him on how handsome he looked.

When he reached the table, she got up and took his hand. "Dance with me?"

"I can't hear the music."

She smirked. "Then you will have to follow my lead."

"I always do." He put his hands on her waist and leaned to kiss her lips.

She made a face as if what he'd said was complete nonsense. "You're the bossiest, most dominant man I've ever known."

He leaned and whispered in her ear. "Only in bed, my love. Have I ever not followed your suggestions?"

Syssi frowned. "There must have been some that you didn't."

Shaking his head, he led her to the delineated dance floor, where several couples were swaying to the music. "You can't think of even one, can you?"

"Not off the top of my head." She wrapped her arms around his neck. "But you are the boss, so don't pretend like you are not."

Kian chuckled. "If that's what you are comfortable believing, I won't argue with you."

Jacki

"Shall we dance?" Kalugal took Jacki's hand and led her to the dance platform.

Wrapping her arms around his neck, she looked into the beautiful blue eyes of her husband. "Our first dance as a married couple. Or is it mated?"

"Married, mated, I don't care what we call it. All I care about is that you are mine, and I am yours. Let's waltz."

She leaned to whisper in his ear. "I don't know how."

He whispered back. "Kick your shoes off and step on my feet."

Doing as he suggested would have required zero effort on her part, and it would have even been fun, but taking the easy road and letting Kalugal do things for her wasn't how Jacki wanted to start their married life. She accepted that he was smarter, more knowledgeable, and more experienced than she was. But that only meant that she could learn a lot from Kalugal, not let him do everything for her simply because he could do it better.

"How about you whisper the steps in my ear until I get it? I want to learn."

Kalugal's smile was full of pride and approval. "Of course. But you need to relax and follow my lead." He put one hand on the small of her back and took her hand with the other. "Step forward with your left foot, and now step forward with your right, so it's parallel to the left. Bring your left foot to your right. Now step back with your right, now with your left, so it's parallel to your right, and bring your right foot to your left."

It was confusing at first, but after Kalugal repeated the instructions several times, Jacki got the hang of it. "You can stop whispering."

By now, their first dance as a married couple had already been joined by Lokan and Carol, Wonder and Anandur. Then Amanda had dragged the reluctant Dalhu onto the dance floor. Syssi and Kian arrived last.

"But I'm enjoying it. It feels intimate even though we are surrounded by people. I'll just whisper sexy things instead."

Jacki loved having Kalugal's cheek pressed to hers too, but as he'd pointed out, they were not alone, and she didn't want to get all hot and bothered in the company of immortals and their super-sensitive noses.

"Don't you dare. I don't want to blush."

"But you look so lovely when you do."

"Tell me how much you love me."

"I adore you." Kalugal pulled her closer against his body. "And I lust after you. I can't wait for everyone to go home, so I can take my bride to bed."

"Patience, my prince."

He chuckled. "I like it when you call me your prince."

When the waltz ended, Kalugal bowed to her, and everyone on the dance floor clapped.

"Dinner is served!" Rufsur called out from the veranda.

"Come." Kalugal wrapped his arm around her waist. "We should be first in line. No one is going to take anything until we do."

Jacki was too hyped up to feel hungry, but she didn't want to keep her guests waiting. "Okay."

At the buffet, Atzil stood behind the long table looking like a drill sergeant, his legs planted firmly on the floor, his head held high, and his square jaw looking squarer than usual.

"Thank you for preparing this wonderful dinner," Jacki said.

He cracked a smile. "Eat first, and thank me later." He leaned closer. "Your pledges were beautiful. Congratulations."

"Thank you."

As they took their plates to the table, Lokan and Carol joined them a few moments later, and then Syssi and Kian.

"The airshow was fantastic," Kalugal said. "Thank you."

Smiling, Kian draped a napkin over his trousers. "Not my doing, but you're welcome."

"I loved the heart and the banner," Jacki said. "Did William make it happen?"

She hoped it meant that he had no hard feelings. His mini crush on her had been sweet, and she'd let him down as gently as she could. Still, no one enjoyed rejection.

"The one and only." Kian cut a piece of potato and put it in his mouth.

"Is that all you are eating?" Kalugal motioned at his plate, which was piled with side dishes, but none of the beef and salmon.

"I'm vegan. That's all I can eat."

Kalugal frowned. "You should have mentioned it. I would have told Atzil to make something special for you."

Kian waved a dismissive hand. "I can always manage with the side dishes. I don't want to create extra work for anyone because of my culinary preferences."

"It's an odd choice for an immortal. We are carnivores by nature."

"We are omnivores, and we have a choice. I choose to stay away from animal products."

"Is it for health or moral reasons?"

"Both."

Kalugal shook his head. "I would love to hear the reasoning behind your decision. Immortals are at the top of the food chain, and we shouldn't subsist on vegetables."

"You are young, Kalugal." Kian smiled indulgently. "I bet that you didn't grow up with farm animals."

"I did not."

"I'm a very old immortal, and when I was young, there were no supermarkets to buy your meat at. You either hunted it or raised it, and I've never enjoyed taking a life, human or animal. I'd rather avoid it if I can, but there were times when I had no choice."

Kalugal tilted his head. "What about immortal life?"

Kian's wicked smile sent chills down Jacki's spine. "I have no problem whatsoever with killing enemies who seek the annihilation of my people."

"Most of them are just doing what they are told," Lokan said. "They are soldiers."

"You don't know your people as well as you think you do." Kian put his fork down and wiped his mouth. "I don't know whether it's the brainwashing, or the compulsion, or the genetics of those who fathered them, but many of your men thrive on cruelty. As I said, I'm old, and I've seen plenty of the atrocities Doomers have committed."

"Humans are no better," Lokan said.

Kian sighed. "Regrettably, you are correct. In fact, they are worse because there are so many of them, and they can perpetrate much more damage than all the Doomers combined. The difference is that they don't pose a direct threat to me, and they don't actively seek my people's demise."

Kalugal didn't seem to agree. "Only because they don't know that you exist."

Kian

Throughout dinner, Kian kept glancing at the sky, noting the change of guard as the drones circled back and forth on their scheduled battery replacement rotations.

He also kept putting his hand on the phone in his pocket, expecting it to vibrate with a new message. The vans passing by Kalugal's place might have been a non-issue, but it had been enough to cause a disquiet that refused to abate.

And that was despite the fact that he no longer suspected Kalugal of planning an attack. More than an hour had passed since the two vans had driven by the property, so if there had been such a plan, it would have been already executed.

"You seem tense." Syssi put a hand on his arm. "What's going on?"

"It's nothing. Magnus texted me before dinner started about two vans passing by the property."

"Maybe someone is moving out or in."

"Not likely at this time at night. But it might have been deliveries to neighboring houses."

"That sounds like a reasonable explanation. So why are you still tense?"

He shrugged. "You know me. I'm always on the alert."

"Maybe dancing will loosen you up." Syssi rose to her feet and tugged on his hand.

With most of the wedding guests still eating at their tables, the dance platform was deserted, but as soon as he and Syssi started walking toward it, Kalugal and Jacki joined them, and then Lokan and Carol.

"It's so nice to celebrate with family." Syssi put her hands on his shoulders.

Dipping his head, he kissed her cheek. Having Syssi in his arms was an antidote to stress. She was like a soothing balm on his nerves, a breath of fresh air, and as they danced, the knotted muscles in his shoulders and back started to relax. But then his phone vibrated, and all that hard-won calm disappeared in a flash.

"I need to get it." He let go of Syssi and pulled out his phone.

One of the vans from before just passed by the house and kept going, but Roni sees it from the drone, and he says it's parked on the street on the other side of the house.

Kian tapped Kalugal on the shoulder. "Do you have a delivery coming?"

"No, why?"

"A van just stopped next to your backyard fence."

"That's odd." Kalugal lifted his hand and motioned for Rufsur to come over.

As Rufsur started walking toward them, both of Kian's earpieces malfunctioned at once, emitting piercing shrieks, or so he thought until everyone around him clapped their hands over their ears, including Kalugal and his men, and then fell to the ground writhing in agony.

The only ones standing were him, Anandur, and Brundar.

It took another split second to process that they were under attack and that he needed to shield Syssi and their unborn child.

Dropping over his wife, Kian covered her with his body and added his hands to hers over her ears.

Then as soon as it had started, the shrieking stopped. Or maybe it just stopped in his earpieces?

Quickly, Kian pulled one out, but all he heard were the groans of everyone around him.

Kalugal was the first one to sit up. "What the hell just happened?" he yelled at the top of his lungs while gathering Jacki into his arms.

Under Kian, Syssi stirred, and he shifted off her. "Are you okay?"

She shook her head and pointed to her ears. "I can't hear anything."

Slowly, everyone started rising, first to sit on the ground, and then to push up on shaky legs. The only two remaining slumped and looking unconscious were Jacki and Jin. Their human ears were less sensitive than those of the immortals, but they also lacked the immortals' rapid recovery ability.

"Where is the doctor?" Kalugal yelled again, his voice sounding panicky. "Jacki needs help."

Kian removed the other earpiece and put both in his pocket.

Kalugal was not the enemy.

But who was?

His phone vibrated.

Pulling it out of his pocket, he read the message from Magnus.

Roni shot the device emitting that sound. There are casualties. More vans are pulling up next to it. We are almost there.

"Fuck." Kian looked at Kalugal, but the guy was useless at the moment.

Rocking Jacki in his arms, he seemed to be hanging on to sanity by a thread.

Instead, Kian grabbed Rufsur and showed him the message.

The guy nodded and lifted his arms high in the air, motioning for his men to take out their phones.

That was some quick thinking.

Everyone's ears were out of commission, and the only way to communicate was via texts.

Typing so fast that his fingers blurred over the screen, he started running toward the back gate, with some of his men following behind, and the others running in the opposite direction, heading for the front of the house.

"Yamanu's shroud is down," Anandur yelled. "We need to hustle."

"I'm okay." Yamanu lifted his arm. "I'll have it back on in a couple of seconds."

Kian lifted his hand and motioned for the brothers to come closer. "Any idea what the fuck that was?"

"No clue," Anandur said. "But if not for Roni, that could have been one hell of a clusterfuck."

Kalugal

The ringing in Kalugal's ears was driving him nuts, but none of that mattered. Jacki opened her eyes, and they were full of tears. She was in pain, and he didn't know what to do.

The doctor finally made it to them, but the only thing she had was a small flashlight.

Crouching, she mouthed, "I'm going to check your ears."

Jacki nodded, which was a good sign. She knew what was going on and was responsive.

Kalugal let out a relieved breath.

The doctor shone her flashlight into Jacki's left ear, and then her right. "The eardrums didn't rupture." She turned the flashlight off and moved it from side to side in front of Jacki's eyes. "Good, you're tracking."

The ringing in Kalugal's ears was subsiding rapidly, and he was now able to hear the doctor clearly.

"Jacki is in pain. What can you do for her?"

"Unfortunately, nothing. I don't have anything with me." Bridget lifted her head and looked toward the back fence. "I think your presence is needed. Rufsur is waving you over."

"I don't want to leave Jacki."

"I'll take care of her. You need to take care of the situation, whatever it is." The doctor put her flashlight back in her purse, and then lifted Jacki off his lap. "I'll carry her to the house."

Wonder rushed over. "Let me. Others might need your help." She took Jacki out of Bridget's arms. "I've already put Jin on the living room couch."

"I can walk!" Jacki yelled, either unaware of being loud or thinking that the others were suffering a hearing loss similar to hers.

He kissed her cheek. "Let Wonder carry you. She is very strong."

Jacki made a face, either because she couldn't hear him or because she was in pain, but she nodded and wrapped her arms around Wonder's neck.

With Jacki taken care of, Kalugal sprinted toward the back of his property. Whoever was responsible for ruining their wedding was going to pay.

Exploding through the back gate, he skidded to a halt.

Two old humans were sprawled on the sidewalk, bleeding, and a younger human was slumped over the wheel of a van that was riddled with bullets. Pieces of broken equipment were strewn about.

"What's going on?"

Kian waved a hand at the two old men. "One is dead, the other one is injured. They fired a noise cannon at us, and Roni shot it down from the drone. The dead one was holding it, the other one and the driver got hit as well. What do you want to do with them?"

In the distance, Kalugal heard police sirens, which meant that the shrouder had gone down as well, and they were exposed. The sirens still sounded very faint, so they had time, but not much.

"Move them into the house. Is your shrouder back on line?"

Kian nodded. "Yamanu is on it. But there are six vans in front of your property, and seven operatives that my men detained. They need to either be moved inside or driven away. And we need to take care of this one too."

They had about ten minutes to do that before the police arrived, and the back gate was good for foot traffic only. The bullet-ridden van would have to be driven around and through the front gate.

"Rufsur, get inside the van and drive it through the front. Kian, tell your men to get the other vans inside as well. They can park on the grass."

Rufsur opened the vehicle's door, moved the injured driver aside, and got behind the wheel.

"Let's take them inside."

Anandur lifted the injured man, and Brundar the dead one.

"Where do you want us to take them?"

"Into the bunker." Kalugal turned to his own men. "Clean up the mess as best you can and then get inside and lock the gate."

"Yes, boss."

"Follow me." Kalugal motioned for Kian and the brothers.

"As soon as everything is out of sight, I can tell Yamanu to switch from shrouding to thralling," Kian said. "He can thrall the police to think that they have checked the report and that the noise came from a faulty exhaust pipe."

"Your guy's talent is extraordinary. I need to be heard to achieve the same result."

Kian smirked. "I know."

"Can't he thrall them to drive in a different direction before they get here?"

"Unfortunately, his thralling ability is limited by distance."

"I was afraid of that," Kalugal said. "That's why we can't leave the vans outside. The police cars have cameras mounted on them, and they record everything. So even if they don't see anything while driving by the house, they will see it later when they go over the footage. Also, the recording might be streamed live to a monitoring center, which could be out of my shrouding range as well."

Kian nodded. "We also don't want them colliding with invisible vans while trying to park in front of your house."

Jacki

As Wonder put Jacki down on the couch, Shamash rushed to her with a glass of water. His lips were moving, but she couldn't hear what he was saying.

"Thank you." She tried to sit up and take the glass, but her head was spinning, and she dropped back down.

Taking it from Shamash, Wonder lifted Jacki's head and brought the glass to her lips.

Still nauseous and struggling to keep dinner from coming back up, she was afraid that even water might induce the puking that she was trying so hard to hold down. But her mouth was dry, and the water was cold.

Jacki took a tiny sip, just enough to wet her lips. It felt wonderful, but perhaps that was enough for now. Letting her head drop back against Wonder's strong arm, she closed her eyes.

Big mistake.

The spinning got worse, as did the pulsating pain in her ears.

When she groaned, Wonder pushed another pillow under her head.

The elevated position helped.

"Thank you," Jacki murmured and closed her eyes again.

As the minutes passed, the pain in her ears gradually subsided to a manageable throb, but she still couldn't hear anything over the ringing.

Hopefully, it was temporary.

When Wonder put a cold, wet towel over her forehead, Jacki pulled both edges over her poor ears, but it didn't help with the throbbing that was located somewhere in her ear canal.

What was that horrible sound?

She'd never heard anything like it. Heck, she didn't know anything could produce a sound so loud.

Had it been an attack? By whom?

Jacki suspected that it had something to do with her, and the guilt caused an uncomfortable feeling in the pit of her stomach that had nothing to do with nausea.

It was her fault.

Lifting her hand, she looked at the silver cuff and wondered whether it was still working. What if that sound had damaged it?

What if it had malfunctioned even before, and she'd been broadcasting a signal? What if the attack was because the director and his cronies had come looking for her?

Opening her eyes, Jacki turned her head and looked at Wonder, who'd moved to sit on the coffee table next to her. "Did anyone get hurt?"

Wonder lifted her hands, gesturing that she didn't know.

"Is Jin okay?"

Wonder nodded, shifted to the side, and pointed at the other couch. Jin was lying in a similar pose to Jacki's with a compress on her forehead, but instead of using a stack of pillows, her head was resting on Arwel's lap.

His handsome face wore a worried expression, and he was stroking Jin's hair.

Lucky girl. Jacki wished Kalugal was with her, but he was probably taking care of the situation.

Was he okay?

Shifting her gaze to the right, Jacki saw Mey, who was sitting on a chair next to Jin and Arwel, and when she shifted it to the left, she saw Syssi and Amanda each occupying an armchair.

Everyone looked worried, but not panicked, so the situation was most likely under control.

The only casualties seemed to be the two humans. Her and Jin.

The good news was that Jin was in a similar state to her but not worse. She was alive, and not too seriously hurt.

Thank God. Jacki let her eyelids slide closed again.

There was a third casualty, though. Her wedding party was ruined, but that was such a petty concern. If that horrendous sound had lasted for even a few seconds longer, everyone's eardrums would have ruptured, and they would have suffered irreversible hearing loss.

Or worse.

With all the immortals down, someone could have just walked in and killed them all, or taken them prisoner.

That someone was probably the director or the people he'd sent to do his dirty work for him.

It was the only explanation that made sense.

Wendy had betrayed them, telling the director that they had been taken by an organization of people with paranormal talents, which had probably made him salivate with greed.

It was an ingenious idea to use a sound attack, a nonlethal weapon that could topple all the paranormals at once no matter how strong their talents were. He couldn't have known that the paranormals were immortal, but apparently, the weapon worked just as well on them as on humans.

Simmons had thought that he could capture many talents with one well-planned attack, saving time and money compared to recruiting them one at a time. And thanks to the trackers he'd implanted in her and her friends, he knew where to find them. The party could have ended like the red wedding in *Game of Thrones*.

Talk about guilt.

Not only had she led the director to Kalugal and his men, but her wedding also provided the perfect setup for him to maximize the number of captured paranormals.

But what in damnation could have made that noise?

Some new secret weapon that had been developed in the underground city?

Except, Jacki couldn't imagine anyone authorizing an attack like that on a group of civilians. Simmons must have lied and made up some crazy story to get approval.

Or, maybe not.

The director was well-connected, and he knew some very high-ranking people both in the military and in the government.

Who knew how deep this thing went?

God, this was such a mess.

They all needed to leave this lovely house and hide somewhere. Perhaps Kian could offer them refuge?

He could convert more of his underground facility's classrooms and offices into bedrooms, so all of Kalugal's men could find shelter there.

Suddenly, the thought of hiding underground seemed very appealing. And the sooner they moved, the better. She had to find Kalugal and tell him that.

Gritting her teeth, Jacki gripped the side of the couch and lifted herself to a sitting position.

"What are you doing?" Wonder asked.

Wow, Jacki actually heard what she said. Even though Wonder's voice sounded as if it was traveling through a pool full of water, Jacki was ecstatic to hear anything at all.

"I heard you."

Wonder smiled. "I'm glad. Now, lie back down. Bridget said that you need to rest."

"I need to talk to Kalugal. Where is he?"

"Still outside. He and Kian and the rest of the guys are cleaning up the mess."

"What do you mean?"

"It was an attack. Several vans with armed operatives have been taken. And I heard that there were casualties. Theirs, not ours."

"Where are they taking them?"

"To the bunker," Arwel said. "Where else?"

Kian

Once the dead, the injured, the thralled, and the vans they'd all arrived in were inside the gate, Kalugal signaled for it to be closed, and Kian told Magnus to ground the drones.

He was taking a risk. But at this point, the danger from without was much more pressing than the one from within.

The police sirens were getting damn close.

Everyone had already moved inside the house or into the bunker, and Kalugal had ordered the lights switched off in the back and front yards.

Sitting on an upholstered bench in Kalugal's foyer, Yamanu stared at the wall in front of him unseeing, his pale blue eyes nearly white against the backdrop of his dark skin. His pupils had shrunk so much that they were nothing but a pinprick inside his large pale irises.

Kian tapped him on the shoulder. "You can switch to thralling now."

When Yamanu nodded, he turned to Kalugal. "Can you shroud the property?"

Kalugal shook his head. "I don't have much practice in that. I'm good at shrouding myself and those near me and projecting that fake image over a large distance. Shrouding places is a completely different talent."

His cousin was being so frank with what he could and couldn't do that Kian was hard-pressed to keep suspecting him of subterfuge. And even though taking a leap of faith with Syssi present was the last thing Kian wanted to do, he didn't have much choice.

It was an emergency situation, and they needed to combine their forces to solve the mess and cover it up.

As three police cars stopped in front of Kalugal's property, and a moment later, all three turned the sirens off, Kian wondered what Yamanu was projecting into their heads.

Kalugal's phone rang. "It's the intercom."

"Hello?" He answered with a Russian accent and a voice that sounded sleepy and irate.

"Good evening, sir. This is Officer Perez. Your neighbors reported gunshots. Have you heard anything?"

Since Yamanu's shroud went down only after the noise device had fired, they might have not heard it at all, only the gunfire that followed.

"Damn teenagers and their bloody motorcycles. You need to catch these hoodlums. They make holes in the exhaust pipes to make a ruckus and scare people half to death."

"I'm sorry, sir. Did you happen to catch their license numbers?"

"I was asleep. By the time I got to a window, they were gone."

"Next time they pass through, please try to write down at least one of the license plate numbers."

"I will do my best. Good night, officer."

"Good night, sir."

Kalugal ended the call, and a couple of minutes later, the police cars left.

Kian chuckled. "You are an excellent actor."

"Thank you." Kalugal dipped his head. "Shall we go see who our uninvited guests are?"

Kian arched a brow. "Are you inviting me to your bunker?"

"I am." Kalugal nodded. "There isn't much you can learn from just looking around. Besides, your people are already there. I also don't intend to stay in this house for long. Especially not after this." He opened the front door and motioned for Kian to step outside.

"Just a moment." Kian turned to Yamanu and put a hand on his shoulder. "You can stop thralling."

The Guardian let out a breath, and his eyes refocused. "Good. I want to get back to Mey and to check on Jin."

Kalugal shook his head. "Jacki and Jin are in worse condition than the rest of us because they don't heal as fast as we do, but Bridget told me that they will be fine in a day or two. She doesn't expect any permanent damage."

"Good to know." Yamanu walked toward the living room.

Kian followed Kalugal out the door. "Even if they suffered permanent damage, the transition is going to take care of that."

"True." Kalugal cast him a sidelong glance. "But unlike Jin's transition, Jacki's is not guaranteed."

"Nothing in life is guaranteed." Kian waved a hand at the vans parked on the grass. "You never know where the next blow will come from. I'm glad that you changed your mind about moving."

Kalugal nodded. "Relocating my collection is going to be a major pain in the rear, but I need to think about Jacki's safety. I've just learned the hard way that I can't protect her against all threats, not even when I'm right here. And I do need to leave the house from time to time."

He stepped on the lift's platform, waited for Kian to join him, and pulled out his phone to activate it.

"Is that the only way into the bunker?" Kian asked, knowing that it wasn't.

As the platform shook and started its descent, Kalugal smirked. "Of course not, but I don't want you to see the safety measures I have at the other entrances. I was very creative with those." He chuckled. "Actually, I stole ideas from several movies, but the creative part was making them real. The booby traps are truly ingenious, and I'm not saying it to toot my own horn."

The platform stopped at a sprawling garage containing an impressive assortment of luxury cars.

"I see that artifacts are not the only things you collect. Is that a Bugatti Veyron?"

"It is, and I'll gladly give you a tour after we deal with our uninvited guests."

Kalugal

"Where did you put them?" Kian asked.

"Phinas was in charge of that. We will find out in a moment."

There were only two rooms large enough to hold the eight operatives and the two old men, one dead and one injured. One was the meeting room, and the other one was a classroom. There was also the extensive storage and his wine cellar, but Kalugal hoped Phinas hadn't used those.

Betting on the classroom, he headed there first, and he was right.

Partially.

The operatives were there, as well as Kian's bodyguards, but the dead man and the injured one weren't.

Anandur pushed away from where he was leaning against the wall, and the blond followed.

"Where are the old men?" Kian asked.

"The dead guy is Director Edgar Simmons," Anandur said. "We put him in the small classroom to the left of this one. The injured one is Doctor Elijah Roberts, and Phinas told us to put him in the cell. Bridget is taking care of him as best she can."

Phinas nodded. "I've sent Heblon to get the doctor what she needs from the pharmacy. If it's closed, I told him to break in."

"I'll be damned." Kian shook his head. "I had a feeling that it was Simmons."

"Who else could it have been?" Anandur smiled smugly. "I knew all along that he was behind the attack. I was just surprised that he took an active part in it."

"What about the men?" Kalugal pointed at the operatives who sat slumped on the floor, their backs against the wall. "Who are they?"

"Kian's men thralled them into a stupor before transferring them to us," Phinas said. "I thought that you would want to interrogate them yourself. But this one we know." He pointed at one of the men. "This is the guy who's been snooping around the property. We've already established that he's a private operator."

Kian regarded the men with a frown. "From the look of them, they are ex-military."

That seemed like a good guess. The men were in their mid to late forties, but they were all physically fit and still wore their hair military style. They were also in uniforms.

"Did you check their documentation?"

Phinas nodded. "Their wallets contain driver's licenses and credit cards. No military identification. The uniforms are probably from a surplus store."

"Is Roberts conscious?" Kian asked.

Anandur shook his head. "Bridget wanted him to sleep, so I thralled him."

"I want to talk to her." Kian headed for the door. "I need to know if he's going to survive."

Kalugal opened it for him. "After we do that, I want to question the head of the team and check how much he knows. After that, we need to scrub their memories and get rid of them."

"Those men have families," Kian said. "I suggest that we find out where each of them lives and drop them off near their homes."

"Should we thrall them to think that they got drunk and can't remember where they've been?"

Kian shook his head. "When I used civilian operatives, I thralled them to believe that they went out on a secret mission and agreed beforehand to get hypnotized to forget it."

"Smart. I like that."

As they reached the cell, Bridget came out to meet them in the corridor, leaving Turner in the cell to watch over Roberts.

"Is he going to live?" Kian asked.

"The injury isn't severe, but he has a heart condition, and that complicates things. Once Kalugal's guy returns with the equipment I asked for, I'll need a volunteer for a blood transfusion."

Kalugal grimaced. "We need Roberts alive so we can get information out of him, but I'm not too happy about giving him a blood transfusion. He's a doctor, and he's not stupid. An immortal's blood might have an unusual effect on him, and he could figure out that something is up."

Bridget leaned against the wall and crossed her arms over her chest. "It might save his life because it will speed up his healing from the injury. It won't do anything for his pre-existing condition. And I'm not worried about traces of it remaining in his system. The effect doesn't last long."

Fascinating. Kalugal had no information on the subject, and now that he had a human wife, it was a good time to find out. Perhaps he could help Jacki recover her hearing faster.

"Forgive my ignorance, but how long exactly would the healing effect last?"

"Four hours tops. After that, our blood loses its extra properties."

"Do you know why?"

She smiled sadly. "I wish I did, but I don't. I dedicated my life to researching what makes us different, and all I can tell you is that it's programmed into our genes."

"Naturally. What I wonder, though, is whether immortals and humans originated from the same ancestor and then we were modified to be superior, or did we create humans and modify them to be inferior."

As Bridget prepared to answer, Kian lifted his hand. "As fascinating as the subject is, we have work to do. This discussion will have to wait for another time."

"Regrettably, you are right, cousin. I just have a few more questions for the doctor. Was Roberts awake and aware at any time after his injury?"

She shook her head. "He lost a lot of blood and went into shock. I asked Phinas to get into his head and thrall him into a sleep mode to lower the stress."

"I assume that you stopped the bleeding?"

"Of course. But I need to get the bullet out and stitch him up. And the same goes for the van's driver. His injury is minor, so I bandaged it and left him in the room with the others."

"Let me know when Roberts is ready to talk."

"It's not going to be anytime tonight. With the blood transfusion, he might be able to talk tomorrow, but I suggest a gentle approach. In his weakened state, added stress might kill him."

"Does he know that Simmons is dead?" Kian asked.

"No, and I advise against telling him right away. That alone might be enough to cause him cardiac arrest."

"No problem." Kalugal pushed his hair back, dreading the answer to his next question. "Is Jacki going to regain her hearing? And if not, can my blood help her recover it?"

"The ringing might linger for a day or two, but she's already doing better. Wonder texted me that Jacki and Jin can both hear, and they are talking too. I believe that they will be back to normal in no time."

Kalugal let out a breath. "So, nothing else needs to be done?"

"Once this is all over, you may want to take Jacki to a specialist and check. Just in case."

"I will. Thank you, doctor."

Bridget smiled. "Just doing my job." She pushed away from the wall. "I'd better go back to watching my patient."

Kalugal turned to Kian. "It seems like the only one we can interrogate at this time is the team's leader."

Kian

Kalugal pulled out his phone. "Phinas, bring the team leader to my office."

"Yes, sir."

Kian would have liked Turner to join the interrogation, but there was no chance the guy was going to leave his mate without protection. Now that the crisis was over, Brundar and Anandur, who'd been with Bridget up until now, resumed their duty as his bodyguards and followed him and Kalugal.

Turning into another hallway, Kalugal opened the door, and the lights came on automatically. "Welcome to my command room." He motioned for Kian and the brothers to go in.

The office wasn't nearly as opulent as Kian had expected it to be, but the computer equipment was state-of-the-art.

Kalugal pulled a chair out for him. "I know this is underwhelming, but I do most of the work from the house, and my office there is much nicer."

"I was wondering about that." Kian sat down. "You seem to enjoy the finer things in life."

"I can afford to." Kalugal smirked. "Even after shelling out twenty-five thousand a day to your charity."

"Now that you and Jacki are mated, I assume your contributions will stop. You no longer need to bribe her to stay with you."

"True, but knowing that I was helping people get back on their feet felt good, so I decided to establish a charity in Jacki's name. She's going to be in charge of it, and it's up to her where she wants to funnel the money. She might decide to keep sending it to you."

Kian doubted the decision had anything to do with Kalugal's charitable inclinations. He was probably doing it to keep Jacki happy. But that was fine. The money would still go to good causes, and it didn't matter what the impetus was.

After a quick knock on the door, Phinas entered with the human. "Where do you want him?"

"On the couch."

The team's leader shuffled in like a zombie. His eyes were unfocused, and his jaw was slack.

Whoever had thralled him had done a hatchet job.

"What's his name?" Kalugal asked.

"Hector Ushman," Phinas said.

Kalugal swiveled his chair to face the guy. "I want to ask you some questions, Hector, and I need you to pay attention and answer truthfully."

As the guy's eyes refocused and he nodded, Kian wondered whether Kalugal's compulsion had overridden the thrall, or was it layered on top of it.

"Who hired you?"

"Doctor Simmons."

"Where does he know you from?"

"A mutual friend recommended me to him."

"Why?"

Hector shrugged. "I'm still new in the field, so I keep my rates low to attract clients. I think that was the deciding factor for the old coot."

"What did he ask you to do?"

"First, he wanted me to check out this address and report what I'd seen. When I did, he said that I got the address wrong and sent me to snoop around another place. When I told him about the party and the sixty chairs I'd seen being delivered, he asked that I gather as many able-bodied men as I could and rent several vans."

"Did he tell you why?"

"He said that it was a suspected terrorist cell and that they were kidnapping key personnel from his facility."

Kalugal leaned back and crossed his legs. "If this was the case, he would have gotten a SWAT team or a commando unit to do the extraction, not a group of middle-aged retired soldiers."

"I didn't ask questions. I was hired to do a job, and no one was supposed to get hurt. All I cared about was getting paid."

"Weren't you concerned? Eight men armed with handguns is not a large enough force to tackle a terrorist cell."

"Simmons told me that he was going to stun everyone in the party using the LRAD. My team's job was to carry the people out into the vans and then drive them to a facility in West Virginia." Hector shook his head. "I should have known that the man was nuts and that there were no terrorists. I told him that the party was canceled and that there was no one in the house." Frowning, he looked around the office. "Where am I?"

"You are dreaming, Hector. Go back to sleep."

The guy's eyes closed and he slumped sideways on the couch.

Kalugal turned his chair around and looked at Phinas. "You can take him back to the classroom. Get some blankets to cover the floor and put him and his men to sleep."

"Yes, boss." Phinas lifted Hector and slung him over his shoulder.

Once he was gone, Kalugal turned to Kian. "Since they were supposed to drive the vans to West Virginia, no one is expecting them back tonight. Tomorrow morning, we will do as you suggested and drop them off near their homes."

"We can do that tonight."

"I'd rather not. I don't want to deal with it while I'm tired, and I want to go back to Jacki."

Smart guy.

Kalugal was calculated and cautious. Rushing to get rid of the problem might lead to mistakes, and those mistakes might bite them in the ass later.

The urgent stuff had been taken care of, and the rest could wait for the morning when they all could think more clearly.

"You are right. Let's get back to our mates. But first, I want to check whether Bridget has everything she needs and Roberts is going to survive."

Kalugal tilted his head. "Are you going to donate him your blood?"

"I don't value his life that much. One of your men will do."

Kalugal

When Kian and Kalugal got back to the cell, Bridget had already gotten her equipment and was busy pulling the bullet out of Roberts' ribcage. "He is lucky that it missed his heart and his lungs." She waved them off. "Go, I'll come up to the house when I'm done."

"Stay with her," Kian told his bodyguards.

Anandur nodded.

"She is perfectly safe here." Kalugal motioned for Kian to follow him. "And she has her immune mate with her."

He wondered why Kian had allowed the guy to stay with the doctor. Turner was his defense against compulsion and the one holding the remote to Kalugal's cuff. Had Kian finally realized that he had nothing to fear from him?

"I know. But I want Turner to come with us." Kian waved the guy over.

Apparently, his cousin was still suspicious.

Turner didn't look happy to leave Bridget, but he did as his boss commanded.

"I can have a room prepared for them down here," Kalugal offered.

"I hope Bridget can leave Roberts for tonight. I want to take everyone back to the hotel."

"I understand. But if you wish, your party can stay here. I will have to move some of my men into the bunker to vacate rooms in the house, though."

Kian glanced back at the corridor they'd just left. "This is not the same way that we got here."

"We are going back to the house through the tunnel."

Kian raised a brow. "Aren't you afraid that we will see all of your booby traps?"

"On the contrary. I wish to boast."

As they reached the door and Kalugal activated the mechanism that opened it, Kian looked impressed. "That's one hell of a door."

Kalugal opened the way. "That's nothing. There is another one ten feet ahead, and you don't want to know the hell that would rain on anyone who makes it through the first one."

"I can imagine." Kian waited for him to open the second one as well.

From there, it was up the stairs and a regular door.

"What's in here?" Kian asked as they passed the library, which was currently occupied by some of his men. "Is this your office?"

"No, it's the library. But since the living room is probably taken by your party, my men found refuge in there." He chuckled. "Usually, I'm the only one who uses it, and since Jacki arrived, she's been spending time with me in there as well. But it's not my men's favorite hangout place."

As he'd expected, Kian's party was indeed in the living room, and so was Jacki.

"Kalugal!" She tried to get up and swayed on her feet. "We need to move!"

He rushed to her and wrapped his arm around her. "Take it easy, love. We are safe for now."

"But they found us!"

He helped Jacki back down and sat next to her. "I don't think we have anything to worry about at this time. After all, Simmons is dead and Roberts is injured."

The little color she had on her face drained away. "What did you say?"

Kalugal looked at Arwel. "No one told Jacki?"

Arwel shook his head. "She didn't look like she could handle it."

Apparently, they didn't know his mate as well as he did. Right now, she had trouble hearing, but she was not fragile.

Speaking loudly, he enunciated every word. "Simmons and Roberts arrived with a device that made that ear-splitting noise, and they brought along several men to carry us out once we were incapacitated. Luckily, the guy who operated the drones shot down that hellish device, destroying it. But since Simmons was holding it, he got hit and died. Roberts was standing right next to him, and he got hit as well, but he is likely to survive."

Jacki let out a breath. "So, it's over." She lifted her arm. "I can take this freaking cuff off."

"Not yet, my love. Someone might replace Simmons, and I'm sure the information about your last known location is stored in the program's computers, as well as the fact that you and your friends have transmitters in you."

"Not for long," Jin said from the other couch. "As soon as we transition, our bodies will reject foreign objects."

He smiled. "I'm glad to see that you are doing better as well."

"What? You need to speak up." She put her hands over her ears. "The damn ringing is almost gone, but there is a hum that is almost as annoying."

Atzil walked in with a big tray of tea and coffee cups and started distributing them. "Is anyone hungry? There is plenty of food left over from dinner."

In response, he got a lot of head shaking.

"Thank you, Atzil." Kalugal took a cup of coffee. "I'm sure that you are exhausted. Go to sleep. If anyone needs anything, I'll show them where the kitchen is."

The indignant look that Atzil cast him was the most disrespectful the cook had ever dared to act toward Kalugal. "I'm not too tired to take care of our guests."

"As you wish."

"Thank you, boss. I also need to finish cleaning up the buffet tables, and my helpers are clearing the backyard." He scurried away.

"Poor Atzil," Jacki said. "He worked so hard to make this night special for us, and it was ruined."

Kalugal patted her knee. "Look on the bright side. At least our wedding party will never be forgotten."

Jacki

When Bridget entered the living room together with Brundar and Anandur, all eyes turned to her.

"How is Roberts doing?" Kian asked.

Jacki still heard everything as if the sounds were traveling through water, but she understood most of it as long as it was spoken loudly and clearly.

"All patched up and sleeping." Bridget joined Turner on an armchair, the two of them squeezing in side by side. "I left one of Kalugal's men to watch over him for a little while, so I could take a break."

"Did you give him the transfusion?" Kalugal asked.

"I did." She shook her head. "It has been a long time since I used such crude methods. I felt like I'd gone back in time."

"Whose blood did you use?"

"Ruvon graciously volunteered."

Anandur snorted. "Grudgingly agreed was more like it, but he did it, and that's what's important."

"Ruvon is a good man," Kalugal said. "They all are." He glanced at Rufsur and nodded, silently congratulating his lieutenant for a job well done.

Resting her head on Turner's shoulder, Bridget looked at Jin. "How is your hearing?"

"Much better, thank you. I hope this freaking ringing will be gone by tomorrow."

The doctor lifted her head and frowned. "On a scale of one to ten, how bad is it now?"

"Compared to how it was in the beginning, it's a four."

"That's not bad." Bridget turned to Jacki. "What about you?"

"The ringing is gone. What's left is a hum, and I hear everything as if the sound is traveling through water. "

"That's good, but if both of you don't feel markedly better by tomorrow, you should see a specialist."

Atzil must have been listening in because he walked in with another tray of coffees and desserts. "Would you like some?" He stopped in front of Bridget.

"Yes, thank you." She cast him a grateful smile. "It was a long day, and it's going to be a long night."

"What do you mean by long night?" Kian asked. "Are you planning on staying here?"

"I have to. Kalugal doesn't have anyone with even basic medical training, and Roberts is still not out of the woods, so to speak."

"I'll stay with Bridget." Turner tightened his arm around her.

Kian didn't look happy. "I will have to bring in some of the other Guardians here. I can't leave you two unprotected."

Next to Jacki, Kalugal stiffened. She knew that Kian's words had hurt him because she felt offended on his behalf.

After all that had happened, and after the way they had all worked together against a common enemy, Kian should be more trusting of Kalugal.

Turner lifted the remote to Kalugal's cuff. "I still have this." He cast him an apologetic glance. "It's just a precaution. It's not personal."

"Right." Kalugal snorted. "It has nothing to do with me or my ability to compel. But I guess I'm lucky that during the attack you didn't fall on the remote and activate it accidentally."

"Believe it or not, I was mindful of it as I went down."

Kian seemed uncomfortable, but he didn't offer an apology. Come to think of it, he really couldn't leave Bridget and Turner unprotected. The doctor might not know much, but Turner was Kian's right-hand man, and he knew everything that was going on. Kalugal couldn't compel him, but he could make him talk by threatening to harm Bridget.

Jacki knew that Kalugal wasn't going to do any of that, but Kian couldn't take the risk.

"I can stay to watch over Bridget and Turner." Dalhu spoke up for the first time since they'd gathered in the living room. "Arwel and Yamanu can stay as well."

"Thank you," Kian said. "But let's have the bachelors do that. I'm sure that your mates don't want to leave without you." He smiled at Amanda, who was glaring daggers at her guy.

Dalhu glanced at her. "Yeah, you're right. My first duty is and always will be to Amanda."

That earned him a bright smile and a passionate kiss.

A little too passionate, in Jacki's opinion.

"Get a room, you two." Anandur threw a cookie at the couple.

Clearing his throat to stifle a chuckle, Kalugal turned to look at Kian. "You can bring a few men inside the bunker if you wish. But my offer to vacate some rooms for you still stands. We have a lot to discuss, and we are all too tired to do it now. I suggest that we work on a plan over breakfast tomorrow morning."

"We can get back here early." Kian wrapped his arm around Syssi's shoulders. "The hotel is not far away, and all of our things are back there. I bet the ladies want out of these beautiful saris. They don't look comfortable."

Syssi nodded. "I can't wait to take a hot shower, get into my pajamas, and dive under the blanket."

"Yeah, me too." Jacki sighed. "And tomorrow, I hope to wake up without the damn humming sound in my ears."

Syssi

Syssi had slept like the dead, and if not for the delicious smell of coffee, she would have kept on sleeping until noon.

But it was too late for that. The smell had woken her enough for her to become aware of how full her bladder was, and she had no choice but to get up.

Throwing a robe over her pajamas, she rushed into the bathroom, barely making it to the toilet in time.

One of the joys of pregnancy, and she didn't mean it sarcastically. Every reminder of the life growing inside her was precious, even the too-frequent visits to the bathroom.

Thank God that the baby was still too tiny to be affected by that horrendous noise. According to Bridget, the baby's ears were not formed yet, and it would take another month until she could hear sounds.

That might be true physically. But in the metaphysical realm, Syssi was sure that Allegra could hear every word, and she conducted entire conversations with her daughter, albeit one-sided.

When she was done in the bathroom, Syssi padded to the suite's common area.

Mey and Jin were already there, sitting at the dining table with their mates, and so were Lokan and Carol. Callie and Wonder were in the kitchen with Anandur and Brundar, and Kian was on the couch, reading his morning newspaper.

He lifted his head and smiled. "Good morning."

"Was I the only one who stayed in bed?" Syssi walked over and sat on his lap.

Kian dropped the paper and wrapped her in his arms. "You needed the rest. The stress last night couldn't have been good for the baby."

"Allegra is fine. Her ears have not developed yet."

"Maybe not, but she could be affected by the stress hormones your body produced. From now on, I want you to stay as calm as you can possibly be."

"Oh, I'm planning on it." She pushed to her feet and walked over to the dining table. "Today is going to be all about lazing in bed with a good romance novel, preferably something funny."

"I have one for you," Callie walked in with a steaming mug of coffee and put it in front of Syssi. "*The Bride Who Lost her Shoes*."

Syssi arched a brow. "That's the title?"

"Yeah. Make sure you're near a bathroom when you're reading it. You'll laugh so hard."

"Then maybe it's not such a great idea." Syssi had trouble holding it in her bladder as it was. "But I'll give it a try. After everything that happened yesterday, I could use a good laugh."

Kian sat next to her and wrapped his arm around her shoulders. "I need to leave soon, but if you need anything, call me."

"Who are you taking with you?"

"Anandur, Brundar, and Lokan." He glanced at Dalhu. "Do you want to come as well?"

"No, thank you."

"I want to come," Amanda said. "I wanted to check out Kalugal's men, and I didn't get to do that last night."

Kian didn't look too happy, and Dalhu even less so. But both knew better than to argue with Amanda. It was just as futile as arguing with Annani.

"If you're going, then I'm coming with you," Dalhu said.

"Of course, darling. I wouldn't go without my protector." She leaned and kissed his clean-shaven cheek.

Syssi would have preferred for Dalhu to stay.

Yamanu and Arwel were fine Guardians, and they were more than enough to keep the ladies safe, but Syssi would have felt better having Dalhu around.

Somehow, he seemed invincible, even more so than the brothers, and that was saying a lot.

"I want to come too," Carol said. "I can help Amanda take notes."

Lokan glanced at Kian with an expression that said, 'please help.'

"Lokan is going to be busy helping us with the captured operatives."

"I know." She crossed her arms over her chest. "I didn't offer to help Lokan. I offered to assist Amanda with her matchmaking mission."

Instead of having a confrontation with Carol, Kian pulled his phone out. "I need to check with Bridget on how Roberts is doing." He typed a quick message.

If he had expected Lokan to convince his mate to stay behind, that wasn't happening. Apparently, Lokan had learned that compromise was key to mated bliss and kept quiet.

"I feel sorry for Simmons," Syssi said. "I know that he was a bad guy, but still."

Carol gaped at her. "You are too nice for your own good, Syssi. The ass-wipe wanted to capture all of us and take us to his program. Can you imagine what he would have done to make us cooperate?"

"He couldn't have done anything. As soon as we recuperated from the attack, we could have easily overtaken the men he brought to transport us."

"Not if he kept us all drugged. It takes a lot to achieve that, but he had Roberts with him, a medical doctor, and he would have adjusted the dosage."

Syssi shivered. "Yeah, I didn't think of that. Thank God for the drones and for Roni." She leaned on Kian's arm. "And thank God for Kian's paranoia. We wouldn't be sitting here and having coffee if he didn't insist on extreme security measures."

Kian put his phone down. "Actually, it was Kalugal's idea. He wanted us to come, and he knew that I wouldn't allow it unless I believed it was safe, so he suggested that we use the drones like we did during the hostage exchange. You need to thank him, not me."

"I'm grateful to both of you. If you had refused to come, there would have been no drones, and Kalugal and all of his men and Jacki would have been taken."

As the return text arrived, Kian read it and nodded. "Bridget says that Roberts is doing well and we can interrogate him. Ruvon's blood did wonders for him."

"I didn't know that our blood could do that," Callie said.

"I didn't know that either." Kian put the phone back in his pocket. "Bridget says that it's a temporary effect and only works in very specific cases."

"That's a shame." Syssi sighed. "I thought that we could help Fernando. He's dying."

For a long moment, no one talked.

It was a miracle that Fernando had lived for as long as he did. And it was all thanks to Nathalie and her dedication to her adoptive father. Andrew had been wonderfully supporting through it all, and it was going to be hard on all of them, but especially on Phoenix. She was too young to understand death.

"We should get going." Kian kissed the top of her head and pushed to his feet.

The brothers followed, and so did Dalhu and Amanda, Carol and Lokan.

Carol just took it for granted that she was going with them, and that was that.

"Good luck." Syssi accompanied Kian to the door. "I just want to put this entire episode behind us and go home."

"So do I." He wrapped his arms around her and kissed her lightly. "But there's still a lot of work to be done."

Kian

Kalugal's gate opened as soon as Anandur drove up to it, and once their two cars were in, the gate closed, and the front door opened.

"Good morning." Kalugal motioned for them to go in. "I'm so glad you decided to join us as well." He smiled at Amanda and Carol. "Jacki will be happy to see you."

"How is she feeling?" Carol asked.

"Much better. Her hearing is almost back to normal. Come, join us for breakfast. Bridget and Turner and your three Guardians are already in the dining room." He sidled up to Kian. "Are those the three burly bears?"

Kian chuckled. "I have no clue. I wasn't the one who assigned them. Why don't you ask Jacki?"

"I don't want her to know that I'm jealous."

"I think she knows."

Kalugal's dining room was big, but this morning it was crowded, and as Kian and the rest of their party entered, the three Guardians got up to make room for them.

"Good morning, boss," Gregor said. "Do you need us to stay, or can we go?"

"You can go."

He had the brothers, Turner, and Dalhu with him. Hopefully, that was enough.

While everyone said hello, Rufsur and Phinas stood up, and friendly handshakes were exchanged between them and the three departing Guardians.

If not for Kian's mistrust of former Brotherhood members, he would have enjoyed seeing that. But as usual, he suspected that things were not as they seemed.

"Good morning." The cook, together with another man, came in to clear the dishes and put down new place settings.

"Poor darling." Amanda put her hand on his arm. "You've probably worked half the night to clean up after yesterday, and you are already serving breakfast."

The cook looked flustered. "I'm good. I enjoy hard work."

"How is Jin doing?" Jacki asked

She wasn't talking as loudly as she had last night, which meant that her hearing had improved a lot.

"Jin is doing better," Kian said. "She is resting, as should you."

Kalugal cast her a look that said, 'I told you so.'

She rolled her eyes. "I wanted to say hi to everyone. When you go about your business in the bunker, I'll rest." She looked at Amanda. "Are you going with them to interrogate Roberts?"

"I have more important things to do." She moved closer to Jacki. "I want a tour of the house and introductions to its inhabitants." She winked. "Carol and I are going to take notes."

Dalhu looked like he had just sucked on a lemon, and Kian would have saved him by inviting him to join them in the bunker, but someone needed to keep an eye on Amanda and Carol.

"I can show you the library," Jacki said. "That's the coolest room in the house, and it has thousands of books." She glanced at Kalugal. "Is that okay?"

He took her hand and kissed it. "This is your house now, Jacki. You can show Amanda and Carol every nook and cranny, except for my office, that is." He cast an apologetic glance at Amanda. "I'm sure you can understand why it has to stay off limits to visitors."

She waved a dismissive hand. "I'm not interested in your office. But I would love to see your artifact collection."

His eyes brightened. "It would be my pleasure, but perhaps some other time. We have urgent issues to attend to." He turned to Kian. "I want Simmons's men out of here as soon as possible."

"They are good to go," Bridget said. "I didn't realize it last night, but in addition to the driver of Simmons's van, several had minor injuries. They didn't go down easily, and our Guardians didn't hold back while apprehending them. The thralling part came later. But there was nothing serious, and I patched them up."

"Good." Kian tapped his fingers on the table. "Their memories need to be thoroughly scrubbed, and new ones implanted." He looked at Lokan. "Can you handle that?"

"Sure thing."

"These are ex-Marines," Kalugal said. "They are not stupid, and we need a good story. I liked your idea, Kian. We should use that."

"What is that?" Lokan asked.

"The story is that they were hired for a secret mission and agreed to get hypnotized to forget it. They will remember agreeing to that and to a certain amount of money they were supposed to get paid."

"We can give each one an envelope with cash," Kalugal said. "Simmons had a lot of money in his briefcase, and I can add a bonus on top of that."

Kian nodded. "Good. So that's settled." He looked at Lokan. "Feel free to embellish the story, just make sure that they all remember the same thing."

"No problem."

"Rufsur, you can prepare the envelopes with the money," Kalugal said. "And you'll need eight drivers. Seven men to drive the vans and operatives to their respective destinations, and one more to pick our guys up. After they deliver Hector and his men to a location near their homes, they should put the men behind the wheel and thrall them to wake up fifteen or thirty minutes later."

"We need to tamper with the GPS on the vans," Kian said.

Kalugal grimaced. "Right. Can your hacker do that? I know some people, but it will get done faster if your guys get on it. They would also need to do the same to the operatives' phones. Or we can just take them away and destroy them."

"That would look suspicious given the story we are going to plant in their heads," Kian said. "It's better to erase the data. I'll need the phone numbers and the GPS registration numbers."

"I'll get them," Lokan said. "Tell Roni that he needs to erase the data from the cloud as well."

Kian chuckled. "He doesn't need to be told. Roni knows what to do."

"Don't expect, inspect." Kalugal leaned back in his chair. "It never hurts to remind people. Even the smartest among us can get distracted, or forget, or get preoccupied with something else."

Turner nodded. "I agree a hundred percent."

Jacki

Atzil showed up with a fresh coffee carafe as soon as the men left. "More coffee?"

The poor guy kept stealing glances at Amanda like an awestruck teenager. The problem was that Jacki wasn't the only one who'd noticed.

Dalhu didn't look happy, and at one point she'd heard him growl, which meant that everyone around the table had heard it too.

"Please." Amanda smiled at him brightly. "What brand are you using? It's delicious."

Kian's sister was drinking up the attention and ignoring her mate's displeasure.

"It's from a private roaster that Kalugal discovered. We get weekly shipments."

"What is its name? And do they ship to Los Angeles?"

"I can write the name down for you." Standing awkwardly with the carafe in hand, Atzil seemed unsure of what to do next.

"Come sit with us, Atzil," Jacki offered.

"Yes, please do." Amanda motioned to the chair next to her.

With Amanda on one side and Carol on the other, Atzil was between a rock and a hard place, or between matchmaker number one and number two.

"What made you become a chef?" Carol asked.

Atzil shifted in the chair. "I'm not a chef, just a cook, and I do it because someone has to, and Kalugal doesn't allow humans in the house."

Amanda lifted a brow. "Kalugal does his own laundry? Somehow I can't see that."

Jacki chuckled. "Shamash does it for him. And he also cleans the master suite. The rest of the house and the bunker are maintained by the other men. They have a schedule they follow, and Rufsur ensures compliance."

"Interesting." Amanda tapped a finger on her chin. "It's the same for us. Kian doesn't allow outsiders into our village either, but I'm lucky to have Onidu."

"Is he a servant?" Atzil said.

"He's my butler."

Atzil nodded. "Like Shamash is for Kalugal. You and Kian are the bosses of your community, so naturally, you don't do your own household chores."

"Not exactly." Amanda lifted her coffee cup and took a sip. "Kian is the boss. I'm not. But I don't want to talk about me. I want to talk about you and your friends." She leaned closer and whispered loudly. "Carol and I are here to see who of our friends might be good matches for you and yours." She put a hand on his arm. "And you're lucky to be the first one we chose to interview."

Atzil cast a questioning glance at Jacki.

"Don't look at me. I didn't get to meet any of their single friends, so I can't help you with inside information."

Swallowing audibly, he turned to Amanda. "Why start with me? Rufsur and Phinas should be first. They are the highest ranked."

"I don't care about that." Amanda put her hand over her chest. "Compatibility and what's in the heart are more important than status and rank." She cast a loving glance at Dalhu. "On the face of things, my mate seems to be a simple man. He was just a junior commander of a small team in the Brotherhood, but he is so much more than that. Dalhu is a fearsome warrior, a talented artist, and he loves me and cherishes me with everything that he is. I couldn't have asked for a better pairing."

Jacki had a feeling that Atzil had stopped listening after Amanda had said that Dalhu was a former Brotherhood member, and he was gaping at the guy with wide eyes.

"You were a Brother?"

Dalhu nodded. "What of it?"

"How did you end up with the goddess's daughter?"

"Sheer dumb luck, or maybe the Fates orchestrated our meeting."

"It was the Fates." Amanda took her mate's hand and clasped it. "And the Fates also brought Kalugal and Jacki together. Nevertheless, that doesn't mean that we should just sit back and let them do all the work. We can help to move their agenda along."

Atzil squared his shoulders. "I'm not only a cook. Before I volunteered for the position, I was also a fearsome warrior."

Amanda smiled. "Many clanswomen would love to have a man who can cook. That's actually your best selling point." She gave him a once-over that made Dalhu growl again. "And you are very handsome too. I'm sure that your superb physique is not the result of lifting heavy pots and stirring spaghetti sauce."

Jacki felt bad for Atzil.

Amanda was appraising him as if he were a prize bull for sale, and Carol was not much better.

While Amanda was doing all the talking, Carol was taking notes on her tablet. And given the looks she was casting at Atzil, she was estimating his height and weight.

Except, given the big grin on his chiseled face, he didn't mind. "Working in the kitchen and cooking for the men is not easy, and I don't have much spare time. But I train for at least two hours a day."

"Awesome," Carol said. "Would you mind if I take a picture of you?"

"Not at all." He flashed her a bright smile.

She snapped a couple with her tablet and motioned for him to stand up.

Jacki was about to say something and save him the embarrassment, but Atzil not only got up, he also posed for the camera while flexing his impressive muscles.

After going over the pictures she'd just taken, Carol looked up and grinned. "This gives me a great idea. We can make profiles for all of Kalugal's men, and then do the same for the clan's single ladies. We will create the first immortal dating app."

Kalugal

"Nice cars." Lokan waved a hand at Kalugal's lineup of luxury vehicles.

Was there a note of jealousy in his brother's tone?

There shouldn't be. Even though Lokan's pay from the Brotherhood could never match what Kalugal was making, he was old enough to have accumulated a small fortune. Provided that he'd been prudent with his money, he could most likely afford to buy a luxury car or two.

"Thank you. I enjoy collecting the best. Whenever I can, I purchase the first one released." Kalugal opened the door and motioned for the group to enter.

Bridget and Turner were already familiar with the layout and headed directly toward Roberts' cell. But it was Lokan's first visit, and even though he was trying to act nonchalant, it was quite obvious that he was observing and committing to memory every detail.

Kalugal didn't want to read too much into it. It was probably a reflex, something that his brother did in every new place and situation.

Hivak waited for them in front of Roberts' cell. "Good morning, doctor. There has been no change. Per your instructions, I've listened to his heartbeat and his breathing, and when I took a break, I had someone else replace me."

"Thank you." Bridget smiled. "With no monitoring equipment, an immortal's hearing is the next best thing."

Kalugal filed her remark for the future. In the new place that he was going to build for his mate and his men, he would have a clinic and purchase all the latest medical equipment for it. The only problem would be getting a doctor to run it. Perhaps he could use a compelled human until one of his men completed his medical education.

The question was who. None of them was particularly studious. But that was something to ponder later.

"Hivak, please take Lokan to the captured men and assist him in any way you can. We need to get their phones and the GPS numbers from the vans."

"Yes, boss."

After Lokan and Hivak walked away, Kalugal entered the code on the keypad and opened the cell.

"Anandur and Brundar should stay outside," Bridget said. "The place is too small for all of us to get in."

Kian looked at Kalugal. "Perhaps you should move Roberts to a different room. It's not like he can escape, and you don't need to keep him locked up for psychological reasons, either. You can make him talk regardless of his state of mind."

"I don't want to move him yet," Bridget said. "Not unless you have a proper gurney."

"We can lift the bed and carry him with it," Anandur suggested.

That wasn't a bad idea. The top bunk had already been removed to allow Bridget easier access to her patient, so lifting the bottom one and carrying it out wasn't a problem.

In fact, since Kalugal wasn't going to use his bedroom in the bunker, he could put Roberts in there. Except, there was one more thing to consider.

"Is there a chance that he would try to take his own life?" Kalugal asked. "That was the main reason for putting him in the cell."

Kian raised a brow. "Can't you compel him not to attempt it?"

"I can do that now that I can finally talk to him." Kalugal stepped out of the cell and motioned for the brothers to go in. "Lift the bed and follow me."

"Gently and carefully," Bridget cautioned.

"Yes, ma'am." Anandur saluted.

After Turner helped Bridget collect her medical supplies, the two followed the group.

"My quarters are one level down, but we can use the elevator."

"You're putting him in your room?" Kian asked.

"I have no use for it right now, and it's the only one large enough for the bed and all of us to fit in."

"How many rooms do you have in here?"

Kalugal smirked. "I thought that you knew. You said that you've seen the blueprints."

"I did, but I didn't count the rooms. I remember that it's much bigger than what I've seen so far."

Kalugal led them to the service elevator and pressed his thumb to the scanner. "Most of the space is taken up by my collections, the cars, and the artifacts. There are several offices, the big classroom you've seen, and a couple of smaller ones and a meeting room. Other than that, we have twenty-five bedrooms of varying sizes. I designed it so all of us can be down here if needed."

Kalugal exited the elevator and led the group down the corridor to his bedroom. "The living quarters down here are quite basic." He stopped next to his room and opened the door. "We don't even have locks."

Stepping back, he let Kian's bodyguards go in with the bed first.

His quarters were larger than all the others, with separate sitting and sleeping areas, but the furniture was simple, and the bathroom had no tub or even a separate toilet compartment.

"You can put the bed against that wall." He pointed to where the television screen was mounted.

After putting the medical supplies on the table, Bridget and Turner sat on the couch.

Kian turned both armchairs to face the bed, sat down on one, and motioned for Kalugal to take the other.

Anandur and Brundar leaned against the desk.

"Thank you." Kalugal pulled the armchair closer to the bed. "If anyone wants refreshments, please help yourselves. The fridge is fully stocked."

"Perhaps later," Kian said. "Let's get to it. Wake him up."

Kian

"One moment." Kalugal got up and walked over to the fridge. "Roberts might be thirsty." He took a bottle of water out.

Kian wondered whether there was a catheter under the blanket covering Roberts. The guy had been kept out for the entire night and morning, and at his age, he probably couldn't hold it.

Kalugal leaned closer to the sleeping man. "Wake up, Elijah, and look at me."

As the old human's eyes popped wide open, he winced with pain and murmured, "Who are you?" He darted his eyes to Kian, and the scent of fear intensified.

"I'm a friend." Kalugal smiled. "Please remain calm. You are not feeling any pain, and you are in no immediate danger. You are in good hands."

Kian stifled a chuckle.

Kalugal was the old man's worst nightmare, but even though the compulsion was delivered in a friendly and relaxed tone, it worked.

Slumping against the pillows, Roberts let out a relieved breath. "I don't remember what happened. Did I fall?"

"You fell and broke several ribs, but the doctor tells me that you are healing nicely." Kalugal lifted the water bottle. "Are you thirsty, Elijah?"

"Yes." Roberts reached for the bottle with a shaky hand.

Kalugal unscrewed the cap. "You will answer all of my questions truthfully, and you will hold nothing back." He handed Roberts the bottle. "Tell me what you know about the Echelon project."

Roberts lifted his head with effort and took a small sip. "It collects information from all over the world, and the bots scan it for trigger phrases. Other than that, it also accumulates data on financial transactions, even those conducted in bitcoin." He smirked. "Nothing can be hidden from its watchful eyes. The problem is sifting through it all, but the bots are getting better at that every day."

"Do you have access to it?"

"Not directly. I only get data that is relevant to my research."

"And how does that work?"

"I provide the trigger words, and they send me everything that's gotten flagged."

"No questions asked? You can submit any phrases whatsoever, and no one questions your request?"

"Thanks to Simmons and his connections, both of us have a high-security clearance. I didn't encounter any objections yet."

Kalugal glanced at Kian. "That can be very useful. Tell me something, Elijah, are all your trainees currently at the base?"

"Yes."

"Is Marisol with them?"

"Yes."

"If you call Marisol right now and tell her to send the trainees home, will she obey your command?"

Roberts nodded. "She will do whatever I tell her to do, but security is not going to let them out. Anyone who wants to leave the base needs to get approval in writing from an authorized superior, and since Simmons and I are not there, she can't get it."

"Did you and Simmons need approval to leave the base?"

"We are not subject to the same rules. We can come and go as we please."

"I see. Did you use a commercial flight to get here?"

"No. Simmons arranged for military transport."

"What reason did he give for the request?"

"I don't know. He must have made something up. It's not like what we were planning to do was authorized." Roberts frowned again. "Who did you say you were?"

It seemed that he was starting to remember some details. Phinas was a good thraller, but he might not have done a thorough job of erasing Roberts' memories. The other possibility was that Roberts remembered things despite it. The old man had a strong mind, and those were difficult to manipulate.

The good news was that he was susceptible to Kalugal's compulsion, which was stronger and more effective than thralling, so that wouldn't be a problem.

"I'm your best friend and confidant, Elijah. My people saved your life, and we are taking good care of you. You should be grateful and do everything that I ask of you."

Roberts nodded. "Yes, I'm grateful. What do you need me to do?"

"For now, I just need you to answer my questions as best you can, and then you need to rest and get better."

"I can do that."

"Excellent. Tell me about the breeding program. Was it authorized, or was it your and Simmons's brainchild?"

Roberts snorted. "No one would have authorized that. We figured that as long as the participants believed that they were choosing their lovers voluntarily, no one would make a big fuss about it. The trainees were all tested and given a clean bill of health, and we gave the women fake birth control shots. I expect pregnancies soon."

"What were you going to do with the children?"

"Watch them grow and see if combining their parents' talents made them stronger paranormals."

"Let's assume that your experiment works and that the children prove to have stronger abilities than their parents. What's the next step?"

Roberts' eyes brightened. "Than we keep doing that and improving on it until we make enough super-people to change the course of humanity." He sighed. "Not in our lifetimes, regrettably. But we set things in motion. This is what Edgar and I dreamt of doing since we were young men."

"Your own version of X-Men."

"Well, not precisely. We have real expectations. The movies were fantasy."

Kalugal pushed to his feet and took the empty water bottle from Roberts. "Sleep, Elijah." He turned to Kian. "Let's go to my office and discuss strategy. I have some ideas."

"I'll stay here," Bridget said.

Kian looked at her. "Are you sure you need to stay? I would like you and Turner to join us. We could use your input, and Roberts is sleeping."

She sighed. "Fine, I'll come. But someone needs to watch over him."

"No problem," Kalugal said. "I'll send one of my men over."

Kalugal

Kalugal opened the door to his office. "Take a seat." He motioned Bridget and Turner to the couch and then walked over to the bar. "I have a limited selection in here, but I can still whip up a nice cocktail for the lady. What would you like, Bridget?"

She waved a hand. "It's too early for me. Do you have coffee here?"

"No, but I can have it brought in. Would anyone else like a cup of coffee?"

"I'd rather sample your selection." Kian walked up to him. "You have a bar in every room you use, and yet you are not a heavy drinker."

Kalugal shrugged. "I'm a connoisseur, and I like the convenience of having a drink whenever I want it."

"Count me in." Turner joined them at the bar.

"Coffee for Brundar and me," Anandur said. "We are on duty."

"Very well." Kalugal pulled his phone out and called Atzil. "Can you send Shamash with a coffee pot to my office in the bunker? We also need three cups."

"Yes, boss. Right away."

"Thank you." Kalugal put the phone back in his pocket. "Atzil sounds more flustered than I've ever heard him. I wonder what Amanda is doing to him."

Kian grimaced. "I guess your cook is her first matchmaking victim."

"The guy has my sympathies." Anandur chuckled. "When Amanda is on a mission, she doesn't let go."

Kalugal nodded and smiled, but his mind was already on a different subject.

As he poured the drinks, he toyed with a new idea that had started brewing in his mind during Roberts' interrogation.

Having the guy under his compulsion opened several interesting possibilities. First, it might solve all of their problems with the program without having to shut it down. Secondly, through Roberts, they would have access to the infamous Echelon system.

After he'd handed out the drinks, and Shamash delivered the coffee, Kalugal sat down and crossed his legs at the ankles. "I have a new idea that trumps all of our previous plans."

Kian leaned back in his chair and smiled. "I have a feeling that I know what it is, but let's hear it."

"With Simmons gone, Roberts will most likely get to head the program, and we can use him to do whatever we want with it. I can compel him to go back and pretend that nothing happened, stop the breeding program, fire Marisol, and destroy any information picked up by the Echelon system that can be detrimental to us."

"I like it," Turner said. "As long as he heads the program and we control him, we have full access to all the information they gather."

"What happens when he dies?" Bridget said. "He's not young, and he has a coronary disease."

Kalugal waved a hand. "Then we do the same with the next director. That's the perfect solution. We can't bring down the entire Echelon system, and we don't want to. The information they gather on suspected terrorist attacks or nuclear threats from other countries can potentially save millions of lives. But we can make sure that the information about paranormal phenomena goes through us first, and we decide what gets filed away and what gets discarded as nonsense. Basically, we will run the program and use the access it has to Echelon to gather information on paranormals, and possibly even unaffiliated immortals."

"I love it. We will use Roberts like a puppet on a string," Kian said. "We have to make sure that he gets to run the program. And that means that we have to come up with an iron-clad cover story for Simmons's death and

Roberts' injury and absence." He looked at Turner. "That's your expertise. What do you suggest?"

"We can keep one of the rented vans, drive Simmons's body to some remote location, and stage an accident in which the van will catch fire, and his body will burn." He looked at Bridget. "You'll need to remove the bullets. If anyone conducts a thorough investigation, we don't want them to find those."

"I can do that. I will even stitch him up, just in case."

Turner took a sip of his drink. "Roberts could say that he had a car accident and was hospitalized. We can plant fake records in a hospital of our choosing. In fact, he could call Marisol and tell her that he is recuperating and will be back as soon as the doctors discharge him."

"What do we tell him about Simmons?" Bridget asked.

"We can thrall him to believe whatever we want." Kalugal got up and walked over to the bar. "Here is a possible story." He poured himself another drink. "They came to San Francisco to check out a possible new recruit, who turned out to be a fake, and then Simmons went to visit a friend and didn't come back. Roberts is worried about him because he doesn't answer his phone. He's afraid that his friend suffered a heart attack because Simmons was complaining about chest pains and refused to get checked."

Bridget shook her head. "As you've noticed, the guy is not easy to thrall. You will have to compel him to tell that story, but you can't make him believe it."

Kalugal shrugged. "Whatever works. I don't care what he believes as long as he manages to convince the higher-ups that this is what happened." He took a sip of his drink. "Before we finalize the plan, though, I suggest that we run it by Jacki. She is familiar with how things work in the program, and she can point out weaknesses in our plan or the cover stories."

Jin

As Arwel's hushed voice filtered through Jin's semi-awake state, she reached with her hand, expecting to find him in bed next to her, but he wasn't there, and the spot was cold, which meant that he'd been awake and out of bed for a long time.

The good news was that she could hear him even though he was sitting on the couch and talking on the phone quietly. The bad news was that she still felt like crap, and not just because of her ears.

A distant hum was all that remained from yesterday's trauma, and she wasn't nauseous, but her throat ached, and she felt feverish.

Could it be that the strep throat had returned?

The bacteria was nasty, and it could lie dormant until something weakened the immune system and then attack again.

Was there a chance that Bridget had one of those wonderful shots in her doctor's bag?

Except, Bridget wasn't there because she'd stayed the night at Kalugal's, watching over Roberts.

Damn. Director Simmons was dead.

Jin still had a hard time wrapping her head around that. Not that she felt pity for him. He deserved to die for what he'd planned to do to her family and friends.

Thank God for Kian's suspicious and super-cautious nature.

When a shiver shook her body, Jin wasn't sure whether it was the fever's fault or imagining what could have happened if not for Kian's paranoia. If he had forgone the drones, they would all be in West Virginia by now, locked up, and forced to do God only knew what.

"Good morning." Arwel closed his phone and walked over to the bed. "Did you sleep well?"

"I did, but I'm not feeling good."

Frowning, he sat on the bed. "Are your ears still ringing?"

"They are almost back to normal. But my throat hurts, and I feel feverish. I'm afraid that the infection might have returned. The streptococcus bacteria is a stubborn sucker."

He put a hand on her forehead. "You feel warm. I should call Bridget."

Jin pulled the blanket up. "It's not an emergency. She is probably busy with Roberts, and I can wait until she comes back." She yawned. "I'll just go back to sleep."

"You should eat something. It's nearly noon."

"I didn't realize that it was so late. Why didn't you wake me up?"

"You needed the rest." He pushed to his feet. "I'll order breakfast for you. What would you like?"

"Tea and orange juice."

"You need to eat something."

She wasn't hungry, but Arwel would just keep insisting. "Fine. I'll have an omelet. Did you eat?"

"I waited for you to wake up."

"Why? How long have you've been awake?"

"Hours."

"Silly man." She slapped his arm. "You must be starving."

"I am." He picked up the bedside phone and dialed room service.

Arwel must have ordered every item on the breakfast menu. The person on the other end probably thought that he was ordering for twelve people.

She waited until he was done. "You shouldn't have waited for me."

"I didn't feel like eating alone."

That wasn't good. When Mey and Jin were still living with their parents, they had a neighbor who would only eat in company. But because both his parents worked long hours and the kid wouldn't eat until they got home, he looked emaciated. Sometimes their mother would feel sorry for him and invite him over for dinner.

Hopefully, Arwel was not going to turn it into a bad habit. It was nice to eat together, but it wasn't always possible. After her transition, Arwel would go back to work, and Jin intended to dedicate a lot of time and effort to her and Mey's future business endeavor.

Jin pouted. "Now, I feel guilty because you went hungry. Please don't do stuff like that. What will happen when you go back to work? You won't eat anything until you get home at night?"

Arwel lay down next to Jin and pulled her into his arms. "It's not something you should get upset about. I could've ordered, but I preferred to wait. That's on me." He kissed her forehead. "I'll go down to the hotel's gift shop and get you fever reducers if they have them. Maybe they will hold you over until Bridget returns."

"I hope she has an antibiotic shot with her." Jin cuddled up closer and buried her nose in his shirt. "I love your smell."

"I didn't put any cologne on."

"I love your natural scent. To me, it smells like home and sex."

Pulling back a little, Arwel arched a brow. "Is that an invitation?"

Regrettably it wasn't, which was another proof that she was sick. Typically, they started each morning with sweet, unhurried lovemaking.

"I'm sorry. Can I get a rain check? I feel really crappy."

"Of course." He kissed her forehead again, then looked into her eyes. "What if this is the start of your transition?"

For a moment, Jin's heart fluttered with excitement, but then she remembered that a sore throat was not one of the symptoms, and her heart sank.

"I wish. But I don't think this is it. Bridget said fever and body aches, which I have, but she didn't say anything about a sore throat, and right now, that's what bothers me the most." She put a hand over the front of her neck. "I hope the tea gets here soon."

Kian

After Bridget had checked on Roberts again, and Kian verified that the location tracking on the operatives' phones had been dealt with, their group left the bunker and headed to the house for lunch.

"I'm surprised that your cook managed to prepare anything with my sister and Carol pestering him." Kian waited for Kalugal to close the two-foot-thick door to the tunnel.

"He had no choice. If lunch wasn't ready on time, there would have been a riot." Kalugal motioned for them to follow him up the stairs.

"What's going on with Lokan? Is he still busy with the men?" Turner asked.

"He's outside, sending the vans off. He's going to join us for lunch in a few minutes." Kalugal opened the door at the top of the stairs. "I'm glad that part is done. I didn't like having a bunch of humans in my house."

Kian nodded. "I understand how you feel. I wouldn't have wanted them in my village either."

When they got to the dining room, the rest of their group was already sitting at the table.

"We came up with a wonderful idea," Amanda said.

Kian cringed. "Do I want to hear it?"

"It's a really good one. We are going to create an immortal dating application. Each single immortal will have a profile, Kalugal's men and our single ladies, and they will be able to check each other out and correspond before meeting in person. That will save us a lot of guesswork."

"That's brilliant, Amanda," Kalugal said.

"Thank you." Carol fluffed up her hair. "It was my idea. We already spoke with William, and he said that his geek squad can create the application. Amanda and I will compile a questionnaire for each single immortal to fill in, and naturally, there will be pictures."

"What's a geek squad?" Kalugal asked.

"William's trainees." Amanda smiled. "They prefer to be called the genius squad, but the geek squad kind of stuck. He has five young guys that he's teaching twice a week, and they help him out with time-consuming tasks that are not too difficult. They are all computer engineers, but William is providing them with continuing education that they couldn't get in any university."

Bridget's phone rang at the same time that Lokan walked into the dining room.

He kissed Carol's cheek and pulled a chair next to her.

"It's Arwel." Bridget frowned. "What's going on? Have Jin's symptoms worsened?"

Bridget was sitting on the other side of the table, so Kian couldn't hear Arwel clearly, and he had to wait for the call to end to get an update.

"Jin might be right. Strep has a tendency to come back," Bridget told Arwel. "I'll check on her when I get to the hotel. If her symptoms worsen, call me." She ended the call. "Jin has a sore throat and a fever."

"Could it be the transition?" Jacki asked.

"It might. Normally, a sore throat is not one of the symptoms, but since Mey's transition was unusual, I wouldn't be surprised if Jin's is as well."

"Unusual in what way?" Kalugal asked.

Bridget shook her head. "That's personal information that I'm not free to disclose."

Disappointed, he glanced at Jacki.

She shrugged. "Don't ask me. I don't know anything."

It seemed like a good time to change the subject, and Kian turned to Lokan. "Are all of Simmons's men on their way home?"

He nodded. "All done. I thralled them first and then added compulsion in case they happen to remember anything."

"Thank you," Kalugal said. "I'm glad that part of the cleanup is over. Let me fill you in on what we decided to do with Roberts." He looked at Jacki. "Feel free to interject at any point if you think that we got something wrong."

Jacki nodded.

"Roberts will become our puppet. I will have complete control over him, and the entire paranormal program will essentially become ours. The first thing to go will be the breeding program. He will tell Marisol to release the trainees and then fire her."

"No more drugs, either," Jacki said.

"Of course. I will also instruct him to destroy all the information about you, Jin, and your two friends. Hiding will no longer be necessary. In addition, I will get him to supply us with leads on new paranormal talents, so we will have access to potential new Dormants." He looked at Kian. "For my trouble, I ask that my men get priority access to the potential female Dormants."

Kian had been expecting that. "Only for the first ten. After that, we renegotiate, and I want full access to the information gathered."

Kalugal nodded. "Agreed."

"You will need to reinforce the compulsion periodically," Lokan said. "Following our father's example, I would say once a month should do it. The good news is that you don't have to actually meet Roberts face to face to do that. You can do it over the phone."

"That's true," Kalugal said. "But on the other hand, his phone, the cellular as well as the landline, might be under surveillance. I will have to compel him to call me from a secure line."

"I think that's too risky," Jacki said. "What if he doesn't call?" She looked at Kalugal. "You must have access to him whenever you please. Things might come up that will need immediate intervention, and you don't want to have to wait for the scheduled call."

Kalugal looked at Kian. "What do you think? Should I give him a satellite phone and instruct him to have it on him at all times?"

"That's not a good idea," Turner said. "If the device is discovered, Roberts will be questioned, and his access to information will be blocked."

"I have a suggestion," Jacki said. "In case you need to contact Roberts urgently, you can call his home number and pretend to be a telemarketer for whatever. A hearing device. But that will be a trigger for him to get out of the house and go to a nearby supermarket. In there, one of your men will hand him a secure phone, and you will continue from there. Maybe you even want to station a couple of men in West Virginia to keep tabs on Roberts."

Kalugal

Kalugal was so proud of his clever wife. "I love the way you think. That's the best solution. Roberts and the access we will have through him to the Echelon system is invaluable. That's certainly worth stationing two men near his house."

Jacki smiled. "I'm glad I could help."

Atzil rolled in a cart. "Are you ready for lunch? Or do you want me to keep it warm until you're done talking?"

Kalugal waved a hand at the table. "Please serve lunch. We can eat and talk at the same time." He chuckled. "Just not with our mouths full."

Jacki pushed to her feet. "Let me help you."

His wife still had a lot to learn about being the lady of the house. Her job was to sit at the table and converse with their guests, not to serve them.

Kalugal took Jacki's hand. "Let Shamash help Atzil." He tugged her back down. "We have important things to go over."

Shamash rushed out of the kitchen with a pitcher of lemonade. "I'm on it."

When everything was served, Amanda looked at Atzil. "Why don't you join us?"

"Thank you, but I can't. I have forty-something men I still need to feed. This is just the first round."

"Maybe you can join us after lunch for coffee?"

"If I can." He glanced at Kalugal for approval.

"I'm sure you can spare a few minutes to have coffee with us. Let your helpers take care of the rest."

Atzil nodded. "Yes, boss."

"What about Marisol?" Jacki asked as Kalugal passed her the casserole. "She knows a lot about the program, and you can't thrall her to forget or compel her to cooperate. I don't know if it's safe to leave her with all that information, especially since she will be bitter as hell over being fired. She's made a fortune working for the program."

Kian smirked. "I thought that you didn't want to off anyone."

Her eyes widened. "That's not what I had in mind. She is a potential Dormant too. Maybe one of your men would be interested in her."

Kian grimaced. "That one is a rotten apple. I don't want her in my community, and you shouldn't invite her into yours."

"Maybe not invite her here, but you can send someone to flirt with her," Jacki suggested. "Perhaps one of the two men you send to keep tabs on Roberts. If Marisol has a new love interest, maybe she won't be as bitter. Besides, we could use her in some capacity. She is a compeller, and we know that she will offer the use of her talent to whoever pays her enough."

Kalugal glanced at Kian. "What do you think?"

"Can you spare another man to keep an eye on Marisol? Because Jacki is right about her knowing too much. She might make a stink just to get back at Roberts for firing her."

"Marisol might be too old to transition," Bridget said.

Turner put his fork down and wiped his mouth with a napkin. "She is younger than I was when I transitioned."

"Yeah, and can I remind you that you almost didn't make it?" Bridget shivered. "Those were the longest two weeks of my life."

He wrapped his arm around her shoulders. "I'm sorry that I gave you such a scare. But you should have known that a stubborn ox like me will never give up." He leaned in and kissed her cheek. "Especially since I had you waiting for me on the other side."

Letting out a contented sigh, Bridget leaned her head on her mate's shoulder. "I'm glad that's behind us."

"You two need to have a wedding ceremony," Amanda said.

Bridget chuckled. "What about you?"

"I'm not planning on having a baby."

Kalugal looked up. "Can immortals plan that? I was under the impression that we don't have any control over it, and that pregnancy is a rare blessing."

"That is true," Kian said. "But our other doctor, Merlin, came up with a way to enhance chances of conception. He makes an elixir that supposedly helps immortals conceive. Although, in my opinion, it's just a placebo."

"It helped you and Syssi," Bridget said. "Your miracle has given all of us hope."

Jacki sucked in a breath. "So Kalugal and I might not have to wait centuries to have a baby?"

"I can arrange for you to meet Merlin," Kian said. "He claims that his potions are custom made for each couple and that different people have different needs. But Merlin is a character, and I wouldn't be surprised if those vile potions of his are nothing but snake oil."

"Are there any side effects?" Jacki asked.

"Except for the gag reflex, none that Syssi or I have experienced. But his potions really taste awful, and they smell and look disgusting too. I think Merlin is testing us to find out how desperate we are for a baby."

Turner nodded in agreement. "One of the worst things I ever had to put in my mouth."

"I don't mind that," Jacki said. "As long as there are no side effects, I'm willing to suffer the taste if there is even a remote chance of the potion helping us conceive."

Kian waved a hand. "You've just proven my theory."

Pushing his plate away, Kalugal took Jacki's hand and gave it an encouraging squeeze. "To be frank, I've never felt more hopeful for the future of my people than I do now. This is indeed a new beginning for us." He smiled at Jacki. "Who knows? Perhaps in a few years, we will have our own clan."

"Don't get your hopes up," Kian said. "It will take much longer than a few years, but you should definitely plan on finding a larger place for your people."

He put his glass down. "Three years ago, when Syssi came into my life, it changed the way I saw the clan's future, and I decided to build the village. I wanted a safe place for us where we could live as a community."

"I would love to have a place like that. How long did it take you to build it?"

Kian chuckled. "Given the scope of the project, not long at all. Because the location was secret and shrouded, I didn't have to bother with building permits and all the other bureaucratic requirements that would have added years to the process. I hired crews from China who were experts in fast building, and I had the place ready in a matter of months instead of years."

"And then you decided to expand the project," Amanda said. "The first phase was fenced off, so we could move into the village while the crews worked on phase two. At the time, I thought that Kian had gotten carried away, but apparently, Syssi's clairvoyance rubbed off on him, and he saw many more clan members getting mates and having children."

"Did they?" Kalugal asked.

"Not as many as I hoped for. I'm not complaining, though. The Fates have been generous with us during the last three years, giving several clan members lifelong companions, but most of my people are still alone. At this time, Syssi and I are the only ones expecting a child."

As everyone's mood plummeted following Kian's dose of reality, a long moment of silence stretched over the dining table.

Except, Kalugal was still more hopeful for the future than he'd ever been, and the distant hum of dissatisfaction that had plagued him most of his life was gone.

They all needed to get some perspective.

"Three years are a blink of an eye for an immortal, and we shouldn't feel discouraged because things are not happening as fast as we would like them to. I'm a great believer in taking the long view, and I'm patient. As long as I know there is hope, I'm willing to wait."

Jacki sighed. "For an immortal, that's the right attitude. But as a human, it's difficult for me to think in terms of centuries rather than years. I hope that once I transition, I will be able to adjust to your way of thinking."

Kalugal hoped so too. His world domination plans were definitely long term, and he might have to put them on ice while securing his men's future.

Squeezing Jacki's hand, he looked at Kian. "Taking the long view also means that I'm not in a rush to move. With Simmons gone and Roberts under my control, Jacki is safe here, and I can take my time building a new home for my people. And since you've already done it for yours, I would appreciate your help with that." He glanced at Jacki. "I would love to build a village for my mate."

"Speaking of Simmons," Turner said. "We need to get rid of the body, and it needs to be done today. Roberts is doing great thanks to the blood transfusion, and we can probably send him home in a couple of days. The staged accident has to happen before that."

"I reserved the van that got hit for that purpose," Lokan said. "Rufsur has men cleaning it up. We don't want any bullets to be found."

"Good." Turner nodded. "I'll take care of the rest tonight." He looked at Bridget. "I hope that you are not planning on staying another night."

"Not unless Roberts takes a turn for the worse." She looked at Kalugal. "If you are going to stay in this house for a while, I suggest that you dedicate one room for a clinic and stock it with medical equipment and supplies. You should also send one of your men on a paramedic course. Even immortals need to get treated for injuries and broken bones."

"I can always bring in human doctors and thrall or compel them to forget."

Bridget shook her head. "You've been living peacefully, and you've been lucky that your men haven't sustained any injuries. But you should know that by the time you get a human doctor here, the injury will heal, and any broken bones will fuse. Without medical intervention, however, the healing might not be done optimally. Bones will have to be re-broken to be reset properly, and that's additional pain and suffering that could and should be prevented."

Kalugal nodded. "You are right, and I would appreciate your or Julian's help in that. I wouldn't know where to start."

"I can order everything for you, but you'll have to pay for it."

"Of course. And I will gladly reimburse you for your time as well."

Bridget smiled. "I would never charge a family member for such a small favor."

Jin

"Jin, sweetie, wake up. I brought you more tea."

"Mey?" Jin croaked. "My throat hurts."

"I know. Arwel told me. I came to check on you."

Jin forced her eyelids to lift. "What time is it?"

"It's after two in the afternoon."

"Oh, damn. I thought that I only closed my eyes for a moment." Jin pushed back on the pillows, reached for the tea mug, and took a sip.

The tea wasn't hot, but it hurt to swallow. "I think I have strep throat again."

"Open your mouth. I'll take a look."

Jin put the mug on the nightstand and opened wide. "Ahhh... It hurt to do even that."

Scrunching her nose, Mey held Jin's chin between her thumb and forefinger and turned her face toward the light. "Your throat is red, but there are no white spots." She patted the sides of Jin's neck. "Your glands are swollen. I hope it's not mono."

Jin shivered. "I hope so too."

The truth was that she had all the classic symptoms. Fever, sore throat, swollen lymph nodes, and body aches. The only thing missing was a skin rash.

Mey had had mono when they'd moved back to New York, and she'd been miserable for two months. One side of her neck had gotten so swollen that she'd had to rush to the hospital for an injection of antibiotics.

The thing about mono was that people could carry the virus in their bodies for years without ever having symptoms, and then something happened to weaken their immune system, and it exploded. And when it did, strep and other nasties took the opportunity to attack.

The other problem with mono was that it wasn't easy to diagnose because it mimicked other more common diseases. The doctors hadn't realized that Mey had it until her spleen had swelled up.

Jin lifted the tea and took another sip. "Where is Arwel?"

"He went to get you something for the fever. The hotel's gift shop didn't have anything, so he had to drive to a pharmacy. Also, Bridget is on her way back to take a look at you."

That was a relief. As the daughters of a pediatric nurse, Jin and Mey knew a few things about various illnesses. But what if this was the start of a transition?

"Did your throat hurt when you were transitioning?"

Mey shook her head. "I felt very weak and achy, and then I developed a fever. Later, my gums started hurting because I was growing these beauties." She flashed Jin a toothy smile.

"Your fangs are cute, and they can barely qualify as such. They look like pointy canines."

Mey shrugged. "I was freaking out because I thought I'd get fangs like the males do. But these are okay."

Reaching into her mouth, Jin patted her gums. "Nothing there. But I wouldn't mind getting fangs like yours. Heck, I wouldn't mind getting a pair like Arwel's." She chuckled. "But if mine also elongate when I get excited, that could be a problem. How would we kiss?"

"Maybe that's the reason why females don't have venom glands and elongating fangs." Mey turned her head toward the door. "Someone is coming."

"That super hearing is something." Jin shook her head. "What I don't get is how come the immortals were less impacted by the noise device given their sensitive ears."

A moment later, there was a knock, and Mey got up to open the door. "Hi, Bridget. Come in."

The doctor strode into the room with her black bag. "Hello, Jin. I stopped by the suite first to bring this." She lifted the bag. "So, what's troubling you?" Bridget sat on the bed next to her and pulled out a thermometer.

"Sore throat, mild fever, achy body. My lymph nodes are swollen too. It feels like the strep, just not as bad."

Bridget put a new earpiece on her device. "How is your hearing? Do you still experience the hum?"

"Very mildly. The sore throat bothers me much more."

"I'll be gentle." Bridget moved Jin's hair back and put the device in her ear. When it beeped, she looked at the readout. "A hundred and one. That's mild." She pulled out a tongue depressor and a flashlight from her bag. "Let's take a look. Open wide."

"Ahhh..."

"Oh, my." Bridget frowned.

It was never good to hear a doctor react like that.

"What's going on in there?" Mey asked.

Leaning back, Bridget pinned Jin with a grim look. "You are growing venom glands."

Jin swallowed and immediately grimaced from the pain. "Are you sure? What if those are just my own glands that are swollen?"

"I've seen enough dormant males go through the transition to know what growing venom glands look like. There is no mistake." She looked at Mey and smiled. "It seems that you were lucky to get only fangs."

"But my gums don't hurt." Jin patted them to make sure.

"They will." Bridget pulled out a tape measure from her doctor's bag and a tablet from her satchel. "I need to take your measurements."

"I'm not going to get any taller, right?"

Having glands and elongating fangs was bad enough, and she was already six feet tall.

Talk about being a freak.

"Mey didn't, but then she didn't grow venom glands either." Assuming a sympathetic expression, Bridget patted Jin's arm. "There is no reason to panic. The venom glands might develop but remain dormant, and your fangs might grow no bigger than Mey's."

"I'm not panicking about that." Jin pulled the blanket under her chin. "Getting taller is scarier to me than having active venom glands and elongating fangs." She looked at Mey. "I guess that I was meant to be a spy or a fighter after all. A businesswoman doesn't need to grow fighting implements."

"That's not true." Bridget measured the length of her arm. "Look at Wonder. She took down Anandur and Brundar, two of our most formidable fighters, but she doesn't want to be a Guardian because that's not where her heart is." The doctor wrote the measurement on her tablet. "We get to choose what we want to do with our lives. You can either go with your natural attributes or not. It's entirely up to you."

Kian

Kian pulled out his cigarillo box. "Anyone care to join me on the veranda?"

After Amanda and Dalhu had taken Bridget back to the hotel to check on Jin, the rest of them had one more coffee and continued discussing the future of the paranormal program. Good progress had been made, and Kian craved a little relaxation.

Lokan eyed the box. "I would like another one of those."

"I need to make some phone calls." Turner pushed to his feet. "In private."

"You are welcome to use the library," Kalugal said. "Shamash can show you where it is."

As soon as his name was uttered, the guy materialized from the kitchen. Kalugal's personal assistant was like Okidu and Shai rolled into one person.

As Turner followed the guy, the rest of them headed out to the veranda and made themselves comfortable on the outdoor couches and chairs.

"Do you have a bar out here as well?" Kian asked.

"No, but I can get you a drink from the main one in the living room. What would you like? I have a nice selection of good whiskeys."

"Surprise me." Kian offered the box of cigarillos to Lokan.

"And for the ladies?" Kalugal asked. "I can make you a couple of Old Fashioneds, or maybe you would prefer wine?"

"I love that cocktail," Jacki said.

Carol cast him one of her charming smiles. "Then I'll have one too."

"I'll be right back." He eyed Kian's box. "Save one of those for me."

"You are a bad influence on your cousins," Anandur said. "Their mother is not going to be happy with you."

The guy's teasing reminded Kian that he still had to give Annani an update about what had transpired during Kalugal's wedding ceremony. She'd probably heard all about it already from someone else, and she would be pissed at him for not informing her right away.

Kian lit his cigarillo and then gave the lighter to Lokan. "I need to report to Annani, but I want to make sure that we have everything under control first."

"We do." Kalugal returned with a tray and put it on the coffee table.

Kian nodded in appreciation. "Hibiki 17. Nice."

Kalugal handed the cocktails to Jacki and Carol and then opened the bottle. "I figured we had cause for celebration." He poured the whiskey into four of the glasses and handed them out. "To the bright future of our clans."

Kian chuckled. "I see that you are fond of the idea. What are you going to name yours?"

"I haven't given it much thought." Kalugal glanced at Lokan. "Perhaps I should call it Areana's clan. Then both of our clans will be named after the goddesses who contributed their genetic material to their formation."

"That's a great idea," Jacki said. "Maybe that will convince Areana to leave your father. She could be like her sister, the head of her own clan."

"That reminds me." Kalugal pulled out a cigarillo from the box Kian left on the coffee table. "I still didn't hear the story of how Carol infiltrated the harem."

Carol looked at Kian. "May I?"

He hesitated for a moment. Now that they had open communication with Areana, infiltrating the harem once more wouldn't be necessary. There was no harm in telling Kalugal how they had done it. If Areana or anyone else wanted to leave, they could help them escape via the cliff.

"Go ahead."

"I'll try to make it short. We had damaging information on a Russian oligarch who was a frequent visitor to the island, and since he's also a major arms supplier for the Brotherhood, he could get away with stuff other guests of Pleasure Island couldn't. He took me with him as his girlfriend, we staged a major fight, and he left the island in a huff without paying his bill. He later called, asking that I be given a job to work off what he owed. But he also specified that he didn't want me to be around men. My punishment for humiliating him in public was to work off the debt for the rest of my life without enjoying male company."

Kalugal lifted a brow. "And that worked? You are a beautiful woman. The head of the brothel would have loved to get you working there."

"I also pretended to be a diabetic with an insulin pump. Besides, Lokan knew the guy in charge of staffing the harem, and he asked him to get me a job there, supposedly as a favor to the Russian. That's how I got in. I expected to find Areana a miserable enslaved prisoner, but she lives like a queen. Navuh loves her and is devoted to her, and he keeps the other immortal ladies only for show. They are allowed relations with the human servants of the harem, and he then claims their children as his own."

"How did you get out?"

She smirked. "I jumped off the cliff."

"I know that cliff." Kalugal frowned. "It's steep, almost vertical, and there are rocks at its bottom. You couldn't have survived the jump."

"We had a team climb up the rock face," Kian explained. "Yamanu got up there and thralled the human guards to believe that Carol jumped. He climbed down with her on his back."

"Areana and Tula were there," Carol continued. "And we made a whole scene about how I was heartbroken over the Russian leaving me. The story was that I committed suicide."

"Brilliant." Kalugal took a puff of the cigarillo. "But I'm surprised my father bought the story."

Kian leaned forward and braced his elbows on his knees. "Carol was supposedly an insignificant human servant. She wasn't worth an investigation. If Areana had agreed to leave, though, a similar scenario would not have worked. Navuh would have searched for her body."

"How did you manage to get your team up to the cliff?"

"We had a semi-submersible and diving equipment."

"Fascinating. But what I don't get is where the two Dormants that Lokan tried to steal fit into the story."

Kian was about to answer when his phone rang.

"Excuse me." He pulled it out of his pocket and looked at the display. "I should probably take this in private." He pushed to his feet and started walking toward the back fence.

"Hello, Mother," he answered when he was halfway there.

"I heard what happened."

"I was meaning to call you once we had everything sorted out."

"What is left to be done?"

"We need to get rid of the body."

"Is there a problem with that?"

"Turner is going to stage an accident. The vehicle will catch fire, and the body will get incinerated. But we haven't done that yet."

"And you have everything else handled?"

"Yes. In fact, the incident played beautifully into our hands and solved a big problem for us."

"Do tell."

Kalugal

While Kian spoke with his mother, Lokan told Kalugal about his plan to kidnap the two Dormants.

Jacki regarded him with thinly veiled hostility. "That was heartless, Lokan. I can't believe you were willing to sacrifice them like that."

To his credit, Lokan didn't shy away from the criticism. "I've gained some perspective since then, and I wouldn't have done it knowing what I know now." He took Carol's hand and put it on his chest. "But it all ended better than well. If I hadn't schemed to kidnap Ella and Vivian, I wouldn't have been captured, and I would have never met Carol or my brother." He looked at Kalugal, and then turned back to Jacki. "And without me, you would still be in the program and would have never met Kalugal. So in a way, my dastardly plans brought happy endings for all of us."

Jacki let out a breath. "I didn't sense any hostility toward you from Ella and Vivian, so if they are willing to forgive you, who am I to hold a grudge, right?"

Kalugal wrapped his arm around Jacki and kissed the top of her head. "I think the Fates navigated things very cleverly to bring us all together."

"Kian is coming back," Carol said. "Annani probably chewed his ear off for not calling her earlier. She hates it when he leaves her out of the loop. Not that she ever is. She knows everything that's going on."

"Is she clairvoyant?" Kalugal asked.

Carol chuckled. "I don't think so. She's just very good with that little cellphone she keeps in her pocket."

"Annani wants to talk to you." Kian put his hand over the microphone. "Don't do anything stupid."

"Like what?"

This was unexpected and somewhat unnerving.

Kian looked at the cuff still locked around his wrist.

"You can call Turner in here if you're worried about me pulling something."

Kalugal had wanted an audience with Annani, but not without preparing for it properly first. Perhaps he could use the time it took Kian to get Turner to gather his thoughts.

"I would, but when Annani wants something done, she wants it done immediately." Kian handed Kalugal the phone.

Covering the microphone with his finger, he whispered. "What do I call her?"

"Clan Mother," Lokan said. "Relax. Annani is not nearly as scary as Kian wants you to believe she is."

Taking a calming breath, Kalugal brought the phone to his ear. "Hello, Clan Mother. It's an honor to speak to you."

"Oh, Kalugal. Let us dispense with the formalities. Talk to me like you would with a friend, and call me Annani, or Auntie Annani." She laughed, the sound almost identical to her sister's.

Otherworldly and enchanting.

"As you wish."

"I was very upset when I heard about your ruined wedding. Then I had a wonderful idea. Since you and Jacqueline have just pledged yourself to each other, and it was not an official ceremony, we can regard it as your engagement party. You can have a proper wedding with me presiding over it."

Kalugal glanced at Kian, who was shaking his head.

"Thank you. That is a lovely idea, but perhaps we should wait with the ceremony for after Jacki's transition."

"Yes, of course. There is no rush. Whenever the two of you are ready, let me know, and I will have Amanda plan a proper wedding for you. Naturally, it is going to be in the village square, with as many clan members as can attend."

Kian shook his head again.

"Is it all right if I put you on speakerphone? This should be planned together with Kian."

"My son is probably hovering over you and shaking his head. But that is okay. You can put me on speakerphone."

Just as Annani imagined it, Kian stood over Kalugal and lit up another cigarillo.

"I can't allow Kalugal and his men into the village, Mother. You know how important it is to keep the location secret."

"Of course I do. But not even your people know where it is. You can bring Kalugal and his party into the village in the same way most clan members come and go."

Kalugal stifled a chuckle. His cousin was paranoid in the extreme. Even his own people didn't know where they lived? How was that even done?

Seeing the confusion on his face, Kian explained. "We use self-driving cars. They are programmed to take over several miles before reaching the secret entrance to the tunnel that leads to the village, and the windows turn opaque."

"Clever. But can't they guess where it is located?"

"They know the general area, but the village is shrouded, and the entrance is hidden. It's all very sci-fi." Kian sighed. "We will revisit the issue after Jacki transitions."

"Very well," the goddess said. "Good luck, Jacqueline."

"Thank you," Jacki croaked and then cleared her throat. "Other than successfully transitioning, I would love nothing more than for Your Highness to preside over our wedding."

Annani laughed again. "If you wish to use a formal address, I prefer Your Awesomeness, or Your Fabulousness. But for now, you can call me Clan Mother. After we meet and become friends, you shall call me Annani."

"Yes, Clan Mother." Jacki bowed to the phone.

"Goodbye, everyone," Annani chimed.

As the goddess disconnected the call, Kalugal and Kian let out simultaneous relieved breaths.

"Will I be invited to the wedding?" Lokan asked.

Kian shrugged. "No offense, but I'm not looking forward to inviting forty-eight former Doomers into my village. But if I can't convince Annani to drop it, then one more doesn't make a difference."

When Kian's phone rang again, Kalugal expected it to be Annani again, but it was Bridget.

"Jin is transitioning," the doctor announced. "She is doing fine, so no need to worry. I just thought that you would want to know."

"Thank you."

"*Mazel tov*," Anandur said when Kian disconnected the call. "It's about time."

"Indeed." Kalugal nodded. "I'm happy for her."

"What's going on?" Jacki asked.

He'd forgotten that she couldn't hear what was said on the other side of the line unless the speakerphone feature was turned on.

"Jin has entered the transition process."

"Oh, my goodness." Jacki's hand flew to her chest. "I need to be with her."

Jin

When Arwel walked through the door, Jin almost cried with relief. Not because she'd missed him so much, but because he brought pain relief pills.

"Gimme." She extended her hand.

"Don't you want to tell Arwel the good news?" Mey asked.

"Painkillers first."

Arwel looked at Mey. "What good news?"

"You heard the lady. Give her the meds first." Mey refilled the mug with more warm water.

"Here." Arwel handed her a container of Motrin. "I also got Advil, Tylenol, DayQuil, NyQuil, Chloraseptic, and Strepsils."

Jin popped four Motrins and followed with the lukewarm tea. "Give me the Chloraseptic, please."

He popped one tablet out and handed it to her.

It didn't help much, but hopefully, when the Motrin kicked in, the combination of the two would do the trick.

"Bridget was here. Do you want the good news first or the bad?"

He frowned. "What bad news?"

"Apparently, my sore throat is not caused by streptococcus. I'm growing venom glands."

"What?" Arwel sat on the bed next to her. "Venom glands?"

Jin nodded. "Bridget is sure of that. What she is not sure of is whether they will be functional. She says that even though I'm growing them, they might not produce venom."

"What about fangs? If you have venom, it makes sense that you will also grow fangs that can deliver it."

Jin grimaced. "It's a possibility." She looked at Mey. "The freak sisters never disappoint. We must always be different than everyone else."

"I should leave you two alone." Mey rose to her feet.

Jin took her hand. "If I feel better after the Motrin does its thing, I'll come up to the suite. I'm sick of staying in bed."

"Good. We can have dinner together." Mey looked at Arwel. "Except, Bridget said that you two should head home as soon as possible. She wants Jin to be near the clinic in case things take a turn for the worse."

"They won't," Jin said more for Arwel's sake than Mey's.

He looked so worried. She only hoped that he was concerned about her going through the transition and not about having a freak for a mate.

When the door closed behind Mey, Arwel kicked his shoes off and lay down next to her. "Cheer up. You are transitioning." He kissed her temple, probably afraid to touch any place else.

"What if I get fangs like yours? Is it going to weird you out?"

He smiled. "Weird me out? No way. It'll be kinky." He waggled his brows. "I'll also get to experience euphoria and multiple orgasms. Who wouldn't want that?"

"What if my venom doesn't work like that? What if it's only good for fighting? I'll have to join the Guardian force."

"That would be a bummer, but let's not worry about it yet. Bridget said that the glands might not produce venom, right? And then you will not grow big fangs either."

Resisting the urge to pat her gums with her finger once again, Jin ran her tongue over them. "So far, my gums are not swollen. So maybe I will not get fangs at all." She chuckled. "Mey and I divided the freakishness between us."

Arwel wrapped his arm around her waist and pulled her closer. "I like it that you are not like anyone else. My mate is one of a kind."

Smiling, she kissed his chin. "I forgot to ask Bridget if we can have sex while I'm transitioning."

Arwel laughed. "I bet that you are the only Dormant to ever think of asking her that. And it also means that the Motrin is working, and you are feeling better."

"I am." She rubbed herself against him. "And I want to shower. Want to help me?"

"You are serious, aren't you?"

"Hey, it could be our last chance before I'm really out of commission. How long does the transition usually last?"

"To fully transition takes months, but the main event can last between a couple of days to several weeks. Every Dormant is different. But for the males, it usually takes several weeks to grow the venom glands, and six months until their fangs reach full length and are ready to use."

Collapsing on her back, Jin groaned and threw an arm over her eyes. "Lucky me. I get to transition like a guy, which means freaking growing pains. God only knows when we will be able to have sex again."

Jacki

Casting an apologetic glance at Kian, Jacki tugged on Kalugal's hand. "Can I have a word with you?" She looked at Kian again. "I'm only stealing him for a few moments."

Kian smiled. "No need to steal. He's all yours."

Turner was still in the library, so Jacki pulled Kalugal toward his office.

"What is it?" He looked at her with amusement dancing in his blue eyes.

"I want to go see Jin."

He shook his head. "Kian, Lokan, and I still have a lot of work to do. Besides, I can't leave the house before we dispose of Simmons's body, and that is not going to happen until later tonight."

"Ugh. Don't remind me."

"You are not sorry that he's dead, are you?"

"Not at all. It's just that talking about disposing of his corpse creeps me out. I really don't want to be here when that happens."

Kalugal smiled. "Oh, now I see where you're going with this. Your excuse is that you don't want to be in the house when it happens."

"It didn't even occur to me until you said it. I just want to visit Jin and see what it's like to transition. And I don't need you to come with me. If you let me borrow one of your cheaper cars, I can drive myself to the hotel."

"By yourself?"

The look of panic in Kalugal's eyes was comical.

Leaning in, she kissed his lips. "I'm not leaving you forever, my love. I'll be gone for a couple of hours, three at most."

He put his hands on her waist and drew her closer. "I need you here. The idea of you not being near me upsets me."

It was sweet that Kalugal was suffering from separation anxiety, but it was important that she set boundaries from the get-go.

Jacki had no intention of living in a gilded cage, especially now that she was no longer a fugitive.

"The hotel is only fifteen minutes away. And since Simmons and Roberts are no longer looking for me, I'm free to come and go as I please."

"Not yet. Don't forget that they filed a fake police report, and if you are stopped, you might get detained. You also don't have documentation."

"Right. I forgot about that. Didn't you ask Kian to bring my fake documents to the summit?"

"I didn't. We decided not to get married using our fake names, so there was no need." He smiled. "I'll make us both new documents, and we can share the same last name. You can choose whichever one you like."

"Awesome. But what do I do until then? I don't want to be a prisoner in the house."

"I can have Phinas or Rufsur accompany you to the hotel, and you will have to put the wig and glasses on. Come to think of it, I'll send two more men to act as your bodyguards."

She rolled her eyes. "That's overkill, but I can live with it. Can they take me there now?"

Kalugal sighed dramatically. "Every moment without you will be agonizing."

"Nice try." She kissed him again. "I love you, but we can be apart for a few hours."

"A few? You said two."

"I said two to three. Jin invited me to join them for dinner."

"Then, it's probably going to be longer than three." He sighed, but then a smirk lifted the right corner of his sexy lips. "Since I am being so agreeable about it, I expect to be rewarded later tonight."

"You are funny." Jacki wrapped her arms around Kalugal's neck. "I'm the one who will be rewarded. Regrettably, I can't give you the same pleasure you give me. I don't have fangs and venom."

"Oh, my sweet, beautiful Jacqueline. You give me more pleasure than I could have ever imagined just by being you."

Vlad

"What are you making?" Wendy walked into the kitchen.

His arms covered in flour, Vlad blew a strand of hair away from his eyes. "I'm making dough for bread, and when I'm done with it, I'll leave it to rise and make chocolate cupcakes." His bangs flopped down again.

"Yummy." She lifted on her toes and pushed the strand of hair behind his ear. "Here. Now it'll stay out of your face."

"I need a haircut."

"I can give you one."

He chuckled. "No, thanks. I look weird enough as it is."

"I could use one," Richard said. "If Vlad's mom decides to show up, I don't want to scare her off." He smoothed his hand over his beard. "Or maybe I should keep the rugged look. What do you think, Wendy? Does it make me look sexy?"

She walked over to him and lifted a bunch of messy hair. "You look like a caveman. I'll give you a haircut and a beard trim."

"Do it on the porch," Bowen suggested. "Less cleanup."

Vlad didn't like the idea of Richard and Wendy alone outside, and he liked her touching the guy even less.

Except, he couldn't object without sounding like a possessive asshole. But maybe there was another way to prevent that from happening?

"Do you even have scissors?"

"I found a sewing kit in the bathroom's medicine cabinet. It has a decent pair of scissors."

"Let's do it." Richard got up, grabbed a chair from the dining table, and carried it out to the porch.

"I'll get the scissors." Wendy ducked into her room.

When the two had gone outside, Bowen walked into the kitchen and leaned against the counter. "I have news that I didn't want to share in front of Wendy. The director is dead."

"When did it happen?" Vlad washed his hands and dried them on a dishtowel. "And how?"

He hadn't told anyone that the director was Wendy's uncle. She'd shared the information in confidence, and since it was irrelevant anyway, he felt that it wasn't worth betraying her trust over.

"Yesterday, he and Roberts, that's the other head honcho of the paranormal program, showed up at Jacki and Kalugal's wedding with a long-range acoustic device. They blasted the party with decibels powerful enough to disable everyone there, including the all-powerful Kalugal, and cause permanent ear damage. If not for Roni shooting the device with a drone, Simmons and Roberts could have walked in and collected everyone in the party like fallen flies. And since they came with several vans and a team of ex-Marines, that's precisely what they had in mind."

"So Roni shot Simmons?"

Bowen nodded. "He was the one holding the device."

"What are they going to do with the others?"

"I don't know. The chief's next update will probably have something about that."

"Do you think they will shut down the program? I mean, with the two heads gone?"

"It's possible. Ask your girlfriend what she thinks will happen."

"I thought that you wanted to keep it from her."

Bowen shrugged. "I just didn't want to be the one who tells her. It's better if she hears it from you."

That was truer than Bowen realized. For better or worse, Simmons was the only family Wendy had other than her abusive father and an absent mother that might be dead.

"Yeah, you're right. Wendy should hear it from me."

"Just don't forget to omit the immortal part from the story. Simmons and Roberts thought that they could capture a large group of paranormally talented people. They didn't know that they were attacking immortals. The disturbing part is that the device they used worked just as well on immortals as on humans."

"Are Jacki and Jin okay? They must have been hit the hardest."

"In fact, they weren't hit as hard as the immortals because their ears are not as sensitive as ours. But we definitely recuperate faster. They are both doing fine."

"Good. I can at least tell Wendy that her friends are okay."

Bowen ran a hand over his chin. "The news is actually better than that. With Simmons and Roberts gone, no one will be looking for the escaped trainees. Wendy and Richard are free to go if they want to. The question is whether we tell them that or not."

That was a problem.

If he told Wendy that she was free to go and that no one would come searching for her, she might do it. To keep her from leaving, he would have to tell her about her potential dormancy.

But was she the one?

With no prior experience, Vlad had nothing to compare it with. What if he felt so strongly about Wendy just because she was his first girlfriend?

Until he was sure that she was the one, he couldn't tell her.

Richard was an even bigger problem. Nothing was keeping him with them. If he was told that he was free to go, he would.

Leaning against the counter, Vlad crossed his arms over his chest. "Right now, we are just assuming that it's safe for them to go. Until we know it for a fact, it would be irresponsible for us to claim that it is, true?"

Bowen nodded. "I see where you're going with that. As long as we are not absolutely sure that it is safe for them out there, we keep it to ourselves."

W endy took a step back and looked at Richard. "That's much better."

It wasn't a professional haircut, but at least he no longer looked like a hobo.

"Can I take a look?" Richard started to get up.

"Don't move. I'll get you a mirror."

"Okay." He sat back down.

Opening the door, she had a clear view of the kitchen, where Vlad and Bowen seemed to be deep in conversation, and by the vibe she was picking up, it was something serious.

"What happened?" She closed the door behind her and walked up to them.

Bowen and Vlad exchanged glances.

"Are you done with Richard?" Vlad asked.

"Almost. I came in to get him a mirror, but then I saw the two of you looking somber like something bad has happened. So what gives?"

"I'll let your boyfriend fill you in." Bowen unfolded his arms and pushed away from the counter.

"Damn you guys. You are scaring me. Are Jin and Jacki okay? Did something happen at the wedding?"

With her sensory feelers at full receptive mode, Wendy got her nonverbal confirmation. "Tell me already."

"Jin and Jacki are all right, but something did happen at the wedding. Let's go to your room." Vlad took her hand. "This concerns Richard as well, but we can tell him later."

Now that she knew that her friends were fine, Wendy's panic subsided, and she remembered that Richard was waiting for her. "Maybe you should tell us together. I told him that I would be right back."

Vlad nodded.

Out on the porch, Richard was still sitting on the chair like she'd told him to, his shirt covered in hair clippings. He looked at her empty hands. "Couldn't find a mirror?"

"Vlad has something he needs to tell us."

"Let's sit down." Vlad led her to the bench.

"Something happened last night at Jacki's wedding. Simmons and Roberts showed up with a bunch of men and a device that generates a loud sound at a harmful level."

When Wendy gasped, Vlad paused and looked at her.

"Don't mind me. Please, continue."

Vlad nodded. "They aimed the noise device at the party and incapacitated almost everyone there. One of the guests must have been wearing earplugs and had a gun. He shot the device."

"Thank God." Wendy let out a breath. "Is everyone okay?"

"Except for Simmons. He was holding the device."

"Is he injured?"

Vlad clasped her hand. "I'm sorry, Wendy. He's dead."

"Good riddance," Richard said. "That old dude was twisted, and he got what was coming to him."

"Are you okay?" Vlad looked at her with concern.

Wendy wasn't sure how she felt. She'd been grateful to her uncle for saving her from her father, but she'd never liked him, especially since he'd started lusting after her.

His death didn't bring sorrow. Mostly, it felt like a door that she'd kept slightly ajar had been slammed shut. There was no going back to the program, and the only path open to her was forward.

It was a relief.

Apparently, in some cases, not having options was actually a good thing.

Wendy nodded. "The director wasn't a good man, and he must have planned something horrible for your people. So I can't really feel sorry for him."

"I know exactly what he wanted to do," Richard said. "Once everyone at the party was down on the floor, he would have come in with his hired goons, collected them all, and loaded them on a plane to West Virginia. How many people were at that party? Fifty? Sixty? A hundred? That's a lot of headhunting money saved that he would have otherwise had to pay Marisol for recruiting that many talents." Richard fanned his T-shirt to dislodge the hair clippings. "Always follow the money. That's usually the motive behind every nasty move."

Wendy nodded. "He would still have to pay Marisol to compel them to cooperate."

"Maybe, but not her full fee. Besides, people like us are hard to find. I'm sure most of the potential talents Marisol sees are duds. People talk about stuff they read, movies they see, and they throw trigger words left and right."

"Poor Jacki." Wendy shook her head. "Her wedding was ruined."

Richard snorted. "Are you sure that you didn't have something to do with this? You looked mighty pissed that she didn't invite you to the wedding."

"How can you say something like that? Even if I could get to a phone, which there is no way I could, I don't know where Jacki is staying. Besides, I would never intentionally ruin her special moment."

"How about unintentionally?" Richard cocked a brow. "Maybe you jinxed it?"

"Ugh. You're so mean. I should have cut all of your hair off."

Richard laughed. "I'm just messing with you." He pushed to his feet. "But just in case you are still in a combative mood, the hairdressing session is over. Thank you."

"Your sideburns are uneven."

"I'll shave them off."

Wendy shrugged. "Suit yourself."

When Richard closed the door behind him, Vlad wrapped his arm around her shoulders. "Are you really okay? Simmons was family." He whispered the last part.

"Thank you for not telling anyone about it."

He nodded. "I didn't think it made any difference as far as our safety."

"Still, I don't want people to know that I was related to that jerk." Wendy sighed. "Are you sure that you want to be my boyfriend? I have nasty genes. An abusive father, a drug-addicted mother, and an evil, pedophile uncle."

"We are more than the sum of our genes. You decide the kind of person you want to be."

"I want to believe that. But I'm afraid of what's lurking inside me."

Jin

"Congratulations!" Syssi pulled Jin into a gentle hug. "I'm so happy you are finally transitioning. I was starting to worry."

"Really? Why? With Mey as my sister, there was no question of me not being a Dormant." Jin sat on the couch between Mey and Arwel.

Syssi shrugged and went back to her armchair. "We know so little about the process, and sickness can prevent it from happening. Thank the Fates that you are healthy and that the transition has started, but I had all kinds of crazy thoughts running through my head."

"Like what?" Mey asked.

"Like a heart condition, or undiagnosed diabetes, or worse. The transition can't happen if the body is not healthy." Syssi glanced at Bridget. "Am I right?"

The doctor shrugged. "We have too small of a case sample to reach definite conclusions, and each one of them is different. For some Dormants it's true, but not for others. There are other factors involved."

"But it makes sense," Syssi insisted. "The transition is a difficult process, and it takes a tremendous toll on the body. Just as someone with coronary disease is not likely to survive running a marathon in Death Valley, he or she is not likely to survive the transition, and that's why the body will not enter it. It's a protective mechanism."

Bridget chuckled. "The problem with common sense is that it's based on what we know. But there are many things we don't know. According to your logic, it is safe for anyone to attempt transition because if they can't handle it, their bodies will just not respond to the venom."

"Maybe that's really the case?" Syssi asked.

Bridget shook her head. "It's not, and even if it was, I wouldn't chance it. But luckily for Jin, other than the streptococcus infection she had, she is perfectly healthy. I gave her a physical."

"I didn't know that." Syssi pushed to her feet. "Anyone want something to drink?"

"I would like some tea," Jin said. "It helps with the throat pain."

Syssi frowned. "Why is your throat hurting?"

"Didn't Mey and Bridget tell you?"

"Tell me what?"

"I'm growing venom glands. That's how Bridget knew for sure that I'm transitioning."

Syssi's hand flew to her chest. "Oh, wow. That's just..."

"You can say it." Jin grimaced. "Freaky as hell. And it hurts." She pulled out a container of Motrin from one pocket and a sheet of throat lozenges from the other. "Without these, I wouldn't be here, sitting on the couch and talking to you.

Arwel wrapped his arm around her shoulders. "Those just take care of the pain. You should conserve your strength."

Jin stifled a chuckle.

He hadn't been too concerned about it when they'd made love in the shower.

Bridget yawned and shook her head. "I need to get some sleep." She rose to her feet.

"Can't you stay awake until dinner?" Syssi asked.

"I wanted to, but I'm just too tired. Save some for me." She walked into her bedroom and closed the door.

"When are Jacki and Carol getting here?" Wonder asked.

Jin glanced at her phone and checked the time. "I invited Jacki to join us for dinner at six, and it's almost time."

"I ordered champagne to be delivered," Syssi said. "Your transition is a cause for celebration."

"I hope."

"They are here." Yamanu lifted his head from his laptop. "They've just entered the lobby. Carol and Jacki have a couple of Kalugal's men with them."

Jin chuckled. "I wonder why Kalugal feels that Jacki needs bodyguards when she's visiting us."

"They are newly mated. He's probably freaking out because she is leaving the house." Syssi headed to the kitchen. "I still remember how hard it was in the beginning to be away from Kian even for a little while." She stopped and turned to look at Jin. "Don't worry. It gets easier with time."

Mey nodded. "When Yamanu left to do the shrouding during the exchange, I cried like a little girl."

Yamanu got up and walked up to her. "You didn't tell me that." He pulled her into his arms.

"Of course not. You left me in charge, and I was pretending to be brave."

The knock at the door arrived at the same time Syssi came out of the kitchen with Jin's tea.

"Hello, everyone." Carol entered with Jacki and the two bodyguards behind her. "I hope you don't mind the extra dinner guests." She turned to the men. "For those who haven't met him yet, this is Phinas, Kalugal's third-in-command, and this is Chad." She put a hand on his arm. "What's your designation?"

He shrugged. "I'm just a simple soldier."

Phinas dipped his head. "We don't wish to intrude on your dinner. Chad and I can stay out on the balcony."

"Nonsense." Amanda waved them over to the table. "Sit right there next to Dalhu and Yamanu. This is a wonderful opportunity to create your profiles."

Carol clapped her hands. "Oh, goodie. I should have thought of that."

"I'm sorry," Phinas said. "But what are you talking about?"

"Atzil hasn't told you?" Amanda shook her head. "I was sure he would spread the good news." She got up and sauntered up to the two. "Carol and I are creating a dating application for immortals. We will create profiles for all of Kalugal's men, and all of the local clan's single ladies. Isn't that fabulous?"

"That's an awesome idea." Jin pushed to her feet and embraced Jacki. "How are your ears?"

"Almost back to normal. And yours?"

"My ears are fine. It's the other stuff that isn't." She tugged on Jacki's hand. "Come sit with me, and I'll tell you all about it."

Arwel got up. "I'll sit with the guys."

"You can stay." Jin patted the spot next to her. "This couch is big enough for the four of us."

"That's okay. I want to hear more about that dating app."

Jacki

Jacki waited impatiently for Jin to explain. What was wrong? She'd said that her ears were fine, but other stuff wasn't. Did it have to do with her transition?

"Remember how I told you that Mey and I are the freak sisters?"

Jacki cast a quick glance at Mey. She wasn't smiling.

"What's wrong?"

"I'm growing venom glands."

"Is that a bad thing?"

"Female immortals are not supposed to have fangs or venom, but Mey and I are the freak sisters, and we have to do everything differently. Mey didn't get venom, but she got the fangs."

This time Mey smiled, exposing a pair of tiny fangs that looked more like sharp canines.

"They are kind of cute. Do they grow larger?"

Mey shook her head. "I was lucky. That's as big as they are going to get."

Jacki glanced at Phinas and Chad, but the two were busy answering Amanda and Carol's questions and not paying attention to the conversation happening on the couch.

"I might get big ones like the males." Jin sighed. "And to sweeten the deal, I might get taller as well. Just point me to the nearest circus."

"Don't be silly," Mey said. "I know it's an adjustment, but you are still going to be beautiful, and you most likely will not grow taller. I didn't."

"Did you?" Jin asked Syssi.

"I wish. But I didn't change at all, and neither did Callie. Right?"

Callie nodded. "No visible changes. Just the cool stuff like super hearing, super strength, the ability to smell emotions, and the like."

Jacki grimaced. "The smelling part still creeps me out." She glanced at the men and then leaned closer to Jin. "How are we supposed to act cool and unaffected when they can smell us?"

Syssi laughed. "There are advantages to that too. You don't have to say anything. Just by sniffing you, your man knows whether you are in the mood or not."

Jacki cast a quick glance at the men again. "I can live with that. What I can't accept is everyone else sniffing my reactions as well."

Callie waved a dismissive hand. "It's a small price to pay for immortality and all the benefits that come with it. But I should warn both of you. Don't drive until after your transition."

"Why?" Jacki asked.

"I passed out and got into a car accident. I'm lucky to be alive."

Jin's eyes widened. "What happened? Did the transition take you by surprise?"

"I didn't know anything about it. Brundar and I were together, but he wasn't allowed to tell me anything. I didn't have any paranormal abilities, so he was sure that I was just a human, and he was trying to keep our relationship a secret. Then one day, I went to the mall, and on the way back, I started to black out for a couple of seconds at a time. I thought that I was just closing my eyes while stopping at a red light. But then one time must have lasted longer and boom. I don't remember what happened, but I was taken to a hospital. Brundar and Bridget came, and she suspected that I was transitioning, so they got me discharged and took me to the clinic."

"Did you get paranormal abilities after you transitioned?" Jacki asked.

"Unfortunately, I didn't. I hoped that I could do something cool, but I guess my only talent is cooking."

"I don't have any paranormal abilities either," Wonder said. "Most of us don't."

This was news to her. "So how come those abilities are indicators for Dormants?"

"Only in some cases," Syssi said. "Generally speaking, humans with paranormal abilities have a greater chance of being Dormants, but not all are. Some are just talented humans. That's why it's almost never a sure thing. In Jin's case, it is because her sister already transitioned, and they have the same mother."

"Are there any other indicators?" Jacki asked.

"Affinity. Dormants and immortals feel a special connection. It's like recognizing a member of your tribe. But it's not always sexual, it could also be a friendship."

"I felt an affinity toward Kalugal even before I met him, but that was because I thought he was handsome and sexy, and that smirk of his…" Jacki fanned herself with her hand. "When I looked at his pictures, I felt as if he was flirting with me with that smirk, and my reaction was quite intense. Then I met him, and I thought that I was doing a great job of hiding my attraction. I didn't know about his super nose. Imagine how embarrassed I was to discover that he knew all along that I wanted him."

Jin patted her knee. "No harm done. You two are married now, and you are going to live happily ever after."

"Yeah, provided that I transition." Remembering Annani's call, Jacki smiled. "I almost forgot to tell you. Annani called Kian and demanded to speak to Kalugal.

She wants us to have a proper wedding ceremony with her presiding over it."

"That's awesome!" Jin clasped her hand. "When and where?"

"Kalugal said that we should wait until after my transition, and then Annani suggested that we do it in the village. Kian wasn't too keen on the idea, but she insisted, and I think he agreed."

Jin frowned. "What do you mean? He either agreed or not?"

"It wasn't a definite yes, but he didn't say no either."

"Don't worry." Syssi leaned forward. "When Annani wants something to be done, it's done. There is no arguing with her. You will get married in the village."

Kalugal

"I'm back." Jacki walked into the library together with Phinas. "Oh, I'm sorry. I didn't realize that you were still in a meeting."

Kalugal felt his shoulder muscles relax. "We are almost done." He pulled her into a quick embrace. "How is Jin?"

"Freaking out." Jacki smiled. "Anyway, I'll leave you guys to finish up." She kissed Kalugal's cheek. "Unless you need me here, I'm going upstairs." She glanced at Turner. "I hope that the unpleasant task that you were charged with is done."

"It is."

"Thank you. I'll sleep better knowing there is no corpse in the house."

"You're welcome."

"Good night, everyone." Jacki waved before walking out.

"I'll join you soon," he called after her.

"We should head back to the hotel," Kian said.

"Before you do, let's drink to the successful completion of phase one." Kalugal opened another bottle of Hibiki and poured it into eight Glencairn glasses. "Help yourselves, gentlemen."

Thanks to Turner, Simmons's accident had been successfully staged, the van careened into a ravine and exploded, and a call had been placed to 911.

"You have great taste in whiskey." Anandur distributed the glasses to everyone.

Kalugal took a small sip and swished it around in his mouth. Fine whiskey was meant to be savored, not gulped.

"Has the police report been filed already?" Kian asked.

"Not yet," Turner said. "It will most likely appear tomorrow."

"Anything we should worry about?" Kalugal leaned against the game table and crossed his legs at the ankles.

Turner looked at him as if the question was a personal affront. "I don't leave any loose ends. You can consider the case closed."

"I do." Kalugal lifted his glass. "That's what we are drinking to."

Kian pulled out a chair and sat down. "Roberts is healing rapidly, and we can send him home tomorrow. We need to finalize the details of his compulsion."

"I've made a partial list." Kalugal pulled out his phone. "I'll text it to you. Feel free to add items or remove them."

"Should we compel him to release the kids?" Lokan asked.

Kian raked his fingers through his hair. "I'm not sure. I know it's a lot to ask of you, but we need to check if their families were coerced into signing them up for the program. If the parents and the kids did it voluntarily, and drugs will no longer be used, it's not our place to decide for them. Also, we need to remove the compulsion from the other trainees, so they can decide whether they want to stay in the program or leave."

"There are only two underage kids, right?" Lokan asked.

Kian nodded. "Andy, that's the fourteen-year-old who looks like he is twelve, and Spencer, who is seventeen and reads auras."

"I remember them. Find out their home addresses, and I'll give their parents a visit. For the others, I will need to make another trip to West Virginia while they are on an outing and take care of everyone at one time."

"I appreciate that," Kian said. "I know that you are a busy man."

"Make Roberts give them more vacations at home," Anandur suggested. "And more outings too."

"Right." Kian nodded. "We can use those outings and vacations to introduce some of them to our people. Except, some are too old to attempt transition even if they are Dormants."

"You should take Carol with you when you go to remove the compulsion." Kalugal smirked. "She can compile profiles for the eligible trainees and add them to the dating application she and Amanda are planning to launch."

"That's not a bad idea." Kian walked over to the bar and refilled his glass. "It will take some of the guesswork out of the process. Our people could choose who they want to meet."

"We need to add trigger words to the ones they are feeding Echelon," Turner said. "We should add words like immortal and fast healing. Maybe we will stumble on unaffiliated immortals."

"Add fangs to the list," Rufsur said. "And glowing eyes."

Phinas snorted. "That would be a mistake. Do you have any idea how many romance novels, movies, and television shows feature vampires? There will be tens of thousands of triggers, and we won't be able to check them all. Quality trumps quantity."

Rufsur lifted a brow. "How do you know all that? I get the television shows, but what about the rest?"

Looking uncomfortable, Phinas waved a dismissive hand. "Don't you remember the Twilight craze? Even *Saturday Night Live* did a skit on that. Team Edward vs. Team Jacob, and all that crap."

Rufsur shook his head. "I think we have here a closet Twilight fan."

Phinas shrugged. "I'm secure enough in my masculinity to admit that I enjoyed the books and the movies. Although, I have to admit that I didn't like the actress they chose to play Bella. She was too skinny."

"I liked Kristen Stewart in that role," Lokan said. "She wasn't beautiful, but that was the whole point. Bella Swan was supposed to be a plain Jane."

Rufsur made a gagging sound. "Someone bring me a puke bucket."

Hiding a smile, Kalugal took another sip from the Hibiki. To see his brother and his lieutenants horsing around was surprisingly heartwarming and a much-needed relief after the serious stuff they had been dealing with since last night.

Jacki

As Jacki soaked in a bathtub full of bubbles, she wondered what strange attributes she would gain with her transition, if any. Syssi's visions had intensified after hers, but since most were very disturbing, she tried to avoid them.

Completely understandable.

It must be so upsetting to foresee horrible events and feel helpless to prevent them. Besides, Syssi was pregnant. An expecting mother should try to stay calm and positive as much as she could. Maintaining a good attitude throughout pregnancy was just as important for the baby as eating right and getting plenty of sleep.

Luckily, Jacki's visions were much milder in nature, and she wasn't worried about their effect on her mental state. They were usually about small things, and until the one about Wonder's caravan, the worst one had been about Allison's car accident.

Usually, they were also about future events, not past.

Witnessing what had happened to Wonder's caravan had been awful, but it wasn't as bad as watching something like that happening in the future and being powerless to do anything about it. So yeah, it had been painful to see, and Jacki had been seriously shaken, but at least she hadn't felt guilty for not trying to stop it or helpless to prevent it.

The events had already happened, and there was no changing them.

So if her transition triggered more such visions, she could deal with that. Having a window into the past could actually be cool.

Perhaps her past visions could even help Kalugal find more artifacts?

That would make him happy.

Smiling, Jacki scooped some of the bubbles and blew at them. It would be fun to travel with Kalugal to distant places. She wasn't too excited about digging in the dirt, but she probably wouldn't have to.

On hot days, she could wait for him in an air-conditioned hotel room.

Wearing absolutely nothing.

As her imagination filled in the rest of the details, her hands glided up to her breasts, and she cupped them, then tweaked her nipples. But the sensation wasn't exciting even with her eyes closed, imagining that those were Kalugal's hands and Kalugal's fingers.

It just wasn't the same.

With a sigh, Jacki dropped her hands and watched the water ripple, lapping at her breasts, teasing them with gentle kisses without providing relief.

As the bathroom door opened, Jacki's first instinct was to duck under the water and hide, but she shook it off. The only one who would enter without knocking was Kalugal, and she actually wanted him to see her naked.

Heck, she wanted him to do much more than look.

Last night, her ears had hurt, and she'd been exhausted from all the excitement. She had fallen asleep long before Kalugal came to bed.

He'd held her, kissed her cheek, and let her sleep.

Tonight, she felt fine, and sleeping was the furthest thing from her mind.

"That looks tempting." Kalugal started on the buttons of his shirt. "May I join you?"

Her eyes riveted to the muscular chest he was slowly exposing, Jacki licked her lips. "You don't have to ask."

"I'll always ask permission." He opened another button and smirked. "Especially when I want to tie you up, or spank you, playfully, of course."

Jacki's nipples pebbled, and her core contracted. "Why would you want to do that?"

"Because it turns you on and adds to your excitement." He shrugged the shirt off, revealing his chiseled chest. He was nearly hairless, with only a light smattering of hair painting a downward trail.

Her eyes riveted to his defined abs, Jacki wondered how the hell he could have known that?

Kalugal couldn't read her mind, he couldn't thrall the information out of her, and since she'd gotten to his house, Jacki hadn't read a single kinky romance. At first, because he obviously didn't have any romance books in his library, and then when he'd given her a tablet and a phone, she hadn't dared to use the devices to purchase kinky romance eBooks.

If he had access to her search history, which she was pretty sure he did, he could have seen what she was reading, and that would have been mortifying. Even though she wanted to share everything with her husband, admitting her secret fantasies was just too embarrassing.

But what if he'd been just guessing to gauge her response? Her scent would tell him everything he wanted to know.

Fortunately, Jacki was in a bathtub full of bubbles, and the flowery smell might mask the scent of her arousal. This time, she could deny it and possibly get away with it. But that would be lying, and the next time Kalugal brought it up, her secret would be out.

Instead, she could phrase her response in a way that would neither confirm nor deny it.

"Are you basing your assumption on statistical probability? Have any of your sex partners been into kinky stuff?"

Kicking his shoes off, Kalugal unbuckled his belt. "To some extent, the majority of women enjoy gentle dominance." He pulled down the zipper. "But some don't enjoy it at all, and some don't like it gentle. Every woman is unique." He dropped his pants together with his silk boxer shorts.

Her eyes glued to her husband's impressive erection, Jacki swallowed. "Define gentle dominance."

"Scooch." He put a hand on her shoulder and slid into the bathtub behind her.

Cradling her between his legs, his hard shaft pressed against her bottom, Kalugal pulled her back against his chest and wrapped his arms around her.

As he cupped her breasts, Jacki closed her eyes and let her head fall back on his shoulder.

His hands gliding over the soapy, wet skin, massaging gently, and his thumbs moving back and forth across her hard nipples, he kissed her shoulder at the spot where it met her neck. "Gentle means that I will only do what brings you pleasure. Except, sometimes, a little spice enhances the experience." He nipped the spot he'd just kissed, lightly pinching her nipples at the same time. "Like this."

Jacki moaned.

"More?" he asked.

As his fingers rolled and tugged, alternating between soft and gentle and a little rough, the fire inside her flamed hot, and the only coherent thought she had left was a resounding yes.

Kalugal

Kalugal's instincts never failed.

Perhaps it was because he was attracted to women who enjoyed a little kinky play. Or maybe there was something unique in the plethora of subtle scents that women emitted that he was good at interpreting. Or perhaps he was just reading subconscious clues.

Then again, as long as women were provided with an environment that was safe both physically and mentally, most were willing to try new things and explore their fantasies.

Except, trust was contingent on full and unconditional acceptance, which was rare. People were judgmental by nature, and although everyone craved complete approval from others, they rarely gave it even to those closest and most dear to them.

No wonder so many spent their lives in self-denial. No one wanted their fantasies ridiculed or marginalized.

To the casual observer, Jacki seemed outspoken and assertive, but a closer look revealed her eagerness to please.

His first clue had been her reaction to the fake attack he'd subjected her to.

Jacki's initial response to the kiss he'd forced on her had been arousal. But that was when she thought that he'd just gotten carried away a little and that a kiss was all he would demand. When he'd escalated things and pushed her down on the couch, her arousal had vanished, and fear had taken its place.

Even though he'd had no other way to verify that Jin's tether was gone, Kalugal still felt remorse over what he had done to Jacki. It was a miracle that she'd forgiven him so quickly.

The truth was that when he entered the bathroom, he had no intention of introducing Jacki to the spicier side of lovemaking. She wasn't ready, and he needed more time to build up trust and to prove to her that she had his total and unconditional acceptance.

But perhaps he could give her a little taste and whet her appetite.

Smoothing his hand down Jacki's belly, Kalugal cupped her center. "This is too soon for you to try anything adventurous. Let's start with a simple surrender." Kissing her neck, he slid one finger inside her. "Can you do that?"

"I don't know what it means," she murmured.

"It means that all you need to do is relax and enjoy. I'm going to take care of you."

Jacki turned her head and kissed the underside of his jaw. "That's easy. But isn't it unfair to you?"

"I'll let you in on a secret." He nibbled on her ear. "For me, and I suspect for most men, giving our ladies supernova orgasms is extremely satisfying." He trailed kisses down her neck. "Nothing makes me feel more like a man than sending a woman soaring on an orgasmic cloud, and not by injecting her with my venom. It's a cool trick to have, but to me, it feels like cheating because it doesn't require any effort or skill on my part. Where's the challenge in that?"

The mention of the bite had Jacki instinctively turn her head a little and elongate her neck. "Your opinion of men is too flattering. I don't have personal experience, but I've heard my girlfriends complain about how selfish their boyfriends were in bed."

"So they were lousy lovers and your girlfriends should've dropped them." He circled her clit with his thumb. "A man's job is to please his woman."

Jacki moaned. "And what's the woman's job?"

"To let go, enjoy, and shower her lover with praise."

"You are amazing." She giggled.

"Yes, I know. And that's a good start." He pushed two fingers inside her.

"Oh, this feels so good. I love your hands on me, and your fingers in me. And I love your mouth and your tongue and your manhood." She giggled again. "Especially that."

Kalugal chuckled. "I didn't mean continuous praise. Just when you feel like it."

"I feel like it now."

Gripping her hips, he lifted her and turned her around to face him. "I love you, my Jacqueline." He pushed up into her.

"Yes," Jacki gasped and lowered herself the rest of the way. "So good."

As he pumped into her, and the water sloshed out of the tub, Kalugal had a passing thought that it could leak down to the library below, and some of the books in there were irreplaceable treasures. But even that wasn't enough to make him stop.

Pumping into Jacki with abandon, listening to her moans of pleasure, and watching the ecstatic expression on her face, he felt consumed by her, by the moment, by the joining of their bodies and souls.

The lovemaking was beautiful, it was meaningful, and it overshadowed every other experience he'd had with any other female.

Holding Jacki up with one hand, he reached between their bodies with the other and pressed his thumb to her swollen clit.

As her inner muscles clamped around his shaft, he pumped up even harder, squeezing her ass with one hand and rubbing the thumb of the other over her engorged clit.

Jacki cried out, and her sheath gripped his shaft almost painfully, spurring his own release.

Letting go of her bottom, Kalugal gripped the back of her neck and opened his mouth wide to deliver the venom bite. But even though he was driven by instinct and barely conscious of what he was doing, at the last moment, he remembered to lick the spot he intended to bite.

As his fangs pierced her skin and his seed jetted into her, Jacki screamed, but it wasn't in pain. She'd climaxed again even before the venom entered her system.

Holding her tightly to him, he shared his essence with his mate, and it felt as if he was sharing his soul with her as well.

They were one.

Jacki

It was dark when Jacki woke up, but Kalugal's eyes cast a soft glow on the white duvet cover, and the reflection illuminated the rest of his handsome face.

His arm was draped over her torso, her leg was over his, and they were both naked under the duvet.

"We are no longer in the bathtub." Remembering the water sloshing over the lip, Jacki cringed. "Did we flood the library?"

"We didn't. I should give my thanks to the builder of this home for a job well done. Nothing leaked, but there is a pile of wet towels in the bathroom the size of a grand piano."

"I'm sorry that you had to do it alone. I would have helped if I could." Jacki frowned. "Not that I'm complaining, but will I keep passing out for hours after sex?"

"I don't know." Kalugal caressed her back. "I've never been with a woman enough times to check whether the effect of the venom loses its potency. You will have to ask your friends. Or, if you want, I can ask Kian or one of the other clan males who is mated to a former Dormant."

"No, that's okay. I'll ask Syssi tomorrow when I go to visit Jin again."

When his face fell, she cupped his cheek. "It wasn't so bad today, right? You survived the separation."

"It's five in the morning, so it was yesterday. But it was difficult. My shoulders and back were tense the entire time, and it felt as if something wasn't right. It was quite disturbing. How about you? Were you tense?"

Jacki smiled apologetically. "Frankly, I wasn't, not about that. Jin was freaking out about growing venom glands and potentially getting even taller. We all tried to make light of it, but I get why she's so upset. I wouldn't want that either. I just hope that my visions will become stronger and more meaningful. Anyway, after that, Callie told me and Jin about passing out while driving during her transition. She got into a car accident and was taken to a hospital. Bridget and Brundar had to spring her out of there and get her to the clan's clinic." Jacki shook her head. "She could have died before turning immortal. Brundar hadn't told her anything because she didn't have any paranormal talents. He thought that he'd fallen in love with a human."

Kalugal's arm around her tightened, and he smashed her against his body. "Now, I'm doubly glad that I didn't let you drive to the hotel."

"Yeah, I'm glad too. Callie told me and Jin her story as a warning not to drive until after we transition."

"Wait a minute." Kalugal's hand on her back paused. "Did you say that Jin is growing venom glands?"

"Yes. And it has never happened before. Mey's canines fell out during her transition, and she grew a pair of cute little fangs, but they don't elongate, so it's not a big deal. Bridget said that Jin might get fully functional ones."

"That's interesting." His hand on her back resumed the slow caressing. "I wonder whether it's a genetic mutation or did they inherit it from a deviant ancestor. Does Bridget know?"

"If she does, she didn't say anything, and Mey didn't offer an explanation either."

"Their talents are also very different. I don't know of any immortal that can do what they do. But on the other hand, I've been away from the island for over eighty years. Perhaps some of the new generation were born with new talents."

"Lokan should know that, right? He is still part of the Brotherhood."

"He is, and I will try to persuade him to jump ship like I did. It's too dangerous for him, especially since he is living with Carol. Our father has spies everywhere, and he will become suspicious."

"Is there a way to detect that she is immortal? Because she and the other women look like regular humans." Jacki scrunched her nose. "Except for Amanda. She is just inhumanly beautiful, and so is Kian."

Rolling on top of her, Kalugal affected a scowl. "More beautiful than I am?"

"No way. You are the most gorgeous man I've ever met or seen or even dreamt about."

He smirked. "That's the correct answer, my Jacqueline." Dipping his head, he kissed her lips. "Are you ready for another round of fabulous lovemaking?"

"Always, my love."

Kalugal

"That coffee smells wonderful." Jacki walked out of the bedroom in her night robe.

"What are you doing up so early?" Kalugal pulled her into his arms. "I was sure that you were going to sleep until noon."

Jacki smiled impishly. "Oh, so that was your plan. You wanted to exhaust me with nonstop lovemaking, so I'd forget about visiting Jin. But it didn't work." She kissed him on the lips. "Your venom is like a shot of energy. I feel as if I slept the whole night."

She hadn't.

There had been the five o'clock in the morning lovemaking, then a short nap, and then another one at seven.

Frankly, he was tired. Not because of the sex, of course, he could go on many more times, but because of the lack of sleep. Except, there was no way Kalugal was going to admit it.

He was a demigod, and he had a reputation to uphold.

Cupping her lush ass, he smirked. "If that's true, after three injections, you should be ready for the fourth."

"Again, nice try. I know that Kian is going to get here around ten, and that's in less than fifteen minutes."

"That's long enough." He lifted her and started walking toward the bedroom.

Jacki laughed. "Put me down. I want to have a cup of coffee with you before Kian gets here."

"Coffee can wait."

"No, it can't."

With a resigned sigh, he let her slide down his body, making sure that she felt how hard he was, just in case she was wondering if he could go for another round.

"That's not going to work either." She slapped his arm.

He tapped his nose. "It did work."

"Ugh. That sense of smell of yours is so annoying. I can't hide anything from you." Jacki sat on the couch and rearranged her robe, covering her beautiful, long legs.

"You can hide plenty, just not your arousal." He walked over to the coffeemaker, poured her a cup, added cream and sugar, and stirred.

"What can I hide?"

"Your thoughts." He handed her the cup. "Your intentions."

"But not if I get excited by them. Then you will smell it."

"Only if the excitement is the result of naughty thoughts. I can also smell when you are sad or anxious or frightened. But I won't know the cause unless you tell me."

She tilted her head. "Isn't that strange for you? You are so used to just reaching into someone's head and getting what you need."

"I don't do that unless the information is vitally important and I can't get it by just asking or compelling them to reveal it. Very rarely, I encounter a person who doesn't respond to compulsion but can be thralled. Besides, I only have access to recent memories or very vivid imaginings. I see them as movies. Thoughts are different, too jumbled and racing all over to paint a coherent picture. If someone has a thought when I'm right there and it's very visual and linear, I can read that."

"Is it the same for all immortals?"

"For most. A very strong telepath might tune into thoughts, and a strong empath can tune into emotions. But those are specific talents that I don't possess."

"But all immortals can thrall, right?"

He nodded. "There are degrees of that too. Most can also shroud, but only themselves and only for a few minutes. Yamanu, who can shroud an entire city block for hours, including sounds and smells, is one of a kind. He can also thrall an entire city block, which is unique."

Frowning, Jacki took a sip from her coffee. "Maybe Yamanu is a demigod too?"

"He is not one of Annani's children. So, no. He is just a very talented immortal."

"Maybe his father was a demigod?"

"Not possible. Up until recently, the children born to the clan were all fathered by humans, and although an immortal can thrall a human female to forget his fangs, he can't thrall an immortal female. If any of the clan females had encountered a male of our species, they would have remembered it."

"What if the father was like you? He could have compelled Yamanu's mother to forget his fangs."

Smiling, Kalugal wrapped his arm around Jacki's shoulders. "There is no one like me. I'm one of a kind."

"Not true. Your father can do the same things that you can."

"Don't remind me. I don't like to think about him and the genes I inherited from him and my grandfather."

"You are a good man, Kalugal. You're not like them."

"Ah, but what if the crazy gene lies dormant, just waiting for some trigger to bring it out? Perhaps my father and grandfather were decent men until they were hit over the head with some calamity that loosened the screws in their otherwise brilliant minds?"

Jacki put the cup down and took his hand. "I don't believe that being bad is genetic."

Lifting their entwined hands, Kalugal kissed the back of Jacki's. "Unfortunately, you are wrong. Genetics play a greater role in shaping who we are than anything else. I just hope that the genes I inherited from my mother are pure enough to offset the bad ones that I inherited from my father."

Jacki

"Why are you crying?" Jacki rushed in and hugged Jin.

Jin put a hand over her mouth. "I'm not."

She was, and Jacki didn't need immortal senses to see that her friend's eyes were red.

Behind her, Phinas and Chad stood at the entrance to the hotel suite, unsure of what they were supposed to do next.

"Hi, Jacki." Arwel walked in from the balcony. "Phinas, Chad, why don't you join us on the terrace?"

It seemed like all the men were outside, giving Jin room to be miserable with her sister and girlfriends, or just hiding from the tears. Except, even though Arwel closed the French door, they could probably hear everything.

Freaking immortals.

But at least they couldn't smell anything from out there.

"Your eyes are red." She took Jin's hand and cradled it between hers.

Still covering her mouth with the other, Jin sniffled. "I cried before. I'm not crying now."

"Okay. Why were you crying before?"

Jin opened her mouth, pointing to the gaps where her canines were missing. "They fell out during the night. I was lucky I didn't swallow them. I'm growing freaking fangs, my gums hurt, my throat hurts, and I'm miserable."

Jacki glanced at Arwel through the glass door. The guy's usual expression was tinted with a shade of suffering, but today there was an additional layer of guilt to it.

Was Jin blaming him for what was happening to her?

"Hey, no need to panic. You might grow cute little fangs like Mey's. They are adorable, and I'm sure Arwel will find them sexy."

"That's what he keeps saying, but it's just talk." Jin leaned closer to Jacki's ear. "If they end up being long like his, it will be like me having a dick. Arwel will feel like he is having sex with a dude."

Unable to help herself, Jacki laughed. "Not the same, sweetie. Definitely not the same." She leaned to whisper in Jin's ear. "You are still the sheath, and he is still the sword. It just happens that both are decorated with thorns. If you grow really big ones, I mean."

"I like the analogy," Amanda said. "I told Jin that she is overreacting. Transitioning wreaks physical and emotional havoc." She cast Jin a pitying look. "It's just your hormones talking, darling."

"Oh, yeah? How would you like to have elongating fangs and venom glands like the men?"

Amanda put the magazine she'd been flipping through down on her knees. "I would love that. I don't think it's fair that we don't have them. Fangs are weapons that the guys always have at their disposal. We, on the other hand, have to rely on pepper spray, or a handgun, or on our men. All are fine, but in some instances, there is no substitute for fangs that can inflict real damage."

"I agree," Syssi said. "Although, in my case, I don't think I could use fangs even if I had them, and the same goes for a handgun. Maybe I could use pepper spray because it's nonlethal."

Amanda snorted. "A so-called nonlethal weapon had us all writhing on the ground, helpless. If not for Roni, we would be in the government facility in West Virginia by now. In our case, those are more dangerous than conventional weapons."

"Kian had his earpieces in," Syssi said. "And so did Anandur and Brundar. The three of them could have overpowered Simmons, Roberts, and their hired goons."

"They were wearing earpieces only because Kian is paranoid, and the same is true for the drones. Imagine what would have happened if Kian trusted Kalugal and didn't take all of these precautions."

Jacki shivered. "I'm so glad about that. I mean, not for Kian mistrusting Kalugal, I think he should have realized by now that Kalugal means him no harm. I'm talking about the safety measures." Another shiver rocked her body.

Jin frowned. "Are you okay?"

"Yeah." Jacki rubbed her arms. "It's a little cold in here. And apparently, I'm more tired than I thought I was. I didn't get to sleep much last night."

"Oh, yeah?" Jin flashed her a gap-toothed smile. "Your hubby kept you awake?"

Jacki nodded. "The venom is like a wonder drug. But I guess the effect is only temporary."

Amanda leaned forward. "It's not cold in here. We've turned the heating on for Jin. Maybe you have a fever?"

Jacki put a hand on her forehead. "I feel a little warm." Her eyes widened. "Could it be the start of the transition?"

Jin laughed. "You've had sex for two days. That's not nearly enough to trigger it. And as far as I know, the transition is not contagious, so you couldn't have gotten it from me."

"Yeah, you are probably right. Maybe I caught a cold, or maybe it's just exhaustion."

"I wish Bridget was here," Syssi said. "At the least, she could have checked your fever."

"Maybe she left the thermometer behind?"

Syssi shook her head. "She took her doctor's bag with her to your place. She needs to check on Roberts. They plan on sending him home today."

Jacki shivered again. "I hope their plan works. What if Marisol can remove Kalugal's compulsion from Roberts?"

"Lokan is going to test it. His compulsion is more powerful than Marisol's. But if he can remove Kalugal's compulsion from Roberts, then there is a chance she can too."

Amanda waved a dismissive hand. "Roberts is going to fire her ass before she realizes that he is under compulsion."

"Yeah, but the first thing she'll do will be to compel him to keep her," Jin said. "She's making way too much money from recruiting paranormal talents to just tuck her tail between her legs and leave. The bitch is going to fight."

"I hope Kalugal's compulsion holds," Jacki said. "So much is riding on it."

"Life is funny that way." Syssi sighed. "Sometimes, the things we dread the most turn out to be a blessing and not the curse we believed it was. We were all so worried about Kalugal's ability to compel other immortals, but it might just save us all. If the program was allowed to continue as is, it could have potentially led to our exposure. But that's still nothing compared to the upside of possibly locating more paranormally talented people who might be Dormants. Our clan, as well as Kalugal's people, need them to thrive. Maybe even to survive."

Jin dropped her head back on the couch pillows. "What I dread at the moment are the freaking fangs and saying goodbye to my bestie. If everything works out well with Roberts, we will leave tomorrow morning. Bridget wants me to be near the clinic." She turned to Jacki. "I'm going to miss you so much."

With tears welling in her eyes, Jacki wrapped her arms around Jin and held her tightly. "Promise that you will come to visit me after your transition. I want to see those fangs."

"I promise. As soon as I'm back on my feet, I'll grab Arwel, and we will come to see you."

"Ahem." Syssi cleared her throat. "Kian might not allow that."

Jin shot her a glare. "Let him try to stop me."

"Hey, don't shoot the messenger. I'm just saying that he might forbid it, and you know why."

Kian

"Stage two is done." Kian walked out of Roberts's room.

The guy's heart was a ticking bomb, and after the amount of pressure Kalugal and then Kian had used on him, Bridget stayed with the guy to make sure he didn't conk out.

During the intense compulsion and then intrusive thrall, Roberts had suffered from heart palpitations, and Kian wondered whether they weren't wasting their efforts on someone who wasn't going to last long.

Kalugal opened his office door. "Now, all that remains to be done is for Lokan to try to remove part of my compulsion."

"I could use a drink," Kian said. "What do you have here?"

"Take a look." Kalugal motioned to the bar. "Whatever you choose, pour one for me too."

"How about you two take a seat, and I'll serve you," Anandur offered. "Both of you could use a rest."

"Fine by me." Kian dropped next to Kalugal on the couch.

They were both exhausted.

Kalugal had gone first, compelling Roberts to do all the things they'd agreed upon. And Kian had taken it from there, performing a thralling job on Roberts with the intricacy of complicated brain surgery.

Roberts wouldn't remember that he was under compulsion, but it was firmly embedded in his mind.

That had been the easy part. The difficult part was erasing the entire plan to capture them from the guy's head and the events themselves.

First, Kian had had to check who else knew about it, like the guy who'd loaned Roberts the long-range acoustic device, and the pilot who'd flown them into San Francisco.

Luckily, what Simmons and Roberts had been planning to do was illegal, so they hadn't gotten approval for any part of it, and they hadn't shared details with anyone either. Even Marisol hadn't known what they'd been up to.

If she had, that would have been a serious complication since she couldn't be thralled or compelled to forget it.

Anandur handed Kian a drink. "Tell us the story that you put in Roberts' head." He handed the other to Kalugal.

Kian took a sip. "That was the most creative work I've done in a while. Syssi would be proud of how imaginative I was." He leaned back and took another sip. "The story had to fit with their trip to San Francisco, explain the missing long-range acoustic device, and Simmons's demise. And it had to be plausible."

"I can't wait to hear it." Kalugal crossed his legs at the ankles.

"Some of the story is even based on the truth, which makes it more believable to Roberts. What I learned from Roberts' memories, is that Simmons had a thing for very young women, and he liked to play out forced scenarios. At his age, the only way he could get that was to pay for the privilege. He'd bragged about his latest escapade to Roberts less than a week ago, so the memory was still fresh in Roberts' mind."

Kian paused to take another sip from the excellent bourbon. "So far, we are still dealing with facts. Here is how I embellished the story. One of his prior service providers had been underage at the time, but he didn't know that, thinking that she was over eighteen. It had been a trap. The entire thing had been recorded, and she threatened to go to the police with the tape and also spread it online. Simmons asked Roberts to help him get rid of the problem."

Kalugal chuckled. "I can guess where you went with that. Simmons made a deal with the girl or her pimp to bring cash money to them. But instead of money, the suitcase contained a long-range acoustic device. They were going to use the device to stun her and her boyfriend, aka pimp, and take the evidence without paying. Except, that's not believable since the girl and her guy would have kept a copy."

"Precisely. That's why that was not good enough. I did some reading up on that device, and apparently, at certain frequencies, it can cause more than hearing loss. It can kill. That's how they were planning to get rid of the problem permanently, and the cause of death would not have been clear."

"Bravo." Kalugal raised his glass. "That will ensure that he tells no one about it, even if in your story they ended up not killing their targets."

"Correct. But according to the scenario I implanted in his head, they killed the couple." Kian looked at Turner. "We will need to plant a fake police report about two unidentified bodies found with severe damage to their eardrums."

"Did you use a specific location? I'll need it for the report."

"I'll give it to you later." Kian put his empty glass down on the side table. "The hardest part was to explain what happened to Simmons, and I'm not entirely happy with that. But I hope it will do. The brakes on the van they were driving malfunctioned. Roberts managed to jump out before it careened into the ravine, but Simmons was trapped inside. Roberts lost consciousness and woke up in the room he is now in."

"Why was he brought here and not to the hospital?" Turner asked.

"His rescuers, meaning us, were into some illegal activity as well, and we couldn't bring him to a hospital. I hinted at mafia. We patched him up as well as we could, and we are sending him home. End of story."

Kalugal uncrossed his legs and leaned forward. "It sounds like a B-movie script. Do you think it will hold?"

"I did the best I could. The story is plausible, and I put in many vivid details for him to remember. I haven't done such an intricate thrall in a long time."

Kalugal

An hour later, Lokan walked into Kalugal's office together with the doctor. "Your compulsion holds. I compelled him to eat a piece of chocolate, and even though his mouth salivated for it, he couldn't even bring his hand near it."

Kalugal grinned. "Excellent."

It was good to know that lesser compellers like Lokan and Marisol couldn't override his compulsion. After Kian had told him the story of how a thirteen-year-old kid had overridden Lokan's compulsion and freed his mother and sister from it, Kalugal had been a little worried.

Shifting sideways, Turner made room for his mate, and when she sat down, he wrapped his arm around her shoulders.

Kalugal loved seeing those small displays of affection between the clan couples. Hopefully, the Echelon system would provide solid leads on potential Dormants, and his men would also find mates. After all, access to the system was possible only thanks to him and his power of compulsion, and he'd negotiated for his men to get the first pick of the females.

"Is Roberts well enough to travel?" Kian asked.

Bridget nodded. "Thanks to Ruvon's blood, Roberts' wound healed without a mark, at least as far as what's visible. But he will still feel tenderness in the area."

"That's okay," Kian said. "He will attribute it to falling out of a moving vehicle. His patchy memory can also be explained by trauma to the head from the fall."

When Bridget lifted a brow, Kian told her the scenario that he'd implanted in Roberts' head.

The doctor shook her head. "He is too smart to believe that. The first part about the blackmail is okay given what you found out about Simmons's proclivities. But the part about the mafia helping Roberts and providing him with medical treatment? Not likely. Mafiosos don't help random strangers they find lying injured on the side of the road."

Kian shrugged. "That's the best I could come up with, and I made sure that it sticks. His rescuers didn't want to call 911 because of who they were, but they felt bad about leaving him to die. Even if Roberts finds it unbelievable, he will be convinced that it really happened the way he thinks he remembers it."

Kalugal glanced at his phone. "Is there anything else anyone wants to say to Roberts before Rufsur takes him to the airport?"

"I'm done with him," Kian said.

"So am I." Kalugal typed a message to Rufsur, telling him to proceed. "I want Roberts out of my house already."

Bridget put her head on Turner's shoulder. "I'm glad this is finally over. Can we go home today instead of tomorrow? I'm worried about Jin not having immediate access to the clinic. If she loses consciousness while we are still here, it will take us about three hours to get home and have her hooked up to the monitoring equipment, and that's too long. Besides, I'd rather sleep in my own bed."

"I don't see why not," Kian said. "I can have Charlie come pick us up tonight."

"Hold on." Kalugal lifted his hand. "Why would Jin lose consciousness? She is young and healthy." He turned to Kian. "You said that the transition isn't dangerous for the young."

"I didn't say that. What I said was that the older the Dormant, the more difficult the transition. Syssi was only twenty-four when she transitioned, and she lost consciousness for twenty-four hours. Callie was twenty-two or three, and she had episodic blackouts. Nathalie, on the other hand, was thirty when she transitioned, and she just flew through it. So you can never know."

The entire time Kian had been talking, Kalugal had been watching the doctor, but she had seemed to agree with everything he'd said.

That wasn't good.

Kalugal had assumed that Jacki's transition would progress without a hitch because of her youth and her health, but apparently that wasn't guaranteed, and she might encounter complications.

What was he going to do if that happened?

He couldn't even take her to a human hospital or bring in a human doctor. They wouldn't know how to help her.

Bottom line, he needed Bridget to stay.

Perhaps he could compel her?

If he could have a private moment with her, he could make her say that it was her idea.

But it was too late for that. Bridget was done with Roberts, and she'd just asked Kian to go home tonight.

Maybe he could appeal to her compassion. "I know this is a lot to ask, but I need you to stay until Jacki transitions. As you are well aware, we don't have anyone who can help Jacki if her transition doesn't go smoothly. And I can't take her to a human hospital either."

Bridget shook her head. "Even if I stayed, there isn't much I could do for her outside of a clinic. Perhaps you should wait with Jacki's induction until you have one set up. I can send Julian to help you do that and also train one of your men in the basics. Then when Jacki enters transition, he or I can fly over and keep an eye on her."

Kalugal pushed his fingers through his hair. "It might already be too late." He lifted his eyes to Kian. "I would be forever grateful if you agree for Jacki and me to come to your village and stay until she safely transitions. I don't mind if you want to keep me locked up in a room with guards wearing earplugs watching me. I just want Jacki to be safe."

As all eyes turned to Kian, his cousin had no choice but to nod. "I can't say no, but I need to come up with safety measures." He turned to Bridget. "We'll leave tomorrow morning. By then, I hope I'll have it figured out."

Kalugal released a silent breath. "Thank you."

Jacki

"Are Kian and his crew still here?" Jacki asked as Phinas parked the car.

"Last I checked with Kalugal, they were all in his office."

"Good. I want to say goodbye."

Chad opened the door for her and offered her his hand. "I can take you there."

"Thank you, but I know the way."

"I'll come with you," Phinas said. "I want to say goodbye as well."

It was probably just an excuse to accompany her, but she couldn't refuse. "Okay."

Walking down the corridor, Jacki wondered whether she should ask Bridget to check her temperature. She was feeling only mildly sick, and she didn't want Kalugal to worry, but what if the mild fever was the first sign of transition?

What if it started and she had no one to help her because Bridget had gone home?

Suddenly feeling faint, Jacki listed toward Phinas and grabbed his arm for support.

"What's wrong?" He looked at her with worried eyes. "Are your ears still bothering you?"

"Not much, but that's probably the reason for the dizziness. I think that the inner ear is responsible for balance, and it might still be affected by what happened to it two days ago."

"I'm sorry, but I have no clue." Phinas looked at her apologetically. "You should tell the doctor." He started walking again.

Could the fever be connected to that? Ear infections caused fever, but could loud noise cause infection?

That was unlikely. Then again, her fever was so mild that she might be imagining it, and the rest of her symptoms might go away after she had some sleep.

As they reached Kalugal's office, Phinas knocked on the door and then opened it, probably after hearing Kalugal telling him to come in, but Jacki hadn't heard a thing, which had probably nothing to do with ear damage.

Immortals and their freaking bat hearing.

"Jacki!" Kalugal walked up to her and pulled her into his arms as if he hadn't seen her in weeks.

Holding her tightly to him, he breathed her in for a couple of seconds and then kissed her cheek.

"Young love," Anandur murmured. "How sweet."

Ignoring the comment, Kalugal let her out of his arms but took her hand and led her to an armchair. "How is Jin doing?" He sat down and pulled her onto his lap.

It was a bit embarrassing to sit like that in the company of Kian and Turner and the others, but no one reacted to Kalugal's move one way or another.

That was probably because they were all used to public displays of affection between mated couples. Even Bridget and Turner, who were the most reserved of the bunch, often shared the same armchair.

Jacki got comfortable on her husband's lap. "Jin's canines fell out, and she's freaking out." She glanced at Bridget. "Do you think she will grow big fangs like the men?"

Expecting Bridget to say that it wasn't likely, Jacki was surprised to see the doctor nod. "I don't see why she would grow venom glands but no mechanism to deliver the venom. But who knows? We will have to wait and see."

Jacki grimaced. "I'll have to be satisfied with pictures. I don't know when I'll see Jin again."

"Tomorrow morning," Kalugal said. "The two of us are going to Kian's village."

Turning around to face him, Jacki gaped. "When was that decided?"

"Just a few moments ago. I realized that you might enter transition at any moment, and we don't have a doctor or a clinic here. Kian has graciously agreed to host us until after your transition."

"I didn't say that," Kian interjected. "My invitation isn't open-ended. I'm willing for you to stay for up to two weeks. If Jacki doesn't transition during that time, she probably isn't a Dormant."

Maybe now was the time to mention that she was feeling a little under the weather?

"You can't go with just Jacki and no bodyguards for protection," Phinas said.

Kalugal shifted, moving Jacki so he could look at Phinas. "If Kian wants to do me harm, a couple of bodyguards are not going to help. I'm taking a leap of faith, and so is he."

"You can bring a couple of men if you want," Kian said. "My sister would love to start her matchmaking program."

Kalugal's brow lifted. "How exactly is she going to do that when my men and I are locked up?"

"You were the one who suggested that I lock you up. Not me. I have no intention of doing that."

Turner cleared his throat. "We haven't discussed yet the safety measures you mentioned before."

"I know, but I've been thinking. Kalugal and Jacki and their party can stay in one of the houses in the new phase.

Jacki and Kalugal already have cuffs, and William can fit them on the two men they bring with them as well. We will know where each of them is at any moment, and Onegus will assign guardians to monitor their activity."

Turner didn't look happy. "That would have been fine with any normal immortal. But because of Kalugal's special ability, I would need to babysit him twenty-four-seven, and I don't have time for that."

"I don't want you to watch me around the clock either," Kalugal said. "It's a leap of faith for all of us. All I can do is vow not to use my powers against the clan in any way. And there is this." He lifted his cuff.

"People." Jacki chuckled. "You are all being silly. There is a much simpler solution. All you need is a couple of guards with earplugs to follow us when we leave the house."

Kian shook his head. "Kalugal can compel their own friends to attack them. If he wants, he could have the entire village under his command."

"No, I can't." Kalugal sighed. "I can compel twenty immortals at once, maybe a little more, but not by much. I'm not nearly as powerful as my father."

If looks could kill immortals, Kalugal would be dead right now from the daggers Phinas's eyes were shooting at him. "Why the hell did you reveal that?"

"Because if I'm asking Kian to take a gamble on me, I have to extend him the same courtesy."

Wendy

"Dinner is ready," Leon called.

Turning the television off, Wendy tried to remember what she'd done all day long, but everything seemed to be one big blur.

The guys had kept her busy with bow practice, she remembered that because her shoulder ached like crazy, but she couldn't remember whether she'd hit the target, or what they had talked about. She also remembered making hotdogs for lunch because her stomach was still protesting being fed junk.

Or maybe it wasn't the hotdogs' fault.

For some reason, the full impact of Simmons's death hadn't hit her yesterday, but it had today.

She literally had nowhere to go and was completely dependent on Vlad and his people. In the program, she'd at least had a contract that provided her with a place to stay and a good income for the next five years.

Now she had nothing but a vague promise of a job in one of the hotels the organization apparently owned.

Wendy felt adrift.

Vlad had kept casting her worried glances, and she'd tried to reassure him with forced smiles, but she hadn't fooled him. Even though he claimed no empathic abilities, he was attuned to her and read her moods way too easily.

Even now, he was still looking at her as if she was on suicide watch.

"Did you have a nice nap?" Bowen asked.

"I didn't sleep."

He lifted a brow. "I didn't hear the television."

"I put it on mute and read the subtitles." She didn't read a single line, but it was a good enough excuse. "I know the sounds bother you guys."

"Only the screaming." Leon put in front of her a plate with a hamburger and store-bought French fries.

That was what happened when it wasn't Vlad's turn to cook.

They'd already finished all the meals that Kian's butler had made for them, and had to fend for themselves.

Vlad passed her the ketchup bottle. "If you put enough of it on the fries, they won't taste as bad."

"Thanks."

Bowen chuckled. "Any culinary disaster can be saved with ketchup."

Leon sat down and put a paper towel over his lap. "If you don't like what I make for you, you're welcome to do it yourself. Cooking is not part of my job description."

Wendy felt bad. They were all taking turns with the domestic chores and doing the best they could. Her hotdogs and coleslaw weren't any better than what Leon had slapped together, and the guys had all been nice about it.

"The hamburger is delicious. I just don't like frozen French fries."

"Neither do I," Leon admitted. "But we are out of potatoes. I need to go grocery shopping."

"It has been almost a week since we got here," Wendy said. "Aren't we supposed to go back tomorrow?"

Bowen wiped his mouth with a paper towel. "Do you miss living underground?"

"I don't. I like it here, but we can't stay in this cabin forever."

She wouldn't have minded if it were only her and Vlad. That could have been romantic, and maybe they could have even moved past kissing and graduated to more serious necking, or even gone all the way and had sex.

Her entire world had been turned upside down, and the safety net she'd believed she'd had turned out to be an illusion, and it dawned on her that playing it safe was a loser's game.

That didn't mean that she would let caution fly out the window completely, but Vlad was as safe as she was going to get. He was sweet, respectful, and non-threatening.

Wendy would never find anyone she would feel safer with and still be attracted to.

Even though Vlad wasn't aware of his own appeal, she thought that he was sexy. So what if he was too skinny? He was strong, both in character and physically, and he was protective of her. What girl wouldn't find that attractive?

Duh, the idiots who hadn't bothered to look beneath the surface.

Their loss was her gain.

Except, she and Vlad were sharing a small cabin with three more guys, and it was just too awkward to even think about having sex.

Leon and Bowen never slept at the same time, so one of them was always awake in the living room, and if they could hear her television shows, they could also hear Vlad and her in her bedroom.

Bowen reached for his second hamburger. "I need to call the boss and ask him what's the plan. We stay until he tells us to get out of here."

"Fine by me. I'm not in a rush to give up fresh air and sunlight." Wendy bit into her hamburger.

What if she snuck into Vlad's bedroom through the bathroom? His room didn't share a wall with the living room, just the kitchen, so maybe whoever was on guard duty wouldn't hear them.

But that meant that she had to initiate, and it was a bold move Wendy wasn't ready for. It was much more natural to invite Vlad over to her room. She could suggest that they watch something together or play a video game, and then they might start kissing, and then necking, and things would progress naturally. If she went into his room, her intentions would be too obvious. Unless Vlad invited her, but he hadn't done so yet, which probably meant that he wasn't ready.

Vlad

"Do you want to play Fortnite?" Wendy wiped her hands on the dishtowel.

Vlad wanted to play, but not a computer game, and as an empath, Wendy knew that.

"Sure. I just need to wipe the table clean."

They'd been going on walks and holding hands, and oftentimes they found a quiet spot and kissed for a really long time. Luckily for him, Wendy liked to keep her eyes closed when they kissed, and she also liked it when he took charge.

So far, he had managed to hide his elongating fangs from her, and he was even learning to control them better. But if things got steamier, he doubted they would obey his command and not elongate.

"I'll set it up." Wendy smiled. "Are you okay with Fortnite, or do you want to play something else?"

"Whatever you choose is fine."

"Okay."

Vlad let out a sigh.

He needed to solve the fangs problem, and then one of them had to grow a set and make the first move, or they would never get past this awkward stage.

Since he was the one who'd been born with them, it made sense that it should be him. Except, Wendy had trust issues, so it would be better if she initiated.

He could imagine several scenarios. Maybe while they were kissing, she would take his hand and put it on her breast?

Or maybe she would tell him to touch her? That could be even sexier.

Or perhaps she would just drop a hint, like saying that she needed him.

Hell. Just thinking about it made him so hard that he could barely walk. Which, as usual, triggered the other responses that he wanted to hide from Wendy.

It was a chilling reminder that who did what first was the less significant part of his problem.

"What are you thinking about?" Leon nudged him with a smile.

"It's not hard to guess." Vlad looked at Richard, but he and Bowen were absorbed in a boxing match on the tube, shouting encouragements at the fighter they were rooting for and cussing at his opponent. Neither was paying attention to the conversation taking place in the kitchen.

"No, it's not," Leon said quietly. "Just make a move. She wants you. You want her. So what's the problem?"

"These." Vlad opened his mouth and pointed.

"Yeah, you have trigger-happy fangs. That's a problem. When you get older, you'll be able to control them better."

"What do I do in the meantime?"

"Thrall the girl. It's allowed for the purpose of hiding who we are. We all do that."

"It's not the same with Wendy. She is not a one-night hookup, and I can't keep thralling her after every time my fangs make an appearance."

Leon nodded. "You need to call Kian and ask for permission to tell Wendy." The Guardian rubbed his chin. "I think it's safe to thrall a human every other day, or maybe every third day. You need to check with Bridget. But since Wendy can't run off, you can go an entire week or even a little longer before doing that."

"What if she is the one? What if we have sex, and I bite her, and she transitions?"

"She won't transition if you use condoms. Until you are sure that she is the one, you shouldn't induce her."

"Yeah, I know that part. Do you or Bowen have condoms?"

Leon shook his head. "I don't, but maybe Bowen does." He turned to his friend. "Hey, Bowen, can you come over here for a second?"

"What do you want?" the Guardian asked without turning his head from the television.

"I need to ask you something."

With an annoyed expression on his face, Bowen strode into the kitchen. "Make it quick."

"Do you have condoms?" Leon whispered.

"Why would I have them? And what do you need them for?"

"I don't. Vlad does."

A huge grin split the Guardian's face. "Congratulations, kid. It's about time."

Vlad's ears caught on fire. "Nothing happened yet. I have trigger-happy fangs, and I can't keep hiding them from Wendy. They start elongating as soon as we kiss. I've gotten better at controlling them, but if we do more than kissing..."

"So, do you have condoms or not?" Leon asked.

"I don't. Why would I have them? Every woman I take to bed is on some kind of birth control."

"What if you accidentally induce a Dormant?" Vlad asked.

Bowen shrugged. "What are the chances of that? One in a hundred million? I have a better chance of dying in a plane crash than hooking up with a random Dormant. Only one plane goes down per five million flights."

"That's fascinating information." Vlad pushed his bangs back. "But what am I supposed to do?"

Bowen clapped him on the back. "I'll get you some. What size do you need?"

Vlad didn't even know that they came in different sizes. "I have no clue." He glanced at the bulge in his pants.

Bowen followed his gaze. "A large should do it. But I'll get you an extra-large just in case. You are a tall guy."

Should he feel flattered?

"Thank you." He smiled sheepishly. "I don't know if I have the guts to go into a store and buy them myself."

Leon chuckled. "It's just one of those things an immortal has to do to protect his partner from transitioning prematurely. Just think that when you go into a pharmacy to get them and hold your head high. You are a good man, and you are doing what's right."

"Good advice. Thank you."

"The nearest place I can get condoms for you is forty-five minutes away." Bowen pulled his car keys out of his pocket. "I'll see you in an hour and a half. Don't do anything you shouldn't until I come back."

Vlad's ears started to melt from the heat. "It's not urgent. You can go tomorrow, or the day after. Nothing is going on yet."

"I've got you, kid." Bowen clapped him on the back again. "I consider it my duty and my honor to usher you into the rest of your immortal life."

"Thanks. I owe you."

"My pleasure."

When Bowen walked out the door, Richard looked towards him. "Where are you going?"

"A grocery run."

"Get me some beef jerky, will ya?"

"No problem." Bowen closed the door behind him.

Leon cast a quick glance at Richard, making sure that the guy was still watching the match. "Call Kian and ask permission."

"I can't call Kian directly. Can you do that for me? What if he's busy?"

"I'll text him and ask him to call you. But just in case he does that right away, you need to tell your girlfriend that you'll join her for computer games later and find a private spot to talk."

"Can I use the motorhome?"

"Of course." Leon's eyes flashed with an inner light. "That's also a great spot to get some action going. I'm sure Wendy would prefer the privacy."

Vlad really hated having the Guardians and Kian involved in his intimate life, but what choice did he have? He needed to get permission, and he needed advice.

As Leon took out his phone and started a text to Kian, Vlad knocked on Wendy's door.

"Come in."

He opened it just a crack. "Leon wants me to clean the motorhome. I'll try to do it as fast as I can."

"Don't worry about it. I'll just watch something until you are done."

"It shouldn't take long." Or so he hoped.

What if Kian called him the next day? How long should he wait in there?

Leon was right about the motorhome being a great spot for necking, though, and cleaning it was not a bad idea. Grabbing a roll of paper towels and a bottle of Windex, Vlad headed out.

Jin and Arwel had left the motorhome clean, so all he had to do was get rid of the dust. Even the bedding had been replaced, and it smelled of laundry detergent and dryer sheets. The fresh scent was fake, but it wasn't unpleasant.

His phone rang as he walked into the small bathroom, and he dropped the bottle of Windex in his rush to pull it out of his pocket.

"Hello?"

"It's Kian. You wanted to speak to me?"

Damn. That gruff voice always stressed him out even though he knew that it was Kian's regular tone and that the guy wasn't angry.

"It's about Wendy. Can I tell her about who we are?"

"Is she the one for you?"

"I think so, but I'm not sure."

"Until you are sure, use condoms. Anything else?"

"Can I tell her, though? My fangs elongate every time I get excited, and it's really difficult to do anything without Wendy noticing them. It's a real pain, and I don't want to thrall her every time we kiss, which we do a lot."

Kian chuckled. "That's a predicament. You can tell Wendy about who we are and why you have fangs and what they are for, but don't tell her about her potential dormancy. That should only be done when you are convinced that she is the one and you are ready to take the final plunge and commit to her. Naturally, you want the same level of commitment from her as well."

"Got it. Thanks."

"No problem. But you don't have long to make up your mind. It's not safe to thrall away more than two weeks worth of memories, and some Dormants take that long to transition. Give it a few days, and if you are still unsure, erase her memories, or better yet have one of the Guardians do that."

"Of everything?"

"If you want to erase just the memory of what you've told her and the bites, you'll have to do that every few days. But there is also a limit to how many times you can do it without causing her damage."

"So basically you are telling me that I should decide whether she is the one or not. But how would I know?"

"If after you make love to Wendy, you are still unsure, then she is probably not the one for you, and you'd better erase her memories right away."

Wendy

Why was Vlad cleaning the motorhome so late in the evening? Was someone coming?

Maybe Bowen and Leon had decided to use it after all. When Jin and Arwel had left, there had been a short debate about who was going to sleep in it. But no one wanted to, each for their own reasons.

Wendy was afraid to sleep there by herself, and the guards wouldn't have allowed it anyway. Richard had said that he was comfortable in the loft and didn't want to move his stuff. Bowen and Leon claimed that they were perfectly fine on the living room couch because only one of them slept while the other kept watch.

After Vlad's mom had bailed out, Vlad took the bedroom that had been supposed to be hers, and there was no reason for him to move to the motorhome either.

Wendy had thought that he would try to sneak into her room through the connecting bathroom, but her boyfriend was a perfect gentleman.

Who knew that she would want a guy to be a little less gentlemanly?

But maybe she was being brave only because Vlad was so considerate, polite, accommodating, and not pushy in the least. If he were more forward, she would have probably gotten scared.

Ugh, how were they going to move forward with their relationship while both of them were so full of insecurities?

Jin was so lucky. She didn't have any hang-ups, and as soon as she'd laid eyes on Arwel, she went after him without a moment of hesitation. The two had jumped into bed after knowing each other twenty-something hours.

If only she had balls like Jin.

Her envy of Jin was so strong that Wendy was starting to think she might have inadvertently jinxed Jacki's wedding because of it. She was a little jealous of Jacki too, but not nearly as much.

Jin's forwardness and her take-no-prisoners attitude was how Wendy would have liked to be. Perhaps she could try to emulate her behavior?

To seduce Arwel, Jin had worn a sexy bikini. Maybe she should put on something sexy as well?

Like what, though?

Her pajamas were a pair of sweatpants and a T-shirt, and she would look silly wearing a swimsuit to bed.

Perhaps a sexy movie would put them both in the right mood?

Except, she didn't remember watching anything titillating lately. The last time she had gotten excited by a show was when she'd accidentally stumbled upon hentai. At the time, she hadn't known that porn anime even existed, and since the title had piqued her curiosity, she had checked it out. That one had been nice, romantic and well-made, so she'd checked out another one, and another.

Some of them were really depraved, though, and she wondered how a society of people who were so polite and proper like the Japanese could harbor such perverted fantasies.

It had only reinforced her conviction that all men were beasts on the inside. After all, the creators of hentai were all guys, and in real life, they probably bowed to their elders, spoke politely, and were model citizens.

Appearances were misleading.

On the other hand, for the past week she'd been living in close quarters with four men and spending most of her days with them. She'd gotten to know them pretty well, and they were all decent guys.

Vlad was more than decent, though, he was wonderful, and the lust he felt for her didn't scare her because it was packaged together with love and protectiveness.

Love. He hadn't said the words yet, but she knew how he felt.

Did she love him back, though?

What was love anyway?

If Wendy had any female friends to talk to, she could have asked. But she didn't have a phone to call anyone, and even if she did, she wouldn't call Jin or Jacki, who were her only options. If they didn't think she should have been invited to Jacki's wedding, then they weren't her real friends.

Mey could be a good person to talk to, but without a phone, that was irrelevant.

As a triple knock on the door announced Vlad, Wendy got up and opened it.

"Sorry it took so long." He looked flustered.

"It wasn't long at all." She closed the door behind him and sat on the bed. "What made you clean the motorhome? Is anyone coming?"

He sat next to her and wrapped his arm around her. "Not tonight. I called Jackson and invited him and Tessa over, but he said that they could only come Saturday night, and I wasn't sure we would still be here. Roni is working on some important project, and he can't get away either. But after Bowen said that we might be staying longer, I figured that Jackson and Tessa can come over on Saturday, sleep in the motorhome, and go back on Sunday. When I told Leon, he said that I should clean it before inviting them to stay overnight."

"Did you call Jackson?"

"Not yet. I wanted to check with you first."

Right. Leon wouldn't have made Vlad clean the motorhome tonight for guests that might or might not arrive Saturday evening.

Wendy had a feeling that Vlad was making the story up on the spot. She didn't get the sense that he was lying, but if he wanted the motorhome to be ready by Saturday night, he had all day tomorrow and the next day to clean it.

What if he did that for them, so they would have a private spot for necking?

Vlad

"I'm okay with them coming," Wendy said. "But you should check with Bowen and Richard as well. They'll probably say yes, but you need to ask."

"True. I'll do that."

Vlad let his bangs fall over his eyes, hiding his face from Wendy. Not that it was going to help with an empath who could sense that he was fibbing.

Why the hell was he doing that?

He'd just gotten approval from Kian to tell Wendy the truth about immortals and who he was, but instead of taking her hand, looking her in the eyes, and revealing his secret, he was telling her half-truths about cleaning the motorhome for Jackson and Tessa.

Perhaps he wasn't as ready as he'd thought he was. His problematic fangs had created a sense of urgency that might have been artificial.

Wendy hadn't told him that she loved him yet, and he hadn't told her either. Perhaps they should keep things simple and old-fashioned.

If they just kissed and did nothing else, he could keep his fangs under control, and there would be no need to tell Wendy anything until their relationship reached the stage when revealing his secrets was appropriate.

Except, he had a feeling that Wendy was just as eager as he was to move to the next stage, at least as far as intimacy went, and he doubted his ability to impose restraint on both of them.

Reaching with her fingers, Wendy pushed his bangs out of his face. "I have a question, and I know that it's kind of personal, but we are a couple, and we should know personal stuff about each other, right?"

Tensing, Vlad nodded.

If she asked about his fangs, he could answer her without violating the rules.

"Have you ever watched porn?"

Damn. That came out of nowhere.

"I don't watch that."

Wendy rolled her eyes. "Come on, everyone does it. You shouldn't be embarrassed to admit it."

"I really don't."

"Why? Is it a religious thing? A prohibition on masturbation or something?"

How could he answer that without mentioning his need to bite? Masturbation released only part of the pressure and was more frustrating than satisfying. That was why he tried to stay away from stimulation and not actively seek it.

Dropping his chin, he let his bangs slide down and cover his face again. "I don't find masturbation satisfying. That's why I don't watch porn. What about you?"

Did girls even watch porn? He didn't know, and he also didn't care if Wendy indulged in it, but he needed to deflect the spotlight from himself before he was burned to a crisp by it.

"Girls don't need visuals like guys because sexual stimulation is more cerebral for us, or maybe because we have better imaginations, but I stumbled upon a few hentai." Wendy blushed. "That's what animated porn is called. A couple of them were very nice and romantic, so I looked for more, but many were really perverted, and that kind of soured the entire thing for me."

Vlad knew what hentai was, and he wasn't surprised that Wendy, who was an anime addict, had watched a few.

He cast her a sidelong glance. "Why did you ask?"

Wendy's cheeks got even rosier. "Because we both lack experience. How are we supposed to know what to do?"

What was implied in her question was clear, and his response to it was powerful and immediate.

As blood surged into his groin and venom slid into his fangs, causing them to start elongating, Vlad's instinct was to get out of there as fast as he could and not come back until he was back in control.

Instead, he shifted away from Wendy and cast a shroud around himself. She would still see what she expected, and as long as she didn't touch his mouth, his secret was safe.

"What's just happened?" Wendy asked.

"What do you mean?"

He knew precisely what she saw. That was why shrouding should always be done away from watchful eyes. But it was either that or running off.

"You shimmered for a moment. It was like a projection that winked out and then returned. I also can't feel you like I usually do."

Maybe it was time to fess up after all?

Not yet.

Wendy knew that he could shroud, and she probably guessed what he'd done, but not the why of it.

The best thing was to make a joke out of it. "You've got me. I'm an alien on a planet millions of light years away from earth, and what you see is my projection. I'm so powerful that you can even touch and smell me."

Only because he was actually there.

He wasn't as powerful as Yamanu, who could fool all human senses.

Rolling her eyes, Wendy slapped his shoulder. "I know that you shrouded yourself. Why did you do that, though? If you're hiding an erection, that's just silly. I know that you are attracted to me, and your response is natural."

He could say that yes, he was hiding a boner, but then Wendy would tell him to drop the shroud, and he couldn't do that.

"It's more than an attraction. I love you."

Smiling, Wendy reached for his hand. "I know. And I love you too. Now, drop the shroud and let me see your face. I don't care if you are as red as a tomato."

"Not yet. I need to tell you something first."

"That you are an alien projection? You've already told me that."

"Actually, it wasn't entirely a joke. I'm not an alien projection, but I might be an alien. At least partially."

"Pfft." Wendy snorted. "You don't have to make up stories to impress me. I love you just the way you are." She took his hand and put it on her chest between her breasts, causing another surge in arousal. "You are quirky, handsome, talented, both artistically and paranormally, and you are the nicest person I've ever met. Nothing you can tell me can top that."

It was nice to hear, but what he was about to tell her might be a downer, not an upper.

"I have fangs."

"I know that. I've seen them. So what?"

"You've seen them in their resting state. They elongate."

Wendy

"Okay..."

Vlad was starting to weird Wendy out.

She shouldn't be surprised, though.

When someone seemed too good to be true, it was because he wasn't true, and she'd fallen for a guy who was missing a couple of screws.

"Promise that you won't freak out when you see them, and I'll drop the shroud."

Wendy stifled the urge to roll her eyes again. Vlad believed that he had real vampire fangs, and she shouldn't make fun of his psychosis. Maybe if he admitted that to Vanessa, she could give him something to get rid of his delusions. But until then, Wendy was going to pretend as if everything he was telling her was real.

"I promise."

He clasped her hand as if to hold her so she wouldn't run away when she saw his imaginary vampire fangs. "Here goes. One, two, three..."

Wendy gasped but then chuckled. "Nice party trick. You put in fakes while shrouding yourself."

Vlad groaned. "No, I didn't. I'm not fully human. I'm immortal, and so are Bowen and Leon and all the others you've met from my clan. We are not an organization of paranormally talented people. Some of us don't have any paranormal talents other than thralling and shrouding. But don't tell Richard. If you do, we will have to thrall him to forget it, and doing that too often can cause brain damage."

He sounded sincere, and oddly what he'd said resonated with some subconscious suspicions she'd been having. The people she'd met had other oddities besides their paranormal talents. They didn't behave like most of the people she knew. The differences were subtle, and they could be attributed to growing up in a different country, or maybe even the sort of upbringing they'd had. But there were enough of them to raise tiny red flags all over the place.

"You can pull on them if you want," Vlad said. "They will not come off. Just be careful. They are very sharp."

As he opened his mouth wide, Wendy leaned closer to take a better look. If those were fake, they were movie prop quality. She couldn't see a seam between the top of the fang and the gums.

Reaching with two fingers, she gave one a gentle tug. It didn't budge, but Vlad groaned as if she'd just touched his erection.

"Did I hurt you?" She looked up and gasped for the second time that evening. "Your eyes are glowing."

It wasn't metaphorical. One eye was casting blue light and the other green.

She knew he wasn't wearing contact lenses, and even if he were, she'd never heard of ones that could emit light.

"When I get excited, my fangs elongate, and my eyes start to glow. Sometimes in that order, and sometimes in reverse. It also happens when I'm very angry, but that's rare. Mostly I have that reaction when I'm around you. I've had a hell of a time trying to hide it."

There was no denying it any longer. Vlad was an alien who had fangs and glowing eyes, and she'd been surrounded by his kind ever since she'd escaped the program with the other recruits.

They'd all seemed so normal, though, or as normal as paranormally talented people could be. And they weren't evil bloodsuckers either.

Or were they?

Maybe they'd fed on her and then erased her memories? In movies, if a vampire didn't suck his victim dry, that was what he did. And the shrouding was just another name for the vampires' glamour.

Except, she was an empath. They couldn't have hidden their blood lust from her, and there had been none.

"Why tell me now?"

"Because I couldn't hide it anymore. Once we go beyond kissing, I won't be able to control my fangs. I didn't want to freak you out without warning, so I asked for permission to tell you."

"From Bowen?"

"No, from Kian. The security of our clan depends on secrecy, and no one is allowed to spill the beans without getting permission first."

Wendy shook her head. "Why would he allow it? I've been proven untrustworthy." Then she remembered that the director was dead, and she no longer had anyone to tell even if she wanted to. "Did Kian allow it because my uncle is dead?"

"Maybe. I don't know. I explained the situation with my fangs, and he agreed."

"So, not all the men of your species have that problem?"

"They do to a lesser extent. I have what's called trigger-happy fangs."

Wendy felt like giggling but stifled the urge. Was that the equivalent of premature ejaculation? Vlad had admitted that his fangs elongated when he got excited, so there was some connection between them and sex.

"Why do you have fangs to begin with? Do you need to drink blood in addition to eating regular food?"

"No, the fangs are for injecting venom. Not that I ever have. But that's because of a lack of opportunity, not because I can't. Every immortal male grows fangs around the time he reaches puberty, and they become functional about six months later."

"What are they for? I mean, obviously, they are for biting." She shook her head. "Scary. But never mind that. Venom usually means poison, but I assume that's not what's going on because Jin would be dead by now. And speaking of Jin, how come I didn't see any bite marks on her? She and Arwel got busy every night. He is also an immortal, right?"

Vlad

"Vlad nodded. "Arwel is an immortal, that's correct."

"Is Jin?"

"She is not."

Soon Jin would transition, but Kian had told him not to tell Wendy about dormancy yet.

"So, what is the venom for?"

Vlad's ears got hot. "For the ladies, it supposedly triggers the best orgasms and euphoria. But it can also be used in a fight. The kind of venom produced depends on the stimulation. Aggression produces venom that can incapacitate an opponent, and sexual stimulation produces the kind of venom that induces the good stuff."

The sudden scent of fear indicated that Wendy hadn't reacted well to his explanation. She'd been okay so far. Why had talk about orgasms scared her?

"What happens when a male gets aggressive with a female?" Wendy asked. "What kind of venom is produced then? Can he kill her?"

Given her past, of course, that was where her mind would immediately go. Vlad shook his head. "I've never heard of that happening."

"That doesn't mean that it hasn't. Men get violent and hurt women all of the time, and it has nothing to do with sex. Rape is an act of violence. Are immortal males different?"

Running a hand through his hair, Vlad thought how to best answer her truthfully.

The problem was that he didn't know.

If an immortal perpetrated an act of violence against a human female, who was going to find out about that?

There had been a few cases in the Bay Area, which Doomers had been responsible for, but those had been premeditated to lure Guardians. Did Doomers rape and kill human females?

He would have to ask Dalhu or Robert, but right now, he didn't have an answer for Wendy. All he could tell her was what he knew of clan law on the subject.

"We have very strict rules about using our powers. We are not allowed to thrall a partner to have sex with us. Consent must be given freely and explicitly, and males are allowed to only thrall away the memory of the bite to keep our existence secret. Females don't have active fangs, so that's not a problem for them. That's also the reason why most immortal females don't bother to even learn how to thrall. But since I can't be sure that everyone always obeys the rules, I can't tell you that it never happens. What I can tell you is that if someone is caught breaking them, the punishment is extremely severe."

She arched a brow. "How severe?"

"I'll give you an example. An immortal teenager who didn't make sure to get consent before touching a human girl's breast was sentenced to whipping. They were kissing, and he got carried away. And you know who reported him?"

"The girl?"

"No, his own mother. That's how important the rule of consent is to us, and it's drilled into our heads, starting with the onset of puberty."

"Whipping seems excessive for touching someone's breast, especially if it was done during kissing. He wasn't a random stranger, and she agreed to the kiss, right? I know that what I'm saying is not politically correct, and that consent for one thing does not mean consent for another, but still. A whipping?"

Vlad nodded. "It happened a long time ago, and girls were not supposed to let guys touch them. Still, a whipping for an offense like that would have been excessive for a human. Not for an immortal, though. We have immense power over humans. We can thrall most to do what we want, and teenage boys are difficult to control.

In that, we are not so different from humans. It's very tempting to use our powers to gain an unfair advantage, so the deterrent must be brutal. Besides, the whipping might hurt an immortal just as much as a human, but an immortal will heal in a few hours instead of days, and there will be no mark left on his skin."

"Would you think I'm a bitch if I said that I applaud whoever made those rules?"

"Not at all. I applaud her too."

"Her?"

Vlad hesitated for a moment before revealing the biggest secret of all. "The head and founder of our clan is a female. A goddess, one of the only two surviving gods on earth. The other is her half-sister."

Wendy's eyes widened. "Get out of here. A real goddess? Like Athena or Venus?"

"Precisely. The gods were real."

"What happened to the others?" She chuckled. "Did they go home?"

"No, they were killed. One god conspired against the others and dropped a weapon of mass destruction on their assembly. They were all killed except for the founder of our clan, who escaped before that happened, and her half-sister, who was on her way to marry the god who killed the others."

"That sounds like a plot from one of my anime shows."

Vlad chuckled. "Now I get why you are not freaking out about all this. The anime you watch exposed you to many fantastical worlds. Your mind is open to the strange and unusual."

"Who knew that it would be good for anything other than distraction, right?"

He nodded. "It can be good for other things as well. Maybe it will inspire you to write a story that could be turned into an anime series."

Wendy grinned. "That could be cool. I can write the story of your clan, modified, of course, to obscure its existence, and you can illustrate it." She flopped down on the bed. "We will make millions."

He lay down next to her. "It could happen."

She turned on her side and propped her head on her hand. "So if gods can die, immortals can die as well, which means that you are not really immortal."

"We don't age, and we don't get sick, and we can recover from most injuries, but not all. So yeah, we can be killed. It's just not easy to do."

"How much are you allowed to tell me?"

"I can tell you everything." Almost. "You can't go anywhere, and if for some reason you choose to leave, Bowen will remove your memories."

"Why not you?"

"I'm not skilled enough to do that. And it would be too difficult. I don't want you to leave. And I don't want you to forget me."

"I don't want that either." She leaned in and kissed his lips. "Your fangs have retracted. They are back to their normal size."

"If you keep kissing me, they will elongate again."

"Later. Now I want to hear the whole story."

"It will take a long time."

"I'm not in a rush to go anywhere."

He nodded. "It all started with the gods taking humans as mates because there weren't enough of them. The children born to them had some of the godly attributes, but they weren't as powerful…"

Kalugal

As Jacki leaned against the bank of drawers and wiped her forehead, Kalugal rushed to her side. "What's wrong? Are you feeling worse?"

Ever since she'd told him last night that she wasn't feeling well, Kalugal had been vacillating between worry and optimism.

But that was when her symptoms had been mild. Now it seemed that she'd taken a turn for the worse.

"I'm dizzy."

He put a hand on her forehead. "You're burning hot."

Lifting her into his arms, he carried Jacki to the bedroom and laid her down on the bed. "I'm calling Kian. He needs to send Bridget over."

"Why? We are going to see them in less than an hour. There is no point in dragging the doctor here and making everyone wait."

"I'm calling anyway."

Jacki waved a dismissive hand and slung her legs over the side of the bed. "I need to finish packing."

"Stay!" He pointed a finger at her. "I'll finish packing for you."

"Ugh. You're so bossy." Jacki lifted her legs back on the bed.

Sitting next to her, he dialed Kian's number.

"Are you on your way?" His cousin sounded as gruff as usual, and Kalugal wondered whether he was still using the voice translating application when talking to him.

Probably not. Kian hadn't used it the entire two days they were dealing with the mess after the attack.

"We are still here. Jacki hasn't been feeling well since yesterday, and now her temperature's shot up. I want to ask Bridget what to do."

"Hold on. I'll put her on the line."

"Hello, Kalugal. Let me talk with Jacki."

"Of course." He handed her the phone. "Bridget wants to talk to you."

"Hi, Bridget. I'm really sorry that Kalugal bothered you. I can make it to the hotel, and you can examine me then."

"Do you have any symptoms other than rising fever?"

"I get dizzy, but that's because of the fever, and I'm also achy, like during a cold or flu."

"What about sore throat, runny nose, a cough?"

"None." Jacki chuckled. "Jin assured me that the transition is not contagious. I'm not growing venom glands."

"No chance of that. But this sounds like the transition to me. Can you hand the phone to Kalugal?"

"Sure."

"Or better yet, just put me on speakerphone. Not that it matters to Kalugal. He can hear me just fine as it is."

"I know. You are both humoring the poor human with her limited hearing." Jacki handed Kalugal the device. "I don't know how to activate the speakerphone feature on your weird phone."

Holding it face up on his palm, he activated it. "Go ahead, Bridget. We can both hear you."

"Since you are going to be here in less than an hour, there is no point in me coming over. There isn't much I can do anyway. I usually just monitor the vitals, which I can do even without equipment while we are on our way to the village."

Kalugal rubbed a hand over his jaw. "Anything I can do? Like applying cold compresses to Jacki's forehead?"

"Jacki sounds fine to me. If her temperature was at a dangerous level, she wouldn't be so lucid. Just finish what you need to do and get in the car. We are waiting for you."

"Thank you."

"You're welcome." The doctor disconnected the call.

Jacki shook her head. "I told you that you were freaking out for nothing."

"I can't help it." He lay on the bed next to her and pulled her into his arms. "You are everything to me. I can't let anything happen to you."

"Oh, Kalugal." She cupped his cheek. "I love you so much. But stop being such a worrywart. This is wonderful news, and we should be happy. I am transitioning. Can you believe it?"

He nodded. "I want to be happy, and I am, but don't ask me not to worry. I won't relax until you are safely on the other side. That's why we are going to the village. I know that you'll be in good hands there."

"I'm so glad that we are going. I can't wait to see the place and meet all the other immortals. I just know it's going to be an amazing experience." She patted his arm. "But we should finish packing and get out of here before they decide to leave without us."

"Yes, you are right. The sooner we get there, the better. I want Bridget to be glued to you." He got up. "Stay in bed. I'm going to pack the rest of your things."

Jacki swung her legs over the side of the bed. "You don't know what I want to take."

"I'll just put everything I've gotten for you in the suitcase."

"Fine. But I'm packing the toiletries and makeup." When he opened his mouth to argue, she put a finger over his lips. "If I faint, you can come to get me and carry me to the car. But it's not going to happen. It's just a fever, and it's not the first time I've had one. It's not lethal."

Letting out a long-suffering sigh, he shook his head. "I don't like it when you argue with me."

Jacki smiled. "Officially or unofficially, we are married now, and you will have to learn to compromise. You are not going to always get everything you want."

Pivoting on her heel, she strode into the bathroom, leaving him behind to ponder her statement.

Kalugal wasn't used to compromising. His men obeyed his commands, mostly without questioning him, and until Jacki had walked into his life, he was the king of the castle, the ultimate ruler over his small group of former Brotherhood members.

Jacki had introduced a pattern interrupt into his orderly life, but it was the best thing that had ever happened to him. His love for her filled his heart with hope and excitement that he hadn't felt since escaping his father's control.

It occurred to Kalugal that things had been stale for a long time. The search for artifacts had provided some interest and excitement, and so had his future plans for humanity. But now that he had Jacki, his former preoccupations suddenly seemed less important.

With only Rufsur and Phinas to share his ideas with, Kalugal had lived in a bubble of his own making, a self-feeding loop of ideas.

Jacki was like a breath of fresh air, and her perspective on things was invaluable to him. So if she thought that he needed to learn to compromise, he would do his best to do so.

Kian

Amanda walked into the suite without knocking. "Are we all packed and ready to go?"

"We are," Anandur said.

As usual, Brundar just nodded.

Kian glared at her. "We've talked about your habit of not knocking before barging in."

For some reason, he'd woken up in a sour mood, which made him react to the small annoyances. With Syssi's help, he'd learned to ignore those, but today his nerves felt raw.

He should be happy.

Everything had worked out fine. The paranormal program was no longer a problem, Kalugal and he had reached an understanding and set up a framework for future cooperation, and Jin and Jacki were both transitioning.

Except, there were a thousand and one things that could still go wrong, and he'd spent half the night awake thinking of all the ways in which their plan to use Roberts could fail.

"Pfft, Kian. You're such a stick-in-the-mud." She sat next to him on the couch. "This is not anyone's home, and since you are sharing the place with three other couples, I know that there is no chance of catching someone having sex on the living room couch." She lifted her chin and looked at him from under her lowered lashes. "Unlike you, my darling brother."

He grimaced. "Don't remind me. I thought that Dalhu was torturing you. I wish I could erase that episode from my mind. Speaking of your mate, where is he?"

"Packing his art supplies." Amanda leaned back and crossed her arms over her chest. "You should remember that episode because it's a perfect example of how assumptions can affect your judgment. If you weren't convinced that every Doomer was evil, you would have realized that I screamed in pleasure, not pain."

"Did you forget that he also kidnapped you? It wasn't only my hatred for Doomers that influenced my reaction. Anyone who harms my family, or even just intends to do so, should be ready to pay the price."

"Yeah, but there are mitigating circumstances. Like Dalhu falling in love with me and being willing to go through hell to atone for his sins. Or like Lokan, who definitely had been plotting against your extended family, and yet you forgave him because he told you where Navuh's island was."

"I didn't forgive Lokan. I'm cautiously cooperating with him because he is bonded to Carol and because he is very useful to us. I sleep better at night, knowing that he will warn me if his father is planning a move against our clan."

"But you forgave Dalhu, right? Even though his crime was worse than Lokan's?"

"I did. But Dalhu was just a simple soldier who was obeying orders. Unless he'd been ready to defect, Dalhu had to do what he was told. Besides, he atoned for his sin, and I consider him a friend now. Lokan, on the other hand, was acting on his own behalf and pursuing his own agenda with no regard for Ella's or Vivian's life. And what made it even worse was that he knew Ella, he befriended her in order to lure her into a trap."

"Yes, but that's not the entire story." Amanda uncrossed her arms. "Lokan's actions were guided by the Fates. If not for his schemes, none of this would be happening." She waved her hand in a circle. "We wouldn't have known that Areana was alive, Arwel wouldn't have found Jin, Yamanu wouldn't have found Mey, and we wouldn't have found Kalugal or Jacki." Tilting her head toward him, Amanda smiled. "And I expect many more pairings to come out of this. Imagine forty-something new couples, and with Merlin's help, many new babies."

The thought had occurred to Kian, but his conclusion was different than Amanda's. If Kalugal's men mated with clan females, it would mean a gain for Kalugal and a loss for the clan because the couples couldn't live in the village.

First of all, because it was a security risk that Kian wasn't willing to take. And secondly, because Kalugal wanted his independence and wouldn't move into the village even if Kian invited him to stay.

Should he even encourage the matings?

Probably not.

He would much rather hunt for Dormant males for the clan females, and have them join his community. The idea was to grow the clan, not shrink it.

Except, now that Amanda and Carol had started working on their immortal dating application, it would be one hell of an uphill battle to make them drop it.

"Hi, Amanda." Syssi stepped out from their bedroom. "Where is Dalhu?"

"He's finishing up packing his art supplies, and then he's going to take our luggage down to the lobby."

"Kian and I are packed and ready to go as well. We are just waiting for Kalugal and Jacki to get here."

When a knock sounded on the door, Anandur pushed to his feet. "I'll get it."

As Lokan walked in with Carol, the waterworks started before anyone even said hello or goodbye.

"I'm going to miss you all so much." Carol rushed into Syssi's open arms. "It was so wonderful to be together again."

Behind her, Lokan shifted from foot to foot. "You're not saying goodbye forever. You can visit your family and friends whenever you want."

"I know." Carol wiped the tears away with her thumbs. "But it's not the same as living in the village and seeing everyone every day."

Wonder pulled her into a hug, practically lifting the petite Carol a foot off the floor. "You can come back and take over the café whenever you want."

"I wish I could." Carol cast a sidelong glance at her mate. "But as long as Lokan remains in the Brotherhood, he needs to be in Washington."

Lokan shook his head. "Would you seriously go back to working in the café?"

Carol snapped her fingers. "In a heartbeat."

"Even if we moved into the village, I wouldn't allow you to do that. You are my mate."

Kian stifled a chuckle. Lokan had just earned himself a one-way trip to the doghouse for an unlimited stay.

"Excuse me?" Carol put her hands on her hips and glared at her mate. "Did I hear the word allowed? Do you really think that I need your permission to do anything I want?"

"No, of course not. What I meant to say was that I would have been displeased with your decision, and I would have tried to dissuade you from working in the café."

Nice try, but it wasn't going to get him out of the doghouse and back into Carol's good graces.

Jacki

As soon as Jacki and Kalugal entered the suite, Bridget took charge. "Let's check your temperature." She pointed to the couch and whipped the thermometer out of her doctor's bag.

While Anandur waved Rufsur and Hivak to join him and Brundar at the dining table, Lokan walked up to Kalugal and pulled him into his arms. "It was good seeing you." He slapped his brother's back. "We should get together sometimes."

"I would like that." Kalugal sounded a little choked up. "After Jacki transitions and we get back here, you and Carol can come to visit. Or we can visit you in Washington if that's more convenient."

Bridget pulled the thermometer out of Jacki's ear. "A hundred and two. That's high, but not dangerous. Let's check your other vitals. Would you be more comfortable in one of the bedrooms?"

She would, but then she would miss out on the conversation between Lokan and Kalugal.

"It's okay. I'm not shy."

Kalugal turned around and lifted a brow. "What kind of examination are we talking about?"

Bridget waved him off. "I'm just going to listen to Jacki's heart and her lungs and then measure her blood pressure. I only need her to roll her sleeve up. I can do the rest over the blouse."

Kalugal nodded his approval as if anyone had asked his permission.

They really needed to have a talk about boundaries, and what he was allowed to butt into and what wasn't his damn business.

"Calm down," Bridget murmured. "What got you so upset?"

"Bossy husband."

Naturally, Kalugal heard her and turned around. "I'm not bossy. Is it wrong for me to want to protect my wife's modesty?"

"I'm an adult, Kalugal. It's up to me to decide what I consider modest."

Carol sat next to her and took her hand. "No fighting, kids. We are saying goodbye, and I'm sad, and I don't want to remember sour-puss faces when I recall these moments."

She was right. Besides, Jacki knew that she was overreacting. Her snappiness had more to do with her feeling sick, weak and anxious rather than anything that Kalugal had said.

"Don't be sad. As soon as I'm okay to travel, we will come to visit you, or you will come to us."

Nodding, Carol carefully wiped away a tear.

"Roll up your sleeve, Jacki," Bridget commanded and then slapped the blood pressure cuff on her arm.

No one was addressing the big elephant in the room, but the next time she and Kalugal met up with Lokan and Carol, it should be at their wedding in the village.

The goddess had said that as soon as Jacki transitioned and felt okay, she would come to the village and marry them in a proper ceremony.

Would Kian allow Lokan to come?

If he was letting Kalugal and two of his men into his secret village, then why not Lokan?

But it wasn't her place to say anything. She was the reason Kian was letting them into the village, and she should be grateful for that.

Syssi came and sat on Jacki's other side. "How are you holding up?"

"I'm anxious."

Bridget removed the cuff. "Your blood pressure is normal, and so are all of your other vitals. For now."

"Can I take something for the fever?"

"You can have some of my stash." Jin walked into the room and tossed her a container of pills.

Bridget caught it before Jacki had a chance to even lift her hand. "Don't overdo it with those. You are not in pain, and your fever is not dangerous."

"Yes, ma'am."

As Bridget pushed up from the ottoman she'd used as her doctor's stool, Jin took her place. "I can't wait for us to get to the village, so Bridget can knock me out with some serious stuff." She pulled another bottle out of her pocket. "These are pretty useless for the pain."

"Oh, Jin." Jacki leaned toward her and took her hand. "And here I am feeling sorry for myself when all I have is a fever. You are going through so much more."

"Yeah." Jin sighed. "I'm the toothless wonder."

At the dining table, Wonder giggled. "Hey, I'm a freak too. You, Mey, and I will form the freak club."

"I want in," Amanda said.

"What's weird about you?"

She struck a pose. "I'm unnaturally beautiful." She'd meant it as a joke, but it was true.

Syssi grinned. "And I'm the pregnant lady who has conversations with her baby even though she is the size of a nut and doesn't have ears yet. I'm joining too."

Carol fluffed her curls and batted her eyelashes. "I'm unnaturally sexy. Save me a spot."

"What about you, Bridget?" Syssi asked. "Do you want to join the freak club?"

"Sorry, ladies. But I don't have time for clubs."

Syssi waved a dismissive hand. "She's no fun to play with. What about you, Callie?"

"I'm still thinking. I'm not special in any way, and I don't even have a paranormal talent."

"Not true." Syssi lifted a finger. "You can make Brundar smile. That's definitely a paranormal talent because no one else can do that. Not even Anandur."

Callie laughed. "Okay, then I'm in."

Syssi leaned toward Jacki and motioned for the other ladies to huddle closer. "Anandur has been trying to get Brundar to laugh for years. I think that Brundar doesn't react to his brother's jokes, not because he doesn't find them funny but because he wants to annoy Anandur. That's Brundar's version of humor. Dry and sarcastic."

Jacki appreciated what Syssi was doing.

Sometimes humor was the best medicine. Jin was smiling, and Jacki felt a lot less anxious.

Whatever happened, she was surrounded by friends who cared about her and would fight for her.

It felt good, but regrettably, she was going to enjoy this feeling of community only for a short time. After she transitioned and the wedding was over, they were going home.

But that was okay.

Once the dating application was up and working, and Kalugal's men started pairing up with clan females, they would build their own community. It would probably take a long time, but it would happen.

Kalugal

Kalugal felt naked without his phone, or his laptop, or his tablet.

Kian had instructed him to leave all electronic devices behind and promised to give him, his men, and Jacki new ones in the village.

If anyone needed him, they could reach him by calling Kian.

He understood his cousin's caution, but after all they had been through together, having his luggage checked, and getting a pat-down had left a bad taste in his mouth.

Even Jacki had to go through that, but at least the one doing the patting down was Bridget, so it wasn't that bad.

"Do you remember when I had to search Jacki?" Rufsur asked.

"Don't remind me."

"I was very respectful."

"I know. But you saw my mate in her undergarments."

Rufsur shrugged. "So what? It was as if she was wearing a bikini."

"I don't want any men to see her in a bikini, either."

Jacki turned around. "We really need to talk about that Neanderthal attitude of yours. It's unbecoming." She pushed her chin up and walked up the stairs without waiting for him.

When she disappeared inside the plane, Rufsur chuckled and slapped him on the back. "Someone is in trouble."

"What did I say wrong?"

"Haven't you heard about Women's Lib?" Amanda sauntered by him. "You should read up about it."

Shaking his head, he followed Dalhu up the stairs.

The former Brother wisely stayed out of the conversation, pretending that he hadn't heard anything.

The interior of the jet wasn't as luxurious as Kalugal had expected from the clan, but it was as well-appointed as any self-respecting, first-class cabin on a commercial airline, which was perfectly fine with him. It wasn't as if he had a private plane of his own, but perhaps he should.

When he took the seat next to Jacki, she turned to him and smiled apologetically. "I'm sorry for snapping at you. For some reason, every little thing annoys me now."

"Are you scared of flying?"

Jacki shook her head. "I was scared the first time. It was when Marisol flew me to West Virginia. But when the clan helped me escape, we hopped from airfield to airfield using small private planes, and I've gotten over it."

"Is it the temperature? Aren't the pills helping?"

"They do, but I'm restless and itchy." She pulled her hair forward and reached behind to tug on the collar of her blouse. "Like this damn tag. It's scratchy, and it's driving me crazy."

"Let me help you." He reached for it with the intention of ripping it off.

"No, don't. You will tear the fabric. I just want to fold it inside out."

"It's the transition." Syssi released her seatbelt. "Don't be surprised if you get weepy for no reason. It's like getting your period but times a hundred." She pulled out a pouch from her purse. "I have a sewing kit with scissors."

Kian beamed with pride. "Syssi is always well prepared. Whatever you need, just ask, and she'll pull it out of her purse."

Syssi chuckled. "That's an exaggeration." She leaned over and cut the tag off.

"Thank you." Jacki let out a relieved breath. "You're a lifesaver."

"You're welcome. By the way, I don't know if Bridget mentioned it, but one of the perks of turning immortal is no more periods."

Kalugal really missed his phone. If he had it, he could've pretended to be reading messages or emails and not listening to the conversation.

Jacki frowned. "How can we get pregnant with no ovulation?"

"This is nature's way of preserving our eggs. They drop only when there is a chance of pregnancy. When you get to the village, you can make an appointment to see Merlin. He's the expert on immortal fertility."

Kian chuckled. "He's more like a witch doctor, but I'm not complaining. He helped us get pregnant."

The pilot poked his head into the cabin. "Everybody, please sit down and buckle up. We are next on the runway."

When he ducked back into the cockpit, Kalugal leaned toward Kian, who was sitting across the aisle from him. "Is the pilot one of yours?"

"Of course. That's Charlie. Besides him, we have three other pilots."

"I should have one of my men take flying lessons. I like the idea of owning a plane."

Kian raised a brow. "I would have expected a guy like you who loves expensive toys to have a selection of private jets."

"Somehow, it never occurred to me. I enjoy flying commercial incognito. You get to meet a lot of interesting people when you fly first class." He smirked. "And everyone likes talking to Professor Gunter."

"Who's that?"

"That's me, of course. That's my archeologist alter ego."

"The old, pudgy man with glasses?" Wonder asked. "The one I saw in Egypt?"

"Indeed, it was I, Professor Gunter, a renowned archeologist." Kalugal affected a heavy German accent.

Jacki giggled. "You sound so funny."

"Do I, *liebling*?"

When Jacki giggled again, Kalugal decided that he would use his German accent as often as he could. He loved hearing her laughter.

As the plane reached flight altitude, Kian unbuckled and pulled a couple of sleep masks from the compartment in front of his seat.

Dangling them from his fingers, he extended his arm over the aisle. "I know that you think I'm paranoid. But I want you and Jacki to put these on and take a nap. Anandur is making sure that Rufsur and Hivak do the same."

With a long-suffering sigh, Kalugal took the masks and handed one to Jacki. "Like it or not, we are going to take a nap."

"No problem." Jacki took the mask, lowered her seat until it was fully reclined, and then put it over her eyes. "Wake me up when we land."

Wendy

Vlad must have talked half the night, and at some point Wendy had drifted off to sleep, and apparently so had Vlad because he was sleeping next to her in her bed.

They were both fully dressed and on top of the blanket, but Vlad's arm was draped around her, and it felt nice.

"Good morning," he murmured with his eyes still closed. "I'm sorry that I fell asleep in your bed."

"I'm not." She pushed his bangs away from his face. "It's nice waking up with you. What time is it?"

"It must be late." He looked at the open window. "I hear the guys practicing outside."

She chuckled. "Naturally, I can't hear anything with my inferior human ears."

"They must know that I stayed the night. Does it bother you?"

"Nope. None of their business. We are both adults." She narrowed her eyes at him. "How old are you? Are you really twenty?"

"Yes. I'm a baby immortal."

"Hold on." Wendy lifted a hand. "When did you go through puberty? And please don't tell me it was a couple of months ago. That will make me feel like a pedophile."

"Immortals go through puberty at the same age humans do."

"Oh, good." She let out a breath. "I need to use the bathroom."

"Me too. I'll go to the one upstairs."

In the bathroom, Wendy squeezed toothpaste onto her toothbrush and looked at herself in the mirror. Her eyes seemed brighter than usual, and the creases between her eyebrows were gone.

Life was full of surprises.

The girl who'd planned on a life of spinsterhood was dating Superman.

Vlad was faster and stronger than an average human, he had better vision and hearing, and he could thrall and shroud.

Immortal.

A descendant of gods.

Wow.

How had she gotten that lucky? What had she done to deserve him?

Nothing.

It meant that there was a catch and that what seemed fantastic now would eventually make her miserable.

Having a Superman boyfriend was cool, and if she had friends, and if she was allowed to tell anyone about him, she would have done some serious bragging.

But the truth was that his immortality was a problem.

She couldn't marry Vlad and have a couple of kids with him even if she wanted to. He would forever be a twenty-year-old while she would age.

Still, she could adopt Jin's attitude and live for today. Vlad loved her, and she loved him back, and that was more than she'd ever hoped for.

If Kian was as good as his word and gave her a decent job in one of the clan's hotels, she and Vlad would date and spend time with his immortal friends, and maybe with Jin and Arwel too.

How old was Arwel?

Now that she knew he could be any age, she suspected that he was much older than he looked. The guy acted very old-fashioned.

And what about Bowen and Leon? How old were they?

Damn, she had so many questions.

That also explained why Vlad had to lie about his mother being thirty-six. Stella probably looked much younger than even that. And Vanessa really was Jackson's mother, and she hadn't had any plastic surgery done.

After brushing her hair, Wendy went back to the bedroom for a change of clothes, but Vlad was already back. "I brewed coffee. Do you want some?"

"Oh, yeah. I wanted to shower and change, but I'll have coffee first."

"Great. Would you like me to make you an omelet?"

"Maybe later." She followed him out of the room. "Right now, I just want coffee and for you to pick up from where you left off last night."

"I don't remember what the last thing I told you was."

"I don't either. At some point, I fell asleep." She chuckled. "I think my brain was full to capacity, and it shut down."

"It was a lot to absorb, and I just gave you an overview. There is so much more."

Wendy pulled out a chair. "Maybe you should slow down and give it to me in small increments."

When Vlad's pale cheeks reddened, Wendy snorted. "Come on. I know that you want to, so just say it."

"Say what?" Pretending innocence, Vlad poured coffee into two mugs.

"That's what she said."

"If you say so."

"As if that's not what you were thinking."

"It wasn't." He put the mug in front of her.

As she considered what other thoughts her comment could have triggered, Wendy felt a blush wash over her face. And then it got even worse when the thought turned into a visual in her head.

Vlad

Wendy's innocent comment had caused a chain reaction that had them both flustered while drinking their morning coffee.

The scent of her arousal triggered his own, and as his fangs started elongating, Vlad wondered whether Bowen had gotten the condoms for him last night and where he'd put them.

"Your eyes are glowing," Wendy murmured into her mug. "Are your fangs growing as well?"

He opened his mouth.

"Oh, wow. That was fast." Her blush deepened. "Let's talk about something else. How old is Arwel?"

"I don't know for sure, but I guess it's a few hundred. I know that he was born in Scotland."

"And Yamanu?"

"He's older than Arwel, but I don't know by how much. Age is irrelevant to immortals, and it's not something that comes up in conversation."

"Okay, then no more talking about age. Except, how old is your mom for real? You must know that."

"Three hundred and one."

"Wow." Wendy put her cup down. "And you are her only child?"

"Yes, and she counts herself lucky. It's very difficult for immortal females to conceive. Nature makes sure that there aren't too many of us."

"Right. I hadn't thought about that. If none of you ever die, then you just keep multiplying. How does that work?"

"Some of us died. But you are right. Even with our extremely low birth rate, in many thousands of years, we might overrun the planet." He rubbed his jaw. "Maybe that's why we are naturally aggressive?"

As Wendy recoiled, he realized that it had been the wrong thing to say. "Those are just impulses. We are very civilized."

"What do you mean by aggressive? How does it manifest?"

He shouldn't mention sex. That would have Wendy running for the hills.

"We have fangs. That's like always carrying a weapon. Maybe if there were too many of us, immortal males would fight each other. I don't really know. But I'm sure nature has an answer for that. If you take rabbits for an example, they are defenseless, so the way they survive is by rapid procreation. With us, it's the opposite."

Wendy grimaced. "I once saw a nature show about infanticide. Do you know how widespread that is? Lions and primates and other species kill the young of their competitors, and it's all about sex. When a lion takes over a pride, he kills the cubs of his predecessor because lactating females are not fertile and he wants to mount them. He kills their babies and then has sex with them. How twisted is that? And the same happens with primates. In some species, the females kill the babies of other females, so there will be less competition for resources."

"That's terrible. I didn't know that."

Wendy crossed her arms over her chest. "Of course you didn't. They don't teach stuff like that in school, and people grow up thinking that everything in nature is wonderful and that only humans are bad. Wrong. The whole ecosystem is cruel and horrible."

Apparently, that was not a good topic for conversation either. What could he say to lighten the mood after that?

"Would you like me to make you a sandwich?" That should be a safe topic.

Wendy sighed and uncrossed her arms. "I want to shower first. But if you are hungry, go ahead and eat."

"That's okay. I'd rather eat with you."

She smiled. "I've seen the quantities you eat, and now I know where it all goes. It fuels your incredible speed and strength. I also know that the popcorn machine that you lifted off me would have crushed me and that a regular human wouldn't have been able to move that fast."

That was a positive change of topics.

Smiling, Vlad nodded. "For some reason, I'm even stronger than most immortal males, and it's totally wasted on me because I have no desire to become a Guardian."

"What's a Guardian?"

"Guardians are the clan protectors and law enforcers. You've met several of them. Bowen, Leon, Arwel, Yamanu, Anandur, and Brundar. They are all Guardians."

"What about Dalhu? Amanda's husband or boyfriend. Is he a Guardian?"

Vlad chuckled. "No. He used to be a Doomer, that's what we call our enemies, but he fell in love with Amanda and crossed over."

Wendy scratched her head. "I remember you saying something about enemies, but it must have been when I was falling asleep because I can't remember it."

"Do you remember the story about the Clan Mother?"

"The goddess." Wendy shook her head. "That's so surreal."

"So she was engaged to a god named Mortdh..." Vlad stopped and listened. "The guys are coming in. I will have to continue the story some other time."

"Okay," Wendy whispered.

"Hello, kids." Bowen walked in with a big grin on his face. "Did you sleep well?"

Jacki

As an unbearable pressure in Jacki's ears woke her up, she covered them with her hands and yawned, but it didn't help.

"Pinch your nose and blow." Kalugal's voice sounded as if it was reaching her through a pool of water. "Just don't force it. Do it slowly."

"Okay."

She did as he suggested, and her ears popped open. Yawning again, she reached for her sleep mask, but then remembered that it was serving as a blindfold.

"Can I take the mask off?"

"When we land," Kian said. "Which should be..." the wheels connected with the runway "...right now."

Jacki took the mask off and looked out the window, but there wasn't much to see. It wasn't an airport, not even a rural one. Just the one landing strip that their plane was coming to a stop on, a hangar, and a bus.

"Nice," Kalugal said. "You have your own airstrip. But shouldn't we wear the sleep masks all the way to the village?"

Unbuckling, Kian pointed to the bus pulling up to the plane. "Remember the opaque windows I told you about? This bus is equipped with them as well."

Kalugal released his seatbelt and got up. "I hope the driver's windows are not."

"Of course not."

Standing in the aisle, Mey stretched her arms over her head and turned to her sister. "Do you want to come with Yamanu and me, or do you want to ride the bus with Jacki?"

"The bus." Jin patted Jacki's shoulder. "I want to be there when Jacki sees the village for the first time. Maybe I can show her and Kalugal around." She glanced at Kian. "Is that okay?"

He shook his head. "They need to get settled first. William will come over to the house that has been prepared for them and put cuffs on Rufsur and Hivak."

"Both of you need to stay put and rest," Bridget said. "The walkabout can wait for after your transitions."

"Yes, doctor." Jin saluted and then leaned to whisper in Jacki's ear. "I can show you all the important stuff on the way to your house."

Mey pulled her sister into a quick hug. "I'll come over to check on you later."

As the pilot opened the door, Mey and Yamanu disembarked first.

With how close the bus was parked to the plane, only a few feet separated its open door from the foldout staircase. The middle-aged driver, whose name Jacki had forgotten, was loading the luggage into the belly of the bus, handling each suitcase with care as if there were breakable items inside.

"Who is that?" Kalugal asked.

Jacki shrugged. "The driver. He is also Kian's butler."

Kalugal chuckled. "I meant, what is he? He is obviously not immortal, and he is not human either."

"That's Okidu," Kian said. "I'll tell you about him on the way."

"That should be interesting." Kalugal followed Jacki into the bus.

When everyone was seated, the driver closed the partition separating the driver's seat from the rest of the cabin. A moment later, the engine turned on, and the windows slowly turned opaque.

Kalugal, who'd taken the aisle seat, leaned toward Kian. "You know that sight is not the only way to figure out a direction or a location."

"I wasn't born yesterday. But unless you have GPS installed in your brain, you need to know where the origin point is to estimate the distance and direction. That's why I asked you and your men to put the sleep masks on."

"Smart. Luckily for you, I don't have a GPS chip installed. But what if that's someone's special talent? A natural ability to ascertain global positioning."

"I've never heard of it, but you have a good point. I'll discuss it with William. Perhaps he can install an interference device."

"Is that what you are using in your village?"

"What William did to camouflage our community is beyond the scope of my technical knowledge. I wouldn't be able to explain it."

Jacki sincerely doubted that. Kian just didn't want to provide Kalugal with information that he could later use to discover where the village was, or use the same technology to cloak the new community he wanted to build for his people.

"When I build my own village, I would appreciate William's help in installing a similar system."

The same thing must have occurred to Kalugal, and Jacki tensed as she waited for Kian to answer that. Would he be a jerk about it? Or would he finally start treating Kalugal as family?

"Sure. But I suggest that you consult with him before you acquire a property. Each site has different challenges, and if you know ahead of time what's the most suitable location, it will make William's job easier in the future."

Releasing a relieved breath, Jacki leaned her head against the headrest and closed her eyes. Kian's willingness to help Kalugal build his own secure place was a sign that he was starting to think of his cousin as an ally.

"What kind of challenges are we talking about?" Kalugal asked. "Does it have to be out in the boonies? I don't want a long commute to meetings if it can be avoided."

Was Kalugal fishing for information that would help him figure out the village's location?

She didn't think that he had any malicious intent, but Kalugal loved a challenge, and he loved solving puzzles. Finding out the location by asking a supposedly innocent question would be just the kind of thing that would appeal to his intellect.

Jacki cast her husband a sidelong glance, but his expression revealed nothing unusual. Except, Kalugal was a very good actor, and she didn't know him well enough to discern whether he was being genuine or not.

"You'll have to compromise," Kian said. "Our previous location was much more convenient in that regard. What I do now is to try to bundle my meetings in the city into one or two days a week."

"So boonies it is. What other challenges?"

Jacki stifled a chuckle. He sounded like a contestant on a game show who'd just figured out the first clue.

"It depends whether you want to be off the grid or not," Kian said. "Power and water supply are important considerations. Solar panels take up a lot of space, are reflective, and they can't be hidden because that will render them ineffective. Wind turbines are too big to hide."

"So, what's the solution?"

"A small nuclear reactor installed deep underground for safety."

Kalugal

Kalugal had learned some valuable information about the village, but not enough to puzzle out the location.

He already knew that the clan's base was in Los Angeles, and from Kian's answers, he'd learned that it wasn't in the urban center but in some remote location. It was off the grid, which meant that it had its own water supply. Maybe they had a well?

The nuclear power generator was an ingenious solution, and he wondered how they'd managed to install one. Obviously, Kian hadn't bothered with permits.

"I'm impressed," Kalugal admitted. "That's a ballsy move to power your village with nuclear."

Kian shrugged. "As long as a strict protocol is maintained, it's a safe and clean way to generate power."

Kalugal doubted he could coax more clues from Kian that would help him solve the puzzle, and asking questions would make the guy even more suspicious than he already was.

Perhaps it was best to leave that puzzle for now and move to the other one that piqued his curiosity.

"You promised to explain about your driver. What is he?"

Next to him, Jacki opened her eyes and looked at Kian. "Is Okidu a cyborg?"

To Kalugal's surprise, Kian nodded. "That's a good guess."

"What do you mean? Is he a cyborg or not? Because I'm not aware that such technology exists. He acts and looks too human."

"You are right. The technology doesn't exist. Okidu is an ancient relic, one of seven who were gifted to my mother by her betrothed."

"How fascinating. You have in your possession a piece of technology from the gods' home planet. I'm so envious."

That was better than any artifact Kalugal had discovered so far or hoped to discover in the future. Okidu was a much more advanced technology than the gods' tablet Kalugal had been searching for.

"Why do you think that Okidu is an alien technology? Perhaps he was made by an antediluvian civilization that became extinct."

Kalugal waved a dismissive hand. "The gods were aliens, and they brought with them alien technology. Unfortunately, your clan seems to own the only remnants of that technology. I knew that you have a tablet, but you also have seven cyborgs. Did you try to make more of them?"

Kian shook his head. "My mother believes that they are sentient beings and refuses to take one apart to see how he is made." He cringed. "Frankly, I wouldn't have been able to do that even if she allowed it. I grew up with them. To me, they are people."

"I can understand that, but there are ways to find out how they are built that don't involve taking one completely apart. Maybe X-rays? MRI machines?"

Kian sighed. "We are afraid to do anything that might have an adverse effect on the Odus because we don't know how to fix them."

"That's a shame." Kalugal leaned back.

"It is what it is," Kian said. "Maybe it's better that way. Humanity is not ready for advanced artificial intelligence that looks and acts so deceptively human."

Jacki rested her head on Kalugal's shoulder. "I'm with Kian on that. Humans will find a way to use the nice butler cyborg as a weapon. I much prefer him to stay like he is now."

As Kalugal stroked Jacki's hair, he tried to imagine an army of cyborgs who all looked like Kian's butler. Middle-aged men didn't look threatening, but he'd seen the ease with which the butler lifted the luggage. He was at least as strong as an immortal male. Probably stronger.

"Do the Odus have any fighting capabilities?" he asked.

"They can learn anything that you wish to teach them, and they do that fast. So turning them into weapons would be easy, but it would also be such a waste. I think they were designed to be domestic help, and that's a much better use for them. If they were supposed to be soldiers, they would have been modeled after someone tall and muscular, and not an older, stocky man or a woman." Kian smiled. "They can morph their facial features and body shape to appear either male or female."

"Can they make themselves look younger or prettier?" Jin joined the conversation.

Kian shook his head. "I've never seen them do that, so maybe that's not an option. Maybe it was also done on purpose so their owners wouldn't feel attraction towards them. They don't have the right equipment for that."

Kalugal chuckled. "After turning them into soldiers, that is the next thing humans would have done. Turned them into sex toys."

"That's gross," Jin said. "But I totally agree. Every new technology that comes out, some pervert finds a way to turn it into porn. Like virtual reality. As soon as the headsets became available, porn games were created."

Syssi cleared her throat. "The technology is even more advanced than you imagine. Have I told you about the Perfect Match virtual reality studios?"

"What are they?"

Kalugal could answer that. "Virtual hookups. You fill out a questionnaire, and the software matches you with the best sexual partner out of everyone it has in its database. Once a match is found, both partners are invited to a virtual sex session designed to fit their fantasies. It's pricy, and only the rich can afford it at this time." He sighed, "I wanted to buy that startup, but someone beat me to it."

"That was you?" Syssi chuckled.

Kalugal narrowed his eyes at her. "Are you the secret investor who bailed them out?"

"We are," Kian said. "But don't feel bad. Without William's help, they would have folded, and you would have lost your investment. They weren't able to work out the bugs on their own."

Syssi shook her head. "It really is a small world. We could have found you a long time ago."

"Not really. You would have met my avatar and wouldn't have known that it was me. But you are right. It is a small world."

"Have you tried the service?" Syssi asked.

"No, but maybe after Jacki's transition, we could give it a try." He dipped his head and kissed her forehead. "What do you think? We could have an adventure in a fantasy world."

She smiled. "I already do."

Jacki

"Thank you. I'll take that as a compliment." Kalugal kissed her forehead again. "You feel a little warm. Do you want to take more pills?"

Jacki shook her head. "They make me sleepy, and this conversation is much too interesting to miss." She lifted her head and looked at Syssi. "As much as I find your virtual fantasy thing fascinating, I'm more interested in the cyborg. It would be so cool if everyone could have a domestic helper at home. If they don't have the right equipment, as Kian politely put it, and if they are programmed so they're incapable of violence, they could make people's lives so much easier."

Syssi looked doubtful. "I love having Okidu, I can't deny it, but I believe that artificial intelligence is dangerous. If they can learn and adapt, at some point they could outsmart humans and immortals alike. The thing is, once the system learns how to learn, it will do it so fast that we won't know what's happening until it is too late."

"Whenever a new technology emerges, it generates fear," Kalugal said. "And that's good because anticipating everything that can go wrong helps design a better product. We still have a long way to go with artificial intelligence, and thinking about the dangers and incorporating safeguards is part of the process."

"We can't anticipate everything," Syssi said. "Take Okidu for example. He had a little accident while helping retrieve Carol from the island. He fell into the water, shut down, and rebooted after several hours. He has been acting strangely ever since."

"Define strange?" Jacki asked. "Not that I know what's normal for him."

"Little things. Like he used to hover over Kian and me just waiting for us to give him something to do. Now he slinks into his room the moment he's done with his chores."

"What about you, Kian?" Kalugal asked. "Have you noticed that? You've known Okidu since you were born."

Kian shrugged. "He seems more aware. But that's not an objective observation. I think that what messed him up was switching masters and not the reboot. For the duration of Carol's rescue, I told him to obey Turner, and then Turner told him to obey the diver team's leader. After having only me as his master for nearly two thousand years, that was too much of an adjustment."

Jacki stifled a gasp. Kian was freaking ancient. Two thousand years old?

Wow!

Syssi must have a daddy issue.

"That's two stories I can't wait to hear." Kalugal rubbed his hand over her arm. "How long do we have until we reach the village?"

"Long enough." Kian smirked. "You didn't think that we were going straight there, did you? Okidu is taking a roundabout route to the village."

Ugh, Kian and his suspiciousness was really annoying.

Kalugal didn't seem to mind, though. In fact, Jacki had a feeling that he'd been expecting that. Would he have done the same in Kian's place?

"Good." Kalugal crossed his legs at the ankles. "Then you can tell me all about Okidu's part in Carol's rescue and about his accident and subsequent reboot."

By the time Kian finished telling the story and answering Kalugal's questions, the bus had stopped.

"Are we there?" Jacki asked.

"Almost," Syssi said.

There was a slight jerk, and then they started moving again, but not for long. A few minutes later, the bus stopped again, and the windows became clear.

"Are we in an underground garage?" She looked at the concrete walls and the thick supporting columns. "It's huge."

"It's quite sizable." Kian got up. "Welcome to the village."

Syssi slapped his arm. "Not yet. Save it for when they actually get to see it."

The bus's door opened with a hiss, and the cyborg butler poked his head inside. "As you have requested, master, all three golf carts are waiting outside the pavilion's doors. You and your guests can go ahead, and I will bring the luggage up."

"I don't need the golf cart," Jin said. "How about you, Jacki? Are you okay to walk for fifteen to twenty minutes?"

"I'm not sure," Jacki admitted. "I feel a little woozy."

"You should take more pills." Kalugal turned to Bridget. "What says the doctor?"

"The pills are up to Jacki. But I recommend taking the cart." She smiled apologetically at Jin. "I know that you want to show your friend the village, but Arwel can drive very slowly, so you'll get to do that without walking."

"But walking is healthy, and I'm not really sick, right?"

"Walking is wonderful when you are healthy. But right now, you should conserve energy because your body needs it for the transition. You don't want to push yourself."

"You are taking the cart," Kian said in a tone that implied the discussion was over. "Jacki, Kalugal, Rufsur, and Hivak will go with you. Anandur, Wonder, Callie and

Brundar, you are with us." He turned to Bridget. "You and Turner will share a ride with Amanda and Dalhu. Do you want them to drop you at home? Or do you want to join the tour?"

"I'd rather go home if you don't mind. But if anyone needs me, please don't hesitate to call."

Kalugal

As Rufsur and Hivak joined them in the elevator, it occurred to Kalugal that Rufsur had been uncharacteristically quiet throughout the plane ride and later the bus. Usually, the guy joked around and had something to say about everything.

What was his problem?

Was he upset about not being left in charge back home?

When Kalugal had invited Rufsur to accompany him and Jacki to the village, the guy had seemed excited, but perhaps it grated on him that the others had bundled him together with Hivak, regarding them both as simple bodyguards.

Kian, Turner, and the Guardians were well aware of Rufsur's position, but they mostly ignored him as if he was a simple underling.

Rufsur should know better, though. Kalugal had chosen him because of their friendship, and hierarchy had nothing to do with that.

He cast him a sidelong glance. "Are you okay?"

"Never been better."

Kalugal didn't detect any sarcasm in his lieutenant's voice. Was Rufsur on high alert because he and Hivak were all the protection Kalugal and Jacki had with them?

Probably.

They didn't even have phones, and naturally no weapons. Well, except for Kalugal's compulsion power. But they were entering a village full of immortals, and Kalugal couldn't compel more than twenty at one time.

It was a little risky, but not as much as Rufsur feared. Kian was not going to make a move against them for the simple reason that he had no motive to do so. The most valuable thing to Kian was Kalugal's cooperation, so he was no good to him imprisoned or dead.

"You can relax. We are among friends."

"That remains to be seen."

Anandur clapped Rufsur on the back. "Just think of all the single immortal ladies that you're gonna meet. I promise you that they will be very friendly. Maybe too friendly."

Hivak chuckled quietly. "I can't wait."

Rufsur glared at him. "We are here to protect the boss, not chase skirts."

As the elevator doors opened, their group exited into a pavilion made mostly from glass. Kian and those who'd ridden with him were just getting out of the other car.

"Are you sure that your cyborg can handle all the luggage?" Kalugal asked. "There is a lot of it."

Kian grimaced. "Please don't call him that. He has a name, and it's Okidu."

"My apologies. Okidu it is."

"And he can handle all the luggage."

"I can't wait to see my Onidu," Amanda said. "I should have brought him along."

"Is he the other Odu?" Jacki asked.

Amanda nodded. "He's my butler. But he is so much more than that. Onidu practically raised me." She followed Dalhu out the sliding doors.

Jacki leaned on Kalugal's arm. "Raised by a cyborg? That sounds like the title of a science fiction novel."

As they exited the sliding doors, the first thing Kalugal noticed was how quiet it was, and the second was how fresh the air smelled. He could detect a very faint ocean breeze, which confirmed his suspicion that they were somewhere in the Malibu mountains.

He kept it to himself and helped Jacki climb into the golf cart.

Fitting six people inside the small vehicle was a stretch, and he was glad when Jin joined them in the back and sat next to Jacki. He didn't want any of the men squeezing close to her.

"I'm going to be the official tour guide," Jin said.

As Rufsur and Hivak sat up front, Arwel, who was the designated driver, helped Okidu sort the luggage out.

"Are those yours?" Arwel pointed at Kalugal and Jacki's four matching designer suitcases.

"Those are ours. And those two are Rufsur's and Hivak's."

When everything was loaded and secured with cords, Arwel got behind the wheel and turned the engine on.

"Welcome to the village," Kian called from the next cart over.

"Thank you. It is lovely."

"Wait until you see the rest of it," Jin said.

The carts moved barely at jogging speed, with Kian's in the lead, theirs in the middle, and Turner's closing the procession.

"This is the village square," Jin pointed. "To the right are the office building, the café, and the clinic. To the left are the playground, the pond, and the large grassy area where parties are held."

In the café several people waved at them, and even though Kalugal wasn't sure that they were waving at him, he smiled and waved back.

"The café is the center of the social life in the village," Jin continued. "That's why Carol loved working there."

The place was beautiful, perfect for raising children, except there were none. No couples were strolling down the pathways holding hands, and no one was pushing strollers.

It was disappointing, but naturally he didn't comment on that. Kian hadn't volunteered information about how many of his clan members had been blessed with a partner or a child, but it seemed that the number was small.

As they entered the residential area, they stopped to drop Bridget and Turner off, but everyone else continued to the house that had been reserved for them.

"Your house is in the new phase of the village," Arwel said. "It's a little farther away from the center, but it's still just twenty to thirty minutes on foot from the café."

"Where is yours?" Jacki asked.

"Also, in the new phase. We are going to be neighbors."

Jacki

As Kian's golf cart stopped in front of a house decorated with balloons, Jacki pointed. "Are those for us? Who did that?"

"Vivian with Ella and Kri's help." Jin smiled.

So she had known about it, and that was why she'd been so eager to accompany them to the house.

It was a nice surprise.

As Arwel parked their cart, Jin jumped out. "Come on, let's go inside."

Her friend was full of energy as if she wasn't feeling the effects of her transition, but that wasn't the case for Jacki. She'd started hers a day later than Jin and was feeling pretty crappy, but neither of them had the severe symptoms that Bridget had warned about.

Were they just lucky? Or was the worst still to come?

Jacki had a feeling that it was the latter.

As Kalugal got out and offered her his hand, she gratefully accepted it, but even with his help, she swayed on her feet.

"You should be resting." He lifted her into his arms.

"Put me down," she whispered in his ear. "I can walk if I lean on you."

"Nonsense. Isn't it a human custom to carry the bride over the threshold?" He walked up the stairs to the front porch.

"Yeah, but this is not our home."

"It is for the next week or two."

"Welcome to your temporary abode." Anandur opened the door and stepped aside to let them through.

Inside, there were more decorations, including a banner that said 'Congratulations Jacki and Kalugal.' Someone had also prepared lunch and left it on the counter.

Probably Vivian. But where was she?

As Kalugal put Jacki down on the couch, the rest of their party filed in, and a few moments later, Vivian came in with a teenage boy who Jacki assumed was her son Parker, Julian, and Ella.

"Jacki, I'm so happy that you are also transitioning." Vivian sat next to her and Kalugal on the couch. "It's wonderful that you and Jin are transitioning together."

"Yeah, we can be miserable together," Jin said.

Vivian waved a dismissive hand. "Ella and I transitioned at about the same time too, but it took me longer." She shrugged. "Which wasn't surprising since I'm twice Ella's age." She reached for Jacki's hand. "I'm so sorry about what happened at your wedding. Once you're up to it, we should have another party right here."

"Already in the works," Amanda said. "Annani decided that they should have a proper wedding in the village with her officiating over it."

Kian lifted a hand. "Let's wait until Jacki transitions and then talk about parties."

"Yeah, we don't want to jinx it." Syssi sat on an armchair across from Jacki. "You look tired. We should all go and let you rest."

Kian shook his head. "William is on his way. I need to wait for him to put the cuffs on Rufsur and Hivak, and then we can go."

"I want to introduce my son." Vivian motioned for the boy to come forward. "This is Parker."

"Hi." He offered Jacki his hand while looking at Kalugal with open curiosity.

"Nice to meet you." Jacki shook it.

"Hello, young man." Kalugal took Parker's offered hand. "I'm Kalugal, Kian's cousin."

"I know. And you are a compeller like me." Parker smiled shyly. "But I'm not as good as you. You can compel immortals, and I can only compel humans."

"That's a rare ability, and it will get stronger as you get older. Who knows? Maybe someday you'll be able to compel immortals?"

"Don't boost his ego. It's already too big. I'm Ella." She offered Kalugal her hand. "Vivian's daughter."

"I know. I've heard about what my brother had planned to do to you and your mother, and I apologize for it."

"No need to apologize. It all ended well, and I forgave him." She smiled. "I had no choice. Lokan is mated to my best friend."

Kalugal looked at Julian. "What about you? Did you forgive him?"

"It took me longer than it has taken Ella, but eventually, I did."

"It was all fated to happen that way," Syssi said. "While we are waiting for William, would you like me to show you the house?"

Kalugal glanced at Jacki. "Are you up to it?"

She nodded. "The house isn't big, so it's not going to take long."

He helped her up and then wrapped his arm around her waist. "Lean on me."

She didn't argue.

Syssi motioned for Rufsur and Hivak to follow her as well. "This is a three-bedroom house, and you each get a room." She opened one door and then the one across from it. "It's not fancy, but cozy."

"It's more than enough." Rufsur walked into one of the rooms. "It's nicer than the one I have in Kalugal's mansion." He waved a hand in a circle. "There is art on the walls, and an area rug and all the colors match."

"We have a wonderful interior designer," Syssi said. "I should introduce you to her."

Jacki shook her head. "Is there a reason Ingrid gets dibs on all the new single guys? If I were one of the other clan ladies, I would get upset."

Syssi grimaced. "You are absolutely right. It's just that I feel sorry for her. It must be difficult to be passed by for the second time."

"Ingrid didn't get passed on by Richard. She bailed on him."

"That's true. But enough about that. Let me show you the master bedroom. It's on the other side of the house."

As they returned to the living room on their way, Hivak and Rufsur stayed behind, which Jacki was glad about.

Syssi opened the door. "That's the master, it has a very nice bathroom and a good size walk-in closet, for most people that is. Amanda had to convert one of the bedrooms into a closet."

Kalugal arched a brow. "Her home is the same size as everyone else's?"

"Most of the houses in the village have only two bedrooms. Amanda has a three-bedroom house like this one, and so do Kian and I."

Kalugal seemed puzzled. "I would have thought that as Annani's children, Kian and Amanda would get something fancier than the other clan members."

"We did. Ours and Amanda's have small guesthouses for our Odus, and Kian and I also have a lap pool in our back yard. That's the one luxury Kian allowed himself. Swimming relaxes him." She smiled. "And believe me, if asked, every clan member would be in favor of anything that can do that."

Kalugal frowned. "I don't understand. Would there have been resentment from the other clan members if Kian and Amanda resided in more luxurious homes?"

"I don't think so. We just preferred to have a home that is cozy and comfortable. Why build a huge mansion for two people? Or three." She rubbed her tummy. "But if we are blessed with another child before Allegra moves out to start her own life, we would have to build an addition."

"I really like this house," Jacki said. "I think it's the perfect size for a family, and given immortals' exceptional hearing, I especially like that the living room separates the master from the secondary bedrooms."

Syssi smirked. "I hear you. But the insulation in these houses is so superb that an immortal can stand outside the closed door and barely hear anything. A human would hear nothing at all."

"I would like to test it." Kalugal walked out into the corridor. "After I close the door, say something in a loud voice, normal speaking voice, and then a quiet voice."

When the door closed, Jacki lifted a finger. "Can I do that?"

Syssi waved a hand. "Be my guest."

"I love you!" Jacki yelled. "But I don't like your bossiness," she said in a normal voice. "But I forgive you because you are so damn sexy," she whispered.

Vlad

Bowen hadn't said anything about the damn condoms, and it had taken Vlad most of the day to gather enough courage to ask, which was probably the game Bowen had been playing.

Let's watch the twenty-year-old virgin blush.

The guy had been incredibly helpful, but he was also an asshole.

Vlad just needed a moment alone with Bowen without Wendy or Richard around, but that was easier said than done. The cabin was small, the five of them did almost everything together, and either Wendy or Richard was always within hearing range.

Inspiration came when he noticed that the haircut Wendy had given Richard was uneven in the back.

"You should really fix that." Vlad pointed at his neck. "The left side is a full inch longer than the right."

"I'll do it right now." Wendy pushed to her feet.

Richard waved a dismissive hand. "No need. It's not like there are any ladies for me to impress here."

Not good. Vlad needed to persuade the guy to go for it. "Now that I've noticed how crooked it is, it will keep bugging me."

"Fine." Richard pushed to his feet. "Let's do it."

As Wendy and Richard stepped out onto the front porch, Bowen smiled. "Clever way to get rid of both of them at once. Do you want to talk about last night?"

Vlad frowned. "What?"

"It's okay if you don't. But I thought that's the reason you got rid of them."

"I just wanted to ask if you got the condoms."

Bowen lifted a brow. "I left them in the motorhome. I thought that was obvious and that you put them to good use last night."

Vlad's face got hot. "We just talked, and then we fell asleep."

"Did you tell Wendy about us?"

"Yes."

"How did she take it?"

"Good. Better than I expected. It's like she was relieved to find that there was a logical explanation for all the things that didn't add up for her. I think that subconsciously, or even consciously, it bothered her that we weren't telling her the truth and that contributed to her feelings of mistrust."

"Could be." Bowen nodded. "Are you going to induce her?"

"Not yet. Kian told me that I need to be absolutely sure that Wendy is the one before I even tell her about her potential dormancy. And until I do, he wants me to use condoms."

Leon, who up until now had pretended to be a part of the furniture, looked over his shoulder at Vlad. "Do you know how to put them on?"

Vlad shook his head. "How would I? I'm a damn virgin, remember?"

"Nothing to be embarrassed about, kid. I think it's nice that your first girl is going to be your last. But if you don't want to embarrass yourself in front of Wendy, I suggest that you practice in private." He looked at Bowen. "I hope that you bought him enough."

Bowen chuckled. "I bought plenty. You can go to the motorhome and practice in private. I'll keep Wendy busy."

"Thank you. I appreciate it."

"No problem." Bowen clapped him on the back. "By the way, how is your sex education? And I don't mean Bhathian's class. Did you watch any porn?"

"I had enough trouble keeping my fangs from showing up at inappropriate times without adding extra stimulation."

Bowen nodded in approval. "That's actually good. Porn gives a distorted view of what sex should be like. Just go with what feels right and remember to take care of your lady's pleasure first."

Leon snorted. "The only way you'll manage that is by keeping your pants on, and there is a good chance that you'll mess them up."

Vlad groaned. "You are not really helping, guys."

Perhaps he should ask Wendy to find the hentai she'd said was nice and romantic. The server in the cabin did not have any anime, but his phone had a satellite connection, and she could use it to stream from any service.

But first, he needed to get to the motorhome and practice putting a condom on.

"How are you going to distract Wendy while I practice?"

"Don't worry about it. I'll keep her busy for at least an hour." Bowen stepped out to the porch.

Leaving the door open, he leaned and whispered something in Wendy's ear.

She nodded and then patted Richard's shoulder. "You're all done. Bowen and I are going for a walk." She waved and smiled at Vlad. "See ya later."

Dusting off the hair clippings, Richard got up and walked back inside. "Is it even now?" He showed Vlad his neck.

"Perfect."

"Itchy." Richard scratched his back. "I'm going to hit the shower."

Wendy

Bowen's offer of a walk and talk had been unexpected.

Just one day ago, Wendy would have found an excuse to decline. It wasn't safe to be alone with a guy whose motives weren't clear. Usually, an invitation for a walk was the code name for a make-out session, but Bowen knew she and Vlad were serious about each other, and his intention was probably to warn her not to hurt Vlad again.

Besides, he was a policeman of sorts, and he was really old. Did that make him safe, though?

Not really. But her senses hadn't picked up on any malevolent intentions. On the contrary, she sensed that Bowen was amused.

"So, what did you want to talk to me about?" she asked.

"Vlad told me that he shared our secrets with you."

"He got permission from Kian."

"I know. I just want to make sure that you are okay. You seem too calm for someone who's just learned that humans are not at the top of the food chain."

She shrugged. "What did you expect me to do?"

"Maybe freak out a little?"

"If I had never been exposed to people with paranormal talents and seen all the shit they can do, I probably would have freaked out. But after the program and the escape, nothing really surprises me anymore. Maybe I'm numb from too many changes?"

"It could be. Not too long ago, though, you still wanted to go back to the program. What I want to know is whether you changed your mind about it because the director is dead and you have nowhere to go, or did you do that because you fell in love with Vlad?"

So that was what this was all about. Bowen was still suspicious of her motives, and she couldn't blame him for it. She'd acted all lovey-dovey before. And although it hadn't all been an act, enough of it had.

"Frankly, it's both. I think that the director's death was the push I needed to make my decision. As long as that door was still open, I kept one foot there and one foot here with Vlad."

"Do you love him?"

"I do. Vlad is the best person I've ever met. I just hope that he never changes."

"He's twenty. Of course, he will change."

Wendy sighed. "That's what scares me. What if he becomes possessive? Controlling? Unreasonable? What if he becomes violent? He said that immortals are aggressive by nature."

"We are. But that aggression is mainly aimed at our enemies. No one gets into fistfights in our community."

"Really? Even when people get drunk?"

Bowen smiled. "The worst you can expect from a drunken clansman is belting out lewd Scottish ballads and making crude jokes."

She laughed. "That actually sounds like fun. Do you know any?"

He cocked a brow and looked at her down his nose. "Of course I do. But even though you won't understand the words, I won't sing them in the company of a lady. At least not when I'm sober," he added with a wink.

"I'm glad that you think of me as a lady."

"You are not a dude."

"You know what I mean."

He shrugged. "Everyone makes mistakes. Some are more stupid than others, but luckily for you, no harm was done."

"That's not true. Because of me, the director believed that the people who helped us escape were all paranormally talented, and that's why he launched the attack on

Jacki's wedding." Wendy cringed. "Jacki is never going to forgive me for ruining her special day."

Bowen stopped, turned to her, and put a hand on her shoulder. "The director failed, and now the program will probably get shut down, so stop beating yourself up. You are starting a new life. Don't bring guilt and remorse into it."

She let out a breath. "I wish there was a way for me to atone for what I did."

"There is. Be good to Vlad. That kid is golden, and he deserves to be happy."

"I'll do my best."

"Good." Bowen nodded. "Did Vlad tell you about fated mates?"

"No."

"Ah." He resumed walking. "It used to be a belief, a myth of sorts, that every immortal had one special person who was destined for him or her, but that only a chosen few were deserving enough for the Fates to reward them with that most precious of boons."

"Used to? I assume that it was proven wrong."

"On the contrary. We've had several such wonderful pairings in our community lately."

"That's great for them. But why are you telling me that? I'm human. I can't be Vlad's special person."

"Perhaps you can. It's up to the Fates."

"How? Are they like fairy godmothers who come and grant wishes of immortality?"

"Something like that. The belief is that the Fates favor those who have either suffered greatly or sacrificed a lot for others."

Wendy hadn't sacrificed for others, but she'd definitely suffered.

Was Vlad her reward?

It was a comforting thought, but it had no basis in reality.

It was just one of those stupid beliefs that people made up to make sense of pointless suffering.

Vlad

Vlad stared at the pile of condom boxes, wondering if Bowen had bought that many as a joke or as a compliment.

A variety of brands, each in two sizes, all promised a superb undiminished experience, which Vlad interpreted to mean that condoms took away from the fun. When a manufacturer claimed to be better at something than others, it usually pointed to a problem that all brands of the product shared.

Like diet drinks promising no artificial taste meant that they all had it.

Lifting one of the boxes, he held it up in front of his face and grimaced. He didn't like the idea that his and Wendy's first time would be a diminished experience just because he couldn't make up his mind.

Perhaps he should wait until he was sure that she was the one.

Then he could tell her about the transition, and they could have their first time together without an artificial barrier between them.

If not for her betrayal, the decision would have been easy, but he didn't trust his own feelings. Wendy was his first girlfriend, and everyone knew the power of first love.

The hormonal maelstrom, the yearning for physical intimacy, the sheer pleasure of not being alone, all of those mixed together created a powerful elixir that muddled the brain. With time and experience, people got somewhat inured to the potent combination and learned to guard their hearts.

Would he ever know for sure?

Lovemaking with a barrier would not induce Wendy's transition, but it might induce the formation of the bond between them.

If that happened, it would eliminate the last of his doubts.

Condom it is. Vlad chose a box at random, pulled out a packet, and tore off the wrapping.

What was he supposed to do with that? It looked tiny.

It probably stretched.

Perhaps he could find instructions on YouTube. If there was a video about how to kiss a girl for the first time, there was probably one about the proper use of condoms.

After checking that the door was locked, Vlad pulled all the window shades down and sat on the couch.

Typing the search phrase, he didn't expect to find many suggestions, but surprisingly, there were many clips to choose from. He selected the one with the most views.

As Vlad watched the guy demonstrate putting a condom on a zucchini, he laughed so hard that the entire motorhome shook. The zucchini was mounted on a stick, had a large mushroom stuck on top of it, and had two wrinkly tangerines flanking its bottom.

After several minutes and deep breaths to stop shaking from laughter, Vlad pulled his pants down and followed the instructions.

The thin, easily breakable membrane didn't do well with his long guitarist's fingernails, and the first condom tore, and so did the second, and the third.

He succeeded with the fourth.

Two things became very clear. One, he needed to clip his nails and file them smooth, and two, condoms were a pain.

Maybe he should just make up his mind, or wait with sex until he did.

Except, inducing Wendy's transition was not the only thing unprotected sex could result in. He could get her pregnant, and they were both too young for that. With the low fertility rate of immortals, that was a remote chance, but it could happen.

Perhaps Wendy could go on the pill? Or take a contraceptive shot? That way, they could forgo the condom and induce her transition without risking pregnancy.

The only problem with that was the wait.

Wendy had hinted that she was ready, and if he kept delaying things, she might think that he didn't desire her, or that there was some other problem.

Was the small inconvenience of using condoms worth all that trouble?

With a groan, Vlad pushed his bangs back.

If Wendy wasn't on birth control pills, and there was no reason for her to be because she was still a virgin, he could use this as an excuse to postpone things. Bridget could send them a prescription, and Bowen or Leon could go to a pharmacy to buy them.

That would give him about two more days to reach a decision. Or maybe even longer than that. What if she needed to take the pills for a few days before it was safe to have unprotected sex?

A quick internet search provided the answer, and it was a definite no. If taken on the fifth day after the start of a period, the pill would be effective right away. Otherwise, it would take seven days.

If Wendy had menstruated recently, Vlad would have known that, and she hadn't, which meant either waiting a week or using a condom.

Good things came to those who waited, right?

Another week would give him enough time to make up his mind whether Wendy was his one and only or not.

Except, that was a lie.

Vlad already knew that she was.

He loved her, and imagining her gone from his life was intolerable. But he needed more time to make sure that he was right, and that he hadn't given his heart to the wrong girl.

Kalugal

Rufsur opened the fridge and grinned. "Thank you, Vivian. She made dinner for us."

"How do you know it was her?" Hivak asked. "Maybe it was the cyborg?"

Rufsur shrugged. "Whoever it was, has my thanks." He pulled out a glass container and opened the lid. "Lasagna."

"I could eat." Kalugal walked into the kitchen and sniffed the dish. "Smells good. What do we do with it now?"

"Pop it in the microwave." Jacki got up from the couch.

He was next to her before she made one step. "You heard Bridget. She said that you need to rest. I'm sure Rufsur knows how to operate the microwave oven."

"And you don't?"

Kalugal shrugged. "I'm sure it's not difficult to figure out."

"You are such a spoiled prince." She plopped back on the couch. "The truth is that I'm tired. It was a long day."

"Indeed."

After their hosts had departed, he and his men had searched the place for bugs, going over every inch of wall, furniture and appliance. Those suckers could be the size of a mosquito, and it had taken them over two hours to discover absolutely nothing.

That was worrisome. Kian was too suspicious, bordering on paranoid, to forgo installing surveillance equipment in the house, not unless he had other means of spying on them.

They had checked his and Jacki's cuffs at home, and although they emitted a signal, they didn't record or transmit voice. Still, it was possible that the ones William had brought for Rufsur and Hivak could do that, but they didn't have the equipment to check.

The other option was that the phones, tablets, and laptops that William had brought for them were bugged. That was why they'd stashed the devices in the pantry, which had the same excellent soundproofing as the rest of the house.

The one problem with that was that it necessitated checking every fifteen minutes or so whether any of them had gotten texts, emails, or phone calls.

Kalugal sat next to Jacki on the couch and wrapped his arm around her shoulders. "After dinner, it's off to bed with you."

"I'm not arguing."

"That's a first." He kissed the top of her head. She really must be exhausted. "If you feel better tomorrow, we can go for a walk."

"That would be nice."

Before leaving, Kian had taken Kalugal aside and explained the rules of conduct. The four of them needed to stay together at all times. If they left the house, the guards posted outside would follow them around. Naturally, the guards had earplugs to safeguard them from his compulsion.

It didn't feel good to be treated with such suspicion, but Kalugal was grateful to Kian for making such a big compromise. Inviting him and Jacki and his two men had been a difficult decision for Kian, and if he needed to put safeguards in place so he could sleep easier, so be it.

The important thing was that Jacki would get the care she needed from an experienced immortal doctor in a proper medical facility.

"Dinner is served," Rufsur announced.

He and Hivak had set the table, and Hivak had even chopped up some vegetables for a salad.

"Is there a grocery store in this place?" Rufsur asked. "There is enough food in the fridge to last us a few days, but if we stay longer, we will need to restock."

"I'll have to ask one of our hosts." Kalugal helped Jacki to the table. "Or you can walk outside and ask the guards."

"They are wearing earplugs."

"You can write the question on your phone and let them look at it," Jacki suggested.

"I'm surprised they didn't put any guards with us in the house." Rufsur lifted the dish and passed it to Jacki.

"Let me." Kalugal took it. "The thing is still hot, and it's heavy."

"I'm sorry." Rufsur cast a sidelong glance at Jacki. "I wasn't thinking."

"That's okay. For once, I don't mind Kalugal being bossy. I'm too weak to lift a pillow."

"Thank you for accepting my help." Kalugal put a generous portion of lasagna on her plate and then followed it with the salad. "So, what do you say about this quaint little home?"

"It's not quaint. It's cozy." Jacki cut a piece of her lasagna. "And the best part about it is the soundproofing."

"On that, we don't have an argument." Kalugal loaded his plate and passed the container to Rufsur. "I need to ask Kian what materials he used. It must be something custom made for the clan. But the house I have in mind for us is much bigger than this one."

"Why? If you build separate houses for your men, you won't need a huge mansion. This feels so much more intimate."

A small house like this didn't fit with Kalugal's self-image. As his name implied, he was a great king, or rather he would be one day when his plans came to fruition.

"I have a different vision for our future."

"Care to share it with me?"

He needed to do that, but not in front of his men. Rufsur was privy to all his lofty plans, but not Hivak.

Except, that wasn't the main reason he wanted to have that particular conversation with Jacki in private. She might not see things his way and start to argue, which shouldn't be done in front of others As king and queen, they needed to present a unified front to the world.

"Later." Kalugal clasped Jacki's hand under the table. "After dinner, I'll serve you tea in bed, and we will talk while you are resting comfortably."

She sighed. "Sounds lovely. I'll just grab a quick shower first."

"Of course."

"I'm done." Rufsur pushed away from the table and took his plate to the sink. "Hivak, you are clearing the table and washing the dishes."

"Yes, sir."

Kalugal regarded his lieutenant with a frown. What was he upset about?

Rufsur had seemed to accept that Jacki belonged to Kalugal and that he would have to set his sights elsewhere. Getting all worked up over something that was a done deal didn't make much sense, and Rufsur was smart enough to realize that.

As Rufsur sat on the couch and turned on the television, Jacki put her knife and fork down. "I'm done as well." She lifted her plate, but Kalugal took it from her hands.

"I'll take care of it. Wait for me before you get into the shower. You are not feeling well, and I want to be there in case you feel faint."

"Okay." She smiled and kissed his cheek. "Instead of a shower, I'll fill up the bathtub."

"Same thing. Don't get in without me watching over you. I've heard of humans who drowned in the bathtub."

"I'll wait."

"Thank you."

As Jacki headed to the bedroom, Kalugal put the kettle on the stove and sat down next to his second-in-command. "What's bugging you?"

"I don't like it here. It's not safe. I know that you trust Kian, but I don't. Not that I have anything against the guy, but he is looking out for his people, not you. And if he thinks even for one moment that you might endanger them, he will not hesitate to strike you down. That's just how things are. The old us versus them."

"What if us are them? After all, we are all related."

"And so is Navuh and every member of the Brotherhood. I like Jacki, you know I do, but she is not worth your life."

"That's where you are mistaken. Jacki is my life."

Jacki

Wrapped in a thick, fluffy towel, Jacki sat on the side of the tub and watched it fill with water.

The pills she'd taken hadn't kicked in yet, and she could feel her temperature rising.

According to Bridget, as long as it didn't get dangerously high the fever was a good sign. Her body was working hard on making changes.

It could have been much worse.

She could have lost consciousness like Callie and Syssi had. She still might, which was why she hadn't argued with Kalugal when he'd told her to wait for him before getting into the tub.

It was nice to have someone looking out for her. She was no longer alone, and if the Fates did right by her, she would never be.

What an amazing thing it was to be part of a couple.

A loving couple, Jacki corrected herself.

Some people were miserable together, and because they knew each other so well, they also knew where to hit so it would hurt the most.

That was the flip side of marriage. It could be the best thing or the worst thing in a person's life. And sometimes it started wonderfully and then one day it wasn't.

Perhaps she should watch her big mouth and not argue with Kalugal so much. She should pick her battles carefully and only insist on the most important stuff.

Little things were not worth getting upset about.

The question was where to draw the line. If she agreed to never wear a bikini in public, for example, it could be an open invitation to other restrictions, and it could end up with Kalugal dictating what clothes she put on every morning.

In a way, he'd already done that by purchasing her clothes for her. Except, she loved everything that he'd gotten her, so there was nothing to argue about.

"Knock, knock." Kalugal pushed the bathroom door open with his foot.

She'd left the door slightly ajar on purpose. With the crazy soundproofing going on in the house, no one would have heard her hit the floor if she fainted.

"I brought us both tea." He put the tray on the vanity. "Thank you for waiting for me." He took her hand and kissed it. "Let me help you get in."

"Are you coming in as well?" Jacki let the towel drop and put one leg over the tub's edge and then the other.

Kalugal swallowed. "You are not well, and if I come into the bathtub with you, I might not be able to keep my hands to myself."

"I'm not sick." She let out a sigh as the warm water enveloped her. "I took three more Motrins before you came. In half an hour, I will feel much better."

Kalugal handed her a tall mug filled with tea. "I apologize for the crude serving vessel, but these big mugs were all I found in the cabinets. There were no porcelain cups."

"Oh, the horror," Jacki mocked. "The great Kalugal is forced to slum it in a commoner's hut."

He smirked. "The great Kalugal will survive the temporary discomfort, but he is very upset to serve his queen tea in such a crude container."

Stifling a chuckle, Jacki took a sip from the tea. "You are such a snob, but I love you anyway. It kind of suits you to act like a royal."

"That's because I was destined for greatness." He got up, turned on the water in the shower, and then sat back on the tub's edge next to her. "You wanted to hear my vision for the future," he said in a hushed, conspiratorial tone.

"Well, this is it. I want to rule the world. Benevolently, of course."

Jacki laughed, but Kalugal didn't smile.

"You're not serious, right? You are messing with me."

"I'm very serious. I look at the world as it is today, and I don't like what I see. It's better than it used to be, but things are not improving fast enough. There is no justification for the ongoing suffering. We have the technology and the knowhow to feed and educate every child wherever she or he is born in the world. And no adult should go hungry either, or have her or his freedoms and opportunities restricted by religious fanatics, corrupt politicians, and other leeches who feast on the blood of innocents."

Wow. Kalugal was not only serious about it, he was passionate. It was admirable that he felt so strongly about human suffering and wished to alleviate it, but as powerful as he was, that wasn't a task for one man.

"Your vision seems to be aligned with the clan's. Perhaps you can work on that together with Kian and Annani. This is too big for one person to do alone. Heck, even the goddess needs help from her descendants, and her progress is slow."

He smiled. "I'm so glad that you understand. I was afraid that you would ridicule my ambitions."

He'd lost her somewhere. "I approve of your vision and the things that you want to fix, but you didn't tell me yet how you want to go about it. I can't imagine how you could possibly effect such a massive change all by yourself."

Kalugal

Kalugal leaned over and kissed Jacki's forehead. "That's one of the many things that I love and admire about you. You are smart, and your thought process is clear. No matter how many layers of bullshit are between you and the truth, you point your laser sharp brain at them and blast them apart to get straight to the essence."

"Thank you, but you are overestimating my mental prowess. I still don't know what exactly you are planning to do."

Kalugal took another sip from his tea and then put the mug on the vanity counter. "My plan is too complex to explain in one sitting, but I'll try." He looked into Jacki's eyes. "Phinas and Rufsur are the only people who I've shared my vision with, and now you. I need you to promise that you will not talk about it, or even mention it, to anyone other than my two lieutenants and me."

"I promise." She reached for his hand. "I'm your wife, Kalugal. You have my complete loyalty, and I'll always keep your secrets safe."

He believed that she meant it, but that might change after he revealed more details. Perhaps the prudent thing to do was to keep talking in generalities and gauge her reaction before delving deeper.

"My eventual goals are very similar to the clan's, but I disagree with the way they go about it. The change is dangerously slow."

"What do you mean? Do you think humanity will nuke itself out of existence?"

"That's one possibility, yes. The growth in human knowledge is exponential, but regrettably, human evolution cannot catch up. Not that immortals are all that superior to humans, as evidenced by my father and his island. If the world is left to its own devices, the suffering and oppression will continue, resources will be squandered by the greedy and powerful, and eventually, humans will destroy this lovely planet we share with them."

"Are you talking about pollution? Deforestation?"

He waved a dismissive hand. "Things are getting better in that regard. The problem is China because they don't give a damn about the rest of the world and keep polluting like there is no tomorrow, but they will be dealt with. I'm not worried about the planet becoming uninhabitable because of industrial pollution. What I'm worried about are the arsenals of destructive weapons, nuclear, chemical, and biological that many rogue regimes have. I'm also worried about the lack of preparedness for natural disasters like massive solar flares, meteors, earthquakes, and the like. And I detest the human rights violations that are rampant around the world."

"What can you do about all that?"

"Take control. Make sure that resources are used properly, and that taxpayers money goes where it's supposed to, and not to line the pockets of corrupt politicians and their friends and families first. You have no idea how much of the available resources are wasted that way. Most people don't go into politics because of ideology. They want the power and the money that come with those positions. I'm going to fix all that. Under my rule, there would be no more homelessness, no more hunger, no more crime. The people will prosper, but the criminals will not, and the politicians and other power grabbers will be held accountable."

"Take control how?"

"With the help of technology. Not right now, but in ten or twenty years, artificial intelligence will make it possible for me to control the entire world."

Jacki narrowed her eyes at him. "You are scaring me, Kalugal. Your vision is benevolent, but your method is not. No one person should have so much power."

"Not even if he wants to use it for the good of all?"

She shook her head. "Power is like a drug addiction. It's corrupting, and if you have no one to answer to, no one to keep you in check, you might end up doing horrible things." She swallowed. "I really don't want to bring it up, but think about your father and grandfather. Maybe the reason they turned crazy and evil was having too much power? There was no one to stop them."

It was a chilling thought.

Kalugal had often wondered about his questionable heritage. His grandfather had been one of the two most powerful gods, and his father was the most powerful immortal ever born. That was where his own power originated from, but the flip side of that was insanity.

Perhaps he was already insane for plotting to take over the world? He didn't feel crazy, and he knew that what he wanted to do was for the good of others.

After all, Kalugal didn't plan on taking credit for any of it. He was happy to stay in the shadows and have his puppets take the spotlight.

"What would you do? If you wanted to fix the world's problems and you had the means to do it, would you sit back and do nothing?"

"I didn't say that you need to abandon your plan altogether. But perhaps you should modify it. You could work together with Kian and Annani, help them achieve your mutual goals faster."

Kalugal didn't like the idea of having to answer to others or seek approval to implement his ideas. That would just slow him down. He knew what he was doing. He just needed someone to be able to stop him if he went crazy.

"I have an idea. You will monitor what I'm doing, and if you sense that I'm turning into my father or grandfather, you'll stop me."

"How? I don't have any special powers. If you don't want to be stopped, I wouldn't be able to do anything."

Regrettably, Jacki was right.

Areana did her best to keep Navuh from drifting all the way to Mortdh's level of craziness, and maybe she was successful in that. But that wasn't enough.

"I need to think about it." Kalugal pushed his fingers through his hair. "The gods had a council, and the head god couldn't do anything without their approval. That didn't end well for them. While they argued about what to do with Mortdh, he annihilated them. The biblical kings had to answer to the religious authority, the prophet, or the holy man, but that's not a good system either."

Jacki sighed and closed her eyes. "We won't solve the world's problems tonight. We can spend a few years thinking about a good solution, right?"

"Absolutely. There is only one problem with taking our time. If the Chinese beat me to it, it's going to be very difficult to wrestle control of the world from their hands."

Jacki opened her eyes. "What are they up to?"

He chuckled. "The same thing I am. They want to take over the world, and they are already well on their way, while I'm still in the planning stage. One thing I am sure of, though, their plans are not as benevolent as mine."

Jacki

As Jacki woke up, she vaguely remembered a bizarre dream about Kalugal ruling over China by shrouding himself to look like its top official. But piecing it together from the disjointed fragments was not happening.

She was burning up, every muscle in her body hurt, and she needed to pee but lacked the energy to even lift her arm.

Where was Kalugal?

How could he have left her alone when she was transitioning and in danger of passing out? He was supposed to watch over her. Bridget had told him not to leave her alone for more than a few minutes.

When the door to the bathroom opened, Jacki let out a relieved breath. Kalugal hadn't left her.

He came over and sat next to her on the bed. "Good morning, my love." He leaned and kissed her forehead.

"Your temperature has risen. Do you want to take more pills?"

"I need to use the bathroom," she croaked through parched lips. "But I can't move."

His expression turned panicked in an instant. "Are you suffering paralysis?"

Despite how crappy she felt, Jacki smiled. "I'm just too weak to move. Can you help me?"

"Of course."

With the frown never leaving his forehead, he carried her to the bathroom and even helped her to get on the toilet. Then he just stood there, looking at her.

"Thank you. Now leave."

"What if you faint? I don't want to leave you alone."

Even if she wanted to, she couldn't pee in front of him or anyone else.

"Give me one minute."

"Fine." His lips pressed tightly together, he turned on his heel and left the bathroom.

Jacki didn't hear the door closing behind him, but she pretended like she had and went about her business. When she was done, she activated the cleaning feature of the sophisticated toilet, which included rinsing and drying.

The thing probably cost more than what she'd gotten from selling her old car.

"I'm coming in." Kalugal strode up to her and lifted her into his arms. "I'll help you brush your teeth and put on your lotions, and then I'll help you to get dressed. We are going to the clinic."

"Can't I just take more pills?"

He set her down on the vanity counter. "I called Bridget, and she said to bring you in."

"I don't want to go." She pouted. "I want to stay here. In bed."

"Would you feel better about going if I told you that Jin is in the clinic?"

"Why? What happened?"

"I don't know. You will have to find out for yourself. Bridget is sending someone with a golf cart in half an hour."

"Am I going to stay in the clinic?"

"Most likely."

"Then you'll have to pack an overnight bag for me."

"I can do that."

She knew he could, and he didn't even need her to tell him what to pack.

Her husband paid attention to everything. He knew which lotions she put on and when, which outfits she liked to wear for what occasion, and even what shoes.

"I love you," she murmured as a tear slid down her cheek.

"Oh, sweetheart." He wrapped his arms gently around her. "I love you more than anything in the world. Don't worry. Everything is going to be all right. Bridget knows what she's doing, and she will take good care of you."

"You are taking good care of me." She put her head on his shoulder and closed her eyes.

The next time Jacki opened them, she was in a hospital room, with all kinds of wires hooking her to different machines and contraptions, and Kalugal's worried face hovering over her.

"You're awake." He sat on the hospital bed and took her hand. "You lost consciousness. Bridget said that it's normal, and your vitals were fine, but I was so worried."

The doctor must have put something in the IV drip that Jacki was hooked up to because she was feeling much better. Her fever was down, and the muscle aches were not as bothersome.

"How long was I out?"

"A couple of hours."

Jacki glanced at the hospital johnny she was wearing. "Did you dress me up before bringing me here?"

He smiled sheepishly. "I wrapped you in a blanket and ran. It was quite the spectacle, with Rufsur and Hivak running behind me, and the two guards that Kian had posted outside running after them. Halfway here, a Guardian with a golf cart intercepted us, and we rode the rest of the way."

She squeezed his hand. "I gave you one hell of a scare, didn't I?"

"You did. But everything is fine now. That's what's important."

"We are not out of the woods yet." Bridget walked into the room. "It's not uncommon for a transitioning Dormant to slip in and out of consciousness." She walked over to the monitor and scanned the readouts. "So far, it looks good."

"Thanks for the meds," Jacki said. "I feel much better now than I felt this morning."

"Your temperature was very high."

"And I was achy all over. I still am, but not as bad as before."

Jin poked her head through the open door. "Can I come in?"

"Of course." Jacki patted the spot to her left. "My bestie and I are transitioning at the same time. How cool is that?" She looked at Bridget. "Can we share a room?"

"The rooms are designed for a single patient. Besides, your mates want to be with you, and we will roll a cot in for the night." She smiled at the three of them. "I'll come later to take your measurements."

"So, what happened to you?" Jacki asked when Bridget left. "Why are you here?"

"I fainted. I didn't lose consciousness, but Arwel freaked out and insisted that we come in. Bridget wanted to hook me up to monitors, but I convinced her to wait until it was absolutely necessary."

"How are your fangs doing?"

"They are still a no show, as you can see. I want them to grow already because the suspense is killing me. Will they elongate? Or won't they? That is the question."

Kalugal

As Kalugal's new phone rang, he walked out into the corridor outside Jacki's room and took it out of his pocket.

"Hello, Lokan."

"How is Jacki doing?"

"She lost consciousness again in the afternoon, just as Bridget predicted. Her vitals are good, and the doctor reassures me that everything is progressing just fine. Nevertheless, I'm worried."

The only time Kalugal had moved away from Jacki's side was when Rufsur had brought him his phone. Kian had relaxed his rules, allowing Rufsur and Hivak to go back to the house, but they had only gone to get the phones and returned to hold a vigil on the bench outside the clinic.

Kalugal wasn't sure whether they did that out of loyalty to him, worry for Jacki, or because they wanted to check out the clan females passing by the clinic on their way to and from the café.

"Carol sends her love and asks that you give Jacki a kiss from her."

"I will."

"Everything will be all right, Kalugal."

"I hope so. I'll let you know as soon as anything changes."

"Thank you."

After disconnecting the call, Kalugal put the phone back in his pocket and returned to sit on the chair he'd placed next to Jacki's hospital bed.

Wonder and Callie had stopped by earlier, voicing similar encouragements, and after that Amanda and Syssi paid him and Jacki a visit with more of the same.

Jacki was young, healthy, and strong. She would transition successfully.

But those were all platitudes. No one knew for sure whether Jacki would make it, not even the doctor.

"May I come in?" Kian's gruff voice was a surprisingly welcome sound.

"Please do."

He walked in with two paper coffee cups from the café and handed one to Kalugal. "Have you eaten?"

"I'm not hungry."

Kian lifted a chair and put it next to Kalugal's. "I remember myself in your position all too vividly. Syssi was unconscious for over twenty-four hours, Amanda was missing, and I was losing my fucking mind."

"Where was Amanda?"

"Dalhu had kidnapped her. But we didn't know that until later. She didn't come home when her butler had been expecting her, and he called to let me know. We figured out the last place she'd gone to before going missing, and William hacked into the security cameras of all the stores on that street. I saw the recording of every goddamned moment of the kidnapping, and it didn't look good."

"I can imagine."

"Can you?" Kian arched a brow. "You don't have sisters, so you have no idea how I felt." He ran his fingers through his hair. "Impotent fury. I knew he was a Doomer because he bit her. She went with him as if he'd drugged her. I had no idea where he had taken her. I didn't know where to start looking."

Something didn't add up in the story. "You said that she walked out with him after he bit her? How is that possible?"

Kian chuckled. "I forgot that you've never had sex with an immortal female. The venom doesn't affect them as strongly as it affects human women. If they black out at all, it lasts only a few minutes, not hours."

"What about the other effects of the venom?"

"The orgasms and euphoria are just as good."

"That's a relief. Jacki is quite fond of the effects."

Kian nodded.

"Hello?" Someone rapped his knuckles on the door. "May I come in?"

Kalugal turned toward the voice and was taken aback. The guy didn't look like any immortal he'd ever seen. Tall and wiry, he was dressed in loose purple pants, an orange button-up with a purple tie, and a white lab coat thrown over the hideous ensemble. But the most striking visual was his super-long white beard, which reached past his belt line.

"You may." Kian waved him in. "This is Merlin. Our fertility expert."

The strange doctor walked over and offered Kalugal his hand. Unlike the rest of him, his hand was elegant and clean.

Not that Merlin was dirty. Everything he wore smelled freshly laundered and his body odor was pleasant. But his clothes were so badly stained that from a distance, it looked like a deliberate pattern.

The guy was a slob, but a clean one.

"It's a pleasure to meet you, doctor." Kalugal gently shook the hand he'd been offered.

A doctor's hands were the instruments of his trade, and Merlin's looked fragile.

"Same here." Merlin pulled out a third chair and put it on Kalugal's other side. "I'm not here as a doctor. I haven't met Jacki yet, and I was curious. But as long as I'm here, I can offer you my services. Come see me six months after the transition, and I'll prepare potions for you and your lovely lady."

"You assume that we want to have children right away. We do, but how did you know that?"

Merlin smirked and leaned back. "Power of deduction, my friend. As someone who grew up without a real family, Jacki craves having one of her own. I bet she wants to have many children."

"She does. But we both know that it's not in the cards."

"You never know. Jacki might be miraculously fertile, or maybe my potions will do the trick more than once or twice." He winked.

Kian

When Kian's phone rang with the ringtone he'd assigned to his mother, he excused himself, walked into Bridget's office, and closed the door.

The doctor wasn't there, and if she returned, he could ask her to leave for a few minutes. His conversations with Annani were better kept private.

"Hello, Mother."

"Good morning. I heard that Kalugal is in the village with Jacki and that she is transitioning."

"You heard correctly."

"I am both surprised and delighted that you have invited your cousin and his mate into the village. How did that come about?"

"Kalugal doesn't have a doctor on staff, and he doesn't have any medical equipment either. When Jin started to transition, he realized that his mate would need medical supervision when her time came, and he asked me, or rather begged me to allow him and Jacki to stay in the village until after her transition. I couldn't refuse, but I made sure to put adequate safeguards in place."

"I am sure you did. Still, it was very kind of you. How are Jacki and Jin doing?"

Kian was sure that his mother knew precisely how both were doing, and her question was meant to steer the conversation in the direction she wanted. Next, she would say that she was flying over to make sure Jacki survived her transition.

"Jin is doing well, or as well as can be expected. She is growing venom glands and probably fully functional fangs as well. She is not thrilled about it, but she is not as upset as her sister was over much less. Jin is a trouper. Jacki is also fine, but she is slipping in and out of consciousness like many of the other transitioning Dormants. Bridget reassures us that she is going to pull through."

"But it is not certain, correct?"

"It never is."

"I am flying over. I should be there in case Jacqueline needs my blessing."

Kian tensed up. The blessing was the code he and his mother used for the goddess's secret blood transfusions, but even though they were talking on the clan's secure network and no one knew what the blessing meant, he was uncomfortable discussing their most closely guarded secret over the phone.

"Jacki's situation is in no way critical. Some of the other transitioning Dormants had a much harder time, and you didn't fly over to bless them."

"These are different circumstances. I already promised Kalugal that I would officiate over his and Jacki's wedding, and since they are both in the village, I could do that as soon as Jacki is well enough. And if I am already coming, I can arrive a week earlier and provide my blessing if it is needed. Jacqueline might not be in danger right now, but her condition might still deteriorate, and her survival is crucial to the future of the clan."

"In what way?"

His mother wasn't clairvoyant, but she had excellent instincts, or gut feelings as she called them.

Annani sighed. "What do you think will happen to Kalugal if Jacki does not make it?"

"He'll be devastated."

"And what do you think will happen to the nascent and beautiful cooperation between you, him, and Lokan?"

"I'm not sure."

"It will fall apart. In his grief, Kalugal could hole up someplace, and in his anger, he might use the incredible power he wields to do harm. Anger and grief over the murder of his adopted son turned Navuh from a semi-decent man into the monster he is now."

Kian felt his ire rise. Explaining evil deeds by past wrongs committed against the evildoer was wrong. People were responsible for their actions, and they had the choice to funnel their pain into doing good or bad,

"Anger and grief over the murder of your husband didn't turn you into a monster. It turned you into humanity's champion and savior. It depends on the person."

"That is true. And I cannot even claim perfect genes as my saving grace. My father was a great leader, but he was not a good man. He was not evil either, but he was ruthless. I guess I was lucky to inherit his leadership ability and my mother's compassion. But we do not know what Kalugal's inner makeup is. Besides, my blessing is such a small favor that it is not even worth discussing."

"That's not true. Your blessing is the biggest deal there is. But I agree with you that Jacki's survival is worth the intervention. If needed, that is. She might pull through all on her own."

Annani laughed. "Oh, Kian. You have no idea how glad I am that for once you agree with me."

"I agree with you often."

"Not before arguing with me first."

"This time, there is no argument. Except, I can't have you staying in the house you used before because I put Kalugal and Jacki in the new phase section. I will have to move Guardians in there and give you a house that's closer to mine."

"I do not wish to uproot anyone."

"I know, and I'm not happy to do that either, but your safety demands it. I'm sure they will understand. When are you planning on coming?"

"I thought about leaving in an hour and arriving at the village by the evening. But you will need more time to move your Guardians, so I will leave tomorrow morning."

"If you don't mind, you and Alena can stay with Syssi and me until the house is ready. Your Odus can stay with Okidu in his cottage. It's not like they need beds to sleep in."

"Of course I do not mind. It would be lovely to spend a couple of days with Syssi and you. "

"I'm looking forward to it." Kian actually meant it. Annani's previous visit had been much less stressful than usual, but that was probably because she had her own place and hadn't driven him crazy by acting irresponsibly with her safety.

"I enjoyed my previous stay tremendously, and I am looking forward to another lovely visit to your beautiful village. I am also eager to get to know Kalugal."

"He's a character. How long do you plan to stay?"

"Two weeks. Perhaps longer if Jacki needs more time to recuperate before her wedding."

"You mean her second wedding. The ceremony wasn't interrupted. The attack happened later."

"I know. But having a big wedding is a wonderful opportunity for Kalugal and Jacki to celebrate with our clan and get to know our people better."

Kalugal

By the time Kian returned to the room, Jin and Merlin had left, and Jacki's condition was still the same. The machines were emitting steady sounds, no alarm had gone blaring out, and Bridget hadn't come rushing in.

Everything seemed to be okay, but Jacki was still unconscious, and Kalugal was still going out of his mind with worry.

"She is going to be fine." Kian put a hand on his shoulder. "I know this seems bad, but it's actually good. Jacki's body has shut down all unnecessary functions, so it can divert all of its energy to the change."

"I know."

That was what everyone kept telling him, but Kalugal didn't trust the reassurances. For some reason, though, Kian's tone now indicated more confidence than it had before.

What had changed?

"The phone call I took before was from Annani. She is flying over. She'll be here either tonight or tomorrow morning, and she will give Jacki a blessing that will ensure her smooth transition."

"That's very gracious of her, and I'm grateful for the gesture. But I'm not a great believer in blessings or conversely in curses. It's all superstition."

Kian sat down and leaned toward Kalugal. "I'm like you. But the proof is in the evidence. Annani's blessing helped Syssi pull through as well as several of the other transitioning Dormants who weren't doing so great."

"Placebo effect?"

"They were unconscious, so no. Belief had nothing to do with it. But Annani is a goddess, and we don't really know all that much about their powers. My mother says that different gods had different talents in varying levels of power. And the older they were, the more powerful they became. Perhaps Annani's energy has healing power, or maybe she can transfer some of it to others when she blesses them."

"That's an interesting idea to ponder. But even if the blessing is just a gesture of goodwill, I will be grateful for it."

"As you should." Kian pushed to his feet. "Can I get you something to eat from the café? They have excellent pastries and sandwiches."

"Thank you. I would love another cup of coffee and maybe a sandwich, but my men can get it for me. They are sitting outside on the bench."

"The café only accepts clan-issued debit cards, which reminds me that I should get them for you and your party. In the meantime, I'll tell Wonder to keep an open tab for you."

"Thanks."

When Kian left, Kalugal leaned back in the uncomfortable chair and closed his eyes.

Kian was putting too much faith in his mother's blessing, which didn't fit his character. The guy was a realist, not a dreamer.

The energy fields he'd used as a possible explanation were not scientifically or even anecdotally proven, but they had been postulated. In Kalugal's opinion, the instances of miraculous healing were mostly hoaxes or compulsion. He could compel someone to feel great for a short period of time, but eventually, whatever was wrong with the body would be impossible for the mind to override.

Still, Annani had a proven record of blessings that helped problematic transitions along.

There could be two possible explanations. One was that the blessing had done nothing, and the Dormants would have pulled through without its help. The other explanation was that the blessing was a cover for something else.

Roberts' fast recovery with the help of Ruvon's blood came to mind. If an immortal's blood could speed up healing in a human, a goddess's blood could help a Dormant to transition.

That's what the blessing probably was, and he was willing to bet that no one was allowed to witness the goddess delivering her blessing.

It was smart of Kian and Annani to keep it a secret even from their own clan. If word got out, she would become the most hunted treasure on the face of the earth.

As always, figuring out a puzzle brought Kalugal great satisfaction, but this time it was even more than that. With Annani's help, there was no more question about whether Jacki would survive.

Provided that her situation didn't deteriorate before the goddess's arrival.

And as for the big secret?

Kian had nothing to worry about. Kalugal would never tell another soul. After all, if Annani's blood had miraculous properties, so did Areana's. They would both be hunted.

Was that why his father had kept her hidden and secluded for thousands of years?

Did Navuh even know what Areana's blood could do?

Kalugal had a feeling that he did.

When Kian returned with two cups of coffee and two sandwiches, Kalugal's stomach growled, and he realized that he'd been famished. His worry over Jacki had extinguished his appetite, but now that he knew she was going to be fine, his belly roared like a hungry lion.

Handing him the sandwich, Kian lifted a brow. "When was the last time you ate?"

"Last night."

"Then, it's no wonder your stomach is making monster sounds." Kian handed him the other sandwich as well. "Here, I can get another one later."

"Thank you. What about my men? They are probably hungry as well."

Kian chuckled. "Don't worry about them. They are getting well fed by the ladies."

"And I thought they were keeping a vigil for Jacki. Apparently not." Kalugal unwrapped the sandwich and took a bite. It was indeed very good.

Kian sat down and removed the lid from his coffee. "My mother intends to stay for a couple of weeks and marry you and Jacki as soon as Jacki is well enough."

"Are you okay with that?"

Kian nodded. "I'll make sure that she is safe." He sighed. "I can only imagine her reaction when I ask her to put the earpieces in."

"Your mother is a powerful goddess. I'm sure my compulsion would have no effect on her. Nevertheless, I will once more give you my word that I will not use it to compel her or any of your people."

Jacki

As Jacki opened her eyes and looked into Kalugal's smiling face, she wasn't sure whether she was awake or still dreaming.

"Hi." He leaned and kissed her forehead.

She lifted her hand and cupped his stubbled cheek. "Are you real? Or am I dreaming?"

With his signature smirk lifting one corner of his mouth, Kalugal put his hand over hers. "I am your dream man. So I'm both."

"Now I'm sure that I'm awake. You weren't as full of yourself in my dream. What time is it?"

"Eleven o'clock Sunday morning. You've been slipping in and out of consciousness ever since I brought you here. But your fever is down, and Bridget thinks that the worst part is over."

"Am I immortal?"

"Most likely, but the doctor has to administer her test to confirm it."

Jacki twisted her lips. "Bridget told me about it. She is going to make a small cut on the palm of my hand. I'm not looking forward to it."

He took her hand and kissed her palm. "I will hold your other hand, and you can squeeze mine as hard as you can."

"I love you."

She wanted to kiss her adorable husband so badly, but she hadn't brushed her teeth since the previous morning, her mouth tasted like sawdust, and her lips were chapped.

He smiled. "I love you more. Are you thirsty?"

"Yes. Very."

As Kalugal poured water from the pitcher, Bridget came in.

"Good morning. How are you feeling?"

"Much better, thank you. Are you going to administer the test now?"

The doctor chuckled. "There is no rush. We will do it after you eat something." She walked to the door and opened it wide. "You can come in, Wonder."

"Good morning." Wonder rolled in a cart. "I brought breakfast."

"Thank you. I'm so hungry."

"Hold on." Kalugal took the remote and raised the bed's back. "That's better, right?"

"Yes."

He handed her a paper cup with water. "Drink this first, and then I'll pour you tea."

Her hand shook from the effort it took to hold the cup up, but Jacki was determined to drink without assistance.

When she was done, she handed the empty cup to Kalugal. "I would prefer coffee if there is any."

"Of course there is." Wonder lifted a thermos and poured heavenly smelling coffee into a cup. "Sugar and cream?"

"Yes, please."

"Knock, knock." Jin walked into the room with Arwel in tow.

He glanced at Kalugal. "Is it okay if I come in?"

"Of course. Take a seat." Kalugal pointed at the chair to his left.

"I heard that you are much better. I am too." Jin sat on the bed next to Jacki's feet. "I'm officially an immortal."

"Congratulations!"

"To you too."

"Bridget didn't test me yet."

Jin waved her hand dismissively. "It's just a formality. But for you the worst is over, while I'm still toothless."

"How long until the new ones come in?" Jacki didn't want to say the F word and upset Jin.

"The points are already out." She opened her mouth wide and pointed with her finger. "Bridget says that in a week or two, I will at least look normal again."

"Just in time for the wedding," Kalugal said. "Annani is either already here or on her way, and she wants to marry us properly as soon as Jacki is up to it."

"Annani is coming?" Jin's eyes brightened. "I hope that Alena comes with her. The goddess is amazing. You are so lucky that you are going to meet her." She looked at Kalugal. "You too."

He arched a brow. "You've met the goddess?"

"Yeah. That's where I was hiding after you kidnapped Jacki and Arwel." She smirked. "You see? Even your compulsion isn't all-powerful. You didn't ask me where I was, and I didn't volunteer the information."

He lifted a hand. "I promised Kian that I wouldn't ask anything that might reveal the clan's strategic secrets. I only compelled you to tell me personal things. I view it as taking advantage of a loophole."

He was good at that. Kalugal was smart and cunning, but he was honest.

Mostly.

"Kalugal is an honorable man," Jacki said. "He does what he promises."

Kalugal

After breakfast was done and everyone left the room, Bridget walked in holding a tray. "Are you ready for the test?"

There were only three items on the tray; a small scalpel, a stack of square pieces of gauze, and a disinfectant, but Jacki's eyes naturally zeroed in on the scalpel.

"I'm more than ready." She pulled her arm from under the blanket and placed her hand on top of it, palm up.

Kalugal took her other hand. "Squeeze as hard as you need to."

Jacki smiled a little nervously. "It's okay. I'm not scared." She glanced at the tray. "The knife is really small."

Her anxiety seemed to be more about the confirmation of her immortality than the small pain she was about to endure.

As Bridget took Jacki's hand and wiped it with disinfectant, she was gentle and slow. But her hand moved with an immortal's speed as she reached for the scalpel and made the cut.

"Ouch." Jacki looked at her hand as the blood welled from the little incision. "It hurts, but not as badly as I thought it would."

For the next several moments, the three of them watched Jacki's palm intently. The blood stopped welling, but it was hard to tell whether the skin was knitting itself back together.

Bridget lifted one of the gauze squares and wiped the blood off. "It's a bit slower than I would like it to be, but it's mending much faster than it would if you were human."

"What does it mean?" Jacki asked without lifting her eyes off her palm.

"It means that your body is still working on the transition."

That was only partially true. From Kalugal's experience, the more diluted an immortal's genes were, the slower he was to heal. Jacki must be far removed from the original gods.

Not that it mattered to him.

The slower rate of healing might have made a difference for a warrior, which Jacki wasn't and would never be.

The important thing was that she was immortal now and wouldn't age.

Except, his Jacki was a smart lady, and she didn't accept Bridget's explanation. "Does it make me a weak immortal? More fragile?"

The doctor nodded. "All it means is that you will heal a little slower from injuries and that you probably won't be able to regrow missing body parts. But since you are not a soldier, that's inconsequential. You will not age, you will not contract human diseases, and you will heal faster than any human from accidental cuts, bruises, broken bones, and the like."

"I didn't even know that immortals could regrow missing body parts."

"Not all of them. If your heart is shredded or your brain exploded, there is no coming back from that. But most other things your body will repair. As I said, it would make a difference to a soldier, so I advise you not to join the Guardian force."

Jacki chuckled. "I have no such intentions."

It took five more minutes until the last sign of injury faded away, and Jacki's palm looked as good as new. Her rate of healing was about a hundred times slower than Kalugal's, which meant that he would have to keep her safe.

"What about my children? Are they going to be weak immortals because of my inferior genetic material?"

Kalugal opened his mouth to protest the use of the word inferior, but Bridget lifted a hand to stop him.

"You are mated to the second most powerful immortal in existence. I don't think you should worry about your children. His genes are more than enough."

Jacki shook her head. "With all due respect, doctor, that's not true. Annani and Areana share the same powerful paternal genes, but they had two different mothers, and Annani is strong while Areana is weak."

She made a valid point, and Kalugal's heart sank, thinking that their children could be more fragile and vulnerable than other immortals.

Bridget smiled the way a teacher smiles at a student who has said something that is untrue or inaccurate. "It is difficult to predict which genes children inherit. Sometimes they can be more like distant relatives than their own parents, inheriting traits that neither of them possesses. It is also possible that Areana's weakness is not genetic but psychological. She might think of herself as weak, and that's what she manifests to the world. Ahn was the most powerful of the gods. It doesn't make sense for his daughter to be so weak."

"Maybe she isn't really his daughter?" Jacki suggested.

"She is. They had methods to check even back then, and Ahn verified his paternity."

"It doesn't matter." Kalugal squeezed Jacki's hand. "Intelligence and strength of character are more important than paranormal powers, and you have both in spades. Our children are going to be brilliant, resourceful, and ambitious."

"Well said." Bridget nodded in approval.

"You are absolutely right." Jacki sighed. "Our children are going to be magnificent." She looked at her palm and rubbed the area of the cut with the fingers of her other hand. "Amazing. There is no sign of it left, and it doesn't even feel tender."

"Welcome to our world." Bridget patted her shoulder. "I'll leave you two alone to celebrate."

Kalugal waited until the door closed behind the doctor before wrapping his arms around Jacki. He embraced her gently, careful around the miscellaneous wires and tubes she was still hooked up to. "Welcome to the rest of our immortal lives together." He kissed her softly. "It's going to be a magical journey, my love, my one and only, my wife."

THE ADVENTURE CONTINUES
EDNA & RUFSUR'S STORY IS NEXT
THE CHILDREN OF THE GODS BOOK 41
DARK CHOICES THE QUANDARY

TURN THE PAGE TO READ THE EXCERPT—>

JOIN THE VIP CLUB

To find out what's included in your free membership, flip to the last page.

Dark Choices The Quandary

When Rufsur and Edna meet, the attraction is as unexpected as it is undeniable. Except, she's the clan's judge and councilwoman, and he's Kalugal's second-in-command. Will loyalty and duty to their people keep them apart?

Rufsur

Rufsur stretched his legs in front of him, crossed his arms over his chest, and leaned back against the clinic's wall.

The bench he and Hivak had been occupying on and off for the past thirty hours was a torture device, but the view was worth it.

The clan ladies passing by were friendly, and so far at least twenty had introduced themselves. All were lovely and seemed eager to sample an immortal's lovemaking prowess, but none had stood out from the rest.

No matter.

The day was still young, and the rumor about the two visiting immortal bachelors was spreading fast. Soon, every woman in the village would come to check him and Hivak out.

Luckily for him and Kalugal's other men, only a few were taken, and since he knew most of the mated females, he could enjoy the view guilt-free.

Rufsur smirked. By the time Jacki got discharged from the clinic, he would have seen every available clanswoman and made his choice.

At least one had to have that elusive extra something he was searching for.

Look at me suddenly being picky.

Until mere weeks ago, Rufsur had never even dreamed of encountering an immortal female, and if he had been fortunate enough to find one, he would have pursued her regardless of her attributes. But now that he had a virtual buffet, he was choosy.

The thing was, he and Hivak were the first unrelated and unattached immortal males to visit the clan, and therefore they had a temporary advantage over the rest of Kalugal's men.

They were a hot commodity, and it would be unwise not to make the most of it.

That was the main reason Rufsur had been sitting for hours outside the clinic, flattening his ass on the hard, concrete bench, and checking out the ladies.

Keeping vigil for Jacki's successful transition was just the pretext.

He wasn't really worried about her. Kalugal's mate was young and healthy, and even though she'd lost consciousness yesterday morning and had been slipping in and out of it ever since, the doctor had reassured them that it was a normal part of the transition process.

Besides, Jacki had the heart of a warrior, and she would make it through just fine.

Nevertheless, Kalugal was stressed out of his mind, and to be there for his friend, Rufsur would have gladly suffered through much worse than sitting on a hard bench.

Naturally, he could get up and stretch his legs, do some pacing in front of the clinic's door, or even get something from the café that was less than fifty feet away. He had already done all of that, and he had also dashed back to the house for stuff that Kalugal had asked for.

But the thing was, Rufsur had noticed that the ladies found it easier to come up and introduce themselves when he and Hivak were sitting down.

Maybe they seemed less threatening from a seated position?

After all, in a different lifetime, Kalugal and his men had been members of the Brotherhood of the Devout Order of Mortdh. Not only was the Brotherhood the clan's sworn enemy, but its members had also earned a well-deserved reputation for being misogynistic pigs.

To approach them even hesitatingly, the clan ladies must know that Kalugal and his men had escaped the Brotherhood during WWII, and that they were not the typical Doomers, as the clan nicknamed Mortdh's followers. And yet, they still regarded them suspiciously. In their eyes, former Brotherhood members were guilty until proven innocent.

Rufsur didn't fault their cautious approach. In their shoes, he would have done the same. In fact, he was also suspicious and considered clan members he hadn't met yet as potential enemies.

Hell, he wasn't so sure that those he'd met and befriended were truly his friends either.

Hivak pushed to his feet. "I'm going inside to check what's going on."

Rufsur shook his head. "Don't. Kalugal would have told us if anything has changed."

"He might be busy celebrating Jacki's successful transition."

Hivak was such an optimist. No one knew when Jacki would complete the first stage of her transition. It would probably take days.

"Not likely. But even if that is true, do you want to walk in on them celebrating?"

Hopefully, Rufsur's gut feeling was right, and Jacki's transition into immortality would be successful, but the odds against it were not entirely negligible.

If she didn't make it, Kalugal would be devastated.

Ruined.

For a time, Rufsur had thought that he had a thing for Jacki, but after seeing his boss fall hard for her, he'd realized that his feelings paled in comparison. What Jacki and Kalugal had was special. The real deal.

Rufsur wanted that too, and that was why he was choosy.

Such a special bond couldn't form with just anyone.

Hivak sat back down. "I'll wait for Kalugal to come out and tell us."

"Good choice." Rufsur glanced at the Guardians who'd been assigned to keep an eye on their group. "Maybe they know something." The two were sitting on a bench on the other side of the clinic's door.

He waved at them. "Any news?"

Jay, the one who looked a little like Beckham, shook his head. "It's too soon."

"That is what I thought." Rufsur enunciated each word carefully, so their translating earbuds would have no problem getting it.

Fearing Kalugal's compulsion ability, which operated by manipulating sound waves, the Guardians assigned to them were wearing the same kind of earpieces that Kian and his crew had worn during the summit.

It was a clever use of existing technology. The clan's tech guy had modified them from translating speech into another language to just repeating it in a machine voice.

Rufsur would have loved to have a pair, but regrettably, they were not for sale. To ensure a perfect fit, the clan's tech guy was custom-making them for each wearer, and it would be hard to explain why Rufsur needed them.

Up until recently, he hadn't feared his boss's compulsion ability, probably because Kalugal had never used it on him before.

But after Rufsur's first experience of trying to break through the voice command that had frozen him in place and rendered him powerless, things had changed. The memory of his impotent rage was going to stay with him for a long time.

Hell, thinking about it still got him angry even though he knew that Kalugal had been just testing a theory. His boss's fake attack on Jacki had looked so damn convincing that it had embedded itself in Rufsur's mind, as did the memory of rushing to her rescue and getting stopped with one damn verbal command.

Perhaps as a precaution, he could purchase top quality earplugs and carry them in his pocket.

Rufsur loved Kalugal like a brother, but the guy was too powerful for his own good, and given his family history, that was potentially dangerous.

Mortdh, Kalugal's grandfather and the god the Brotherhood worshiped, had gone insane because he'd been spurned by Annani. That had pushed him into singlehandedly ending the gods' era by killing all but two—Annani, the clan's mother, and her half-sister, Areana, who was Kalugal's mother.

Navuh, Kalugal's father, was not as crazy as Mortdh, but he was a piece of work nonetheless.

Bottom line, Kalugal had to be watched, and after they had escaped the Brotherhood and Navuh's control, Rufsur had appointed himself as his boss's watcher.

Kalugal's intentions were good, and he was a decent man, but the guy was three-quarters god, brilliant, had the ability to compel other immortals, and carried crazy genes that were a ticking bomb just waiting for the right trigger.

Having a pair of good earplugs might make all the difference between being able to stop Kalugal and failing.

Hopefully, it would never come to that, but it was better to be prepared. If anything happened to Jacki, it might be just the trigger to push his boss over the edge.

As the sound of wheels rolling over pavement pulled Rufsur out of his own head, he looked up and saw Wonder pushing a food cart toward the clinic.

"Hold on." He jumped up to open the door for her.

"Thank you." She pushed the cart through.

"Any news on Jacki?" he asked.

"Bridget called me and asked that I bring breakfast for everyone, so maybe Jacki is awake. I'll tell you on my way out."

"Thanks."

Rufsur went back to his spot on the bench.

Twenty minutes later, the clinic's door opened again, and he jumped up to hold it for Wonder.

Grinning, she rolled her cart out. "I have great news. Jin has officially transitioned, and Bridget is about to test Jacki, who is feeling much better."

Rufsur felt like hugging the woman. Instead, he dipped his head. "Thank you for letting us know. I'm so relieved."

"Same here," Hivak said. "I like Jacki."

"You're welcome, but even though it's just a formality, we need to wait for Bridget to administer the test first."

"Of course."

Rufsur sat back down, but then got up and started pacing. Time slowed to a crawl as they waited for Kalugal to come out and tell them the good news. Finally, when the door opened, and their boss stepped out with a big grin on his face, it wasn't hard to guess the test result.

"Jacki is officially an immortal now."

He pulled Kalugal into a bro hug. "Congratulations!" He slapped his back. "Can we see her?"

"Not yet. Now that she's feeling better, Jacki is concerned with how she looks. She wants to shower and change out of the hospital gown before seeing anyone."

"Do you need me to get her anything from the house?"

"I'll ask her to check what's in the bag you packed for her. If she still needs anything, I'll call you."

Rufsur nodded. "Congratulate Jacki for us."

"I will." Kalugal slapped his back. "You don't need to sit on this bench anymore." He glanced at the two Guardians sitting on the other side of the door. "Perhaps you could invite your new friends to celebrate at the café."

"Good idea."

His boss's intentions were clear—take the opportunity to get friendly with the Guardians and pump them for information.

Rufsur walked up to them. "Are you guys hungry?"

"I could eat," Theo said. "Congratulations on Jacki's transition. Now the four of you can go home."

"So eager to get rid of us already?"

The Guardian shrugged. "I'm tired of this babysitting job."

"I hear you." Rufsur clapped him on the back. "But that's your boss's fault. We came in peace, and we mean no harm. We don't need to be guarded twenty-four-seven."

A female passing by shook her head.

Unlike the other clan ladies, she wasn't much to look at. In fact, it seemed like she was doing her best to appear as unattractive as possible. Her brown hair was pulled back and gathered into a tight bun, her pantsuit was two sizes too big, and her shoes belonged in a museum. They were the kind women wore in the forties.

Maybe she'd kept them since then.

"Who's that?" he asked Theo.

"That's Edna. Our judge."

That explained the drab clothing and severe bun. Still, she could've at least bought a pantsuit that was her size and didn't look like a potato sack.

The woman must have heard Theo because she stopped and turned around.

As she pinned Rufsur with her incredible, soul-penetrating eyes, her intense gaze created a bubble around them, and in that space, nothing existed but the judge and her pale blue eyes. The world around them receded into the background. There were no sounds, no sights, no smells, just her.

She wasn't beautiful, but it had nothing to do with her facial features. It was in her austere expression and the depth of sorrow in her smart eyes.

What had made her so sad?

Whatever it was, Rufsur wanted to fix it.

If he could only wrest a smile out of her, a real one that started from the inside and was more than just a lifting of her thin lips, her beauty would burst free for all to see.

Edna

For over three hundred years, Edna's heart hadn't skipped a beat because of a man, but it did so now.

And for whom? One of Kalugal's men. The one who looked like her Robbie.

She needed Vanessa to examine her head.

At first, right after Robbie had died, Edna had seen his face everywhere, but he had been gone for more than three centuries, and that hadn't happened to her for the longest time.

Besides, her memory of him was foggy, and the resemblance was superficial. There were probably thousands of men out there who looked like that. Taller than average but not huge, broad-shouldered but not overly muscled, brown-haired, brown-eyed, and with lush lips that were easy to lift in a charming smile.

Except, the physicality didn't matter.

Robbie had been special, one of a kind. This man who looked a little like him was just a simple soldier who couldn't possibly contain a soul as big and as bright.

The truth was that there was nothing foggy about Edna's memory of the love of her life.

If she closed her eyes, she could still see Robbie's smiling eyes looking upon her with love and adoration, and on sunny days, the gold flakes in his irises dancing happily just because she was there. Edna still remembered quite vividly the feel of his lips when they kissed, the breadth of his shoulders as she clung to them when he made love to her, the dimple in his cheek when he smiled…

The pain of his loss had dulled over the centuries, but in moments like this, it returned with a vengeance, cutting her raw again.

"Hello." As the man waved and smiled, the dimple in his cheek was shockingly familiar. "I'm Rufsur." He started walking toward her.

Edna's heart skipped another beat. "Delighted to meet you, but I'm in a bit of a rush right now. Proper introductions will have to wait."

Ignoring his offered hand, she turned around and strode off.

Coward.

The mighty judge, whom everyone respected and feared, was scared to shake a man's hand just because he reminded her of someone she'd loved in another lifetime and had broken every clan rule to be with.

Annani should have had her whipped for her blatant disregard of the rules. Back then, they hadn't been written into a code of law yet, but every member of the clan had known what was permitted and what wasn't.

The goddess had chosen to show her mercy, but at the time, Edna would have preferred she hadn't.

She'd craved that whipping with every fiber of her grieving body and soul. The physical pain would have been a welcome reprieve from the suffering.

Maybe that was why Annani had forgiven her. Grief had been the punishment most befitting her crime. She'd fallen in love with a human and had stayed on as his lover for over a year. If he hadn't been killed, she would have never left him.

Eventually, he would have realized that her teasing about being a faerie princess come to seduce him had held a smidgen of truth.

For Robbie, Edna would have risked exposing who she was, and worse, who her people were.

Her biggest regret was that their many nights of lovemaking hadn't resulted in conception. Their child would have been immortal, and her grief would have been more bearable if she'd gotten to keep a piece of Robbie with her forever.

Except, the Fates hadn't blessed their union. Perhaps they even detested it, punishing her by taking Robbie's life.

Was she responsible for his death?

As irrational as the thought was, Edna could never dismiss it entirely, and the guilt added another layer of pain to her grief.

With a sigh, she pulled the door to the clinic open.

There was no point in reliving the past. She was a different person now, with duties and responsibilities, which was what had brought her to Bridget's office on a Sunday.

"Good morning." The doctor arched a brow. "Have you come to check on our transitioning Dormants?"

Not really, but the polite thing would be to inquire about their health.

Edna pulled out a chair and sat down. "How are Jin and Jacki doing?"

Bridget smiled like a proud mother. "As of this morning, they are both officially immortal."

Edna had been counting on Jin transitioning, but this was even better. She needed to talk to Kian and didn't want to call him at home on a Sunday, especially since he was hosting Annani. But if Jin and Jacki had both transitioned, he would come to congratulate them.

"That's wonderful. Is Kian on his way?"

"I was just about to call him with the good news. Why?"

"I need to talk to him, and I was hoping to catch him here. But since I already have your ear, I might as well share my concerns with you."

If she managed to get Bridget on her side, the doctor's vote might influence the other council members to join as well.

"What's on your mind?"

"The alliance is good, and I'm all for it, but having Kalugal and his party in the village is a mistake. Even though Kalugal no longer belongs to the Brotherhood, he is still a potential rival and not to be trusted. In fact,

I'm furious at Kian for inviting him without the council's approval. Such a decision is not at his sole discretion."

Bridget leaned back in her chair and crossed her arms over her chest. "I was there during the summit, and frankly, Kalugal impressed me. He made many more concessions than Kian, and he showed more willingness to cooperate. When the attack happened, Kalugal and his men worked with Kian and the Guardians to clean up the mess. Then we all put our heads together, and we've turned the failed raid attempt into an opportunity to solve the problem of the government's paranormal talents division."

"I'm delighted to hear that Kalugal is a reasonable man and that he is willing to cooperate, but that doesn't make him our friend. He is working with us because it's beneficial to him. When our interests clash, or he no longer needs us, he might turn into an enemy." Edna sighed. "You and I are not naive young women. We've seen so-called friends and allies turning on each other. We've even seen sons killing their own fathers and sometimes mothers in power grabs. Brothers killing brothers. Do you think that we are any better than humans in that regard?"

Bridget shook her head. "We have enough of our own bloody history as proof that we are not. But on the other hand, we can't let fear stand in the way of progress. I think Kalugal and his men will be good for the clan." She smiled. "Especially for the single ladies. Think of all the potential couples. If enough of ours mate his, the family ties will ensure peaceful coexistence."

"Really?" Edna snorted. "You must have forgotten the lessons of Scottish history. Inter-clan marriages were common, but so were the mutual slaughters."

"Those were different times, Edna. The world is not as savage as it used to be."

"Some parts still are, but that's beside the point. Jacki has transitioned, and Kalugal and his party should go home. I support the alliance, but meetings should happen on neutral ground, and proper safety protocols must be followed. No matter how friendly Kalugal appears, our guard should never waver."

Bridget sighed. "You are not going to like this. Annani wants Kalugal and Jacki to have a proper wedding in the village. She wants a big party and to preside over the ceremony. That's why she came. I'm afraid that they are going to stay at least another week, if not longer."

"That's not good."

When Annani decided on something, there was no way to change her mind. Even Kian was powerless to do so, and the small local council held no sway over the goddess at all.

The only way to put pressure on the goddess and have her reconsider was to convene the big assembly. If the entire clan voted unanimously against having Kalugal and Jacki's wedding in the village, Annani would be bound by their decision.

That was not going to happen, though. First of all, it would take at least a week to arrange for all clan members to attend the big assembly. Secondly, not everyone would consider the wedding problematic, and thirdly, the goddess might view it as mutiny.

Perhaps if she spoke with Annani and explained her reservations, the goddess would listen to reason?

Edna pushed to her feet. "I'll talk to Annani, and I'm also going to demand that Kian hold a council meeting. Can I count on your support?"

Bridget pursed her lips. "Let me think about it. You've raised valid concerns, but I'm sure a compromise can be reached. We can hold the wedding in the village, but maybe postpone it by a few days, so enhanced security measures can be put in place."

Kian

"That's great news, Bridget. Thanks for letting me know. Syssi and I will stop by later to congratulate the two happy couples."

The doctor chuckled. "Give it at least two hours. Jacki saw herself in the mirror and freaked out. She needs some time before she's ready to receive visitors."

Kian still remembered how gaunt and fragile Syssi had looked after going through the main stage of her transition. The energy needed for the change to immortality was immense, and in addition to shutting down all unnecessary functions, the body also cannibalized itself by using up fat stores and even muscle tissue.

"What about Jin? Is she okay?"

"Jin is a trouper. She is taking everything in her stride. Her fangs are finally starting to grow in, and surprisingly, that makes her happy."

"Are they going to elongate?"

"I'm afraid so. What she sees now are just the tips, but they are already very long on the inside."

"I guess there is a first time for everything."

"It would seem so."

He'd thought that Mey's small fangs were as strange as it was going to get, but Jin's transition had proved him wrong.

It was still a mystery why the sisters were different than all the other dormant and immortal females. The leading hypothesis was that they had inherited the traits from a divergent godly ancestor, but the question was, who was she or he?

"I assume Jin and Mey's daughters will have fangs as well?"

"It's likely. I'll see you later, Kian."

After ending the call, he returned the phone to his pocket and walked into the dining room where his family was gathered for brunch. "Good news. As of this morning, both Jin and Jacki are officially immortal."

Syssi clapped her hands. "That's a cause for celebration."

"I did not get a chance to give either of them my blessing," Annani said. "But I am happy they did not require my help."

"You can give them a blessing now," Amanda suggested. "Jin definitely needs it."

Alena frowned. "Why is that? Is she having a hard time?"

"No, but she is growing venom glands and fangs. That would upset any girl."

Kian pulled out a chair next to Syssi. "Bridget says that she is taking it well. "

"That's because she is already mated." Amanda reached for another waffle. "If she were single, she would be freaking out. I bet most immortal males would have thought twice before pursuing her."

"Why?" Syssi asked. "Jin is very attractive, and I think she's going to look like a badass with elongating fangs."

Amanda waved a hand. "You know how males are. They like to feel macho, and a female who has the ability to incapacitate them with her fangs and venom might seem unfeminine to them. Just think about Wonder and what a hard time she had because of her incredible physical strength. Now imagine how much worse it would have been for her if she had elongating fangs as well."

Annani nodded. "She would have been an outcast. But those were different times. I am glad that she woke up from stasis to a world where her statuesque figure is not as unusual and her physical strength is not deemed freakish."

"Anandur is special," Amanda said. "Not every male would have been okay with a female who was stronger than him and could kick his ass."

Looking at Kian, Syssi arched a brow. "Would it have bothered you if I had fangs?"

"Not as long as mine were longer."

Syssi laughed. "You are much bigger all over. Of course my fangs would have been smaller."

Alena cleared her throat. "TMI, people. What I want to hear about is the new immortal dating application that Amanda and Carol are working on."

"What is that?" Annani asked.

"It's like Tinder or eHarmony," Amanda explained. "People compile a profile of themselves, and others check them out. If there is a match, they agree to a date, or maybe they just talk online for a while before meeting in person."

"I see." Annani didn't look enthusiastic. "Technology is wonderful, but in this case, it does more harm than good. Those dating sites impede this generation's ability to form meaningful relationships. Still, it might be a good idea in our special case, but it is premature."

"Why do you think so?" Amanda asked. "I thought that you would love it."

Annani sighed. "You know that I have my finger on the clan's pulse, and apparently, not everyone is happy about Kalugal's males snapping up clan females."

"They will be snapping each other up," Amanda said. "I don't get what the problem is. Everyone was lamenting about how there weren't enough Dormants and about how long they would have to wait for mates, and now that we have over forty eligible bachelors, suddenly they are not happy? Is that because they are former Doomers?"

"That's not the reason," Kian said. "Since Kalugal and his men won't live here, the females who mate them will move there. Kalugal's community will grow and thrive, while ours will shrink. We need our females to grow the clan."

Annani nodded. "And that is not the only concern our males have. You promised Kalugal's men first access to the female Dormants from the government's program. The rumor has spread, and with it, resentment."

"I had no choice. Without Kalugal's continuing compulsion of Roberts, getting those Dormants wouldn't have been possible in the first place. Kalugal's request for priority access was justified."

"Crap." Syssi wound a lock of hair around her fingers. "We didn't think it through. In all the excitement, we only saw the positives. I was so happy that the clan females would have access to available immortal males, and the only thing I was concerned about was whether they were good men. But if as a result over forty of our females leave the clan, we will be hastening our own extinction. We can't afford to lose that many."

For a long moment, everyone sat in somber silence.

"You need to renegotiate the agreement with Kalugal," Alena said. "He owes you for allowing him and Jacki into the village."

Kian grimaced. "That's not something I want to use as leverage. It was the right thing to do."

Amanda nodded in agreement. "We can't pull back, but we can make it much more difficult for Kalugal's men."

"How?" Alena asked.

Amanda tapped a finger over her lips. "Forget the dating app. Every guy that wants a clan female will have to agree to being auctioned. The clan females will bid on them, and the winner will get the guy for one night. Naturally, the proceeds will go to our charity, so it will be considered a good deed for the men. Those who find their one and only will move to the next stage. They will have to go through some very inventive and grueling trials to get accepted into the clan."

Dalhu shook his head. "Kalugal will not agree to that. He would be losing men to us."

Amanda shrugged. "Then his men won't get access to our females."

"The single ladies are not going to be happy about it," Kian said. "Rufsur and Hivak have gotten a lot of attention while sitting outside the clinic."

"You have to talk to Kalugal," Annani said. "Perhaps the solution is integrating him and his men into our clan."

"Even if it wasn't a security risk, Kalugal wants his independence. He will never agree to that."

"Don't be so sure." Amanda smiled. "If that's the only way his men can have a shot at immortal mates, they will put a lot of pressure on him. And if Kalugal resists, I wouldn't be surprised if a significant number of them rebelled and asked to join our clan."

Kalugal

"I don't need you with me in the bathroom." Jacki put a hand on Kalugal's chest and gave it a barely-there push. "I'm not dizzy, and my legs are just fine. If I need help, I'll call you."

Unreasonable woman.

"I don't know why you are being so stubborn." He leaned and whispered in her ear, "I know what you look like naked."

"But I don't." Jacki looked down at the voluminous hospital gown. "I have a feeling that I've lost ten pounds overnight, and I want some privacy when I check what I look like under this thing."

He cupped her cheek. "Ten pounds less, or ten more, it doesn't matter. You are always beautiful to me. I love you."

Her eyes softened. "I know, and I love you too. But I really need a few moments to myself. Can you be a sweetheart and give me that?"

Sly woman.

"Fine." Kalugal handed Jacki the duffle bag with her change of clothes. "I'll be right outside the door if you need me." He pulled the chair over and sat down.

She shook her head. "Please, take it back to where it was. You'll hear me just as well from five feet away."

It was more like ten feet, but Kalugal knew that there was no point in arguing with Jacki. It would only upset her, and she would keep insisting until he did whatever she wanted anyway. He could, however, negotiate. "On one condition."

"What is it?"

"You can take as long as you like in there, but say something every five minutes or so to let me know that you're okay."

"It's a deal."

As Jacki closed the door behind her, Kalugal let out a sigh and returned the chair to the side of the bed.

Last night, Bridget had offered to roll in a gurney for him to sleep on, but he'd refused. He'd spent the entire time sitting on the damn chair and listening to Jacki breathe, and now he was stiff and tired and wanted to go home, but not to their temporary lodging in the village.

Much as he was grateful for Kian's hospitality, Kalugal wanted things to go back to normal. He wanted to take Jacki and his men back to the mansion, and resume his work, albeit part-time. Until Jacki's vitality was fully restored, he needed to take care of her. Then, in a month or two, when she was up to it, he would take her on a proper honeymoon to some exotic location.

Right now though, being back in his own home seemed like the best honeymoon possible. He missed the privacy, the peace and quiet, and the comfortable routine he and his men had enjoyed before the summit, the attack, and then the trip to the clan's secret village.

"I'm still okay," Jacki said from the bathroom. "I'm getting into the shower now."

"Thank you for remembering to let me know."

At the sound of a knock, he got up and opened the door. "Kian. I didn't expect you here so early."

Kalugal didn't invite his cousin to come in. Instead, he stood in the doorway and blocked the way. Jacki might get out of the shower with just a towel wrapped around her, and she would be mortified to find a male visitor in the room.

Kian glanced at his watch. "It's after twelve."

Earlier, when he'd called to congratulate them, Kian had said that he and Syssi would visit Jacki in the afternoon.

"Jacki is still not ready to see anyone. She's in the shower."

"I'm not here for Jacki. Annani wants to talk to you. She wanted to meet Jacki as well, but she is willing to wait until Jacki feels up to it."

Kalugal wanted to meet the goddess, but now was not a good time. He looked at the bathroom door. "I can't leave her."

"I can wait until she's done showering."

"I don't want to leave her alone."

"I'll ask Bridget or Jin to come in and keep Jacki company. You can't decline an invitation from the goddess."

Damn. Talk about bad timing. Was Annani doing it on purpose to catch him off balance?

The goddess had already done it once, when she'd informed him that he and Jacki were getting married again in the village with her presiding over the ceremony. The only excuse he'd been able to come up with on the spot had been Jacki's transition. But now that it was behind them, he needed time to figure out how to wiggle out of staying for the wedding without offending the mighty Clan Mother.

It would be a security nightmare for both him and Kian, and neither of them was too enthusiastic about going to all that trouble for a party. They'd already done it once, and it hadn't ended well, though through no fault of their own.

"Can I ask you to wait outside?"

"Of course." Kian dipped his head. "I'll see if Jin is accepting visitors."

After Kian left, Kalugal walked over to the bathroom door and knocked. "Are you about done?"

The door opened, and Jacki stepped out. "How do I look?"

"Beautiful."

She had dark circles under her eyes, and the yoga pants that were normally tight seemed too loose on her hips, but she was still gorgeous.

"You are sweet, but you are also a liar." She padded to the bed and sat on it. "The shower sapped what little energy I had. I'm going to lie down."

"Of course." Kalugal helped her get comfortable and covered her with the blanket. "Kian came to tell me that Annani wants to see me, but I don't want to leave you alone, and I can't refuse the goddess either."

"Naturally." Jacki yawned. "Go. I'm going to take a nap anyway."

"Bridget is here if you need her."

"I know." Jacki lifted the call button. "Don't worry about me. I'm immortal now, remember? I just need to rest."

"True." He leaned and kissed her temple. "I have the phone that Kian gave me. If you need me, call, and I'll come as fast as I can."

Order Dark Choices The Quandary today!

Join the VIP Club

To find out what's included in your free membership, flip to the last page.

The Children of the Gods Series

Reading Order

THE CHILDREN OF THE GODS ORIGINS

1: Goddess's Choice

When gods and immortals still ruled the ancient world, one young goddess risked everything for love.

2: Goddess's Hope

Hungry for power and infatuated with the beautiful Areana, Navuh plots his father's demise. After all, by getting rid of the insane god he would be doing the world a favor. Except, when gods and immortals conspire against each other, humanity pays the price.

But things are not what they seem, and prophecies should not to be trusted...

THE CHILDREN OF THE GODS

Dark Stranger

1: Dark Stranger The Dream

2: Dark Stranger Revealed

3: Dark Stranger Immortal

Dark Enemy

4: Dark Enemy Taken

5: Dark Enemy Captive

6: Dark Enemy Redeemed

Kri & Michael's Story

6.5: My Dark Amazon

Dark Warrior

7: Dark Warrior Mine

8: Dark Warrior's Promise

9: Dark Warrior's Destiny

10: Dark Warrior's Legacy

Dark Guardian

11: Dark Guardian Found

12: Dark Guardian Craved

13: Dark Guardian's Mate

Dark Angel

14: Dark Angel's Obsession

15: Dark Angel's Seduction

16: Dark Angel's Surrender

Dark Operative

17: Dark Operative: A Shadow of Death

18: Dark Operative: A Glimmer of Hope

19: Dark Operative: The Dawn of Love

Dark Survivor

20: Dark Survivor Awakened

21: Dark Survivor Echoes of Love

22: Dark Survivor Reunited

Dark Widow

23: Dark Widow's Secret

24: Dark Widow's Curse

25: Dark Widow's Blessing

Dark Dream

26: Dark Dream's Temptation

27: Dark Dream's Unraveling

28: Dark Dream's Trap

Dark Prince

29: Dark Prince's Enigma

30: Dark Prince's Dilemma

31: Dark Prince's Agenda

Dark Queen

32: Dark Queen's Quest

33: Dark Queen's Knight

34: Dark Queen's Army

Dark Spy

35: Dark Spy Conscripted

36: Dark Spy's Mission

37: Dark Spy's Resolution

Dark Overlord

38: Dark Overlord New Horizon

39: Dark Overlord's Wife

40: Dark Overlord's Clan

Dark Choices

41: Dark Choices The Quandary

42: Dark Choices Paradigm Shift

Edna and Rufsur are miserable without each other, and their two-week separation seems like an eternity. Long-distance relationships are difficult, but for immortal couples they are impossible. Unless one of them is willing to leave everything behind for the other, things are just going to get worse. Except, the cost of compromise is far greater than giving up their comfortable lives and hard-earned positions. The future of their people is on the line.

43: Dark Choices The Accord

The winds of change blowing over the village demand hard choices. For better or worse, Kian's decisions will alter the trajectory of the clan's future, and he is not ready to take the plunge. But as Edna and Rufsur's plight gains widespread support, his resistance slowly begins to erode.

Dark Secrets

44: Dark Secrets Resurgence

On a sabbatical from his Stanford teaching position, Professor David Levinson finally has time to write the sci-fi novel he's been thinking about for years.

The phenomena of past life memories and near-death experiences are too controversial to include in his formal psychiatric research, while fiction is the perfect outlet for his esoteric ideas.

Hoping that a change of pace will provide the inspiration he needs, David accepts a friend's invitation to an old Scottish castle.

45: Dark Secrets Unveiled

When Professor David Levinson accepts a friend's invitation to an old Scottish castle, what he finds there is more fantastical than his most outlandish theories. The castle is home to a clan of immortals, their leader is a stunning demigoddess, and even more shockingly, it might be precisely where he belongs.

Except, the clan founder is hiding a secret that might cast a dark shadow on David's relationship with her daughter.

Nevertheless, when offered a chance at immortality, he agrees to undergo the dangerous induction process.

Will David survive his transition into immortality? And if he does, will his relationship with Sari survive the unveiling of her mother's secret?

46: Dark Secrets Absolved

Absolution.

David had given and received it.

The few short hours since he'd emerged from the coma had felt incredible. He'd finally been free of the guilt and pain, and for the first time since Jonah's death, he had felt truly happy and optimistic about the future.

He'd survived the transition into immortality, had been accepted into the clan, and was about to marry the best woman on the face of the planet, his true love mate, his salvation, his everything.

What could have possibly gone wrong?

Just about everything.

Dark Haven

47: Dark Haven Illusion

Welcome to Safe Haven, where not everything is what it seems.

On a quest to process personal pain, Anastasia joins the Safe Haven Spiritual Retreat.

Through meditation, self-reflection, and hard work, she hopes to make peace with the voices in her head.

This is where she belongs.

Except, membership comes with a hefty price, doubts are sacrilege, and leaving is not as easy as walking out the front gate.

Is living in utopia worth the sacrifice?

Anastasia believes so until the arrival of a new acolyte changes everything.

Apparently, the gods of old were not a myth, their immortal descendants share the planet with humans, and she might be a carrier of their genes.

48: Dark Haven Unmasked

As Anastasia leaves Safe Haven for a week-long romantic vacation with Leon, she hopes to explore her newly discovered passionate side, their budding relationship, and perhaps also solve the mystery of the voices in her head. What she discovers exceeds her wildest expectations.

In the meantime, Eleanor and Peter hope to solve another mystery. Who is Emmett Haderech, and what is he up to?

49: Dark Haven Found

Anastasia is growing suspicious, and Leon is running out of excuses.

Risking death for a chance at immortality should've been her choice to make. Will she ever forgive him for taking it away from her?

Dark Power

50: Dark Power Untamed

Attending a charity gala as the clan's figurehead, Onegus is ready for the pesky socialites he'll have a hard time keeping away. Instead, he encounters an intriguing beauty who won't give him the time of day.

Bad things happen when Cassandra gets all worked up, and given her fiery temper, the destructive power is difficult to tame. When she meets a gorgeous, cocky billionaire at a charity event, things just might start blowing up again.

51: Dark Power Unleashed

Cassandra's power is unpredictable, uncontrollable, and destructive. If she doesn't learn to harness it, people might get hurt.

Onegus's self-control is legendary. Even his fangs and venom glands obey his commands.

They say that opposites attract, and perhaps it's true, but are they any good for each other?

52: Dark Power Convergence

The threads of fate converge, mysteries unfold, and the clan's future is forever altered in the least expected way.

Dark Memories

53: Dark Memories Submerged

54: Dark Memories Emerge

55: Dark Memories Restored

Dark Hunter

56: Dark Hunter's Query

57: Dark Hunter's Prey

58: <u>Dark Hunter's Boon</u>

Dark God

59: Dark God's Avatar

60: Dark God's Reviviscence

61: Dark God Destinies Converge

Dark Whispers

62: Dark Whispers From The Past

63: Dark Whispers From Afar

64: Dark Whispers From Beyond

Dark Gambit

65: Dark Gambit The Pawn

66: Dark Gambit The Play

67: Dark Gambit Reliance

Dark Alliance

68: Dark Alliance Kindred Souls

69: Dark Alliance Turbulent Waters

70: Dark Alliance Perfect Storm

Dark Healing

71: Dark Healing Blind Justice

72: Dark Healing Blind Trust

73: Dark healing Blind Curve

Dark Encounters

74: Dark Encounters of the Close Kind

75: Dark Encounters of the Unexpected Kind

76: Dark Encounters of the Fated Kind

The Children of the Gods Series Sets

Books 1-3: Dark Stranger trilogy—Includes a bonus short story: **The Fates take a Vacation**

Books 4-6: Dark Enemy Trilogy —Includes a bonus short story—**The Fates' Post-Wedding Celebration**

Books 7-10: Dark Warrior Tetralogy

Books 11-13: Dark Guardian Trilogy

Books 14-16: Dark Angel Trilogy

Books 17-19: Dark Operative Trilogy

Books 20-22: Dark Survivor Trilogy

Books 23-25: Dark Widow Trilogy

Books 26-28: Dark Dream Trilogy

Books 29-31: Dark Prince Trilogy

Books 32-34: Dark Queen Trilogy

Books 35-37: Dark Spy Trilogy

Books 38-40: Dark Overlord Trilogy

Books 41-43: Dark Choices Trilogy

Books 44-46: Dark Secrets Trilogy

Books 47-49: Dark Haven Trilogy

Books 50-52: Dark Power Trilogy

Books 53-55: Dark Memories Trilogy

Books 56-58: Dark Hunter Trilogy

Books 59-61: Dark God Trilogy

Books 62-64: Dark Whispers Trilogy

Books 65-67: Dark Gambit Trilogy

Books 68-70: Dark Alliance Trilogy

Books 71-73: Dark healing Trilogy

MEGA SETS

INCLUDE CHARACTER LISTS

The Children of the Gods: Books 1-6

The Children of the Gods: Books 6.5-10

TRY THE SERIES ON

AUDIBLE

2 FREE audiobooks with your new Audible subscription!

PERFECT MATCH SERIES

Vampire's Consort

When Gabriel's company is ready to start beta testing, he invites his old crush to inspect its medical safety protocol.

Curious about the revolutionary technology of the *Perfect Match Virtual Fantasy-Fulfillment studios*, Brenna agrees.

Neither expects to end up partnering for its first fully immersive test run.

King's Chosen

When Lisa's nutty friends get her a gift certificate to *Perfect Match Virtual Fantasy Studios*, she has no intentions of using it. But since the only way to get a refund is if no partner can be found for her, she makes sure to request a fantasy so girly and over the top that no sane guy will pick it up.

Except, someone does.

> **Warning:** This fantasy contains a hot, domineering crown prince, sweet insta-love, steamy love scenes painted with light shades of gray, a wedding, and a HEA in both the virtual and real worlds.
>
> Intended for mature audience.

Captain's Conquest

Working as a Starbucks barista, Alicia fends off flirting all day long, but none of the guys are as charming and sexy as Gregg. His frequent visits are the highlight of her day, but since he's never asked her out, she assumes he's taken. Besides, between a day job and a budding music career, she has no time to start a new relationship.

That is until Gregg makes her an offer she can't refuse—a gift certificate to the virtual fantasy fulfillment service everyone is talking about. As a huge Star Trek fan, Alicia has a perfect match in mind—the captain of the Starship Enterprise.

The Thief Who Loved Me

When Marian splurges on a Perfect Match Virtual adventure as a world infamous jewel thief, she expects high-wire fun with a hot partner who she will never have to see again in real life.

A virtual encounter seems like the perfect answer to Marcus's string of dating disasters. No strings attached, no drama, and definitely no love. As a die-hard James Bond fan, he chooses as his avatar a dashing MI6 operative, and to complement his adventure, a dangerously seductive partner.

Neither expects to find their forever Perfect Match.

My Merman Prince

The beautiful architect working late on the twelfth floor of my building thinks that I'm just the maintenance guy. She's also under the impression that I'm not interested.

Nothing could be further from the truth.

I want her like I've never wanted a woman before, but I don't play where I work.

I don't need the complications.

When she tells me about living out her mermaid fantasy with a stranger in a Perfect Match virtual adventure, I decide to do everything possible to ensure that the stranger is me.

The Dragon King

To save his beloved kingdom from a devastating war, the Crown Prince of Trieste makes a deal with a witch that costs him half of his humanity and dooms him to an eternity of loneliness.

Now king, he's a fearsome cobalt-winged dragon by day and a short-tempered monarch by night. Not many are brave enough to serve in the palace of the brooding and volatile ruler, but Charlotte ignores the rumors and accepts a scribe position in court.

As the young scribe reawakens Bruce's frozen heart, all that stands in the way of their happiness is the witch's bargain. Outsmarting the evil hag will take cunning and courage, and Charlotte is just the right woman for the job.

My Werewolf Romeo

The father of my star student is a big-shot screenwriter and the patron of the drama department who thinks he can dictate what production I should put on. The principal makes it very clear that I need to cooperate with the opinionated asshat or walk away from my dream job at the exclusive private high school.

It doesn't help matters that the guy is single, hot, charming, creative, and seems to like me despite my thinly-veiled hostility.

When he invites me to a custom-tailored Perfect Match virtual adventure to prove that his screenplay is perfect for my production, I accept, intending to have fun while proving that messing with the classics is a foolish idea.

I don't expect to be wowed by his werewolf adaptation of Red Riding Hood mesh-up with Romeo and Juliet, and I certainly don't expect to fall in love with the virtual fantasy's leading man.

The Channeler's Companion

A treat for fans of *The Wheel of Time*.

When Erika hires Rand to assist in her pediatric clinic, she does so despite his good looks and irresistible charm, not because of them.

He's empathic, adores children, and has the patience of a saint.

He's also all she can think about, but he's off limits.

What's a doctor to do to scratch that irresistible itch without risking workplace complications?

A shared adventure in the Perfect Match Virtual Studios seems like the solution, but instead of letting the algorithm choose a partner for her, Erika can try to influence it to select the one she wants. Awarding Rand a gift certificate to the service will get him into their database, but unless Erika can tip the odds in her favor, getting paired with him is a long shot.

Hopefully, a virtual adventure based on her and Rand's favorite series will do the trick.

Note

Dear reader,

I hope my stories have added a little joy to your day. If you have a moment to add some to mine, you can help spread the word about the Children Of The Gods series by telling your friends and penning a review. Your recommendations are the most powerful way to inspire new readers to explore the series.

Thank you,

Isabell

FOR EXCLUSIVE PEEKS AT UPCOMING RELEASES & A FREE COMPANION BOOK

Join my *VIP Club* and gain access to the VIP portal at itlucas.com
To Join, go to:
http://eepurl.com/blMTpD

INCLUDED IN YOUR FREE MEMBERSHIP:

YOUR VIP PORTAL

- Read preview chapters of upcoming releases.
- Listen to Goddess's Choice narration by Charles Lawrence
- Exclusive content offered only to my VIPs.

FREE I.T. LUCAS COMPANION INCLUDES:

- Goddess's Choice Part 1
- Perfect Match: Vampire's Consort (A standalone Novella)
- Interview Q & A
- Character Charts

If you're already a subscriber, and you are not getting my emails, your provider is sending them to your junk folder, and you are missing out on **important updates, side characters' portraits, additional content, and other goodies.** To fix that, add isabell@itlucas.com to your email contacts or your email VIP list.

**Check out the specials at
https://www.itlucas.com/specials**

Printed in Great Britain
by Amazon